A ROYAL
CRUEL
KING

ROYAL ELITE
SCHOOL

RINA KENT

To the invisibles ones.

AUTHOR NOTE

Hello reader friend,

If you haven't read my books before, you might not know this, but I write darker stories that can be upsetting and disturbing. My books and main characters aren't for the faint of heart.

Cruel King is a new adult romance novel intended for adult readers only. This book has a villainous hero, enemies to lovers, angst, and explicit/ intense sexual situations. If you're looking for a sweet romance, then this book is NOT for you. Aside from the previously published book, this version contains a never-published-before bonus scene.

Cruel King is a complete standalone in Royal Elite world. No book should be read prior to this.

To remain true to the characters, the vocabulary, grammar, and spelling of *Cruel King* is written in British English.
This book is part of a trilogy and is NOT standalone.

Don't forget to Sign up to Rina Kent's Newsletter for news about future releases and an exclusive gift.

He's no fairy tale king.

Levi

Here, little princess. I'm your king.

You have three rules. Bow. Break. Bend the knee.

Fight me all you want, but soon enough, you'll be chanting long live the king.

Astrid

One day I'm Royal Elite School's small fly, the next I'm hunted and left to die.

He doesn't only shred my life to parts, but he's also coming after my heart.

He thinks he broke me, but the new princess will bring the king to his knees.

PLAYLIST

Theme Song
Time is Running Out—Muse

Playlist
The Fear—The Score
Paint It Black—Ciara
Stronger—The Score
King of Nothing—Broadside
Pressure—Muse
Champion—Bishop Briggs
Supremacy—Muse
Mercy—Muse
Undisclosed Desires—Muse
Supermassive Black Hole—Muse
White Flag—Normandie
I Really Wish I Hated You—blink-182
Devil Devil—MILCK
Takeaway—The Chainsmokers
I Think I'm Okay—Machine Gun & Yungblud
Arcadia—Smash Into Pieces
Head Above Water—Avril Lavigne
Something Just Like This—Coldplay & The Chainsmokers
Hurricane—I Prevail
For Reasons Unknown—The Killers
Boyfriend—Ariana Grande & Social House

Find the Playlist on Spotify.

A ROYAL ELITE BOOK

CRUEL KING

ONE

Astrid

You may be noble, but stay away from King.

This is the last place I should be.

Alcohol, drunk teenagers, and thumping music.

A party.

Not to be dramatic, although I probably am, this place is like my worst nightmare wrapped in super-expensive watered-down alcohol.

Now, I'm not that much of a fun-ruiner, although my best friend, Dan, would say otherwise.

Spoiler alert, don't believe anything Dan says. He's into drama and all that jazz.

But I promised him I'd attend one party before the summer starts. Since Dan is part of the football team, I expected him to take me to their usual thing—not that I know what that is, but I had an idea it'd be in some posh house in London.

However, the sneaky wanker chose *the* party. AKA the mother of all freaking parties in Royal Elite.

When Dan and I walked inside, I had to double-check to see if we were somehow trespassing into the Queen's holiday mansion and if I should tell Her Majesty that I saw the drunk captain of the rugby team piss in her pool.

To say the place is huge would be like saying the Vikings

are tiny. Okay, that was lame, but I kind of insert the Vikings in any similes I make.

Golden arcs decorate the entrance and all the way to the massive lounge area. The vaulted ceilings and the sweeping stairs only add to how ridiculously grandiose this place is—even for Royal Elite's level. Jeez. To top it off, there are butlers serving drunk teenagers more drinks than they need.

I mean, I come from money. Scratch that. Dad is rich, I'm not. However, this is on a whole different level. Even for me.

When Dan said it was party night, I thought we'd crash in one of the popular 'elite' houses.

We'd drink their expensive liquor, try to pretend that we belonged to the same school that has the future prime minister and parliament members in the making, and then piss off to nurse a hangover.

But Dan forgot to mention a tiny detail about the location of the party.

It's in the middle of freaking nowhere.

I stopped following the twists and turns Dan took with his car the moment we were out of London and no road signs came into view.

For a moment, I thought Dan was taking us to some gypsy party.

Well, this sure as hell isn't a gypsy party.

The mansion is hidden behind tall pine trees on top of a hill—no kidding. The owner is either way too private or way too gothic.

Or both.

Aside from the attendees' cars, there's nothing in sight. Now that I think about it, this would be the perfect opportunity to mass murder everyone.

I can totally see this as the opening scene of a horror film.

You need to stop watching all those gory films. I can almost hear Dad scold in my mind. Oh, right. He's not Dad. He's *Father.*

That should summarise the formal nature of my relationship

with Lord Clifford. He may or may not kill me for coming to this party without his permission.

One more reason why I follow Dan's demonic plots.

I sip from my second drink. I had one shot with Dan as soon as we arrived, but then he buggered off, so now, I'm walking around with this cocktail. There's barely a burn at the end, but I have a high tolerance, so this is nothing.

I need a distraction from the scene around me. I can't believe Dan left me—probably to go shag. Worst wingman ever.

The entire school is gathered here. Some sway to the loud, offbeat music. Outside, a few of the rugby team cannonball into the kidney-shaped pool—that has piss in it. Others howl as they play a drinking competition that I wish I had the guts to participate in.

But then again, nothing is worth jeopardising my current position in the school—I'm part of the invisible folk. You know the type: those who no one actually cares if they miss a class or two—or an entire year. And I'd like to remain that way, thank you very much.

Invisibility is a cool superpower that allows me to breeze through without any bullshit or drama.

However, if I was going to remain that way, I should've probably chosen a less noticeable best friend than Daniel. In my defence, when I discovered his popularity, he'd already super-glued himself to me as my wingman.

Even with his popularity, I'm invisible enough that his harem of girls don't notice me when they're hitting on him.

Some of the Royal Elite students present here are still wearing their pristine uniforms with red ties and navy blue jackets. On their pockets, the school's golden logo is embroidered. The lion in a shield, topped by a crown, is a sign of both the power and corruption simmering within the walls of the school.

There's a reason the uniformed people are alone in a circle, probably discussing books. I would join in, but I doubt they'd like it when I tell them they're not supposed to wear a uniform to a party.

Even I, a total 'party terrorist'—per Dan's words—have opted for jean shorts, fishnet stockings, and a simple black top. Oh, I also wore my favourite white basketball trainers that Mum painted black stars on.

My heart shrinks at the thought of her. I take a deep breath of the alcohol and the designer perfumes permeating the air.

Fun. This is supposed to be a night of fun.

My idea of fun includes either my art studio or marathoning the latest gory film.

Just saying.

A long howl at the entrance wrenches me back to the present.

The chatter weans and the crowd parts like the Red Sea did for Moses.

When the kids trip over each other to make way, I'm not surprised to see the football team waltzing in like freaking England's champions. Only, wait. I think they did win a game that would lead them to some sort of a school championship today.

This could or could not be the celebration party for their win.

Another tiny detail that Dan forgot to mention.

I'm not going to kill my best friend.

I'm not going to kill my best friend.

Screw it.

I retrieve my phone and type.

Astrid: You're dead, Dan. Better start picking your funeral song.

Daniel: Resistance by Muse. U know that. What got ur knickers in a twist?

Astrid: Football party? Give me a fucking break. I'd rather choke on my own vomit.

Daniel: First, eww. Second, did I mention eww? Third, stop being a drama queen, crazy bugger.

Astrid: Where are u?

Daniel: Convincing Laura Davis to suck my dick. Heard she deep-throats like a pro.

Astrid: You're a pig. *disgusted emoji*

Daniel: What? It's on my list of things to do while I'm still in school.

Astrid: I'm beginning to think that ur list only has sex missions on it.

Daniel: There's nothing better than fucking.

Astrid: I'd rather watch gore.

Daniel: Astrid, I love u, but u're weird.

Daniel: Gotta go, Laura is giving me the look.

Great. I'm really on my own while Dan is banging his random girl for the night.

My head gets fuzzy—not sure if it's because of the drink or something else. Even the football team, who are fist-bumping the eager crowd and grabbing a random butt here and there, become hazy.

All I keep hearing are the multiple shouts of "King!"

There are two of those at Royal Elite School, also known as RES. According to Dad—sorry, *Father*—I'm to stay away from anything with the last name King.

When I became Lord Henry Clifford's 'public' daughter, he had two rules for me:

You will not disgrace the Clifford surname.

You will stay away from the King surname.

Ordinarily, I wouldn't listen, but the two kings of the school represent everything I loathe.

Unrestrained power.

Reckless behaviour.

Corrupted wealth.

They're probably the ones who own this ridiculously wealthy mansion. Old money is everything in RES and the King name is the definition of it. Even Dad's old money and aristocratic blood don't compare to theirs.

I don't wait for the team's grand entrance.

Invisibility 101: Never mingle with the popular crowd.

I make a beeline towards the back hallways of the mansion, but the cheers and the "Go Elites" follow me all the way through.

The obsession with the football team in this school makes me twitchy. I mean, come on, they're school kids, not the freaking Premier League Titans.

But again, sports have never been my thing. I'm all for art and creativity. I'm a far cry from being an athlete, and Dan always makes fun of how even a small run gets me all out of breath and panting.

As I walk down the half-empty hallway, my head feels fuzzy and disoriented. I see double of the couple making out near a door.

I sway and bump into something.

"Watch it!" someone grunts and I mumble something in return.

Shit. I don't feel good.

I reach for my phone to call Dan. The numbers turn into blurry, wavy lines. I blink and fall against a wall.

I hit Dan's number and the rings sound like they're coming from an underground room. He doesn't pick up.

Come on, Dan.

I try again, but the more time that passes, the hotter my skin becomes. My clothes feel like pieces of lava on my flesh.

I hit Dan's number on my phone again. He still doesn't pick up.

I remember that we agreed to meet at the car park, so I opt to wash my face and head out there.

My hand shakes while I clutch the phone and make my way down the hall, searching for the washroom. There's something else Dan mentioned about tonight's party that somehow flashes into my fuzzy head.

Don't go into the pool house. It's restricted access.

I don't know why I'm thinking about that now. After all, this is far from the pool house.

Couples stand on either side of the wall, making out and

whatnot. I push the first door to my right and stop. The sound of flesh slapping against flesh and unmistakable moans make me slam it shut immediately.

I try the next, and the next, but they're all either locked up or occupied.

And I might have pissed off a few couples.

My clothes stick to my heated skin and my legs turn wobbly and weak, hardly able to carry me. A summer vibe song blurts from the speakers and buzzes through my ears.

A rush of energy washes through me and a weird urge to dance takes a hold of me. It's with effort that I resist the pull and continue on my way.

After a trip down the similar halls, I spot one of the football team's players following a girl out of an isolated room.

Thank God.

I run towards it as fast as my legs allow.

As soon as I'm inside, I head to the door on the right and almost cry with joy when it turns out to be a washroom.

The automatic tap opens, and I splash water on my face over and over, but there's no extinguishing the fire expanding all over my flesh.

I know something is wrong with me, I just don't know what. Could it be the cheeseburger I had with Dan on the way over?

All I know is that I need to go home. Now.

With one last splash of water, I trudge back to the exit.

I should've heard the male voices. I should've hidden in the bathroom for a bit more.

Hell, I should've never gone into 'the room' in the first place.

The moment I open the door, pale blue eyes peer into my soul.

King.

The same king I was warned to stay away from. He's watching me with a smirk and a glint in his eyes as if he found his next prey.

"Looks like a little lamb lost her way."

TWO

Astrid

Invisibility 101: Don't mingle with the most popular boy in school.

Holy shit. Are those eyes for real?

It's the first thought I have while staring up at the eldest of the school's two kings. The blue of his irises are so pale, it's almost grey, but not really. It's like a cloudy sky with a promise of some blue. It's impossible to predict whether they'll darken into a storm or clear into a mesmerising day.

And it has absolutely nothing to do with how much I love the colour blue or how his eyes have one of the rarest variations I've ever seen.

I'd take hours of mixing paint and still not be able to come out with the right colouring.

In my two years in RES, I never paid attention to the 'Kings'. Of course, they were shoved down mine—and everyone else's—throats at school for being the rulers. The kings. The prodigy football players. The future heirs of King Enterprises that own half the country and control the other half through politicians.

You can't escape the King surname in the UK—unless you live in a cave, and even then, their name might follow you there. They dominate *The Daily Mail* and every mail. If I didn't know better, I'd say they're after the Queen's throne. Only, some might argue they're already more powerful than she is.

However, this is my first up-close-and-personal look at a 'King'.

Levi King.

Captain of the football team.

Crowned king of the school.

And attractive as shit.

It's not his eyes, but more like *all* of him. His golden blond hair is short on the sides and long on top, pushed back in a sexy tousled kind of way. His jaw is too sharp for a seventeen going on eighteen-year-old. He's too tall; I have to look up to stare up at him—or ogle the shit out of him, basically. The hard ridges of his shoulders and arms hint at muscles honed by hours in the practice room. He's like a young Viking in dark jeans, a black T-shirt, and the team's royal blue jacket that has the school's lion-shield-crown on it.

Yup, he totally inherited Viking genes from the folk who invaded England's shores once upon a time.

Well, shit. Even with the football team reminder and something Dad said about staying away from the King last name, I want to run my fingers through his hair and see if it feels as silky as it looks.

I open my mouth, meaning to say something—something stupid probably—but nothing comes out. That's weird. I don't feel as funny as I did not so long ago.

If anything, energy buzzes through my heated skin so hard that a tremor runs along my limbs.

I stumble forward and a strong hand clutches my bare forearm.

A bolt of electricity shoots straight to a secret part of me.

Oh, God. That feels *so* good.

"You okay there, Princess?" He removes his hand after steadying me.

I clutch it in mine and put it on my arm. "Do it again."

My voice is too sultry even to my own ears, but I don't care. His touch just elicited something euphoric and I want to feel it again.

My lips clamp around a moan as I move his hand up and down my arm in a long sensual caress.

For the love of Vikings, why does it feel so smooth and hot and…bloody amazing?

I need more.

A lot more.

"What do you think you're doing?" He stares down at me with a look of interest mixed with menace.

Or maybe it's only menace and I'm imagining the interest part because my body needs it right now.

He pulls his hand free from mine and before I can groan at losing the sinful sensation, he advances into me until I'm pressed against the doorframe.

He smells like clean soap mixed with expensive cologne and smoke. I sniff with a loud, embarrassing sound like a drug addict getting a fix.

All that penetrates my hazy brain is his hot as shit presence and the fact that he's way too overdressed for a Viking.

I reach for him in a mindless attempt to remove his clothes. His jacket brushes against my top and my nipples tighten with pulsating throbs.

My movements stop at the humming sensation. That feels so good.

Why does it feel so good?

Worse, why the hell do I want to rub my breasts against his chest—or jacket, I'm not so picky right now.

"You're not supposed to be here, Princess." The rumble of his voice rolls over my hyperaware skin like whips of his tongue.

I nod, not even aware of what I'm nodding at. I just need him to get a little closer.

"Do you know what happens to bad girls who go where they shouldn't?"

I continue nodding, too transfixed by the ethereal blue of his eyes. Are those some flecks of grey in them? If only I had my sketchbook to capture the moment.

Though it would be near impossible to emulate the colour.

Levi grabs me by the arm and this time, a moan escapes my

throat as he drags me out of the bathroom and into the vast room I breezed through earlier.

I'm too focused on his hand on my bare skin and how my thighs have tightened to notice anything around us.

"Look what I found." His voice alerts me to the shapes in the dimly lit room.

The low music thumping from the walls has 'You'll end up dead' in the lyrics as soon as I let the outside environment sink in.

Okay, that's not creepy at all.

Half of the football team are either smoking, drinking, or playing cards. They all look up at Levi's words.

"I thought girls were for later?" one of them asks with amusement. "Not that I mind. You can start with my dick, love."

Eww.

"Naw, come on!" Another throws the deck of cards. He has curly brown hair and is wearing his jacket backwards. "I'm not taking your sloppy seconds anymore, Chris. C'est pas cool."

"I'm your senior, Ronan. Shut it."

"I think she wants me first." Hot breaths tickle down my ear as warm lips brush my earlobe. "Don't you, Princess?"

Um, yeah! Yeah!

Keep doing that, please.

I want to shout that at the top of my lungs, but I can't find the words. I can only close my eyes and lean into his hard chest. Well, hell. He can probably use this thing as a surfboard.

Something at the back of my mind tells me this is wrong— so wrong, but I don't particularly care about that something at the moment.

That something can go suck it as long as King keeps touching me and making me feel good. Torturous, but still so fucking good.

"Wait," a smooth voice calls from my right, where two members of the football team are isolated playing…chess?

He stands up and stalks towards me with infinite ease. His team jacket clings to his broad shoulders. Either he walks too silently or I'm too buzzed to hear his steps.

Because the next thing I notice, he's in my face, looking down at me with sinister eyes that are darker than Levi's. Even his hair is jet-black. He shares Levi's straight nose and the same posture, but he's nothing like him.

While Levi gives the impression of a badass Viking king. His cousin has the aura of a silent serial killer king who may or may not slaughter his people if he feels bored.

The younger of the two Kings, Aiden, watches me for a few long seconds with his hands nonchalantly tucked in his pockets as if he's assessing a lamb for slaughter.

Damn these two cousins and how beautiful they are. Even with menace written all over his face, I can't help noticing the whole deadly charm he has going on.

"You're Clifford, aren't you?" Aiden asks.

"Clifford?" The previous playfulness in Levi's voice vanishes into thin air and his tone hardens.

I hold on to the feel of his hand on my arm as I choke out. "I'm just Astrid. Clifford is Dad's name." I giggle and lower my voice. "Oops. Shh. Don't tell him I called him Dad. He doesn't like that."

Aiden raises an eyebrow as if he's proved a point, but he's not looking at me. "Hands off, Lev."

Silence rolls through the room. Even the other guys stop whatever they're doing and focus on me sandwiched between the two cousins.

Or more like, they're focused on the hostile energy that's brewing between the two kings.

Me? I rub my back against Levi's chest, needing to feel the friction and something else—I just don't know what.

"No." It's a single word, but even in my half-dazed, euphoria-seeking state, I can feel the power behind it.

"Father said —"

"I don't care what he said." Levi cuts him off in a cool tone. "Uncle doesn't tell me what to fucking do."

A few of the guys howl as if he delivered the punchline of the century.

"You're digging your own grave." Aiden shrugs and stalks back towards the chessboard and another player who's been waiting for him.

Levi's arm curls around my shoulder and he pulls me into the hard curve of his side. A shot of electricity runs through me and settles between my thighs as his fingers stroke my bare skin underneath my top.

I suck in a stuttering breath, holding on to the sensation with everything in me.

"Anyone else have any objection to make?" he asks, but he doesn't seem to be expecting an answer.

Levi King's word is law.

Anyone who goes against him will only crash and burn.

The football team's players all come from prestigious tycoon families, both old and new money, but they're nothing compared to the Kings' power.

The only one who can stand up to Levi is another King. Which isn't happening any time soon since Aiden seems to have lost interest in this situation altogether. He sits on his chair, head leaning against his hand as he continues playing chess.

I'm not surprised when not one of the team members say a word.

Levi drags me beside him down the hall. I hold on to every touch like I'll die if he stops.

"Save some for me, Captain!" one of the guys shouts.

I'm too occupied by his arm around my stomach to register anything else.

It isn't until a door closes behind us and Levi releases me that I realise we're in a room.

Alone.

THREE

Levi

A monster isn't born. It's made.

Here, little lamb. I won't eat you.

At least, not yet.

The girl was all over me not two minutes ago, but now that we're alone in one of the private bedrooms in Uncle's sickeningly large mansion, she looks about ready to bolt.

I breeze past her, and she trembles then shrinks back against the wall as if the mere contact is electrifying.

I flop onto the edge of the bed, leaning on one hand, and tilt my head to watch her.

She's pretty in a pop fiction kind of way. Pale rosy lips. Long, silky brown hair and eyes so green, they almost sparkle and shit.

Granted, she's not as pretty as the girls who throw themselves at me and the team all the time, but she's got it going on in a discreet, almost tomboyish kind of way.

With her denim shorts and unconventional trainers, it's like she's stuck at that point between girlhood and teenagehood.

The only difference is, there's nothing immature about her petite figure. She has soft curves and a tiny waist that fit perfectly in my palm earlier.

In the beginning, I planned to play with her, push her buttons and then pass her around for the team.

But after I learned her last name, she became my prey for the night.

Screwing Clifford's princess means one thing—pissing Uncle off.

And I live to piss Uncle the fuck off and see how he looks at me like I'm a rock in his shoe.

The failure.

The king without a crown.

The family's black sheep.

I'm just giving him one more reason to hate me—aside from the grand finale I have planned for his favourite holiday home.

I pat my thigh. "Come here, Princess."

She swallows, the sound echoing in the silence surrounding us. Clifford glances between me and the door for a fraction of a second.

They say the human brain is wired for snap decisions.

It's funny how people make mistakes, thinking they're the right choices.

Like Clifford's princess for instance.

Her brain is obviously telling her to run. Deep down, we can all sense danger, but not everyone focuses enough to relate to their basic instincts.

I should probably thank chess and Uncle's tyrannical upbringing for making me so aware of my surroundings.

Clifford's princess either missed some aristocratic lessons from her lord father or she simply doesn't give a fuck.

It'd be so interesting if it were the latter.

With one deep breath, she abandons the door and takes tentative steps in my direction, red creeping up her neck.

She comes to a halt in front of me, rubbing her arm and peeking down at me through her thick lashes. I grab her wrist and she moans, her eyes fluttering closed.

I stop myself before I yank her to my lap and fuck her senseless.

When she moaned earlier, I thought it was a show or some seduction technique.

I stand and tilt her chin up with my thumb and forefinger, staring straight into her dilated pupils.

No wonder she turns into a puddle whenever I touch her. She's pumped with E.

I push her away and she releases a tiny gasp, her eyes snapping open.

"W-what?"

"I don't do druggies. Run along."

Her brows draw together as if she's offended. "I'm not a druggie."

"Says every druggie."

She tilts her chin up in defiance. "You can't tell me I'm something I'm not."

Huh. Interesting.

She has the attitude that comes with the princess title.

My hand wraps around her waist under her T-shirt so that my skin is touching hers. She fits so fucking perfectly in just one palm. My fingers creep up near her ribs and I stroke her until a shudder goes through her.

"That feel good, Princess?"

"Oh, God, yes." Her eyes flutter closed as she steps so close that I smell lilac on her. "More."

That's what every druggie says.

I know that, should've said that.

But I'm caught in how her lips part, accentuating the pink teardrop in the middle. She's so aroused that I not only feel it in the tremors of her body, but I also smell it in the air.

I'm tempted to yank her top off, bend her over, and fuck her until she forgets her name and screams mine.

But I meant it. I don't do druggies.

Clifford's princess stares up at me and bites down on the corner of her lip. My pelvis crashes against her lower stomach as she moves up and down against my jeans.

My dick hardens as she moans, "Please, more."

Fuck me.

Maybe I can make an exception this time. I'm already corrupted, so I might as well.

But before I give in to my demons, I snap, "Out."

When she stares at me with that slight blush, eyes shining with innocence and pain, a sick thought remains in my mind.

I want to complicate her.

Ruin her.

Crush her innocence.

Then watch it all burn.

But again, that's what I feel about most beautiful things.

If my soul is black, why does the world need colours?

I grab her arm and drag her towards the back door. Her lips part as she struggles to keep up with my strides. When I open it and throw her outside, her lips part.

She wobbles towards me. "No, wait —"

I shut the door in her face, muting all the foggy chaos that erupted because of her presence.

Tonight isn't the time, but it will come.

Clifford's princess and I will have another duel once she's sober and can handle me.

But for now… I smile as I exit the bedroom and return to the team.

It's time for my summer gift to Uncle.

FOUR

Astrid

Not only did I bleed, but you also left me for dead.

My fists bang on the door for what seems like hours. It's like there's no soul behind it. No answer.

No nothing.

I slide down to the ground, regaining my breathing.

So much weird energy buzzes through me, like there's a party going on through my organs. I want to jump and run—at the same time.

I don't know where this place is, but it's dark. The only light comes from the main house in the distance. *Something Just Like This* by Coldplay and The Chainsmokers playing at the party. Somehow, I drifted from the main house and ended up in this adjacent building during my trip earlier. Maybe this is the pool house Dan mentioned.

Normally, I'd make sure there was no one in my immediate vicinity, but normal isn't today.

I jump up and start dancing, twirling between the bushes and riding the wave coursing through my veins.

If someone is invincible enough to jump to the sky, it's me.

The music seeps under my skin and tightens my muscles.

My tank top sticks to my back with sweat the more I twirl and shake my hips like Mum and I used to.

Pressure builds behind my eyes at the memory of her— or the lack thereof. It's been two years and she's becoming more and more like an illusion. Her smile is disappearing and the positive energy she taught me has been replaced by a deep gloom.

While dancing, I pull the underside of my forearm in the direction of the light. It's not clear, but I can almost see the tiny tattoos of a sun, a moon, and a star.

She made the star black because I'm her 'star'. She said she named me Astrid because it means an old Norse star, a super strength that she needed when she had me.

The tattoo is the last memory I have of her.

If I hadn't asked her to come pick me up from an art class late at night, if I hadn't thrown a tantrum when she told me the news, maybe she'd be here now.

Maybe I wouldn't be stuck with Dad and his entitled last name.

If I'd gotten her out of the car in time, if I had called for help in time…

I screw my eyes shut against the grief and the what-ifs. My shrink said guilt-shaming will only consume me without offering a solution. Still, the wave of crushing guilt is as constant as every breath I take. It's lodged in the dark corners of my heart and my soul.

It feels like it was yesterday. The smell of smoke, burnt flesh, and metallic blood.

So much fucking blood.

I continue swaying to the music with less energy. My arms wrap around my middle and I open my eyes, chasing the 'guilt-shaming' away.

I want to take off my clothes and take a dip in the pool.

Sounds like a brilliant idea, me.

I jump and hop amidst the bushes and the dirt path leading to the main mansion.

Dan better show up or I'll kill him. What's the use of a best friend if he doesn't go stupid pool dancing with me?

The bright lights of the house become clearer, and I stop, shielding my eyes with the back of my hand. Ugh. Why so strong? I'm still struggling with the lights when the sound of hushed voices reach me.

"Come on, we don't have time. Do it!"

"Shut it. Everything needs to be perfect."

"Just do it already or we'll be in trouble."

My ears perk up at the hushed whispers coming from between the bushes. They're male, but I don't think I've ever heard them before.

Or have I?

But then again, RES is too big for me to know everyone. Especially since I nailed the invisible role.

Besides, this is the farewell party before summer, so more than likely, all the students are here.

My instinct tells me this isn't a conversation or a situation I should be privy to. And my instincts are always right.

I sneak in the opposite direction towards the blinding light.

A twig crunches under my shoes like in some cliché horror film. I freeze in place, muting my chaotic breathing as best as I can.

"Who's there?" the first hardened voice asks.

"I'm going to check."

"Don't let them escape!"

Oh, for the love of Vikings!

I sprint through the bushes and between the tall trees. Loud footsteps echo behind me.

My heart hammers against my ribcage as if it's about to spill on the ground. The more the footsteps close in on me, the harder I push forward.

I'm not an athletic person. The mere act of running whooshes all the energy out of me like I'm a deflating balloon. Soon enough, I'm panting and sweating like a pig.

"It's over here." One of them calls.

"I'm bringing backup."

Dad is so going to kill me if these guys don't.

Too many gory films, Astrid. You watch too many gory films. There's no way high school students—RES's posh students, no less—would commit murder.

Then I recall that their families' power can get them out of anything. Including murder.

God, I hate everything these rich kids stand for.

I try to run on silent mode, but the twigs continue crunching under my feet as if purposely giving a signal to my hunters.

Branches and the odd tree trunk scrape against my bare arms as I carry on my run.

My pulse pounds in my ears when I reach a small road. I bend over behind a tree to catch my erratic breathing.

Aside from the moonlight slipping through the clouds and the trees, it's pitch-black out here. The mansion's lights and music have completely disappeared.

The footsteps have vanished, too, and so have the voices. Phew. Maybe even my horrible athletic skills have managed to get me out of this unscathed.

Still, my heart won't stop beating fast and hard against my chest cavity.

Thump. Thump. Thump.

I take tentative steps towards the empty road, hoping to find someone for help.

Two steps forward. One step back.

The sound of a night bird—or beast—makes me freeze in place, almost peeing myself.

When I go home, I won't take gory or horror films for granted anymore. It's terrifying as hell in real life.

"This way!" someone shouts.

"No one sees and lives to tell about it," a familiar voice— super familiar—deadpans as numerous steady footsteps sprint in my direction.

I bolt down the road, my heart hammering in my chest so loudly, I can't hear my own breathing.

Run.

Run.

Run!

They say you don't feel it when your life ends.

I do.

It happens in a split second.

One moment, I'm running down the road; the next, blinding headlights freeze me in place.

I want to move. I want to get out of the way.

I can't.

Something hard crushes against my side and I'm flying over the road. I fall with a thud, my hands flopping in an awkward position.

Something warm pools underneath me and sticks to my T-shirt.

Voices scatter all around me along with the loud squeal of someone slamming their brakes.

The metallic stench of blood fills my nostrils, just like that day two years ago.

It's rainy and dark. So fucking dark, I can smell death in the air.

It has a distinctive scent, death. All murky and metallic and smoky.

Mum's head is lolled to the side with blood running all over her neck, smudging the white blazer she was happy to receive last week.

I stretch out a hand, but nothing in my body moves.

I can't reach my mum.

I can't save her.

"P-please… Please…no…please…"

Dark shadows loom over me. They're talking, but it's hushed and I can't make anything of it.

Warm fingers touch my side. I crack my eyes open and make out a small star tattoo like mine on the inside of his arm.

"Leave her," the voice says.

My world goes black.

FIVE

Astrid

They didn't think I'd come back alive.

Two months later,

Back to school.

Back to life, basically.

The past two months were pieces cut from hell. I half-expected Lucifer—the real one, not the TV show—to jump out and inflict some sort of torture.

While all the kids at school holidayed and posted pictures from all over exotic places, I spent my time split between the hospital and rehab.

All of it crashed down on me in such a short period of time, it's like I'm reliving the tragedy from three years ago.

Unlike then, I didn't come out unscathed.

I broke my leg, bruised my ribs, and dislocated my shoulder. According to the doctor and the nursing staff, I was lucky.

Lucky.

Such a weird word.

I even heard my stepmother say that to her countless snobbish friends. I was *lucky* to have escaped death twice.

Obviously, this luck thing isn't hereditary, because Mum died in her first car accident.

Why couldn't I share that *luck* with her?

Dan flings an arm around my shoulder, bringing me back to the present.

The September sky has a beautiful pale hue and the sun actually shines down on us peasants in the UK.

The air smells of autumn's humidity and that tame forest scent—coming from the huge pine trees surrounding Royal Elite School.

Dan and I make our way through the tall double doors, both dressed in our uniforms. Mine has a dark blue skirt and a matching jacket with RES's golden lion-shield-crown on the pocket. A red ribbon is tied around my neck over the white button-down shirt. Dan's is identical except he has trousers and a red tie.

Dan smiles—complete with a left dimple—at all of the female species passing by us and adds a few winks, causing some of them to nearly fall over each other.

He's good-looking in that classic British kind of way. First of all, he has a dimple—that must be why I wanted to be friends with him. People with dimples kind of draw others in like magnets. He takes his time to style his chestnut hair in a way that looks imperfect. Add in his turquoise ocean eyes and he's like a model in the making.

No joke. A scout stopped his mum in the mall and begged her to have their agency represent him.

"Hey, crazy bugger." He pokes my arm. "We can do the final year and we can even do it sideways, too."

I roll my eyes. "Does everything need to have a sexual meaning with you?"

"Hell yeah. Senior year, senior sex life, baby."

I shake my head. Incurable Dan.

For a moment, I'm lost in all the students rushing through RES. Half appear excited—mostly freshman—while the other half look as if they were dragged out of bed.

Oh, and I belong to the second half, thank you very much.

One more year.

Just one more year and I'm out of this shit show.

Dan stops me on the side of the half-covered hall where students are filtering through and catching up on all the fun they had during the summer.

Some discreetly whisper while pointing at me, but it's few and far between.

I may be a Clifford, but I'm not at all that important in RES.

Here's to hoping the accident news will die down soon so I can go back to being my cute, invisible self.

Problem is, there were double accidents that night. The mansion caught fire when that car hit me.

We have a Facebook group for RES' students, from which teachers and the administrators' board are banned. In said group, some have speculated that the hit-and-run driver put the mansion on fire, then during their escape, they hit me.

Other freaks suggested that I'm an accomplice, since, well, Clifford and King are enemies. And boo-freaking-hoo, it appears that the mansion belongs to Jonathan King.

"You returned from the dead." Dan ruffles my hair again. "That alone deserves a celebration. I'll delay my shagging sesh with Cindy if you want to grab a greasy cheeseburger from Ally's?"

"Wow." I gasp in mock surprise, putting a hand on my chest. "You would delay your sexcapades for me? I didn't think you loved me this much, Bug."

"I know, right? The sacrifices one has to make for friendship. You better name your first baby after me. Daniel Junior would look bloody brilliant on paper."

That draws a chuckle out of me, even though I'm not in the mood. This is Dan's way to cheer me up.

Aside from attending the football team's camp, he spent the summer making the rehab sessions less boring and drawing a laugh out of me every chance he got.

He doesn't voice it, but I know he's been feeling guilty about leaving me alone that night. I've been trying to tell him it wasn't his fault, but Dan will just be Dan.

Loyal to a fault.

My shadow to a fault, too.

Or maybe it's the other way around. I'm the invisible one, so I'm probably the shadow in this friendship.

One more year and we'll both be free of our parents and their expectations.

Free. Just the thought pushes a burst of unanticipated energy through my veins.

Dan and I continue our way inside, talking about our classes.

RES's old architecture doesn't reduce any points from its stupid grandiose reputation. Built in King Henry IV's time during the fourteenth century, it was first used for the king's subjects and then fell under the rule of aristocrats and old money folks.

The huge arcs and the half-covered stony hallways evoke a breeze from the past mixed with the present's modernity. It has ten towers, each dedicated to a level. Seniors get four. Freshmen and second years get three each.

RES is exactly its name. Elite's school. The private school of all schools. It's not only about money here, though. If you don't have the brains that go with Daddy's bank account, you're not welcome within its walls.

It has the toughest entrance exams in the country and they're very selective about who they accept into their ranks.

I guess I got lucky.

Or not.

Depending on how you look at it.

For one, education here can help me in breaking free from Dad. But does it matter if he's the reason I'm here in the first place?

"So, party this weekend?" Dan asks with a waggle of his brows.

"Wow. You really think I'd step foot in a party after what happened at the last one we were at?"

"You can't let them bring you down. I bet they want you to stop having fun."

"It was a hit-and-run, Dan. Pretty sure they wanted me dead, not to stop me from having fun."

"You think they're the same people who called help and gave as many details about you as possible?"

"I don't think so."

My 'saviour', as Dan and I labelled him, was the one who had a star tattoo on his forearm. Sort of like the star in the sun-moon-star tattoo Mum inked on me. However, when the responders came to get me, they found no one by my side.

Dan searches my face. "And you still remember nothing about that?"

I shake my head. Because of the fire, the police didn't manage to retrieve any surveillance camera footage.

The facts were, I was drugged and then hit by a car that night. My blood test results showed a considerable dose of ecstasy and some cocaine.

I think Dad was angrier about the drugs—and, therefore, his reputation—than whether or not I remained alive.

Dad thought I used the drugs of my own accord. He didn't have to say it for me to feel it. He thinks I'm a complete disgrace to the Clifford name.

All he did was slap me with numerous therapies, coping, and maintenance. It's like I'm a machine who's supposed to start running again after a few mechanics look into it.

He did the same after Mum's death. He never stopped to ask if maybe I wanted to talk to him instead of some strangers.

To occupy myself, I've been visiting the deputy commissioner—a friend of Dad's—and insisting on finding the bastard who did this to me.

If they think I'll cower into my shell and be a turtle, they'll have a freaking ninja turtle on their hands.

Okay, that was lame, but all my similes are.

Mum and I didn't have much, but we had our dignity. She taught me to never take other people's rights but to not let them take my rights either.

If you don't strike back, people will stomp all over you, Star.

Mum might not be here anymore, but her words are my mantra.

"You're all I got, so don't go all emo on me." Dan fist-bumps me and we make a sound that resembles the 'Big Bang'. "Stay strong, Bugger."

"Strong is all I got, mate." I nudge him with a shoulder. "I wasn't always all rich and preppy like you."

"Yes, Miss Working Class." He grins, saluting as he motions in the direction of the football team's lockers. "I'm over here. See you in class."

I wave at him with two fingers and continue down the hall. Energy pumps through my veins at the idea that all this will be over soon.

One more year.

I'm making my way towards the classroom when a hand slams on the doorframe right next to the side of my head and a tall body blocks my entrance.

My vision snaps to the obstacle and I freeze. Everyone in the hall seems to stop walking and talking altogether, too.

Levi King.

The same hypnotic eyes that pushed me to the brink of death stare down at me with a strange gleam. The other time, I saw interest mixed with menace, but now, it's complete calculation.

"What do you want?" I snap, and a few gasps break around me.

No one snaps at Levi King. Kids here trip over themselves to keep him happy and comfy on his stupid throne.

I'm thankful my voice contains all the venom I feel for this bastard.

He knew I was drugged and still threw me out to be hunted down and left for dead.

Well, he only knew I was on drugs. He couldn't possibly have known someone drugged me unless he was the same arsehole who did it.

But that's the part that remains fuzzy. If Levi drugged me, why didn't he carry on with his plan instead of kicking me out?

A change of heart, perhaps.

But why would he drug me anyway? He and I don't cross paths. Ever.

He lives on the highest position of the food chain and I've chosen the low, comfortable—and very invisible—end on purpose.

What made me visible to him?

That's the only reason I'm not going full offence on him. That doesn't mean I'll take his entitled shit around me, though.

The accident taught me something valuable. I'll not be a secondary character in my own life.

Not anymore.

Levi tilts his head to the side. "Is that any way to greet me after the entire summer, Princess?"

"What do you expect? A chanting of 'Long Live the King'? Sorry, the choir is still on holiday."

His lips twitch in amusement. Even when I'm sober, he's attractive as shit. His shoulders have broadened over the summer—due to football training, no doubt—and I swear he became even taller.

"And here I thought you were still interested."

"Interested?" I repeat, dumbfounded.

"Did you forget?" His voice drops to a shiver-inducing range. "You begged me for more the last time we were together."

My cheeks warm until I feel like I've been thrown into a

pit of flames. He had to bring up the most embarrassing moment of my life.

I lift my chin. "Lapse of judgement. Believe me, it won't happen again."

His fingers clasp around my wrist and he tugs me towards him. I try to twist and pull, but that only makes his grip tighter.

"Let me go," I grit out, hating the audience that has stopped to see the show.

My cheeks flame with hot, flashing anger at being manhandled in public. Way to ruin my top-notch invisible reputation.

"Meet me after school," he whispers in that deep, slightly husky voice.

It's not a request, it's a flat out order. He must be so used to people falling at his feet.

I give up trying to remove my wrist and glare up at him. "Why would I want to do that?"

He taps my nose twice. "Wait for me at the car park after practice."

"No."

"Be there, Princess."

He must still see defiance written all over my face. Instead of cowering away, his eyes shine with mischievousness and something similar to 'challenge accepted'.

When he speaks again, it's loud enough for everyone surrounding us to hear.

"Don't worry. This time I won't make you beg for it." He smirks. "For long."

Scorching heat climbs up my neck and to my face, bathing me in red-hot embarrassment mixed with blinding anger.

His lips widen in a smug grin that says, 'I always win' before he taps my nose again and walks in the opposite direction. Everyone goes out of their way to let him go through as if they actually believe he's the king or some shit.

I stand like a red ball of rage, watching his retreating back with stupefaction as one of the other seniors joins him and soon enough, half of the football team are waltzing alongside him towards the locker room.

Everyone continues gawking at me as if I'm a world wonder—or a mass murderer, I can't be sure which with some of the girls' glares.

"Slut," one of them hisses as she brushes past me.

The anger that should be directed at her or her minions who spout similar insults is burning in the opposite direction.

Towards the locker room and the wanker in it.

King wants me to meet him after school?

I'll be meeting him after school, all right, but he'll be wishing he never issued his royal decree.

SIX

Levi

You could've escaped the battle, but instead, you asked for a bloody war.

Coach yells at the front lines, his voice reverberating over the pitch like he's a general at war. Or maybe he's the strategist.

A royal blue baseball cap with RES's golden crown covering his bald head, he rolls his notes into what resembles a bat that he doesn't hesitate to strike the slacking players with.

We've just finished our first practice game of the season. The main team lost against the second-year team. Two-nil.

Two to fucking nil.

The negative energy radiating off Coach Larson is like a black shroud over my mood.

The two teams stand in straight lines opposite one another as Coach paces between us.

The second team wears neon yellow over the team's jersey while my team has the official royal blue jerseys and white shorts.

"Ladies," Larson snarls, his small eyes and bushy brows give him a meaner, harsher look. "Is this how we're starting the season after last year's defeat?"

"No, sir!" all of us yell.

"I didn't hear you, girls."

"No, sir!" we bellow.

He nods as he continues his back and forth pacing with his hands crossed behind him. The paper bat hits his spine with every move. "The school might put you on a pedestal, but that's only because you're getting Royal Elite's name out there. The moment you stop benefitting the board, the team will be gone."

A few murmurs break amongst the players, but they know better than to interrupt Coach.

"What did you think? Your parents pay for your education, not sports. Royal Elite is all about academics. The only reason they indulge with a few sports teams is because they want to promote that the school isn't all about nerdy, snobbish teenagers. Are we or are we not going to prove to them that we breathe football?"

"We are!"

"Are we or are we not going to win the schools' championship this year?"

"We are!"

"I didn't hear you."

"*We. Are!*"

"Captain." Coach stops in front of me with a dark expression.

He doesn't approve of the way I've been leading the team since the finals' loss in July, but he also knows I'm the reason they're in check. He might be the strategist, but I'm the leader of the troops on the field. Besides, he trusts I won't allow anything to screw this up. We both want that championship.

"I need results."

"You will get them, sir."

Still standing in front of me, he points at Daniel, one of the benched players. "Good game, Sterling. You held the fort."

He smirks in that cocky way that half the sports' players have.

Coach moves to Chris, who's standing beside me, and gives him a harsh glare. "Vans. You're out of the startup line next game." He focuses on the opposite team. "Astor, you're in. Show me what you got, boy."

"Yes, sir!" Ronan grins like a goofball.

Coach Larson heads into the locker room with his assistant managers and the medical trainer trailing after him.

Chris lunges forward, to start a scene with Larson, no doubt.

I stand in his way, blocking his path. He's like a bull, eyes black and jaw clenching. I hit my shoulder against his and shake my head.

"Fuck this, King!" he spits out. "I won't give up my position for a second-year."

Ronan waggles his eyebrows. "Maybe you should've played better, huh?"

My gaze meets my cousin Aiden's bored one and I say in a levelled tone, "Take him away."

"Naw." Ronan jumps in place, ducking on his own. "Come at me, bro."

"Ronan," I warn. He's treating it as fun and games, but Chris is volatile as shit right now.

And most of the time, really.

Aiden clutches Ronan's arm while Xander pushes him from the other side.

"Just to be clear," Xander, a striker and a little wanker, calls over his shoulder as they walk away. "This has been long overdue, Chris. You haven't deserved a place on the team since the summer."

Aiden offers me a knowing glance before he, Xander, Ronan, and Cole stalk to the locker room.

They're nicknamed the four horsemen because whenever they're on the field, they bring conquest, war, famine, and eventually death.

I call them the four fuckers.

Aiden, Xander, and Cole snatched their positions from the seniors. Ronan was the last to join.

The rest of the second-year players follow Aiden and his band of thieves. I might be the captain, but if they had to choose, they'd probably take the 'young' King's side.

Chris continues lunging forward like a train losing its course.

Niall and Alex, two seniors, try to pull him back, but it's like he's on Red Bull—or fucking drugs, judging from his performance.

I swing my fist and punch him in the chest. He stops with stupefaction written all over his face. The rest of the senior players and the freshmen watch for my reaction, unblinking.

"What the fuck was that for?" Chris spits out.

"For losing your place."

"It was Coach, he —"

I get in his face. "Did Coach play with your legs? Did he let Aiden score the first goal and lose the ball to Xander so he could score the second? Did he leave the defence like a pathetic deserted land?"

"Well, no, but —"

"No buts, Chris." I point a finger at his chest. "You've been playing like shit since the quarter-final game and during summer camp. If you don't snatch your place back from Ronan, you're out. For. Fucking. Good. I don't need halfwits on my team."

He opens his mouth to say something, but I'm not listening anymore. The rest of the players part as I make my way to the showers.

Christopher and I are friends. Well, maybe not exactly friends, but colleagues. We both like the high of alcohol, cigarettes, and girls.

We've been rebels against our last names and our families.

I loathe my uncle and he hates his uptight father, who's the metropolitan police's deputy commissioner. Chris and I found each other in detention when we were juniors, and we bonded.

If there's trouble, we shit all over it. Both of us live for that disapproving look on our guardians' faces.

We even bet on whether his father or my uncle will pay the largest cheque to the school to cover all the trouble we cause year in and year out.

But Chris has been spiralling out of control. He's been a knee too deep in the excitement part that he doesn't play decently anymore.

Football isn't only a game for me. It's not a high of the moment and a pumping of adrenaline. It isn't the roaring of the crowd or the chants.

It's a state of mind.

It's the only fucking thing I own in a life that's shackled by Uncle's chains.

Football is the only thing I'm doing for myself, and no one will take it away from me.

For that, I need to handle a certain princess problem that's two months overdue.

Aiden and his arsehole friends walk with me to the car park, chatting about the upcoming game. Or more like, Ronan and Xander are bickering while Aiden and Cole shake their heads at them.

Chris left without even going into the locker room. Half the reason why I unleashed on him in front of everyone is because I know he holds grudges. Here's to hoping he'll release it on the pitch by finally sobering up and snatching his place back.

"I'm telling you, fuckers, I want hookers on my birthday." Ronan taps his chest. "That's the least you can do for all the parties I throw you all year round."

Xander punches his side. "And what, you want one that comes out from the cake, too?"

"Fuck yeah." His eyes twinkle. "All in bunny uniforms, *s'il te plait.*"

"Bestiality alert," Cole deadpans.

"Fuck off, Cole." Ronan glares. "Don't kill the fantasy."

"Okay, hold on. Let me get this straight. So we're getting hookers sent to…a House of Lords' member. Like, hello, hookers' house? Can you send some bunny strippers to Earl Astor's mansion?" Xan laughs. "You realise they might send us the police or, I don't know, some MI6 agents?"

"Chill, arsehole. We'll do it in the summer house." He waggles his eyebrows. "Okay, test time. My best friend will be whoever hires the hookers for me. Raise your hand, but no pushing. I know you all want to."

He turns in our direction to find all of us staring. Except for Xan and Cole, who are laughing.

"Come on. Anyone? Cake bunny hookers are my fucking fantasy."

"And we have to make your fantasies come true because…" Aiden trails off with a poker face.

"Because I'll make your fantasies come true in return!" Ronan pauses. "Wait, no. That didn't come out right. I'm seeing some disturbing images in my mind right now."

Xan waggles his eyebrows. "Like?"

"Like Cole and Aiden's kinky shit. I'm not making that rubbish happen." He pauses. "Back to my fantasy. It's completely doable. Anyone?"

Aiden shakes his head. "Pass."

"Besides —" Cole recovers from his fit of laughter "—you do realise that none of us are old enough to hire hookers."

"Captain is." Ronan meets my gaze with puppy eyes.

"Stop looking at me like that or you'll be the only cake bunny hooker on your birthday," I tell him.

The guys burst out laughing, both Xander and Cole teasing Ronan, who's sulking and swearing that he's not throwing any parties for us anymore.

Aiden falls back in step with me, letting his friends trudge ahead. "I heard you punched Vans."

Except for his friends and me, everyone is a last name to Aiden. He doesn't even bother to learn people's first names.

"Why?" I ask. "You going to tell your *daddy* about it?"

Aiden raises an eyebrow. "Do you honestly think Jonathan needs me to tell him anything that happens in this school?"

I scoff.

He probably has paparazzi on us or some shit. Jonathan King owns this school—and probably everyone in it.

There was a coffee shop that Aiden and I frequented. So what did Jonathan do? He bought the fucking thing.

But hey, he didn't do it blindly just because he's a control freak and wants to cage us from every corner. No. That's not how the tycoon of King Enterprises works.

He studied the place like hell first, and only took over it when he knew that it'd be two hundred per cent profitable.

Oh, and yeah, he abso-fucking-lutely sent his harem of lawyers and his PR team to intimidate the owners into selling.

"You're playing with fire, Lev." Aiden's words bring me back to the present.

I stop and face him so that we're toe-to-toe. Only, I have a few inches on him. "Yeah?"

"One miss." He raises an index finger. "Whether it's alcohol, fights, or any other disaster, and you're done for with *my daddy*. It's checkmate."

My jaw clenches so hard, my teeth hurt. I want to pummel Aiden into the wall and punch that smug look off his face.

Before I can act on the impulse and give Uncle the trouble he's been pining for, Ronan's high-pitched voice breaks the tension. "Oh, shit."

Cole winces as he glances at me over his shoulder.

"What is it?" I walk ahead of Aiden and stop short in front of my black Jaguar.

On the windshield, there's something written in white paint.

'Run along, King. You don't need to beg for it.'

SEVEN

Astrid

I was forgotten until you said my name.

My muscles lock as I make my way down the sweeping marble stairs. I've been living here for more than two years, but it still doesn't feel like home.

It's a tower and I'm trapped.

Nope. Not like Rapunzel or even Disney's *Tangled*. This is the real-life version.

Since Mum's death, I've been nicknamed 'Clifford's Hidden Princess' by the press. Because Dad hid me away for a whole fifteen years, even though he and Mum were married for some time and I'm not an illegitimate child.

Since the public revelation, I started to think that I might truly be a hidden, forgotten princess. Locked up in this mansion.

One more year.

With that splash of hope, I take a deep breath and cross the grandiose lounge area with gold-rimmed chesterfields and high platform ceilings.

I peek through the dining area where my 'family' is having breakfast.

"Morning," I blurt, already heading to the exit. "I'm leaving for school."

"Astrid." Dad's calm but non-negotiable tone stops me in my tracks. "Come eat."

"I'm not hungry."

"Sit down and eat."

I wince at the harshness in his command and my shoulders slump. With careful steps, I cross the gigantic dining room with its flawless marble flooring and stone fireplace. A few of the kitchen staff stand in waiting like an episode from freaking *Downton Abbey*.

I smile at Sarah, the head cook, but it must've come out as a grimace, judging from the deep frown across her blonde brows.

At least I have a friendly face around. It helps that she makes me the most delicious chocolate smoothies and cheesecake.

I flop on the chair at the tail end of the table—which is the farthest seat from Dad's and his wife's. Not meeting their gazes, I start gulping down raw jam and the cheesecake. I scarcely taste anything. The sooner I'm done with breakfast, the faster I'm out of here.

"Honey, slow down." My stepmother's fake caring tone ruins my gluttonous mood. "Don't worry. The food isn't going anywhere."

I gulp the mouthful of the smooth cheesecake, finally tasting the sweetness of it, and cut her a glare across the table.

Victoria has an elegant aura about her. It's in everything she wears or says. Even her tone is a flashback from a period film. Her blonde hair is gathered in a neat French twist. She's wearing a tailored high couture dress that must've cost a Third World country's budget. A dainty necklace surrounds her smooth neckline and the matching earrings dangle from her ears. She keeps bragging that Dad got her the jewellery set for her birthday.

Gag.

She's everything a lord's wife should be. It's like she was made straight from a manual.

Victoria might look ten years younger than her actual age

due to the facelifts and the aristocratic name, but she's nothing like Mum.

My mother was proud of her tattoos and her artistic streak. She was a free spirit meant to fly, not to be trapped in a mansion like Victoria. But, then again, maybe that's why Dad chose her over my mum.

Ever since I came here, Victoria has made it her job to throw jabs about my origins. If I eat fast, it's because Mum kept me hungry. If I refuse the expensive gowns, it's because I'm used to scraps. If I'm acknowledged by anyone, it's only because I'm leeching off Dad's name.

"It's different here, honey." Victoria's lips pull in a conservative smile as she does with the reporters. "You don't have to worry about food."

"I never had to worry about food before either," I say after swallowing another mouthful of Sarah's cheesecake.

Screw Victoria for insinuating that Mum didn't take care of me. She was both my mother and my father rolled into one.

I admired her for raising me on her own and being everything I needed.

When I first showed an interest in sketching, Mum stayed up all night modelling for me. When I was having a bad day, she'd take me on long drives, just the two of us.

Mum was my world while Daddy dearest lived with his *real* family.

"It's fine if you did," Victoria continues.

"We didn't. Mum worked for a living, you know. She didn't freeload off her lord husband."

Victoria's upper lip twitches and I smile to myself. Small victories.

"Astrid Elizabeth Clifford."

I wince at Dad's deadly calm tone. If he calls me by my full name, then he disapproves.

Not that he ever really approves of me.

My fork clinks against the plate as I lift my head slightly to meet his punishing green eyes. The definite proof that I'm his daughter. That his genes collaborated in making mine.

I'll be eighteen a few weeks from now, but I still feel as small as the seven-year-old kid who begged him to stay. The stupid little kid who painted him as my first kindergarten picture.

Henry Clifford is solid and well-built for someone in his mid-forties. His dark brown hair, another something I inherited, is styled back, highlighting his strong forehead and the straight, aristocratic nose.

His pressed navy suit clings to his body as if he were born into one. I certainly don't remember him out of it.

When I was a kid, I used to feel over the moon with joy whenever he showed up.

Now, he just intimidates me.

I don't know when he stopped being my dad and started being his title.

Victoria places her hand on top of Dad's with a sickeningly sweet smile that's giving me diabetes. "It's okay, darling. She'll come around."

Kill me now.

"Morning!" A breeze of potent cherry perfume—that must've cost another fortune—wafts past me.

Nicole kisses her mum and my dad on their cheeks before flopping down on Dad's left.

We're wearing the same school uniform, but she somehow makes it look more elegant with a pressed blue skirt and the shirt's cuffs rolled over her RES jacket. Her blonde hair falls in waves to the middle of her back as if each strand were taken care of separately.

Of course, unlike me, Nicole doesn't eat like a pig. She takes her time to cut and chew while conversing with the adults about her upcoming tests and school activities.

Hanging my head, I push around the remnants of the cheese-cake on my plate, not bothering to eat.

To say I feel like a stranger would be an understatement.

Victoria and Nicole always snatch Dad's attention while I sit here as unnoticeable as a wallflower.

I try to ignore the stab of hurt when Dad offers Nicole a smile he never gives me anymore. All I get from him are drawn brows and disapproving stares.

"Maybe you can study maths with Astrid," Victoria suggests to her in an awfully cheerful tone before she tells me, "I'm sure Nicole can help you get better results."

I would rather choke on my own vomit, thank you very much.

"If you weren't so stubborn to refuse a private tutor, maybe you wouldn't have catastrophic results." The edge of disapproval in Dad's voice is like a knife to my heart. "Why can't you be like Nicole?"

"Why don't you adopt her and spare us all the misery?" I don't mean to say that aloud, but it comes out anyway.

The clinks and clanks of utensils stop as silence stakes claim in the dining area. Even the kitchen staff halt mid-stride.

My ears heat with both shame and anger.

Maybe my own dad should stop comparing me to his perfect stepdaughter.

Maybe he should've left me alone after Mum died.

At least then I wouldn't feel like a stranger whenever I'm around his family.

I snatch my backpack and jump out of my seat before Dad can burn me some more.

Behind me, Victoria tells him, "Astrid is just going to be Astrid."

I wipe a tear from my eye as I make my way out.

I miss you so much, Mum.

Sketchpad in hand, I wait near the entrance of the park for Dan to pick me up.

Since it's early, only joggers come in and out. I like watching the exertion and how much they work for what they want.

Capturing those moments is my passion.

Or rather, *was*.

All the charcoal lines blur into something unrecognisable. The slight tremor in my hand hasn't subsided since the accident. For two and a half months, I haven't been able to sketch anything properly.

No matter how much I try, it isn't there anymore.

The magic has disappeared.

The doctor said there's no physical damage and that all of this is mental. The shrink said that I could be resisting something or that I'm under a lot of stress. My trauma is insinuating itself into my ability to create art.

I wanted to tell him that I have no trauma. That I'm going to find who ran me over and teach them a lesson, and then everything will be totally cool. However, Dr. Edmonds is psycho-analysing me a lot already.

The last thing I need is for him to suggest some psych ward to Dad.

I sigh as I throw the sketchpad back into my backpack.

Sketching has been the only thing that's kept me sane since Mum's death. If I lose that, too, it'll be like losing another piece of Mum.

At this rate, I'll have nothing left of her.

A honk startles me from my thoughts.

Nicole's Audi parks right in front of me, uncaring about partially blocking the park's entrance.

Of course, Nicole drives an Audi. Dad's gift for her eighteenth birthday during the summer. The same summer that I spent recovering from an accident.

Not that I'm bitter or anything.

Besides, since Mum's accident, I've given up on driving altogether.

"I'd offer you a ride, but my car doesn't do losers."

Her friend, Chloe, snickers from the passenger seat while applying lip gloss.

Oh, for the love of Vikings. Nicole and her bitch friend are the last people I need to start my day.

"You have nothing better to do with your time, Nicole?" I raise an eyebrow. "Aside from kissing my dad's arse, of course."

"I just wanted to tell you how right you are for once. Uncle should just adopt me and erase you completely from the family registry. We all know you'll never be able to carry the Clifford name as I can."

I swallow the stab of how accurate her words are and how much they affect me, even when I don't want them to. It's not about the name. It's about how she's going to steal Dad once and for all while I watch.

"And yet, you're still Nicole Adler." I meet her malicious stare. "I don't see a Clifford there. Do you?"

She snarls, but Chloe nudges her arm. "Tell her to stay away."

Seeming to backpedal, Nicole measures me up and down with distaste like she and her mother did the first day Dad brought me to 'their' home.

"Hey, Viking. Stay away from King."

I study my black nails, fighting a fake yawn. Nicole came up with the 'Viking' nickname as a jab at how much I watch the show, but the joke is on her. That TV series has more coolness than she'll ever have.

"Last I checked, he's the one who approached me."

"As if King would ever be interested in a charity case like you."

"Oh, I'm sorry." I raise a mocking eyebrow. "Who holds the family name again?"

"Stay away from King or you'll regret it."

"Regret what?" Dan's voice reaches me before he stands beside me and flings his arm around my shoulder.

People who say that a knight in shining armour can only be a prince or a love interest or whatever are totally wrong. Mine has appeared in the form of my best friend.

Daniel has parked his car down the street and made his way to stand by my side in front of the bullies. Not that I can't handle Nicole and her minion, but Dan knows how much these confrontations exhaust me. It's no good for my invisibility case.

Nicole's face reddens as her eyes bounce from me to Daniel, and back again. "Just what we needed. The loser friend."

"Are we really going down that lane, Nicole?" Daniel asks in a tone that's completely different from his normal carefree one.

She gulps until I swear I almost hear her. That's weird. Nicole hates Daniel as much as she loathes me—if not more. Actually, she marked him as an enemy before I came along, so it's weird to see her not spit her venom as usual.

"Bastard," she mutters under her breath.

"You might want to wipe that." Dan rubs the side of his mouth with his thumb.

Nicole touches her lips. "What?"

"Your bullshit." He turns me around in the direction of his car.

"Do as you're told, Viking!" she shouts at my back.

The best way to have me do something is to tell me not to do it.

I'm tempted to stay close to Levi just to see Nicole's face reddening with exertion, but even that priceless look isn't worth it.

I hate Levi King and everything he represents.

Besides, after the little gift I left on his car yesterday, I'm sure he won't bother me anymore.

However, I'm proven wrong when I arrive at the school and part ways with Dan.

As soon as I open the door to the art studio, I halt at the threshold and scream.

EIGHT

Astrid

I didn't start the war, but I'm fighting to the death.

All the canvases are painted pitch-black.

Every single one of them.

My muscles stiffen as I search around for any possible intruder. But there can't be one, now can there?

RES isn't the type of school where just anyone can come in and pull a stunt like this. Not to mention that I'm the only soul who's around in the early mornings.

"Just like a funeral, huh?"

My spine snaps upright at the sinister tone directly behind me.

The click of the art studio's door closing fills the space and sticks to the back of my throat.

I whirl around and come face-to-face with those hypnotic grey-blue eyes.

Levi King.

Just what I needed on this epic morning.

"You did this?" I throw my arms in the direction of the canvases.

"Who knows?" A smirk lifts his lips the slightest bit.

There's this air of nonchalance about him. A *fuck you* to the entire world surrounding him. He's in full rebel mood with his tousled hair all over the place, but it still has that supermodel look written all over it. There's no tie in his uniform and he has the cuffs of his shirt rolled over the sleeves of his jacket.

How can someone so gorgeous be the embodiment of the devil?

I start towards the exit. "I'm telling the principal."

"Sure thing, Princess. While you're at it, tell him you painted my car's windshield."

I come to a screeching halt and fold my arms. "I don't know what you're talking about."

He pushes off the door and it's like he's gained height. He's become all broad and stiff and…

Threatening. Intimidating.

All humour vanishes from his face, as if I was imagining all the smirks and nonchalant behaviour.

It's scary how well he masters his emotions, what to show and what to hide, when to stalk and when to attack.

Something undecipherable shines in the depth of his eyes and they turn a completely different shade of blue.

Deadly blue.

The type of blue that's infested with sharks.

I keep my position, refusing to let him affect me. But that doesn't stop my limbs from screaming at me to step back.

Levi King isn't someone I want to play games with.

One more year.

If I stay out of trouble and finish this year peacefully, everything will be over.

Any type of conflict will destroy my invisibility game.

Despite my pride, I step back, matching his wide relentless strides towards me. The air ripples with crackling tension that grips me by the gut. With his every step forward, my heart hammers against my ribcage. I feel like the stupid little deer who lost her way from the herd and got herself stuck with a hungry, relentless predator.

My calves hit the easel and I yelp. I grit my teeth at the effect I'm letting him have on me.

"Stop!" I thrust both my palms against his chest and push him.

I might as well be pushing a buffalo.

A very toned one with hard ridges and pectorals and the whole stiff board thing.

He doesn't move back. Not even a step. If anything, he leans closer into my personal space. So close that my hands are the only thing stopping his chest from crushing against mine. So close that he becomes tenfold more beautiful. So close that I smell cigarette and chocolate cheesecake on his breath.

Wait. Is that on me from this morning's breakfast? Because if this bully likes cheesecake, too, I'm retiring from the food.

"What do you want, Levi?"

"It's King to you."

"No, thanks. You have a name, so why does everyone call you by your last name?"

"You don't ask the questions, Princess. You only answer mine, understood?"

I can't believe the arrogance of this bastard. But then again, he's had the school in the palm of his hand for two years. Why wouldn't he think everyone would bow down to him?

"What do you want, *your majesty?*"

He tilts his head at the sarcastic note and I jut my chin upwards. He stares down at my hands on his chest, lips twitching, as if contemplating something. Before he can get any wild ideas, I remove them with a jerk.

Big mistake.

Levi advances into me like the bull from earlier, and I have no choice but to step around the easel and move back. I hit the wall and a shiver draws down my core.

Why the hell do I keep backing myself into corners with him?

Levi slams his hand on the wall beside my head with his

face mere inches from mine. My air supply comes in and out in short bursts. I can't even breathe properly, afraid that this time, my throbbing chest will surely become one with his.

"I told you what I want." His voice drops to a dangerous, low range. "But what did you do?"

I fold my arms, both to stop his chest from grazing mine and to control the hammering of my crazy heartbeat.

My gaze trails in the opposite direction, refusing to meet his eyes. If I do, I have a feeling they'll swallow me whole and never let go.

"I said." His thumb and forefinger squeeze my chin, forcing me to face him. "What did you do?"

I gulp against the feel of his skin on mine. The long, calloused fingers bring back memories of that night.

Hit-and-run night.

For the first time in months, the memories aren't gory and gruesome like in my nightmares.

No.

They're entirely different.

These recollections consume me like a case of drugs gone wrong—or maybe it's gone right.

Goosebumps form on my arms at the memory of how good it felt to be touched by him.

How he elicited those foreign, desperate sensations in parts I didn't know existed.

This same devil made me feel like no one had before.

No. That was the ecstasy. Anyone could've touched me and it would've felt good.

Only now, I'm under no drug influence, though I might as well be. Tingles draw down my spine, and I have no way to fight them off.

All I can do is show him that he can't get to me.

"I told you I'm not meeting you. It's not my fault you assumed otherwise."

He raises one perfect thick eyebrow. "Is that why you painted my car?"

"That was for humiliating me in front of the entire school."

"That's nothing compared to what I could do to you. Be a good little princess and I'll let everything blow over."

"And if I don't?"

"Believe me, you don't want to go there." Something menacing and sadistic shines in his gaze. It's like he wants me to defy him so he can take sick pleasure in crushing me.

That's his type, isn't it? They're so rich and entitled and bored. They make it their job to step on anyone in their path to fend off their boredom.

If he steps on me just because he's bored, I'll make his life a living hell.

He releases my chin, and I hate how the place his fingers touched feels empty and tingling at the same time.

"I heard you're not dropping the accident with the police."

"You know about that?"

Aside from Dan and the odd student here and there, I didn't think my non-fatal accident meant much to RES, especially not to the point that Levi would know about it.

My invisibility game must be getting too weak.

"Drop it," he says in that infuriating authoritative tone.

"Huh?"

"Stop going to the police station, stop digging your nose around. Drop. It."

"Are you out of your mind? You want me to let a criminal who left me to die off the hook?"

"You look fine to me."

"You've got to be kidding me. While you were having fun in your stupid summer camps, I spent my days in physical and mental therapy. Bet none of you thought I'll come back, but I'm here now and I'll make anyone who made me suffer pay. So don't you dare stand there and have the audacity to tell me to drop it. That will never happen, *King*."

I pant after my outburst. My ears and face are on fire and my entire body is stiff, but I don't back down from his demonic stare.

It actually feels super good to give him a piece of my mind. Screw him if he thinks he can make me give up on my justice.

Something undecipherable flashes on his face as he steps back with his head tilted in that unnerving, assessing manner.

"I'll play the game. Think carefully because this is the only time I'll forfeit the first move. What will make you give up?"

"Nothing."

"Nothing, huh?"

"Absolutely nothing."

"Tell me, Princess, is your sense of justice more important than everything else?"

I lift my chin. "Of course."

The unsettling silence returns as he measures me from the top of my head to my shoes. It's not in a sexual way, though. He's like some hitman assessing which way will kill me faster and with less hassle.

When he meets my eyes again, they're darker than a few seconds ago.

Black.

Lethal.

"We'll see about that."

Dread tightens my stomach. "What the hell is that supposed to mean?"

"It means —" he taps my nose twice with an easy smile that would've made him appear welcoming if I didn't already know that a devil lurks inside him "—break or I'll do it for you, Princess."

NINE

Levi

You were caught in a crossfire where only I could win.

"Do you know what happened?"

I stop at the foot of the stairs and smooth my RES jacket. Actually, not smooth. I unbutton the shit out of it so I look like the school's charity case.

The sound of Uncle's voice puts me in a sullen mood. Shouldn't he be already out to ruin some lives?

"Tell me, Aiden."

"Yeah, tell him, Cousin." I breeze into the kitchen and straight to the refrigerator, not sparing either of them a glance.

"Morning to you as well, punk." Uncle shoots the words like rapid fire.

I grab a bottle of milk and don't bother with a glass as I gulp half of it down. The cold liquid soothes my throat after drinking last night.

We have a dining room down the hall, but we don't bother using it for meals. It's only a place for Uncle's gatherings where he can show off his wealth and billionaire status.

Once I swallow, I wipe the side of my mouth and lean against the marble counter, facing Jonathan and Aiden. They sit side by side at the kitchen bar.

Looks-wise, Aiden is a carbon copy of his father. He shares

his jet-black hair and the emotionless dark grey eyes—the King's signature. Mine came out light and wrong because of Mum's genes.

A chessboard made of crystal glass and black stones sits between them. Only a few moves have been made. They're probably picking up an old game. Jonathan and Aiden take weeks to finish a chess game.

Normal families speak about their day. Ours is all about fucking each other over in a chessboard war.

"So what are we talking about this morning?" I tilt my head. "Aside from the usual banter of screwing up my life, I mean."

Jonathan pushes the plate of scones away as if my mere presence has spoilt his appetite. "You're screwing up your own life. If you choose to be nothing, you'll be nothing, Levi. How about you be something different for a change?"

"Do say what *something* means in your definition, Jonathan. Spoiler alert, if that includes following in your steps, I'll pass."

"You'll lose the attitude in front of me." His eyes darken and so does his voice. "I raised you when your mother threw you at your father's feet. I continued to raise you when your father couldn't."

My grip tightens around the bottle of milk until it almost cracks. Still, I keep the carefree tone. "If by raising me, you mean, you spent money on me, then no thanks to you. My father was a King, too."

"A useless one at that," Jonathan deadpans as if he's talking about a pet he disliked instead of his flesh and blood. "This family doesn't need worthless members. If you use the King name, you give back what you use."

"Such as?"

"Study at Oxford."

"Yeah, that would be a no," I say as nonchalantly as I can and take another swig of milk.

Aiden shakes his head, shooting me a disapproving glance

before he goes back to cutting and eating his bacon as if he's all alone in the kitchen.

Screw him and his father.

Jonathan stands and buttons his pressed dark blue jacket. "Our deal still stands, Levi. If you screw up one more time, your trust fund will be suspended until you're twenty-five—as per your father's will."

"A will you forced him to write."

"You're lucky I had him leave you something in his state. Do you think he cared about you or your future?" He pauses for a beat.

One of the intimidation methods that he taught us. *Silence always gets you what you want*, he used to say. *People are compelled to fill the silence and it can be used to your advantage.*

"Having me as your guardian is the best thing that's happened in your life, punk. You'll bend to me."

I meet his harsh stare with my own. "A king doesn't bend."

"One without a crown does."

He strides out of the kitchen like he already owns half the world and plans to conquer the other half. Which is true in a way.

I slam the bottle of milk against the counter and droplets scatter all around. With a deep inhale, I close my eyes to rein in the onslaught of sweeping anger rolling inside me.

A year.

I need shit to stay together until graduation, and then I'm leaving Jonathan's kingdom once and for all.

"You're doing it all wrong." Aiden places his empty plate in the sink beside me. "You think you can take him, but you can't."

"Want to bet?"

"I don't make losing bets."

He leans over, staring at the board. Jonathan blocked Aiden's knights, and any move he makes will cost him either his rook or his bishop.

Typical Uncle. He always starts by making you lose your strongest defences.

"Careful there, Cousin." I raise an eyebrow. "You're under-estimating me."

"And you're underestimating Jonathan. We all have the com-petitive streak, but he's been in this game longer than us. How do you think he expanded his empire? You're supposed to back down when he rises so he doesn't crush you."

"If anyone gets crushed, it won't be me."

"I don't know if you're being an idiot or what, but he won't hesitate to ruin your life. There's nothing that would stop him from stripping you of your inheritance until you're twenty-five. Are you ready to risk being kicked around for a whole seven years?"

"Shut the fuck up, Aiden."

"Just stating facts, Lev." He reaches over the counter, grabs an apple and crunches a big bite. "Play smart, not strong."

I tilt my head to the side, watching him as he chews. "You know about what happened that night, don't you?"

"Sure do." He appears completely unfazed, his dead eyes cal-culating the best way to overthrow his father's game.

Since that incident nine years ago, there's something wired completely wrong about Aiden.

It's like the deity took my little cousin and sent us back a demon on his behalf.

An emotionless, psychopathic demon.

"Why didn't you tell him—your father?"

"I don't have a reason to." He lifts a shoulder. "As I was say-ing, smarter, not stronger. You can't dethrone Jonathan King in a game of muscles. A game of wits, however..."

He leaves it hanging as the corner of his lips lift. He must've figured out a way to protect his defences against Jonathan's ruth-less attack.

But that will probably put his queen in jeopardy. Not that Aiden cares. He's never been shy about bringing out the big guns since the beginning.

"Do you have anything that ties you to that night?" he asks without ripping his gaze away from the board.

"I'm killing all ties." Starting with that damn Clifford princess and her nosing about.

"Exactly." He picks up another apple on his way out and throws it my way. I catch it right above my head as he says, "Play the person…"

"Not the game," I finish.

One of the truest things Dad ever said.

I catch a ride with Aiden for our early practice because my car needs professional help to remove the paint.

As we stop in the car park, I catch sight of honey-brown hair flying in the wind. Aiden steps out, but I remain glued to my seat, watching her easy laughter.

She's tipping her head back, eyes twinkling with spontaneous energy. It reaches me from across the car park and stirs a dark, unhinged side of me.

I want to ruin that.

I *need* to ruin that.

Beautiful things have positive effects on people. Most want to capture such moments and relive them over and over again.

Not me.

I itch to burn them and destroy their ashes until nothing is fucking left.

With Astrid Clifford, that sensation is morphing into something else.

I'm compelled to turn her life as black as those canvases, but a part of me yearns to feel the stuttering of her breath as I barge into her space uninvited.

Aiden hangs his arms from my open window. "Are you coming?"

"Daniel Sterling." I fix the boy wrapping his arm around her shoulder as they walk inside.

I have two thoughts about him.

His arm needs to be broken.

He should be black, too, for witnessing her laughter.

Aiden follows my vision. "He's a senior and is usually benched."

"Or out of practice altogether." He didn't show up to practice yesterday, probably not wanting to waste his time on the final year.

Daniel is the cocky football player type. The type who's using the game to get his dick wet and to have all the attention that comes with it.

He's decent enough and could've snatched his place long ago if it weren't for his half-arsed attempts.

A smile tugs my lips. Guess who'll have my wrath during today's practice?

One point over Clifford's princess.

My phone rings as I reach for my bag. Chris's number flashes on the screen and I hit ignore.

I'm not in the mood for his empty excuses.

He sends a text.

Christopher: Urgent. I have news.

"What is it?" I answer as soon as he calls again.

"I overheard my father with his officers," he whispers, seeming out of breath.

"And?"

Thanks to the fact that Chris's father is the deputy commissioner at the Met Police, we were able to avoid prison trouble all these years.

"It's bad." Chris sounds chilled. "That girl's doctor said she'll be able to remember if she's put under similar circumstances or shown potential suspects. My old man and his colleagues are contemplating it. He told them to push through with the case because she's a lord's daughter. Fuck, King. What if she remembers us?"

"She won't," I grind out. "Keep your mouth shut and come to practice."

"But —"

"Practice, Chris."

I hang up before he can say anything else that'll worsen my already shitty mood.

The anger from this morning rolls over me and all around me, suffocating my breathing.

Seems that the princess refused to listen.

I'll ruin her before she ruins me.

TEN

Astrid

You picked the wrong subject, your majesty.

"**S**lut."

"Whore."

"Entitled bitch."

My face remains blank as all the insults are thrown my way. I think someone even called me a harlot. Who the hell uses that outdated historical term anymore?

Since last week when Levi cornered me in front of the classroom and broadcasted that I 'begged' him for it, the entire school has been out for my blood.

During lunch, I received two offers from guys who assured me they wouldn't have me beg for it.

That's why I'm eating in a secluded corner in the school's garden. I never liked the pretentious air of the cafeteria anyway. Levi turning the entire school against me is more proof of why I'll never belong in this circle.

And by circle, I mean the entire football team who are always following him around like they're the subjects in his royal court.

There's this aura about those he keeps close. They're called the four horsemen by RES and they carry all the destructive energy that Levi needs.

All of them are ruthless in their own way—even the silent ones.

Since the beginning of my invisible days, I've waited for any rebellion against the entitled arseholes.

Hasn't happened so far.

Everyone ends up dropping to one knee like willing peasants.

Even Dan belongs to their circle, so I can't be the type of bitch who badmouths shitty, entitled athletes in front of him.

I can do it in my mind just fine, though.

Sitting cross-legged on the bench, I take a bite of my hamburger and sketch with my free hand. My shrink and physical therapist told me to take it easy, but I'm not good at listening to orders.

Besides, things have been changing with the weird dreams—or nightmares—I've been having lately.

I can't even recall what I've seen when I wake up. I'm just drenched in sweat and feeling claustrophobic.

Dr. Edmonds, my shrink, says I might be witnessing flashbacks from the accident. So I've come up with a theory.

My inability to sketch properly might also have to do with what happened during the accident. If so, maybe I can remember what happened if I push myself to sketch something—any-thing—from that night.

But every time I try, like now, Levi's infuriating face comes to mind.

I scratch out whatever I've been sketching and huff around my mouthful of hamburger.

Muse-killing arsehole.

"Hey, Bugger. What are you doing over here hiding?"

"Avoiding entitled football players. No offence, Bug." What? I didn't say I wouldn't say anything.

He chuckles. "It's taken, damn you."

That's Dan and me. It's a friendship made in heaven. Or in a pool.

The thing is, when I first moved in with Dad, he had Nicole take me to a party so I'd meet friends.

As if I would ever be interested in Nicole's friends.

So, anyway, I didn't want to go, but I'm glad I did.

Of course, Nicole abandoned me as soon as we arrived. The feeling was mutual, thank you very much.

So, I was there, in a secluded area by the pool, minding my own business and drinking diluted tequila. And okay, I might have been staring at my sun-moon-star tattoo and crying about my mum.

Then someone shouted. "Holy shit. Is that a bug?"

That was Dan and he'd mistaken my star tattoo for a bug. I punched him for saying that about Mum's last tattoo. He was drunk, so he kind of fell into the pool and didn't surface, and I thought I'd killed him or something.

So there I was, pulling him out, crying and telling him I didn't want to be a murderer. That's when he opened his eyes, laughing.

I talked to him about Mum and he told me about his grandma that he'd also lost recently.

Since then, we've been inseparable. Best beginning of a friendship ever.

That's why I know that Dan and I are tight, even when I make fun of his team.

But hey, he once saw an impressionist painting and told me it looked like cockroaches had walked on it.

I peek up at him as he slides beside me with a stupid grin on his face.

"What?" I can't help but grin back.

"I have huge news."

Still cross-legged, I face him, his happiness rubbing off on me. "Well? Are you going to make me beg you to say it?"

"That'll work, too." He waggles his eyebrows. "Like you begged Captain."

"Oh, please. Not you, too, Bug."

"What? I'm wounded I had to hear about it like everyone

else. I'm the best friend and should get inside scoop." He shakes his head in mock sadness. "I'm telling you, our friendship is on a rocky path."

I roll my eyes.

"You can fix it by telling me how you begged for it. On your knees? On your back? Sixty-nine? Or maybe —"

I throw a small rock at his chest, shutting him up. "I told you it didn't go that far. It was the drugs."

He's silent for a second. "I don't think the drugs make you want someone you never wanted before."

"How would you know that?"

He shrugs. "Just saying."

"Whatever that means. Are you going to tell me your huge news?"

"Two words, baby." He lifts his index and middle fingers. "Starting. Lineup."

"What?"

"Coach chose me for the upcoming game's starting lineup!"

"Wow, that's great, Dan." I can't fake my enthusiasm, no matter how much I try to.

He laughs before it disappears and he gives me his poker face. "Your disinterest is showing, Bugger."

"Sorry, but I thought you didn't care for the football team anymore?"

"Hell no! I said they don't care for me." He rubs his hands together with mischievousness and achievement written all over his face. "I knew my time would come! No more benching."

"I knew you could do it." I clasp his shoulder in a bro hug. "I'm proud of you, mate."

"Hell yeah, baby. *I'm* proud of me!" He slaps his hand in the air as if he's swatting an imaginary arse. "Can you imagine the number of girls who'll be throwing themselves at me after the game?"

"You're seriously a pig. Is that all you want to play football for?"

"It's a primary reason. My to-do list will expand with this shit." He snatches my half-eaten hamburger and finishes it in two huge bites. "There's also all that glorious cheering and adrenaline. You'll love it."

"Football and I aren't friends, remember?"

"You promised," he says over a mouthful of hamburger.

"No, I didn't."

"First year." He switches to a calm, posh accent like some old BBC News anchor and fakes holding a mic. "When Daniel and Astrid first became friends, Astrid told him she hates football and Daniel told her he hates art. So they agreed to never fake interest for each other. *However*, Daniel promised to attend Astrid's exhibition if she has one. In return, Astrid promised to attend Daniel's games if he becomes a starter."

"Ugh. I did."

"Yes, you did, Bugger." He waggles an eyebrow, doing a mic drop motion. "You're keeping that promise. Saturday night. Home game. We're kicking some arse this season."

There goes my plan to drag Dan with me to a museum.

"This is the captain's last year and he's so going to nail it."

I hit his shoulder again. "Hey, Bug, I might be attending your game, but save me the idolisation of Levi when he's actively ruining my life."

"Maybe you shouldn't push against him. He's King."

"I'm hiding at the back garden for lunch, do I look like I'm pushing?" I sound as incredulous as I feel.

The only reason I'm not challenging Levi is because I don't want Dad to be called in by the school, or worse, to learn I haven't been keeping away from the King surname as he ordered me to.

Besides, invisibility is hard when I have the school's literal king breathing down my neck.

However, I'm keeping my case with the police very much alive. If anything, I asked Dad's friend, the deputy commissioner, to tell me if any other evidence showed up.

Screw Levi if he thinks he can take away my right to know the truth.

"He can be harsh, but he's a cool captain." Dan's voice is filled with awe, and the sad part is, I think it's subconscious. "He vouched for me with Coach, you know."

"Wait." I look up from my ruined sketch. "Levi vouched for you?"

"Yeah, how cool is that?"

"Not at all. Don't you find it weird that he vouched for you now of all times?"

"Nope." He stands, flinging his backpack over his shoulder.

"Dan. The guy probably didn't notice you for two years, and now that he wants to destroy my life, he makes you a starter? Come on, this has set-up written all over it."

"Football, Captain, and Coach don't work like that. A starter was removed and I took his place because I pushed myself to be better."

"Dan—" I rise and clutch his arm "—I'm sorry. It's not that I think you're a bad player, it's just that the timing is weird, that's all. I don't want you to be hurt when things don't turn out the way you're hoping."

"I'll be fine." His voice softens as he drapes an arm around me. "Just stay out of trouble, Bugger."

"Yes, mate." I smile, glad the small fight between us is over.

He's the only person who can make the final year tolerable.

Dan and I part ways once we walk into the school. He has practice and I have a few hours to kill in the art studio before we go home together.

I sure as shit don't want to go home a minute sooner than needed and have to deal with Victoria's honeyed snark, Nicole's venom, and Dad's aloofness.

Someone bumps into me, almost knocking me on my arse. I brace myself at the last second and come face-to-face with none other than Nicole.

"Watch where you're going, bitch," she hisses under her breath and her two friends snicker like it's the funniest joke they've heard today.

I jab a finger at her shoulder and shove her back. "*You* watch it." I lean over to whisper so only she can hear, "Or does the entire school need to know that you and your mother are gold-diggers who stole my father from his family?"

Her eyes widen and I push past her, feeling a little better than I have this entire day.

"Do you think your opinion has any importance around here, *slut?*" she shoots from behind me, but I ignore her and slip into the art studio.

There are two junior students already sitting at their canvases, but they don't bother returning my greeting.

Not only is my newfound visibility a pain in the arse, but it's also the wrong type of visibility.

I'd hoped all this would blow over, but it doesn't look that way.

I sigh as I head to my locker for my apron. This place is my sanctuary; I won't let anyone ruin it for me.

Even if the art teacher dismissed all the black canvases as if they never happened. I had the vague idea that the entire school bowed to King, but I never thought he also had the teachers eating from the palm of his hand.

Naive old me.

The moment I pull out my apron, my temper flares.

'Slut' and 'Whore' are written in red paint all over the white apron.

The junior kids jab each other, suppressing laughter and probably taking pictures.

My fists clench the cloth as a hot, scalding wave rolls over me.

I don't care if Levi did it or if someone else did it on his behalf, but I'm done shrinking back.

He pulled me out of my invisibility cave and he'll regret every second of it.

If he wants a battle, I'm going to give him a bloody war.

ELEVEN

Levi

You don't have long. I'm coming for you.

I step out of the shower with a towel wrapped around my midsection and dry my hair with the one around my neck.

Since today's practice was hardcore, I expected the guys to be planning the best way to party and shag. I'm surprised to find them all gathered in front of my locker.

"He'll flip." Xander whistles.

"No shit." Sean, the goalkeeper, stretches an arm over the locker.

Ronan's naked shoulders shake with laughter. "I want to meet the person who had the balls to do this. *C'est tellement fantastique.*"

"Do what?"

The entire team falls silent at my question and their demeanours stiffen.

"Promise you'll remain calm, Captain." Cole blocks my view even though everyone else pulls back.

"Why do I need to remain calm?"

"Let him." Aiden motions at Cole to move.

When he doesn't, Xander forcibly pushes him back, muttering, "We still need you alive, dickhead."

Inside my locker, all my team jerseys are painted in red. One of them is hanging from the locker. Right above my number ten, where my last name is usually written, 'King' is marked out. Above it, 'Manwhore' is written in bold capital letters.

My hand tightens around the towel in a white-knuckled grip.

That fucking princess.

She's starting to piss me off and I'm no good when I'm pissed off.

"I mean, it's not even an insult." Ronan laughs as he slaps an imaginary arse. "You get the best pussy out of us all. Whoever did this must be jealous."

"Yeah, King." Xander laughs along. "It's not your fault that all the girls throw themselves at you. It's an honour, am I right?"

The rest of the guys hoot and cheer, saying how they'd love to be me.

But that's the thing about appearances, isn't it? They all think it's the family name, the safe funds, the face, and maybe even the talent. They think I have it all. I'm a lucky fucking bastard because all the girls want to be with me.

I cause trouble and get away with it.

I give the world the finger and I'm cheered on.

I fuck a teacher and have the entire school board apologise to my uncle instead of the other way around.

The team doesn't know that the only reason I keep up with the dumb drama is because of the rebellion I've been leading against Jonathan.

They want to be me?

Well, good luck with getting inside my head. Even I dislike that fucking place.

"Get them out of my sight," I say with a calmness I don't feel. The junior members trip over each other to empty the locker.

"Stay calm," Aiden whispers beside me while putting on his jacket.

He must be seeing the demons swirling in my eyes, because he repeats in a slower, lower tone, "You need to stay calm, Lev."

I breathe through my nostrils, trying—and failing—to expel the gloomy, murderous energy running through my veins.

The need to hurt.

To maim.

To fucking destroy.

Even the remnants of adrenaline from the game isn't cutting it anymore.

"We're going to the Meet Up," Aiden announces to the guys.

"Fuck yeah!" Ronan fist-bumps Xan.

"You coming?" Cole asks me with a cautious tone.

I nod absentmindedly.

The Meet Up is Aiden's way to keep me from heading down the other path, but there's one small thing he's forgotten about.

I'm a King and we always get payback.

My gaze roams the locker room to search for Chris, but he must've left right after practice, where he was still as useless as shit.

I go to my bag—that's also painted in red—and retrieve my phone.

Levi: Come to the Meet Up.

Then I toss the device back in my bag, not waiting for an answer. If Chris knows what's best for him, he'll be there.

The guys start filtering out. Aiden stops and points at his locker, telling me silently to change into one of his spares.

I swear the little fucker smirks as he follows Cole and a very animated Ronan out.

"Daniel. A word." I catch myself using the calm, deceptive tone Jonathan taught us and I inwardly curse myself.

He stops and surveys his surroundings as if looking for something.

The rest of the team spare curious glances our way as the locker room empties.

Daniel might have been part of the team for two years, but I've never had one-on-one words with him. I can count the number of times I've actually talked to him on one hand. Sure he comes to Ronan's parties and hangs out with the team, but we were never close.

However, times change.

I sit on the bench and continue drying my hair. Daniel stands as close to the exit as possible while remaining in the locker room.

His build isn't bad, but he doesn't work his leg muscles for long. As a result, his stamina doesn't allow him to play a ninety-minute game from start to finish. That's the only reason he hasn't snatched a starter's position.

He's fast, though, and he can fit as a right back or a midfielder. Coach noticed that he did well in the summer camp. It only took a word from me to convince him that Daniel Sterling could use a shot as a starter in the next game.

"Are you ready for Saturday?" I ask in a friendly tone.

His eyes light up. "Yeah."

"It's one of the rarest chances you'll get, so make it count."

"Will do, Captain." He appears relieved and relaxed now.

My chance to strike.

"That friend of yours. A…something?"

His easy-going demeanour disappears as he stiffens. "Astrid."

"Right. Astrid." Not that I can ever forget her name, considering that she's the thorn in my side who has the ability to fuck up my entire future.

"She…" he trails off, seeming to weigh his words. "I'm sorry for whatever she's done. She's not bad, she's just not originally from around here. She doesn't know the etiquette well."

I pause drying my hair. "She's not?"

"She lived with her mum before Lord Clifford took custody about three years ago. She hasn't lived amongst us since she was a kid."

So the princess hasn't been a princess all along. Interesting. No wonder she didn't exude the rotten, snobbish smell everyone at RES has.

During that party, she seemed so carefree and innocent, and yet, somehow shackled down.

"You're not going to hurt her, are you?" Daniel asks with a slight edge when I remain silent.

"Depends." I stand up until I'm toe-to-toe with him.

"On what?" His shoulders pull back as if he's about to fight me.

Also interesting. Seems that the princess has a loyal friend.

"I want you to tell me something, Daniel. It's in her best interest."

Once Daniel is done giving me the information I need, he leaves and I change into one of Aiden's jackets—that's tighter than mine.

My lips curve in a smirk at the idea of a hunt.

I warned her.

She didn't listen.

The time has come to punish her.

TWELVE

Astrid

If the king drops you, you can only break.

I stand in front of my half-empty canvas, staring blankly.

It's been going this way for hours.

My muse has been escaping me and I don't know how to catch it—or if it was ever possible to catch it at all.

The only painting I did today was on Levi's jerseys. I even took my time in painting the 'Manwhore' all over his 'King' title.

Why am I the only one who gets called names in RES when he's the actual manwhore?

Even I heard about the epic affair last year. He fucked a biology teacher in the lab for weeks until the principal walked in on them.

Said teacher is banned from all schools and she moved out of the country.

True, he was a minor at the time, but why the hell was he treated as a victim?

Not to mention all the girls who always brag about sleeping with the arsehole and how *good* it felt. They've been making my life hell because of him.

The satisfaction from sneaking into the lockers and painting all his belongings in red still hums under my skin.

During these moments, when I'm letting my true free spirit

loose, I can't help but remember Mum. She rooted spontaneity in me and taught me to never put on a mask.

Masks will suffocate you, Star.

She should've thought of the possibility that Dad would have custody of me.

In his house, all I can wear is a mask. The thought of screwing up and letting him down terrifies me.

After all, he's all I have left.

Nicole made sure to swing by the art studio earlier and announce that we're having a family dinner tonight. According to her, it's fine if I give it a miss. In fact, I should miss it since I'll only make a fool out of myself.

I considered showing up just to piss her off, but the thought of Dad's cold, disapproving stares made me change my mind.

I procrastinate until it's almost nine, when RES closes its doors. It's not like I can spend the night in the art studio.

After cleaning the brushes and putting the supplies in the drawers, I close the door on my way out.

Walking down the vast halls, I stick my earbuds in and let *Supremacy* by Muse fill my senses.

An eerie calm atmosphere fills the school's walls at this time of night. The only active students indoors are the book and chess clubs. Many athletes practise outside this late.

This is the best time to enjoy RES's massive architecture and the ancient history of the building. No snobbishness or bullying can ruin the mood.

Dan texted me earlier saying he was going to a 'Meet Up' with the team—which is apparently some secret hangout place for RES's football starters. He offered to pick me up, but I declined and told him to have fun.

Still, I can't help feeling a streak of jealousy and doubt.

Even though Dan has used his position in the team to lure girls, he has never been really that into the game. It feels like I'm losing my best friend to the stupid football team.

Besides, there's no way all these invitations to both the team and their secret partying place are a coincidence.

It could be that I'm being overly paranoid, though. I hate the idea of drifting away from my best buddy. If this is another tactic from Levi, then I'm punching his gorgeous face and totally leaving bruises.

I cross the car park on my way to the side exit. It's the perfect place to catch a taxi without getting all tangled in the traffic in front of the main building.

The bright white light illuminates my way as I retrieve my phone.

Astrid: u having fun?

Daniel: Hell yeah! We're looking at having a threesome tonight.

Astrid: You're a pig.

Daniel: One u love, Bugger.

Astrid: Just so we're clear, I'm so not having fun tonight and u need to make it up to me.

Daniel: Fiiiine! I'll rewatch Vikings with you for the thousandth time.

Astrid: And bring me the scones your mum makes.

Daniel: Nope. Those are mine.

Astrid: No deal.

Daniel: We'll split. *angry face emoji* Stop coming after my scones, damn you.

I smile, sending him a laughing out loud Japanese emoji and tuck my phone in my back pocket.

If sacrificing tonight means stealing some of Aunt Nora's scones from Dan, then I'm game. I always tease him, saying we're only friends because of his mum's scones.

I'm heading towards the exit when the car park goes pitch-black. I stiffen and come to a halt.

I hit Stop on the music and hurry towards where I remember the outside gate being.

My hands turn clammy and my breathing hitches so loudly, I can't hear my footsteps or anything around me.

Dammit. The lights usually stay on until later.

My hand clamps around the straps of my backpack until my nails dig into my palms.

I'd start running, but my limbs are too shaky for that.

It's true what they say about losing one of your senses. When you can't see, everything else becomes heightened.

My ears pick up on the slight rustle of the wind against the pine trees surrounding the school. Or at least, I hope the rustle is because of the trees.

My nostrils fill with the scent of petrol from cars and pine, as well as my own—which is so similar to fear.

The air on my skin feels like razor-sharp objects trying to dig their way inside. No matter how much I swallow, I can't chase away the taste of acid from the back of my throat.

This is becoming terrifyingly similar to what happened that night.

Both nights, actually.

Everything started with darkness.

You can do this, Astrid. You can totally do this.

My pep talk doesn't work. The whooshing of my pulse doesn't slow down and black fills my vision.

A tall, sombre figure blocks my path. I scream, but the sound is muffled by a strong hand blocking my mouth.

I freeze as I'm pulled back, my feet dragging on the concrete with a haunting noise.

Am I b-being kidnapped?

The thought stirs me out of my stupor. I thrash against my capturer's hold, scratching and kicking anywhere I can.

My back is slammed against something hard. Air knocks out of my lungs, and I gasp for non-existent breath.

A claustrophobic feeling creeps up my spine, paralysing me. My entire existence is filled with the large, broad figure looming over me like a dooming Grim Reaper.

I know fear.

I've *lived* it. Twice.

During Mum's accident and my hit-and-run. However, fear isn't a feeling someone can get used to. It's not a feeling that gets easier with time.

If anything, it gets worse.

Now that I've seen fear's face, it keeps changing, so every experience is more horrific than the previous one.

Tremors shoot down my body and I'm shaking like a leaf during a downpour.

"P-please...please..." I mumble against the hand holding me in place.

I should know by now that begging doesn't save you. Begging can make those with sick minds want to torture you some more.

But I have nothing else.

Even if I fight, my captor is obviously way stronger than me.

He stopped my earlier struggles with a mere hand. He can tear me from limb to limb if he chooses to.

His free hand glues against my chest.

My eyes screw shut as tears burn behind my lids.

Oh, God.

Please no.

Please.

Something inside me snaps and any reluctance I had about fighting back disappears. I punch and kick everywhere and nowhere all at once.

I barely hit anything, but I don't stop. I'm crying and punching and kicking like a maniac.

He fists my shirt and my screams turn crazier, even though they're blocked by his hand.

He pulls me forward. I trip, but I catch myself in the last second before falling on my face.

Both hands disappear from my chest and mouth and hushed footsteps retreat in the opposite direction.

Before I can form any thoughts about what's just happened,

blinding lights turn on in the car park. I flinch, squinting to make out my surroundings.

I'm standing near the exit with my back facing the school.

Harsh, shallow breaths leave my mouth as my heart thumps against my ribcage.

Thump.

Thump.

Thump.

I stare around me, spooked, half-expecting a monster to lunge at me from the shadows.

When I stare down, there's a piece of paper stuck to my school jacket.

I snatch it with trembling fingers and read the typed words.

Stay away or pay.

THIRTEEN

Levi

I orchestrated your fall, but I don't feel the grand finale.

My hands remain inert by my sides as Chloe straddles my lap, her flowery perfume so strong, it's nauseating. Or maybe that's due to the shots of vodka I've been gulping down.

The party is in full swing around me. Girls grind on the team members. Some smoke, others drink. I should stop them, considering that it's a weeknight, but fuck if I care.

Hell, I've been drinking like a sailor myself.

The captain in me is a shitty person right now.

The Meet Up is a cottage-like house on the outskirts of London that Aiden inherited from his mother.

Ever since we grew old enough to need a breather from the Kings' mansion and Uncle's merciless grip, this place has become our sanctuary.

Ronan is channelling his inner dancer and MCing the party with his random French sayings.

Xander gambles at the table in the middle of the room with a few other players. But half of the team have taken a girl—or two—and disappeared down the hall.

Rock music thumps from the new speakers Cole installed

the other day. Chris is grinding with a girl, his eyes bloodshot and his smile manic—just like when we returned from the mission.

It's a merry-go-round of fun and games.

Usually, I'd take part in the masquerade and pretend like all of this is what I want it to be.

But I couldn't give a shit whatsoever.

Not when everything is fucking black.

I push Chloe off me, and she stumbles to her feet with a squeak.

Usually, I'd fuck the shit out of her or any of her friends. However, since the beginning of this year, none of the girls have been doing it for me.

Especially now, when everything, even the fucking air, is clawing up my throat and suffocating my breathing.

Ignoring Chloe's protests, I breeze through the crowd, snatching a cigarette from between Cole's fingers on the way out.

As soon as the outside cool air hits me, I take a drag and blow a cloud of smoke in the distance.

I'm not a smoker, but whenever it feels like shit is closing in on me, nicotine chases the fog away. There are also the happy pills some of the guys use, but I promised myself to never get within two inches of that poison.

Not after what happened in the past.

It's one of those nights where everything feels fucking wrong.

Wrong place.

Wrong mindset.

Wrong bloody air.

The only thing that keeps flashing in my mind is the look of horror and despair in those teary eyes as she stared up at me.

The way she begged, even though she's not the type to.

I meant to scare her, put her in her place and teach her that there's no crossing me.

But as I stared at the terror in her gaze and felt her shrink and tremble against me, something strange happened.

I had doubts.

I *have* doubts.

For my entire life, I've been taught to be assertive. Once I plan everything to a T and study all possible outcomes, I shouldn't look twice before forging ahead.

After all, no battles were won by just holding down the fort.

My family is known for its boldness, whether in business, social, or political situations. We don't back down once we set our sights on something.

Tonight shouldn't have been any different.

And yet, it was.

Maybe I took it too far. Maybe I triggered some sort of a trauma that she's struggled to keep buried inside.

Her voice sounded hauntingly similar to that black night.

I run a hand through my hair and toss the cigarette away.

It's over.

It's done.

That should teach Astrid of her place.

Judging from how Daniel is singing out of tune with Ronan, it seems she didn't bother to call or text him.

Not sure if that should delight or anger me.

A part of me is glad the whole thing is done, but the other part, the most confusing fucking part, feels emptier and blacker than it did at the beginning of the night.

This is supposed to be my win, but I don't feel victorious.

FOURTEEN

Astrid

I don't hate you, I hate my weakness.

I hide in the confines of my room underneath the blanket, breathing my own air.

For always chastising myself about feeling strong, I don't anymore.

I've spent the entire night curled into a fetal position, crying until no more tears come out.

There are no words to describe the amount of hate I feel for myself for letting him—or them—get to me.

If I can't even stand up for myself, how am I to survive in the scary, vast world?

Is leaving Dad's house real freedom or am I just deluding myself?

All these chaotic questions have never left me the entire night. I thought about Mum and her strength, but that only brought more self-hatred for not being more like her.

I thought about Dad and his power and how I didn't inherit an ounce of it.

I thought about college and my art and how I have no idea where I'm going from here.

It's all been crashing down on me. I don't know how to stop it—or if I *can* stop it.

Last night, in the aftershock of adrenaline and fear, I learnt something important.

I've never really had control over my life.

All this time, I've been floating like an aimless object with no landing zone in sight.

The door opens and I still, holding my breath. I'm not in the mood to talk to anyone—even Sarah.

She's been checking up on me, but I told her that I wanted to be alone.

The bed dips as a weight settles on the edge. His strong cedar scent gives him away before he speaks.

"Sarah said you're staying in sick today?" Dad asks in his usual calm tone.

I make an affirmative sound without changing my position.

A sigh comes from my left. It's not annoyance, but more like resignation—or something similar. He makes the same sound every time he comes to adjust my blanket at night.

It's the only habit Dad has kept doing since I came to this house.

Every night, he readjusts my blanket as if I'm a child and murmurs, "Night, Star."

I've always pretended to be asleep, or maybe he only comes when he thinks I'm asleep.

He's been doing that religiously, even during the nights when he's caught up late with work. The only time he misses his habit is when he's abroad. Even then, he sends me my goodnight wish in a text.

When he came last night, I resisted the urge to roll over and cry in his arms. I'm still tempted to do it now, but I stop myself.

His 'goodnights' aren't fatherly, they're obligatory. Dad's upbringing and aristocratic name are all about manners and etiquette. I'm sure he gives Nicole her 'goodnights', too.

"Is it because of the accident? Are you having nightmares?" he asks. "I'll call Dr. Edmonds."

The shrink is Dad's solution for everything.

"No, I'm just down with something." *Like my dignity.*

"Look at me, Astrid."

I shake my head, curling further into myself.

"Did something happen at school?"

I can tell him everything. Dad will probably notify the school, and then what? It was completely dark and they weren't stupid enough to leave evidence behind. It'd only bring more of their wrath.

Dammit. I can't believe I'm cowering away from them this easily.

But what did strength give me aside from reliving my nightmare over and over again?

I can't be thrust back into those horrible memories from the accidents. I just *can't.*

"Can you drop the case?" I ask in a quiet tone.

"Why?" Dad sounds suspicious. "You were so insistent on making them pay."

"I just… It's not worth it. I probably won't remember."

"Look at me," he repeats, and I shake my head again. "Astrid Elizabeth Clifford, are you or are you not going to remove that blanket?"

"I want to be alone."

One moment I'm curled into the safety of my blanket, the next, I'm uncovered. I try to pull the cover over my head, but Dad keeps it out of reach.

I face him and he freezes.

Oh, for the love of Vikings. My face must look like a hot mess.

"Why are you crying?" For once, Dad appears out of his element. Awkward, even.

"Just…girl stuff," I lie.

"Yeah. Right. Of course," he says slowly. "Do you want me to bring Victoria in?"

"No!" I snatch my blanket and hide under it again. "Can you call the school and tell them I won't make it?"

"Sure." There's an awkward silence before a warm hand pats my shoulder over the covers. "Call me if you need anything."

And with that, he's out the door. I resist the urge to call after him.

In the few minutes he was here, I wasn't sucked into that endless circle of thoughts.

I close my eyes and pray for sleep.

By afternoon, I feel a bit better. It probably has to do with how I spent most of the day sleeping.

It's one of those rare peaceful days where Victoria has a gathering with other lords' wives and Nicole will be at school all day.

I annoy Sarah in the kitchen, and since she doesn't like anyone in her space, she kicks me out with a chocolate smoothie and a ruffle of my hair.

So I lounge by the pool with my sketchpad in hand. My lips purse and my brows scrunch together as I stare at what I've spent the last thirty minutes sketching.

Levi.

The lines are a mere draft, but it's his outline. It's his side profile and those merciless pale blue eyes.

I can't believe he's the first actual sketch I've made in freaking months. I'm about to rip the paper when a familiar voice calls.

"Hey, Bugger!" Dan's footsteps sound from the pool's door. I thought he had late practice today. He must've ditched after I texted that I wasn't coming to school because I'm sick.

Best friend ever.

"Thank God! I've been dying of boredom." I toss the sketchpad on the chair and jump up. "You better be ready for some Viking marathoning and me kicking your arse at pool."

Dan winces, stopping not far from the door. My eyes widen when the other figure strolls ahead of Dan.

His light devil eyes twinkle and his lips curve into a smirk. "I'm game."

FIFTEEN

Astrid

I'm not playing this game anymore. Stop dragging me to the chessboard.

The last person I expected to see standing in my house is only a short distance away.

He's wearing his uniform in that nonchalant, tousled way and, of course, no tie. I hate how stupid tall he is and how that tugging starts at the bottom of my stomach.

No, not tugging.

It's a rolling wave of anger about to crack me open.

"What the hell are you doing here?" I bite out.

"Daniel mentioned you were sick," Levi says ever so casually while advancing towards me with predatory strides. "I came to wish you better."

More like to ensure that he got me where he wanted me.

"Get out." I motion at the door, throwing a glare at Dan.

I can't believe he brought the devil to our little haven without a warning.

Worst best friend ever.

"Whoa. Slow down, Astrid." Dan gives me a lopsided smile, then offers Levi an apologetic one. "She's not usually like this, Captain."

Sure thing, Dan. I'm not usually bitchy with the one who's out to destroy my life.

I don't know if I want to pull his hair or kick him in the balls for bringing Levi here as if we're long-lost friends.

Dan approaches me and I jab him in the side, earning me a groan. He smooths my hair back and whispers, "Be nice. My game depends on it."

I want to tell him and his game to go suck it, but I'm not that type of bitch. My problem with Levi has nothing to do with Dan. I don't want him to be the collateral damage of whatever war we're having.

Besides, Dan wouldn't have brought him if he'd known what happened last night.

Or at least, I hope not.

The reason I didn't tell him is because I feel cowardly and weak.

"I'm going to see if Sarah has some smoothie left." Dan pats my shoulder one last time and saunters inside before I can stop him.

Damn Dan. I hope Sarah doesn't have any smoothie for him.

It hits me then that I'm all alone with Levi.

The same Levi who terrorised me less than twenty-four hours ago.

My courage from earlier withers away, and I'm back to being the helpless fool from yesterday.

I gulp, doing everything in my might to avoid his stare, despite the holes it's drilling in my face.

"Your father didn't tell you not to mingle with the Cliffords?"

"I don't have a father," he says casually. "But my uncle warned me."

"So why didn't you listen?" I peek at him through my lashes.

His eyes spark with pure trouble. "I'm not good at listening to warnings."

"Then be my guest." I can't help the sarcasm in my voice.

"I'd love to see Dad's reaction when he finds you here. We have Grandfather's shotgun that hasn't been used in a long time."

I flop on the lounge chair and snatch a cold bottle of water. My gaze gets lost in the blueness of the swimming pool as I pretend he doesn't exist.

Easier said than done.

His presence fills the space and ripples with something uncomfortable yet magnetic at the same time.

"Harsh, Princess."

A shadow looms over where I'm sitting, blocking the afternoon sun and sucking the air from my vicinity like the Grim Reaper.

My eyes slide up his body to the pressed uniform trousers, where both of his hands are in his pockets. His messenger bag is flung across his broad chest and rests on his side. I can't help pausing at the way his team's jacket stretches over his developed shoulders like a second skin.

I stop when I finally reach his face.

People as evil as Levi shouldn't be born with such a sinfully attractive face. Why do they get everything when they're supposed to be less than nothing?

"Harsh?" I spit out. "I've been in two near-death situations because of you. How about that for harsh, King?"

"First of all, I had nothing to do with your first near-death situation. You can't blame me for all your misfortunes just because you're bitter."

"You sure didn't stop it."

"I'm not exactly privy to the future, Princess."

"Anyone with enough decency would've helped me that day."

"I'm not sure if you noticed, but I don't have any of that decency."

"Yeah, I learnt that the hard way." I jerk my head away from him and take a long swig of my water. But even the cold liquid doesn't soothe my burning insides.

"About the second time…" he speaks in a low tone. "If I had a repeat, I would've done it differently."

My gaze snaps to his, expecting to find mockery, but there's only that hardened light blue gaze.

The fire that's been brewing inside me weans down in one brutal go.

"Is that an apology?"

He says nothing. Instead, he flops beside me, crowding my space and filling my nostrils with his sinful masculine, clean scent.

It's crazy how much he exudes self-confidence. It's like an inseparable part of who he is.

What he is.

Does he ever question himself?

He's everything I'm not and I hate him for it.

I hate how much he can get under my skin when I'm supposed to push him the hell away.

"What's that?" He motions at my other side.

I scramble to close the sketchpad before he can catch a full glimpse of himself on the drawing.

"Shouldn't you be leaving?" I jerk my chin at him.

"Shouldn't you be more hospitable?" he shoots back with a slight tilt of his lips.

"I hate you, Levi. The mere sight of you makes me want to throw up. You already proved your point, and I'm done playing, so leave me the hell alone." I'm panting after my outburst, but I keep my chin held high.

"You're done, huh?"

"Yeah. It's not worth it anymore."

"Here's the thing, Princess. You might be done —" his lips inch impossibly close to my ear until hot breaths tickle along my skin "—but I'm not."

A shudder draws down my spine at the rumble of his voice coupled with the heat of his words.

My grip tightens on the bottle of water as if I'm stopping my hands from doing something. What, I don't know.

"What the hell do you want from me?" I'm glad my voice doesn't crack like my insides.

"Your fire." His lips graze the lobe of my ear and a zap of shivers shoot through my body. "Your fight." His voice drops to a low, tingle-inducing range. "Your *everything*."

His arm wraps around my midsection, drawing me to the curve of his side as if I've always belonged there.

As if this is the most natural place to be.

I briefly close my eyes at the feel of his contagious body heat. It's like being thrown into a fire pit and enjoying every second of the burn.

How can a cold, merciless psycho have such warmth?

I'm too hazy to think straight, but then I remember how much I hate said psycho. That not twenty-four hours ago, he drove me to the edge of insanity. He can't erase that by pretending to pull me back to safety.

Someone like Levi King doesn't save others. He only gives them the illusion and makes them believe they're out of danger. When they fall for the trick, he pushes them off the cliff all over again.

A king doesn't sacrifice himself. The poor pawns do.

I may have retreated, but I will *not* be a pawn.

Eyes snapping open, I push him and all the devilish things he's inciting in my body away and jump to my feet.

He chuckles as if I just told him the funniest joke.

"I'm warning you. Stay the hell away from me, Levi," I growl.

All humour disappears from his face as he slowly rises to his feet. "I told you, I don't listen well to warnings, Princess."

"Something is so wrong with you."

He reaches out a forefinger and taps my nose twice. "Guess you'll have to fight me and find out what that something is."

I jerk away from him, but that only makes him smirk in that infuriating, provoking way.

"That won't happen."

"Won't happen, huh? Do you want to bet?"

"Screw you, Levi." I fold my arms over my chest.

"I'd be happy to if you stop running away like a coward." With one last tilt of his head, he saunters out the door as if it's his damn house.

Blood whooshes in my veins as I flop down on the chair.

I will not be provoked by him. I will not be provoked by him...

Too late.

I'm totally murdering Dan for this. He'll be my scapegoat.

With one last exasperated breath, I snatch my sketchpad. I'm so going to rip the drawing I made for him to pieces.

My mouth hangs open.

Levi's sketch is gone.

SIXTEEN

Levi

There's no place for a princess on the chessboard, but she barges in anyway.

After the discussion of tomorrow's formation, Coach leaves us to shower and head home. It's the first game of the season and team spirit is at its highest.

You'd have to be blind not to notice that Aiden, Xander, Cole, and Ronan have brought new life to the team. Even I can't deny that their harmonised team play has improved our middle and front lines. It's rare to find second years as starters, but the four of them have proved themselves indispensable.

Once we're gone, they'll have a stellar senior year ahead. If we win this year's championship, there's a high chance they'll repeat it next year.

For the first time in RES's history.

If anyone can pull it off, it's Aiden. The guy has no relationship with failure.

The team members slap each other on the back on their way to the showers, joking and talking about pussy and partying.

I don't feel it.

Any of it.

It's like I'm caught in a vicious, black cycle of my own making that I can't penetrate.

Coach pulled me aside yesterday to inform me that Premier League scouts will show up during this season. He believes I can make it to one of the big ones, but even Coach said the dreadful, 'If your family is good with it' line.

Uncle has made it blunt and clear that there will be no professional football playing, and even if I do get recruited by one of the Premier League's Titans, Uncle has the power to blacklist me from any team that matters.

When you have King Enterprises in the palm of your hand, anything can be done with a push of a button.

My long distant football dream isn't the only thing that's fucking up my mood.

I'm thinking too much, calculating too much, and partying too much. I'm not getting enough sleep. Sometimes, I wake up just to find out I'm still dreaming.

All of that is terrifyingly similar to a certain someone who shall not be named.

I take a quick shower, indulging in some of the guys' vain conversations about alcohol and pussy. Once we're out and changing our clothes, Ronan says, "Party at my place?"

"No," I scold. "Game night, no partying."

"Come on, Captain." Ronan punches the air. "We can kill those Newcastle losers even when we're drunk."

The others yell and shout, thumping their chests.

"No partying and no getting drunk on game night," I say in a deadly tone, making them all grow silent. "Do I have to repeat myself?"

"No, Captain," a few of the juniors answer and the others nod.

"Guess I have to settle with one pussy. *Merde!*" Ronan rolls his eyes. "The sacrifices I have to make for the team."

"How is that a sacrifice?" Cole asks.

"Cole, mate, when I throw a party, I get at least two pussies and a blowjob as a thank you. Now, I'm stuck with only Chloe."

"You're tapping that now?" Xander unwraps his towel and

shoves his feet into his boxer briefs. "I thought she had eyes for Captain."

"He tossed her off his lap last week like a bad habit." Ronan frowns. "I don't know why girls think I'm cool with sloppy seconds."

"Because you are?" Cole asks.

"Because you fuck anything in a skirt?" Xander chimes in.

"That's not true!" Ronan protests.

"Mate." Xander flings an arm over his shoulder. "How many times have you gone to console a girl after she's been rejected just to end up between her legs?"

"Hey, *connard.* Sex is the best form of consolation."

"Right," Cole mocks. "Of course."

It's no use telling him that Chloe still texts me, practically begging me to meet her. He wouldn't care and neither do I.

None of these girls stir anything in me anymore. For them, I'm just a stepping stone so they can say they fucked King. The captain. The local star.

They've always been nothing, so it feels like nothing when I ignore them.

Besides, they're not the ones who've been getting my dick hard since that night a week ago.

Maybe I really am sick.

"Yo, King," Chris whispers from my right.

I leave the guys bickering and lean closer to Chris as I button up my shirt.

"I checked with my old man and that girl's father didn't drop the case," he murmurs. "We should teach her a lesson this time."

I shake my head.

"But they'll —"

"We're only under jeopardy if she remembers, and she doesn't."

Chris taps his foot, surveying his surroundings before he hisses, "If she does, we're done for."

"She won't. It's in my hands now. Drop it."

On that evening months ago when Astrid looked at me with teary, wrenched eyes, searching for a soul I don't have, I didn't sleep.

And in that sleepless night, I came up with a different tactic. If the problem is her memory, I'll take care of that instead of taking care of her.

"We should threaten to rape her," Chris mutters. "Then maybe the bitch will understand to back off this time."

One moment, Chris is talking; the next, I'm throwing him against the lockers with my arm against his fucking throat. He wheezes, face reddening as he struggles. I tighten my arm, cutting off his air supply.

"You won't get near her, touch her, or even fucking look at her," I snarl against his face as his eyes bulge. "When I say to drop it, you. Fucking. Drop. It."

Scratchy noises escape his throat and his colour turns from red to blue. Somewhere at the back of my mind, I recognise that he's suffocating and that I've relayed my message and should let him go, but the unhinged part of me wants to see the life drain from his face drop by bloody drop.

"Let him go, Lev." Aiden clutches my arm and it's then I realise that a few more of the team are pulling me away from Chris.

Or trying to.

I release him and he slides to the ground, coughing and clutching his throat.

Aiden's brow furrows as he watches me with that calculative spark.

I'm known for not getting worked up on the team, so this must be kicking Aiden's head into overdrive.

"Don't fucking show up here again unless you plan to snatch your place back," I bark at Chris and storm out of the locker room.

I need a long drive and a smoke. Or a few.

It'd be best if I don't go back home tonight. Jonathan's face is the last thing I need to see.

Murderous energy looms in my head like a thick fog with no way out.

In the car park, I stop when I spot a petite figure lingering near the exit, right under the bulb.

She must be waiting for Daniel.

Earbuds in and brows drawn, Astrid is focused on the sketchpad in her hands. There's a slight twist to her upper lip when she's in full concentration. It's adorable.

Adorable.

Fuck. I don't remember the last time I ever thought of something as adorable.

Astrid isn't one of those girls who wears her uniform skirt as short as legally allowed or her jacket as tight as possible. She wears it with a quiet elegance that fits her petite frame and rebellious character.

Only, she hasn't been rebellious at all.

She did return to school after I barged into her house, but since then, she's been keeping to herself.

No more distasteful pranks. No more challenges. No more... anything.

And she's been treating me as non-existent. I thought I wanted her to back off and know her place, but now that I think about it, her sudden lack of fight is part of what's been pissing me off.

I've been feeding off her negative energy like a starved predator, and now that she's sealing herself in, I'm tempted to claw inside and pluck her out.

There's something about her that keeps pulling me in and I'm not the type to back off until I see the end of it.

Time to see how much fight the princess has left.

SEVENTEEN

Astrid

Can you fight when the devil pulls you into the night?

Ugh. Not again.

I frown at the sketch in my hands.

Mum was a tattoo artist and did her best pieces when the customers gave her free rein. She used to say that spontaneous art is the best art. A real muse doesn't ask for permission before striking.

Looks like my muse is a freaking idiot.

For the past week, the only face I've been able to sketch properly is Levi's.

His slightly droopy pale blue eyes. The straight, high nose. The sharp jawline. The slight curve in his neck with the tendons and veins rippling. I even included the small mole on his collarbone.

Something is seriously wrong with me.

I'm about to rip it when a shadow looms over me. My head snaps up, and I remove my earbuds. *Super Massive Black Hole* by Muse continues thumping low while I meet a senior's gaze.

He has messy brown hair and a buff physique, especially his shoulders and chest. His name is Jerry Huntington, if I remember correctly, and he's part of the rugby team.

"Yes?" I ask, unsure why he's approaching me.

He smiles like a cartoon character. I'm sure he meant to woo me with it or something. In that case, epic fail.

"The guys and I are going out for a beer, do want to join us?" he asks in a suggestive tone.

"No, thanks." I fling my backpack to the front and stuff my sketchpad and earbuds inside.

"Come on, babe. You'll like it." I catch him licking his lips from the corner of my eye. "I promise."

"I said no," I try to speak as calm as possible, hoping he'll get the freaking hint and go away.

It's not that I'm not interested in boys, but athletes have never appealed to me.

Aside from my freaking muse, of course.

I'm closing the zipper of my backpack when his hand snags around my wrist. His voice turns threatening as he speaks, "I said you'll like it. Don't pretend like you're hard to get. Everyone knows you're a little slut."

"That's enough!" I push at him and attempt to yank my wrist from his hold. "Let me go."

He doesn't. If anything, his grip tightens until my wrist hurts.

I groan, my throat closing around the scream that's bubbling up to be set free. My face heats with exertion and even though I try to rein in my reaction, I can't help the shivers of fear crowding my shoulders.

For the love of Vikings, this can't be happening again.

One moment, I'm trying to free myself from Jerry's hold, the next, a large body slams into Jerry's bulk and pushes him straight to the concrete.

I stare in stunned silence as Levi smashes Jerry to the ground. Although the rugby player is bigger, Levi doesn't show any signs of backing off.

He launches successive blows at Jerry's face and abdomen as if he's a punching bag. It takes Jerry long seconds to gather his wits and hit back. He uses his upper bulk to push Levi to the ground and pin him with a knee to his stomach before he punches him over and over again.

Something twists in my chest at the constant slaps of flesh against flesh.

But maybe it's not because of the violence. Maybe it's because of something else.

Nope. I'm not going there.

Their view isn't so clear with them rolling on the ground, wrestling and punching each other. Soon after, the football team's captain gains the upper hand.

I don't have to see the blackness in Levi's mood to feel it. It permeates the air like a suffocating, impenetrable smoke.

He's not only fighting Jerry, he's out for blood.

"Stop it!" I shout when I'm partially out of my stupor. "Stop!"

Neither of them listens. If anything, their punches and grunts become more violent. At this rate, they'll kill each other.

My gaze strays beyond them in both directions, looking for anything that will help in stopping the two bulls.

When I find nothing, I put two fingers in my mouth and whistle loudly.

Jerry is the one who looks up first. Levi punches him in the face and stands as his opponent falls face-first to the ground.

When the rugby player pushes to his feet, obviously ready for another round, I speak in a loud, clear tone, "I'll call the principal."

"Fucking bitch," Jerry mutters under his breath while dusting off his trousers. "Can't see what's so special about her."

"What did you just say?" Levi is in his face in a split second.

Of course, Levi doesn't give a shit about the threat of the principal. I'm starting to learn that he doesn't give two fucks about anything.

I stride to them and place a hand on Levi's arm. "Let him go. He's not worth it."

Jerry gives a lopsided smirk that smears the blood from his lips over his teeth. "Listen to your slut, King."

Before I can see the gloom on Levi's face, I feel it. No, I *breathe* it in the air.

It's there in the quick rise and fall of his chest. The clenching of his fists. The stiffness of his shoulders.

I stare up at him and gulp audibly.

His gaze is completely black.

Dark.

Deadly.

It's like he could kill Jerry and not feel an ounce of guilt about it.

He starts to push me away, but I block his path so that my back is to his front and I'm facing the rugby player.

"Isn't your father Judge Huntington?" I ask Jerry in my coolest voice.

"Good you know about that." Jerry continues smirking and I gloat at the fact that I'm going to wipe it off. Once and for all.

"I suggest you go home and ask your daddy about the money he embezzled from the Crown Court. Because guess who has evidence? That would be my own daddy. Now, if I go home and tell him Judge Huntington's loser son harassed me, who do you think will pay?"

Jerry's smirk disappears and his face turns ashen. I bet he thinks no one knows about his father's extracurricular activities. It's not that Dad tells us these types of things, but I overheard a phone conversation the other day—when I was sneaking out. The information stayed with me, especially since said judge has been appearing more and more on TV.

Jerry casts a fearful glance at me before he curses and flees the scene.

"Arsehole." I turn around, about to curse Levi, too, but I'm transfixed by the slow but clear lighting of his eyes.

The black has dissipated and is now being replaced by his usual hooded expression.

He's jacketless and tieless. The first few buttons of his shirt are undone as if he couldn't bother to do them. Under the lights, his tanned skin contrasts against the white shirt. Due to his fight with Jerry, he has dust all over him, and bruises on his cheek and collarbone. His right shoulder is drooping to the side like he can't hold it up.

Even in his dishevelled state, he still looks every bit the gorgeous bastard.

"For the record, I don't need you to defend my *honour*," I say with feigned sarcasm and push past him to the exit.

He winces.

Walk away.

Walk the hell away.

"I don't like it." Levi's voice stops me in my tracks.

I slowly turn around to face him. "You don't like what?"

"When others touch you."

My lips part, not knowing how to respond to that.

He takes the decision away when he strides in my direction and looms over me like a damn wall.

"From today on, you won't let anyone touch you." He says the words like he has every right to.

"Let me think about that…" I mock, waiting mere seconds for dramatic effect. "Decree denied, your majesty."

"Astrid," he growls, his hand clasping around my arm. "You don't want to fight me on this."

I'm momentarily stunned by the way my name rolls off his tongue in that slight, raspy tone.

It's the first time he's said my name, and there's something disturbingly intimate about it.

"As if I'm allowed to fight you on anything else," I murmur under my breath.

"You are."

"I am?"

He's taken me by surprise too many times in one night. It's starting to give me whiplash.

Is this another game?

His arm shoots forward and surrounds my waist in a steel

hold. I don't get to react as he yanks me towards him, flush against his chest.

His hard muscles flatten my breasts and I can't help the way they tighten against the material of my shirt and jacket.

My hands push at his shoulders, even while my insides liquefy at his warmth.

"Fight like that, Princess." He shoves my legs apart with one of his and settles his thigh between mine until an unmistakable bulge pushes into the hollow of my stomach. "Do you see what your fight does to me?"

Smothering warmth flushes me from head to toe as I stare up at him with widened eyes.

He's...hard.

For me.

That bit of information throws me for a loop. A whooshing sensation tingles at the bottom of my stomach.

"Levi..." it's supposed to be a warning, but it comes out like a helpless moan. I lick my lips to try to smother it.

"Fuck, Princess." His eyes spark with lust and that black look. "Stop doing that or I'm bending you over right here, right now."

I want to think he wouldn't do it, but this is Levi King. 'Impossible' isn't in his vocabulary.

I attempt to push him away, but I freeze.

Completely.

Thoroughly.

Levi crashes his lips against mine.

His lips are *on* mine.

He's *kissing* me.

I'm too stunned to react as his firm mouth takes claim of the remaining sanity I have left.

His free hand wraps around my nape, and I'm completely at his mercy.

My nails curl into his shirt as he moves his lips against my own. He's not only kissing me, but he's also demanding I kiss him back.

"Open." He nibbles on my bottom lip. "Up."

I keep my mouth in a thin line. On one hand, an unhinged part of me wants to let go and drown in the moment—even if I might die afterwards. On the other hand, the logical part can't forget that this is freaking Levi King.

The same King who's been making my life hell.

I hate the bastard. I shouldn't be kissing him or even entertaining the idea.

But a taste won't hurt.

Will it?

"Open. The. Fuck. Up." With each word, he bites down harder on my lip, sucking and pulling it between his teeth. I'm surprised he doesn't draw blood with his merciless tug.

My lips part in a whimper.

That's all the invitation he needs.

Levi devours my mouth.

He doesn't ask for access. He just barges right in as if he's always had a claim on this part of me. His hot, relentless tongue swirls around mine with animalistic urgency.

I'm lost.

Completely sucked in by everything Levi. The hard ridges of his chest. His strong, powerful hands. And his lips.

Damn his lips.

How the hell did I survive without kissing them before?

Something at the back of my mind tells me this is wrong, but I tune it out.

I'm floating in a foggy air as tingles run down my spine straight to my core. I've been kissed before, but never in my wildest dreams would I have expected to be devoured like he's dying and I'm the only air he can breathe.

My eyes flutter closed and I let myself fall, even knowing it'll hurt when I hit the ground.

But if this is wrong, then I don't want anything to be right ever again.

EIGHTEEN

Astrid

The push isn't painful, the fall is.

I sit in Levi's car—the same car I vandalised. That should mean the sky will fall on the ground any second now.

I'm still stunned from the kiss in the car park. I unknowingly find myself licking my lips as if I'm chasing the taste.

The surreal feeling.

The complete abandonment.

It's like an out-of-body experience, and I still can't wrap my head around it.

As if that isn't enough, Levi kidnapped me to his car, saying that he'll drive me home. He wasn't hearing my half-arsed attempts at reminding him that Dan is my ride. Then the rain started pouring and he pushed me inside the Jaguar.

Of course someone like Levi drives a fast car. Everything about him is. Nothing goes slow when he's around, including my heartbeat, my thoughts, and my memories.

And I'm licking my lips again. Dammit.

I need a night's sleep to think through whatever mess I'm in the middle of.

It doesn't matter whether I back off or not. Levi is the type who slams in head-first, just like he did with Jerry.

The power from earlier still stifles the air like a potent aftertaste.

Even now while driving, he has this constant volatile energy that's barely tucked under the surface. He's like gasoline, waiting for a spark to erupt so he can leave ashes in his wake.

I'm not sure whether I'm the spark or the ashes. Or both.

"How did you learn to whistle that way?" he asks as we stop at a red light.

He has his shirt's sleeves rolled to his elbows and I can't help gawking at his strong arms with veins and tendons rippling under his skin.

I shake my head from the distraction. "Mum used to stop taxis that way and I picked up the habit."

"Did she teach you any other cool tricks like that?" He flashes me a charming grin.

For the love of Vikings, can he stop doing that?

No wonder he has all the girls dropping their knickers—or to their knees—for him.

I like to think I'm above being charmed, but thinking back to how I melted in his arms, my case doesn't look so good.

I stare through the window. "Mum taught me everything I know. My first sketch. My first bike ride. But most of all, she taught me not to kill my fire and to be myself."

"She never thought you'd end up in this plastic world, did she?"

My head cocks his way. "How do you know I ended up in this world?"

He winks. "I can find out anything I want, Princess."

Ugh. The arrogant prick.

"You don't like the life you were thrown into, huh?"

"What's there to like?" My gaze gets lost in the lights and buildings being soaked by the rain. "Everyone here are copies of copies. It's like they strive to be each other instead of their own selves. If anyone tries to rise above the norm, their heads will be chopped off."

Silence greets me, and I tilt my head slightly in Levi's direction. I gulp at the intense look in his eyes as he watches me. It's like a reappearance of the black Levi who beat Jerry to a pulp.

Only now, violence doesn't seem to be his driving force.

It's something much more unsettling and invasive that I feel straight to my bones.

Goosebumps erupt along my skin, and I'm sucking the air out of my lungs instead of breathing.

There's wickedness in the way Levi watches me. A promise. A damnation. And if I'm not lying to myself, there's also a connection. Since that day I stopped and saw him at that party, there's been an invisible line enchanting me towards him.

I tried to push, I tried to pull, but the damn thing won't break. He's trapping me with his cruelty whether I like it or not.

"Uh, did your mum teach you any cool tricks?" *Way to go, Astrid. You sound like an idiot.*

I just had to fill the silence with something or I would've been sucked into his orbit.

My question seems to have done the trick since he focuses back on the road. "My mother threw me at the steps of my father's house in the middle of the night when I was two days old, then she ran away like a thief and never looked back."

"Oh, umm…" I'm flabbergasted, not only by the load of information in one sentence, but also by the apathetic tone he used to say the words.

Just when I'm debating how to respond to such a bomb, he continues, "The only thing I learnt from that woman is that you can become rich if you're knocked up by the right man." He winks. "Not that I can use her tactics."

His complete disregard for something so important is crazy. No. It's terrifying. It only proves how much of a deviant Levi King actually is.

But then again, if his mother, who should be bound by nature to love him, abandoned him, why should he have any compassion for the rest of the world?

"What about your father?" My voice is small, as if a higher range will make him run away.

"What about him?"

Did he abandon you, too? Are you completely incurable?

Before I can voice the questions, the car swivels to the right and I brace myself, almost hitting the roof.

It's then I notice we're headed in the completely opposite direction from home. The road's lights disappear and it becomes narrower and darker like in a real-life horror film.

"Where are we going?" I murmur, trying not to sound as spooked as I feel.

He says nothing.

My back muscles snap upright as my eyes bulge, bouncing between him and the pitch-black road.

"This isn't funny, Levi."

"It isn't supposed to be."

My breathing stutters as distorted images from that night with Mum claw at my inner walls like hungry predators.

"Don't… Don't…"

"You're a good little princess, aren't you, Astrid?" His tone switches to a chilling, apathetic range.

I grip the door handle with shaking fingers as the road darkens further and no cars come into view.

"Levi, stop."

"You should know by now that I don't do what I'm told."

My heart pounds against my ribcage so hard, it nearly falls to my feet.

He keeps going and going *and going*.

I can't believe I fell for his trick. He distracted me with the story about his mother just to have me drop my guard so he could destroy me in the worst way possible like he's always wanted.

My frantic gaze flickers between the black surrounding us, the pounding of the rain, and how he pushes the accelerator until we're almost flying off the road.

I want to fight him. I want to be crazy and force the wheel out of his hand, but I'm frozen.

The night of my mum's accident plays in the back of my head like an old, grainy film.

My eyes blur with unshed tears as I recall the exact moment the car flipped and having to watch her lifeless form lying in a pool of blood.

The car comes to a screeching halt and I jump up, a sob tearing from my throat.

"Not a bad ride, huh, Princess?"

My head snaps his way at the same time as my hand. I slap Levi so hard, my palm stings, and then I'm running in the darkness.

Rain soaks me immediately. My hair sticks to my cheeks, and water rivulets run down my face and neck. My shoes sink in the mud, bogging me down.

Strong hands surround my waist from behind and pull me off the ground until I'm suspended in mid-air.

I thrash against his hold, fighting my tears. I'm thankful that the rain will help hide them. "Leave me the hell alone! I told you I'm done playing your stupid games!"

His lips find my ear and he nibbles on the flesh before speaking in a low, shiver-inducing tone. "And I told you, I'm not, Princess."

Waves of anger, rage, and betrayal roll into one and threaten to spill free, but what's the point if I can't even fight him?

What's the point if he keeps wrecking my peace like a vengeful hurricane?

"Why?!" I scream at the top of my lungs, still clawing and kicking at him. "I was living just fine in my invisibility bubble. Why did you have to make me visible?"

"I made you visible, huh?"

"You did! You screwed up everything."

"You were never supposed to be invisible, Princess," he whispers the words in that rough voice of his.

My skin heats and not even the rain can erase the burn.

"Why did you bring me here? Are you planning to kill me?" I blurt. "I swear I'll turn into one of those vengeful ghosts and haunt you for eternity."

He chuckles, sending shivers along the shell of my ear. "You'll haunt me, huh?"

"Duh. For eternity, mate. You can count on it."

"I can count on it," he repeats with amusement.

"If you hear doors squeaking and sounds in the hallways, that'll be me. If you see smoke in the mirrors, that'll be me, too. Oh, and if you trip and fall in a game? Yup, totally me."

He laughs, the sound echoing around us like a hymn. "That's kind of like clinging, you know."

"I'm game as long as it makes your life miserable."

"Who says it will?" he murmurs the words straight against my earlobe. His breaths tickle my skin, but his lips never touch it.

The freaking tease.

I clear my throat. "So where are we? The cemetery? I'm warning you, my stepmother calls me a cat with nine lives. She does it behind my back, of course, because she has her snobbish image to keep and all that jazz. Don't tell her I know. So anyway, it might take a bit of effort to finish me off."

"Are you always a drama queen when you're nervous?"

"Nope. Only when I'm kidnapped to the middle of nowhere. You know, by a devil's minion and all that."

Still holding me, he spins us around so I'm facing a cottage-like house on the unkempt ground. The car's lights outline the cosy antique architecture with the rain pounding down on it.

"Okay. I've got to admit it's a nice hideout for a serial killer."

"This is our Meet Up," he says, fighting a smile. "Usually, the team would be here if it weren't game night."

"Right. No serial killer activities, I guess." I peek at him. "Why did you bring me here?"

"You asked about my father and I brought you to the best place to feel it."

"Feel what?"

He drops me to my feet, and I slowly turn around.

In the middle of nowhere, under the pouring rain, Levi opens his arms wide and tilts his head back. Water soaks his gorgeous face, the hard tendons of his collarbone, and his Viking hair.

His white shirt becomes completely see-through, sticking to his muscles like a second skin.

And he's smiling.

It's not one of his cruel fake smiles. This one is genuine like he's…happy?

The view grips me by the gut. My heart pumps so loudly, it's a miracle he's not hearing it.

This position. This same position.

I've seen it somewhere.

But where?

"The rain," Levi whispers, still closing his eyes. "My father taught me to feel the rain."

NINETEEN

Levi

You make me lose control and you'll pay the price for it.

Watching Astrid in my space, my compound, stirs a strange part of me.

I lean back against the counter with a glass of vodka in hand as she sits opposite me on the sofa.

Drying her hair with a towel, she surveys our surroundings like a curious kitten.

Aiden and I have kept the place simple with just a few sofas, two poker tables, and a bar. In short, all the fun Jonathan won't allow us at home.

While Astrid drinks in her environment, my gaze keeps flickering to the way her wet white shirt has turned transparent. Her half-naked full, milky white tits push against the fabric. They'd fit fucking perfectly in my palms while I —

"You own this?" she asks.

"Technically, Aiden does. In reality, I do."

"That doesn't make sense."

"A lot doesn't." I'm still ogling her tits and their gentle bounce every time she moves her hand up and down.

"Like you and your cousin? You guys are weird."

"How so?" I ask absentmindedly.

Astrid finally follows my field of vision and crosses an arm over her chest as a blush creeps up her neck. "Pervert."

Fuck me.

I never thought I would ever enjoy seeing a girl blushing, but Astrid is the exception to all the rules.

She's her own rule.

I smirk at the way she glares at me, but even her anger is cute when it's mixed with embarrassment.

The princess can fight whatever we have all she wants, but I've already set my sights on her. She can run, but I'll catch her every time.

Hell, I'll enjoy every minute of the chase, too.

There will be no escaping the king's grasp in his kingdom.

The moment I saw that sorry fuck touch her, I saw black. The kind of black that Jonathan has been doing everything in his might to erase from my life.

But then, the most fascinating thing happened.

Astrid stood up to Jerry and put him in his place with such eloquence and strength that it made me speechless. My pitch-black mood dissipated without my having to put any effort into stopping it.

I don't think she noticed it, but at that moment, she looked exactly like her father when he's putting down his political enemies in the House of Lords.

What? I might have googled her and watched a few videos of her dad on YouTube.

"Why do you think Aiden and I are weird?" I ask, needing to keep her talking.

The way her lips roll around the words reminds me of how I claimed her mouth and how much I want to repeat it over and fucking over again.

Before I claim other parts of her.

Soon.

So soon.

She buttons her jacket, concealing my view of her tits. "I don't know. I just feel it. You're obviously the devil in disguise."

"Why in disguise?"

"Because you appear perfect and gorgeous on the outside."

"Perfect and gorgeous, huh?"

"That wasn't a compliment. It only means that you're not on the inside."

"Still, you think I'm perfect and gorgeous, yeah?"

The slight blush creeping up her cheeks is all the answer I need.

"Whatever. You only look that way because you inherited some Vikings' genes—which is super unfair, by the way. I should've been the one who inherited some."

"Why?"

"Mate! Have you seen them? They're super badass."

"You're doing just fine without the Viking looks, Princess."

"Yeah, right." She rolls her eyes. "Anyway, back to you and your cousin. You're the devil and Aiden seems suspiciously normal."

I laugh, my head tipping back. "If you think I'm the devil, you should search for a higher position for Aiden."

She mulls my words over in that busy head of hers. "Does it run in the family? Being abnormal, I mean."

My jaw clenches, but I mask my reaction and smile. "Sure thing. If it makes you sleep better at night to know we're all defective, then go right ahead."

"You don't have to be a dick about it." She stands, throwing the towel to the side. "I'm trying to figure out why Dad hates you guys so much when he thinks all those negative emotions are beneath him."

"Maybe Lord Clifford isn't such a saint, after all."

She lifts her chin. "Or maybe your family wronged him. I witnessed first-hand how cruel a *King* can be."

Jonathan is the type who destroys anyone who crosses him. It's weird that he's choosing to remain tight-lipped about his grudge against Lord Clifford.

"Take me home."

I abandon my half-full glass of vodka and approach her with steady steps. "Repeat that without the order part."

"So only you are allowed to dish out orders?"

"Basically." I stop when I'm toe-to-toe with her and she has to stare up at me. "Now, rephrase. Here's a hint. Use 'please.'"

"Go screw yourself, *please*."

I grin. "Wrong choice."

My arm wraps around her waist and I dip my head down to hers, needing to taste her lips again.

To feast on them.

To eat her up until there's nothing left of her.

Astrid's sparkly green eyes widen. She jerks a hand up, covering her mouth, and my lips find her fingers.

Instead of pulling away, I kiss the back of her hand, biting and nibbling on her skin like I would've done her lips. I tongue her forefinger and middle finger, thrusting between them and sucking the flesh into my mouth.

A long shudder goes through her. I'm rock fucking hard. My dick strains against my trousers, wanting to feel her bare.

I'm consuming her fingers with my mouth and she's consuming me with that expressive, lust-filled gaze.

Her hand trembles as if she wants to remove it, but something is stopping her.

Maybe it's the same thing that's stopping me from bending her over and burying myself inside her so deep, neither of us would know where I end and she begins.

In one night, I've had a bruised nose and shoulder because of her. I've had my first all-consuming kiss with her. I've enjoyed the rain after a long time also because of her.

I can't begin to imagine what my life will be like if I spend more time with her.

No idea what this fucking obsession with Astrid is all about, but I know one thing.

I'm seeing it to the very end.

TWENTY

Astrid

When it rains, it fucking pours.

My eyes are barely open as I trudge down the stairs. Pain snaps from the back to the front of my head and my nose is partially blocked.

Yup. Totally caught something from being soaked in last night's rain.

Aside from sheer confusion.

The more time I spend with Levi, the better I think I know him. At the same time, it's like I still know next to nothing about him.

For the life of me, I can't figure out why he does everything he does.

Don't they say that on the chessboard, the king's moves can't be predicted? Or did I make that up?

What worries me the most about Levi isn't his acts. It's my reaction to him. Yesterday, I was on the verge of completely surrendering to his sinful touch and lips. Damn those firm, kissable lips.

For the love of Vikings, why can't I snap out of it and stop thinking about that kiss?

He's the devil, remember?

When I get to the bottom, the sound of agitated voices reach me.

"I saw her! She came home in King's car."

"Now, hush, Nicole," Victoria hisses. "Don't say that name aloud in this house."

My feet falter around the corner of the dining room as I contemplate what to do.

They're talking about me, so I shouldn't feel bad about eavesdropping.

"I can't take this anymore. She's not supposed to be here. You said she'd be gone."

"She will." Victoria sounds calm. "This is her last year in the house before she leaves for good."

How did she figure out my plan?

Not that I care. This is all for everyone's benefit. I don't fit in with Victoria and Nicole's posh, impeccable life.

Even Nicole's dead father was some sort of a knight. She and her mother are a picture-perfect family, suitable for Dad's needs.

If he has to choose, he won't choose me.

I ignore the pang that comes with that thought and start to push inside when Victoria's voice stops me. "Her type belongs in the rubbish, just like her whore mother."

Blood pumps in my veins and heat smothers my neck, creeping up to my face.

I barge inside with my fists clenched at my sides and toss my backpack on the chair.

Victoria and Nicole are sitting across from each other with their plates in front of them.

"Take it back," I say with a calmness I don't feel.

Nicole's malicious eyes shoot daggers in my direction as she stabs something on her plate.

Victoria's flawless eyebrows scrunch in mock surprise. "Take what back, dear?"

"You called my mother a whore and you'll take it back."

"You must've misheard, dear." Victoria continues smiling as she sips her tea with no care in the world.

The thing about Victoria is her ability to avoid confrontation and slip her way out of any dire situation. It's probably why she's the perfect wife for a man like my father.

But I'm not the press. She's not getting away with calling my mother a whore.

"I don't know much about my parents' history, but I know that my mum came first." I mimic her cool, infuriating smile. "Maybe we should research who's the home-wrecking whore in this story."

Victoria's face scrunches, but she remains seated. Nicole jumps up, pointing a fork at me. "Did you just call my mother a home-wrecking whore?"

"Oh." I smirk, making sure to meet Victoria's gaze. "You must've misheard, *dear.*"

Nicole makes her way towards me.

"Sit down, Nicole," Victoria scolds.

"You little bitch," Nicole snarls in my face. "You and your slut of a mother were and will always be nothing to Uncle Henry. You're just used tissue that can be thrown away at any second."

I raise my fist and punch Nicole in the face.

It's a knee-jerk reaction. Something that comes in the heat of the moment.

Hearing her talk about my mother that way brings a rolling wave of rage.

No one, absolutely *no one*, badmouths my mother and gets away with it.

Nicole and Victoria shriek at the same time as the younger girl falls against the table, clutching her face.

Nicole straightens with her eyes shimmering. She fists her hands, and I hold my ground.

Bring it. I'm ready for a fight to the death with her right now.

Victoria pulls her daughter back by the collar of her dress.

"Oh, Henry. I don't know what's wrong with Astrid." She caresses Nicole's hair. "It's okay, baby. It's okay."

My muscles lock at the mention of Dad's name. Measured footsteps come from behind me before he stands beside his wife and stepdaughter. His face is so closed, it's impossible to read his mood.

"She called my mother a whore, Uncle," Nicole sobs, showing him the reddening circle around her left eye. "When I told her to stop, she punched me."

"That's not true!" I yell.

"Oh, Henry," Victoria cries. "I think Nicole needs to see a doctor."

"Oh, come on." I stare at her with stupefaction. It wasn't that hard, although I wish it had been.

"I know you don't like us, Astrid." Victoria looks at me with pity-filled eyes. "But I thought we were a family."

"Stop being a hypocrite! You called my mother —"

"Enough." Dad's voice booms in the dining room.

"But, Dad, she —"

"It's Father, not Dad," he grits out.

I fight the sob trying to be set free. "She said my mum —"

"Your mother is dead," he deadpans as if I don't know that piece of information. "She's been dead for three years. I've been trying to give you leeway, but it's not working. When will you learn that your mother is in the past?"

"Never!" My vision blurs with tears. "Just because you forgot about her doesn't mean I will."

"Astrid Elizabeth Clifford. You will stop this instant and apologise to Victoria and Nicole."

Both mother and daughter smile discreetly.

I lift my chin up even as a tear slides down my cheek. "I'll never apologise."

"Then you'll forget about attending next week's exhibition."

No. I've been looking forward to it since my accident. He can't take that away from me. "But you promised."

"And you promised to try and get along with Victoria and Nicole. If you don't keep your promises, why should I?"

"I won't apologise for something they started."

"No apology. No exhibition."

"Fine!" I snatch my backpack and throw it over my shoulder. "But for the record, you stopped keeping your promises since I was seven, *Father*."

I wait until I'm out of the house before letting the tears loose.

TWENTY-ONE

Astrid

If you're the devil, why am I not running? Why am I barging into your hell instead?

The energy in the stadium is beyond infectious. It seeps under my skin and awakens a part of me I never thought existed.

The crowd's chants, the girls' screaming at players, the parents' cheering from their conservative place down below, *Something Like This* by Coldplay blasting from the speakers.

There's so much chaos—aside from Coldplay.

I've never been to a football game before, not only because sports aren't my thing, but also because I never understood the fanatic mindset of most Premier League's fans.

Today seems like a fraction of the Premier League—a younger brother of sorts. A few thousand spectators fill the school's stadium, chanting and carrying the royal blue sticks matching the team's colours.

I'm going to watch till half-time for Dan's sake and then I'm out of here.

"Ugh, some parasites decided to show up."

My head lifts at Nicole's malicious voice. I can't help smiling at the slight bruise on her left eye from this morning. She did her best to hide it with makeup, but it's visible.

Nicole is wearing the team's jersey and jeans. King's number ten. Of course. Her friend Chloe is wearing number thirteen, Astor.

"If we lose, you're dead," Chloe says with a twist in her dramatically red lips.

I roll my eyes and decide to ignore them. The best method to conquer any bullies is to not give them what they seek—a reaction.

After some glaring, they huff and puff, then head up to the 'best' seats.

I retrieve my sketchpad from my bag and snuggle it in my lap. Here's to hoping the other spectators are too busy with the before-game spectacle to notice me sketching in the middle of their beloved game.

I focus on a small boy, probably one of the players' brothers. He's wearing a blue jersey and screaming, "Sean!" over and over. I smile and attempt to capture that spark in his eyes and the care-free flinging of his arms as his mother holds him.

Just as I'm about to get lost in the zone, the music comes to an abrupt halt. The entire crowd stands up, cheering and roaring at the top of their lungs. Since my vision is entirely blocked by everyone in front of me, I have no choice but to stand, too.

The reason for the crowd's transformation must be because of the players filtering into the stadium. I'm going to bet that the players with the white and black jerseys don't elicit this madness. It's the blue ones. The Elites.

I grin as my best friend walks in with his teammates, looking ready to kick some butt.

"Go get 'em, Danny!" I scream at the top of my lungs while everyone else chants the King name. Either Levi or Aiden—or both. Xander, Cole, and Ronan get a lot of cheering, too.

Levi leads the team with sure, confident strides. He still has the bruise around his lip from yesterday, but he looks as god-like as ever with his 'fuck the world' posture.

It's not his confidence or even his last name that makes him untouchable, it's his attitude. I've yet to discover anything that affects him—*really* affects him. And maybe I'm jealous of that. Maybe I wish I had his attitude about life.

He lost both his parents, but unlike me, he doesn't act like it's the end of the world.

But then again, something is wired wrong with Levi.

It feels strange to see him in his lion's den—the stadium—looking all ready to tear someone to pieces. It's like getting more insight into who he truly is.

The two teams stay behind as Levi and another player from the other team advance to the middle of the pitch. Unlike the other players, they both have a neon yellow armband. Pretty sure that means they're the captains.

An older man wearing a black jersey and shorts stands between them. I assume that's the referee. He says something and both Levi and the other player nod.

The crowd grows silent as anticipation fills the air until I can taste it on my tongue. I'm standing here like an idiot, having no idea what the hell is going on.

The referee tosses a coin in the air and nods towards Levi. The crowd cheers as the two players shake hands, then shake the referee's hand and each run back to their team.

I'm entranced by the way Levi runs. It's agile and effortless and so damn beautiful.

Everything about him is thick and hard and mesmerising.

His T-shirt sticks to his back muscles, rippling with every step he takes. His biceps bulge against the T-shirt's short sleeves. I can't see the throbbing veins of his arms, but I can almost feel them all pumped for the game.

His thighs and legs are a sight to behold. All muscular and toned like he's human aesthetics.

Or more like a Greek statue.

Stunning but cold.

All the players take their positions on the pitch. The

kick-start is between Levi and his cousin. The cheering from earlier must've been because Levi won the first ball.

The crowd sits back down, and I do, too.

Although I don't understand much of the game, I can tell Elites are doing better. They approach the goal more and the ball is almost always with them.

Every time Levi or Aiden touches the ball, the girls erupt in uncontrollable screaming. I can't help the rush of adrenaline at seeing Levi commanding his team and giving instructions left and right.

I came here to watch Dan, but I've barely given him any attention. Every time I do, I find myself searching for Levi all over again. Guess who the Worst Best Friend Award goes to?

With my sketchpad on my lap, I keep doing lines and trying to capture the moment Levi throws the ball. He has such a magnificent posture. One of his arms flings back, the other forward. One foot on the grass and the other suspended in the air.

It's like he's about to fly.

The first half ends with a draw.

As the players start filtering back inside, I rush down the stairs and catch the Elites on their way to the locker room. The crowd are shouting encouraging remarks their way. Once again, the Kings and the other three star players get most of the cheering.

Dan has his head tucked down. He must be feeling so defeated on his first game as a starter.

"You can do it, Danny!" I scream so he can hear me. "You're the best of the freaking best!"

Two heads snap in my direction. The first is Dan's. He grins from ear to ear and taps his chest, then points at me.

The second is Levi's and his expression is the complete opposite of Dan's. The pale blue of his eyes darkens and he stares between me and Dan and comes to a stop. He stops walking inside, stops listening to a player who's talking to him.

He just…stops.

Everyone ceases to exist as his gaze focuses on me and me alone.

An odd awareness grips me by the gut at the strange, destabilising look in his eyes and his stiff posture. My air turns suffocating, as if he were able to suck it all away from this distance.

The moment ends when another player slams his shoulder into Levi's. Number nineteen, Knight. Levi winces, breaking eye contact, and lets his teammate lead him inside.

I release a breath I didn't know I was holding and trudge back to my place on the benches.

My fingers tremble as I gather my sketchpad and stare at Levi's silhouette. My cheeks heat and my insides feel like a jumbled mess.

What in the ever living hell was that all about?

He didn't touch me, but I can still feel his fingertips all over my skin and somewhere deep inside me.

I continue sketching as rock music fills the stadium.

I tell myself that I'm finishing the game only because Dan needs moral support.

That's all.

A chubby girl with cute braids sits beside me before the second half starts. Her eyes spark with something similar to both excitement and fear.

"Oh, sorry," she says as if only just noticing me. "Is this seat taken?"

I smile. "No, help yourself."

"Thanks!" She retrieves a bar of chocolate and offers me some. "I'm supposed to not eat these at night. Don't tell my mum or my nutritionist—or anyone, for that matter."

I laugh, accepting a small piece. "My lips are sealed."

"I'm Kimberly. Second-year," she offers. "You're Clifford, right?"

"Just Astrid is fine."

"So, Astrid, I'm not used to seeing you at the school games. Do you come often?"

"'This is my first game."

"Oh." She pauses. "Oooh. You have to know what you're missing out on."

Kimberly spends the next ten minutes trying to shove as many football terms into my head as possible.

"I'm not a big fan either, but I like to come to watch sometimes." There's a dreamy tone in her voice. "My best friend is a fanatic fan of the Premier League, but she never comes to the school's games."

"Why not?"

She shrugs. "She hates them, I guess."

"Here they come!!" someone screams from behind us. "Go Elites!"

Like in the first half, the music comes to a halt and everyone stands up. Kimberly and I follow.

As the second half begins, I can't help noticing that there's something different about Levi. While Aiden and the others play relaxed, he's tense. His shoulders are tight and his instructions are more curt than in the first half.

"I wonder what the captain's beef is," Kimberly says.

So I'm not the only one who notices it.

"He doesn't usually play like that, right?"

"Of course not. He's always cool and confident. He's the captain, after all."

"So he's like a good player?"

"Good?" She laughs. "Try perfect. He's the best player we have and the top centre midfielder in the schools' championship. We're talking Premier League level here."

We're interrupted by cheers because of a triple play from Cole to Xander, and then back to Cole and straight to Aiden. He scores.

A roar grips the crowd and everyone screams—Kimberly included. All the other players attack Aiden, tackling him to the ground and ruffling his hair.

All except for Levi.

He only high-fives his cousin and returns to the starting point at the middle of the pitch.

It's then I notice the defect in his posture. His left shoulder is slightly drooping downwards.

My eyes widen. It's the same one he slammed into Jerry last night.

For the remainder of the game, the four 'horsemen' take possession of the field. Aiden, Xander, Cole, and Ronan seem comfortable in their own skin and the crowd goes rampant whenever they touch the ball.

Levi returns to the backlines a lot. According to Kimberly, it's for defence purposes since they're only one score ahead.

"Does Levi play like this sometimes?" I ask Kimberly.

"Captain? Never." Although Kimberly is talking about King, her eyes never leave number nineteen, Xander Knight. "He'll be scouted by the Premier League. This is his worst performance in years."

"Wait. He wants to play professionally?"

"That's what I heard. They've scouted him since the second year, but I guess he wants to finish school first—oh my gosh, yes! Do it!"

My muscles lock when Levi runs towards the goal with Aiden to his right. The latter raises his hand, but the captain doesn't pay him any attention and forges through.

With every metre he cuts, my heart beats so loud as if I'm the one running and panting.

Steady there, heart. We don't even do running.

When Levi approaches the danger zone, someone from the other team tackles him. Levi falls to the ground with a thud.

"Oooh," the crowd voice their joint disappointment.

My hands turn sweaty as Levi remains on the ground, unmoving.

My breathing comes out choppy and stuttering as Levi's teammates gather around him.

A second passes…

Two...

Three...

Four —

He stands up, leaning on Aiden, and everyone releases a collective breath.

I stare with stupefaction as he dusts off his jersey as if nothing happened.

Besides relief, something morbid and nasty takes refuge inside me. I stand up, grab my backpack, and storm out of the stadium. Kimberly waves back when I mumble a 'bye'.

My heart thumps as I stomp out and straight into the hallway, heading to the art studio.

I slam the door shut and lean against it. What the hell was that all about?

And why am I so bothered about it?

TWENTY-TWO

Levi

I haven't decided whether you're my damnation or my salvation.

"This isn't my captain, King. Get your head out of your arsehole," Coach whisper-yells so only I can hear on his way out of the locker room.

Then my attention moves to the guys, who cheer as they carry Aiden on their shoulders. They drop him, slapping his back and ruffling his hair.

He grins, but it's fake. He doesn't really enjoy any of this. He just does it for appearances' sake. A defence mechanism of sorts.

I button my shirt in silence. The familiar gloomy energy surrounds me like a four-walled prison.

It's not because of the game or even the bitching pain in my shoulder. It's because of those fucking green eyes that didn't leave me since last night.

I might have spent a sleepless night punching the bag in the gym.

I might have stopped myself a thousand times from barging into her house in the middle of the night, and thinking screw it if her father murdered me.

This obsession is becoming dangerous and fucked up. I'm not the type of person who lets anyone else take over my thoughts, my mind, and even my fucking dreams.

And yet, everything has been revolving around Astrid Clifford.

As if that wasn't enough, she had to show up at the game and screw up everything.

I don't know what pissed me off more. The fact that she wasn't there for me, or the fact that she was cheering another guy's name right in front of me.

Whatever it was, it fucked up my entire game in the second half. And now, unreleased energy keeps buzzing in my veins, demanding to be set free.

I might have to fight tonight. Or drink. Or both.

A finger taps my arm. I'm too caught up in my thoughts that the mere gesture takes me by surprise, and I clench my fists.

Aiden's face appears to my right, wearing a frown. "You're turning speedy, aren't you?"

"Piss. Off," I snarl in his face.

He doesn't flinch at my open show of hostility. "This isn't even about the game, isn't it?"

"No, Cousin, it's not about the game. It's never about the game. It's all about my screwed up genes, remember?"

He's silent for a few seconds. That's Aiden. Everything needs to be plotted to a T—including his damn thoughts. "If the chessboard doesn't look to be in your favour, you're the only one who can change its direction."

"Yo, me Kings!" Ronan interrupts us in a mock cockney accent, flinging one arm around Aiden's shoulders and the other around mine. "Party at me place. No objections. Deal? Deal."

He drags us both to the centre of the room and announces, "Victory party at the one and only number thirteen's! Captain approved!"

The guys hoot and carry Ronan on their shoulders.

"Didn't you say you wouldn't throw any more parties for us?" Xan taunts.

"Shut it, Knight." Ronan gives him and Cole a dirty look. "This is my compensation for not having the cake bunny hookers."

I should probably stop them since they need recuperation, but I'm in no mood to ruin their fun on the weekend.

Besides, I need to get myself out of this trance or drink myself to fucking sleep.

"Can we invite people?" Daniel asks from the corner.

"*Mais oui!* The more the merrier, *mon ami.*"

Daniel grins and retrieves his phone. My eyes narrow on his hands. Is he texting Astrid?

My blood pumps harder at the thought. I don't like it.

I don't fucking like it.

I remove myself from underneath Ronan's arm and stride to Daniel.

"Was that Astrid at the game?" I ask in a nonchalant tone.

As if I could ever mistake that tomboyish attitude, her soft voice, or those damn sparkling green eyes.

"Uh, yeah, Captain. She promised to be present for my first game."

And be a fucking cheerleader, apparently.

"Are you inviting her to the party?" I ask.

"I sent her a text, but she won't come. She hates these things."

I don't know if I should feel relieved or pissed off or both.

One hour later, half of the team are shagging in Ronan's guest rooms. He made sure to lock his parents' room. It's been off limits ever since he found Cole or Aiden and their 'kinky shit' in it.

The only ones who remain with me in the pool house are Aiden and Cole, and they're playing chess. I played a game or two, but I quickly got bored.

I had a drink and that turned too boring too fast as well.

Everything is.

I want to get out there and down one more shot or two and fucking fight someone. Not only is Aiden keeping me on a leash, but I know exactly where that behaviour will lead me.

Another lifetime as Jonathan's slave.

So I just stand around, ready to stop any trouble that breaks out amongst the team members.

A girl, Nicole something, has been hanging off my arm since the beginning of the evening. She's wearing my number and staring up at me with big, wide eyes.

I want it to be a different face with my number on her back. Different person. Different fucking eyes.

"On your knees," I order her.

"I'm not a whore." Her lips part, but even those are the wrong fucking ones.

"On your knees or get the fuck out of here."

Her gaze strays to Aiden and Cole, who sit on the opposite side right across from us. They're too engrossed in their game to pay her the slightest bit of attention.

Nicole, who I think is Chloe's friend, drops to her knees between my legs, licking her lips and pretending to be shy. It's so different from how heat crept up Astrid's neck and face. How she genuinely blushed and melted in my arms.

She has a way of getting under my skin and refusing to come out.

I stuff my finger in Nicole's mouth, opening it wide. She sucks, but I tsk. "Stay still."

This Nicole girl does nothing for me. I can't even get it up for her.

I try to imagine it's the princess sitting right here at my mercy, blushing. Like it's gotten a shot of ecstasy, my dick hardens. Those eyes. Those damn fucking eyes are staring up at me like they're about to spark.

Nicole's hand snakes to my trousers' belt as her other one caresses my bulge. It's not her touch that hardens me, it's the image of Astrid being a good little princess. Her small hands grasp me, stroke me, about to suck me off while staring up at me with those —

"Wow, you're so big."

Aaaand Nicole had to ruin it with her screechy voice that's nothing like Astrid's.

What the fuck was I thinking anyway? This isn't her and it never will be.

When I thrust into her throat, I want it to be Astrid. It has to be her.

I clutch Nicole's shoulders, about to push her away, when a small gasp reaches me from the entrance.

I feel her presence before I lift my head and see her. She's still in that denim skirt from earlier with a white top.

Fucking hell. She's as beautiful as a forbidden fantasy.

Astrid's gaze flies from me to Nicole, who turns her head to stare at the newcomer. Her lips part farther before she shakes her head and stares from Nicole to me again.

She doesn't meet my gaze as she blurts. "I…um…thought Dan was here. Sorry to interrupt."

The door shuts behind her quietly and Nicole laughs in that annoying way. That's when I realise what Astrid just saw.

Fuck.

I was so caught up in seeing her here that I forgot the state she saw me in.

"Why the fuck are you laughing?" I snap at Nicole.

"The little Viking has learnt her place both at home and here."

"At home?"

"She's my stepsister, but not for long." Her hand returns to my trousers. "Now, where were we?"

I shove her away until she falls backwards, barely catching her balance.

"But —" she screeches.

"Go swallow someplace else."

I don't wait for her to disappear and stride past her to the exit.

Something tells me I really fucked up this time.

TWENTY-THREE

Astrid

My demons aren't yours to fight.

I will not cry.

I will *not* cry.

I take a deep breath, fighting the moisture in my eyes and the pressure building behind my nose.

I'm not that girl. I'll *never* be that girl.

The crowd seems to thicken the harder I try to push myself out of the maze.

So what if Dan insisted I celebrate his first win as part of the team?

So what if I didn't want to go back home only for Dad to force me into a dinner with Victoria?

Coming here was a big freaking mistake.

Or maybe it wasn't.

Maybe I had to see Nicole between Levi's legs to finally snap out of whatever madness that's taken over me.

Still, my chest aches so much, it's a struggle to breathe.

Why the hell does it hurt this much?

"Here's my girl!" Dan embraces me in a hug out of nowhere, reeking of alcohol. "Ro, Xan, did I introduce you to my BFF?"

"Why, hello there." Ronan—number thirteen—grins with

sparkling brown eyes. "Why have you been keeping such a good-looking lady to yourself, Danny boy?"

"Yeah, Danny. Sharing is caring." Xander grins and it's too sickeningly charming. He has classic pretty boy looks, blond hair, blue eyes, all complete with dimples.

"I'm Ronan." He takes my hand in his and places a kiss on the top. "Don't believe everything you hear about me."

"It's usually much worse," Xander finishes for him.

"Now, hands off Astrid, you pigs." Dan swats them away as if they're flies. "She doesn't like sex."

I jab him, an involuntary blush creeping along my skin as I mutter, "Thanks for broadcasting that, Bug."

I should probably take him away before he spills all my secrets. Dan is a chatterbox when he's drunk.

"Wow, okay." Ronan fakes a gasp. "We need to fix that. I volunteer, *mademoiselle*."

Xander pushes him out of the way. "I'm a month older than you and, therefore, can go first." He smiles. "If the lady would have me, of course."

"My house. My rules." Ronan puffs out his chest, then looks at me. "Why don't you choose?"

I'm speechless, not knowing what to say to that.

"How about a drink instead?!" Dan shouts.

"Hey, I'm a drinking king." Ronan pats his chest. "No one can beat me."

"Astrid can." Dan massages my shoulders. "She has a weird high alcohol tolerance."

That's it. I'm taking a taxi and hauling Dan's arse home.

Ronan's eyes widen. "My hero."

"Wait." Xander gets impossibly close until I smell blueberry pie on him. "You're that girl Captain brought into the pool house at the beginning of summer, aren't you?"

Yup. The night I ruined my invisibility.

Why did I have to stumble into Levi back then?

"Oh. That one." Even Ronan's smile falls and the air shifts from playful to tension-filled.

"She's an artist and hates athletes, so screw off, Ro," Dan continues with a slight slur.

"My mother is into collecting," Ronan offers with a half-smile that doesn't quite reach his eyes. "Do you want to see?"

"Dan?" I ask. I need to talk to him and stop him from broadcasting my damn life to his football friends.

"Yeah, let's go."

Ronan directs us while Xander disappears with one of the girls. They all seem to be throwing themselves at the football team tonight.

Like a certain Nicole.

No. Nope. My mind isn't going there.

Pressure perches on my chest whenever that image pops back in my head.

Dan leans on me, laughing and hooting whenever one of his teammates passes by or waves at him.

We go inside the room Ronan directs us to. It's an office with a mahogany desk and chairs. The walls are covered in impressionist artwork, all of them in shades of white, grey, and black and sorted from lighter to darker.

Interesting choice of colours for a woman. Ronan's mother must be deeply interested in art if she kept this collection.

"What is it?" Dan blinks, fingering a bronze Buddha statue.

"Can we go home?"

"Now?" His brows scrunch. "The party just started."

I want to mention that he's been getting into too many parties lately, but I don't want him to think I'm making all of this about me again.

"I know you don't like these scenes." He approaches and clutches my shoulders. "But it's our last year, remember? We're having all the fun so there will be no regrets. Wait." He wipes under my eyes. "Were you crying?"

"No, yes, I don't know." I bite my lower lip and then I just blurt it all out, from this morning about my fight with Victoria and Nicole straight to when I found the same Nicole sucking Levi's dick.

"Fucking Nicole," he breathes out. "I can't believe he took the exhibition off the table."

My head bows as Dan stands against the desk with me.

"And then she sucked off Captain." He sounds soberer than he did a few minutes ago.

He didn't ask the question, but I nod anyway, my chest tightening at that image.

Daniel remains quiet for a beat. "Why do you care who sucks off Captain?"

My head jerks up at that. "I…don't."

"You most certainly do." He smiles a little with a sense of bitterness. "Otherwise, you wouldn't be so upset right now. Do you like him?"

"Of course not! He's a fucking bastard who thinks he's entitled to everything. I hate his type, remember?"

"Yeah, but maybe you noticed he's not exactly that type?"

I did and I hate him even more for it. Why did he show me layers of himself if he was going to have Nicole suck him off?

"You know…" he trails off.

"What?"

"I heard this from Ronan when he was drunk, but it seems that Captain is under a lot of pressure from his uncle and maybe that has to do with why he's bothering you?"

"Doesn't matter."

"Hey, little bugger. We're not supposed to be running away from our problems, remember?" He nudges my shoulder. "Or there'll be no marathoning Vikings."

"That's torture." I smile, giving him a bro hug. "Go ahead and have fun. I know you're dying to shag someone."

"Thank fuck." He chuckles. "But seriously, are you going to be all right?"

"Yeah, I'll just spend some time here and then come find you?"

"Give me time for a quickie."

I jab him. "I didn't need that image."

He laughs. "See you, crazy."

"Duh, crazy."

Takeaway by The Chainsmokers filters from the door as Dan slips out and closes the door behind him, muting the outside world.

I continue leaning against the table, staring at the opposite wall and the clash of white and black. It's like yin and yang. Good versus evil. An angel versus the devil.

I try to focus some more and read into it, but all I keep seeing is Nicole's smug smirk and Levi's black one. He must've been out of his mind with desire for her.

Maybe he's already having sex with her right now.

I seal my eyes shut, urging the images to disappear.

Too late. I painted the picture, and now, it refuses to go away.

I can't believe I was worried about him earlier today.

Why? Just why would I care about that scum?

I should be focusing on more important things. Such as my hit-and-run accident and trying to remember any snippets from that night.

The chaos from the party filters back into the room. I open my eyes, happy that Dan returned for me. Maybe he had too many drinks and decided to go home.

My breath catches in my throat when the door closes and Levi advances towards me with sure, wide steps.

A chaotic string of feelings pushes through me. I want to hit and claw at him. I want to scream at him, but that will only show that I care, so I pretend to watch the painting of good versus evil as I ask, "Aren't you supposed to be with Nicole?"

He grabs both my hands in his stronger one. "I'm supposed to be right fucking here, Princess."

TWENTY-FOUR

Astrid

It's not me, it's you.

"Don't touch me," I grit out.

His body pushes into mine, hands tightening around my wrists.

The small of my back hits the table as he towers over me, all hard ridges and powerful. However, I feel no intimidation.

Hell, I don't even see him as an irresistible Viking right now. He's just a fucking bastard.

"I told you I'll ruin you." There's malice in his tone. A sharpness that's meant to cut. "I told you I'll break you, but you still didn't back down. You still *taunted* me as if asking me to retaliate harder."

"Fuck you, Levi. Fuck. You. All I ever wanted was to live my last year in peace, but no, you had to ruin *everything*. Did I ask you to take an interest in me? Did I fucking make you? You're the one who set out to destroy me with your stupid games."

"And you're the one who refused to lose." His face tightens as if he's the one who's mad, not the other way around.

"I wasn't born to lose or to become a pawn on your board."

He watches me then, all intent like he's cutting me open and peering inside me. It would be unnerving under different circumstances, but now, all I feel is contempt.

I want to ruin him as much as he's ruined me.

This time, I want to be the predator instead of the prey.

"What you saw isn't what it seemed," he says in a cool tone like we're discussing the weather.

"Sure thing. I definitely didn't see you getting your dick sucked by Nicole, King."

"Don't call me that."

"Isn't that what you demand everyone to call you, *King?*"

"Not you."

His chest comes impossibly closer. My breasts brush against his Elites' jacket with every breath. I try not to focus on how full and tight they feel or how my nipples ache in response.

His fresh scent mixed with a distant whiff of vodka fills my senses.

His presence is like a natural disaster—impossible to avoid and always leaves destruction behind.

And I refuse to be collateral damage.

I struggle against him, trying to head-butt him, but he easily moves out of the way.

"Do you consider me a joke?"

"A joke," he repeats slowly, keeping his merciless hold on my wrists.

"Or am I a conquest? A war you need to win."

"A war is fucking child's play compared to you, Princess."

"How many girls have you told that? Does that include Nicole? You know, with her taking care of the *captain* and all that."

His lips curve into a wolfish smirk. Damn him and how unreal he looks. "Why are you so upset, Princess?"

"I'm not."

"Are you perhaps jealous?"

"Screw. You."

And screw Nicole and screw my heart for ever thumping for this bastard.

He pushes his pelvis into the space where my T-shirt meets

my skirt. Something hard and thick presses against the bottom of my stomach through his jeans.

I can't help the shudder that draws down my spine.

"Do you feel that, Princess? There's nothing I want to do more than to spread your legs and fuck you raw."

His dirty words elicit a tightening at the pit of my stomach. It's like a flashback from that night and I'm barely able to stop myself from rubbing all over him.

Then I recall that a certain blondie was rubbing all over him not so long ago.

I bite my lower lip until I almost draw blood. "Nicole's sloppy seconds aren't on my to-do list."

"Fuck Nicole. Fuck everyone. None of them matter."

"And I do?" I scoff.

"You do."

He pauses, seemingly surprised at his own words. His posture tenses and we watch each other for a second too long, as if we need to soak in the moment.

I'm the first who pulls myself out of the trance. "Leave me alone, King."

"I told you to stop calling me that."

He releases my wrists and grabs me by the hips. His hands are large and strong around my petite frame as he lifts me with ease.

I yelp when he sits me on the desk. He slaps my legs apart, and my denim skirt stretches with the motion as he settles between my parted thighs.

Tiny shivers break out on my skin and down my back.

"Do you know who I thought about when Nicole was between my legs?"

"I don't want to know."

His hot breaths tease the shell of my ear, drawing a shudder from my inner walls. "You don't, huh?"

"I *don't*."

"I'm telling you anyway. When she looked up, it was these

beautiful green eyes." His fingers trace along my eyelashes. "When she opened her mouth, I saw these lips." He trails a forefinger from my eyes to the corner of my mouth, hovering but not touching.

I swallow around the sound trying to claw its way out. My ragged breathing with every draw.

"Then what?" My voice is low, defeated. "You would've fucked her and pretended it was me?"

"She's not you."

The words are barely out of his mouth when his entire posture stiffens like he hates it. He hates that she's not me. That he can't play his games on her and pretend it's me.

And for some reason, that makes me feel a strange sense of accomplishment.

Even the king doesn't always get what he wants.

Levi grabs a handful of my hair in his fist and pulls until my head tilts back. He trails his other hand up my collarbone and wraps it around my throat.

His hold is firm enough to make sure I know he's controlling my breathing. One squeeze and all my air will be gone.

My pulse goes into overdrive until it's impossible not to hear it.

Thump. Thump. Thump.

At this angle, I have a complete view of the clenching in his sharp jawline, the contempt on his hard features, and the black in his pale eyes.

I'm starting to think that for Levi, black isn't a colour. It's a state of mind and being.

A monster hides behind that sinister, menacing look. A monster who'll rip me to pieces if I let him.

Scratch that. He'll rip me apart even if I don't let him.

I've already provoked the king and now, there's no going back to being a mere pawn on the enemies' lines. My best bet is to climb the ranks and *somehow* bring down the king.

He squeezes my throat for a beat. "No one is you, Princess."

My chest rises and falls so hard, I'm glad that my heart is an organ and can't possibly rip its way out of my ribcage, kamikaze style.

I place a hand on his chest in a sorry attempt to push him away. "This can't happen. I hate you, Levi."

"If it makes you feel better, hate me all you want." He runs his lips along the shell of my ear, flicking his tongue out to tease the heated skin.

A small gasp tears past my lips and I can't help angling my neck to the side, even with his hand keeping me in place.

"You and I are toxic," I breathe out in a low tone. "We're nothing alike."

"It's opposite poles who attract," he speaks against my ear, nibbling on the sensitive flesh.

I bite my lower lip against the onslaught of emotions. I clench my thighs, but that only manages to squeeze him harder against my slick core.

"Opposites also destroy each other."

"I'm good with that, too."

I open my mouth to protest. However, any words I'm about to say end in a gasp when his lips claim mine. Unlike the kiss in the car park, this one is more desperate, violent, and out of fucking control.

His teeth clash against mine and his tongue thrusts in like he's always owned this part of me.

Like he's had me his entire life.

I don't fight it this time. I *can't*.

When he pulls on my hair, I tilt my head back and let him kiss me. No. Scratch that. Because Levi doesn't kiss, he devours. He eats me up like I'm his favourite flavour.

Then, a second later, he squeezes my neck and wrenches our mouths apart.

I'm panting and begging for air, but all I can think about is *more*.

I need more.

Our mouths aren't meant for breathing or talking. They were made for kissing.

It's a freaking crime that he hasn't been kissing me all this time. We should've been kissing since that night I was all drugged with him and his touch.

Only, I'm not drugged now, am I?

Levi is the drug. And I'm a victim of my addiction to him.

I'm a victim of his obsession with me and the way he looks at me as if I'm his life's dilemma.

"Don't come cheering for others at my game," he growls the words against my throat.

"W-what?"

"Don't stand there calling another guy's name in my fucking presence."

I smile, incredulous. "Are you obsessed with me or something?"

"Call it an obsession or foolishness or fucking madness," he grunts, squeezing my throat. "But you keep your eyes on me."

I don't get to reply, because his tongue invades my mouth. Conquers it. Smashes it. Like it's his God-given right. Like I was made for him to conquer.

The biggest part of me wants to give back what he takes. I want to kiss him like I can win the battle, too. I want to claw at his defences and pull down his walls.

But that's not who I am, right? I'm not supposed to go on battles and wars. I'm supposed to finish my damn year in peace.

I rip away from his mouth with a groan. "I..."

"Stop denying it." The pale blue of his eyes trap me in an enchanting spell. With one last squeeze to my throat, he trails his hand to my breast, cupping it. "These feel so full, don't they?"

I shake my head even as my nipples harden like never before.

"But look at them pushing against your T-shirt. I bet they want me to feel them, huh?"

He flicks his thumb against my nipple over the cloth. His dirty words and his touch elicit a magnitude of sensations.

Everything feels tenfold sharper.

The desk's wood under me is too hard. The soft light has suddenly become too bright. His intoxicating scent is like opium or a shot of alcohol.

"Lie all you want, but I can feel your arousal, Princess."

I'm about to protest when he pinches my nipple hard.

My head falls back on a moan. "Oh, God."

He continues twirling the nipple, playing, then pinching it as if it's a torture device. And in a way, it is.

Hot breaths tickle my ear as he whispers, "Are you telling me that if I touch you right now, you won't be dripping wet?"

"L-Levi..." It was supposed to be a protest, but I'm too drugged on his dirty words.

Not to mention that the double onslaught on my breast and ear is making me too hazy to think.

"Tell me, Princess, if I push through your folds, are you going to soak me?"

I don't get to reply.

With his grip on my hair, he pushes me back and yanks my skirt to my mid-section, exposing my pale thighs and the black boy shorts.

The spark of lust in his eyes mixes with that strange blackness.

"Levi, you —"

My words die out when he cups me over my boy shorts. I bite my lower lip against the moan. It's like all my nerves have gathered underneath his hand.

"You *are* wet." His wolfish grin makes me draw a stuttering breath.

"How do I make you wet, Princess?"

His fingers inch to the band of my underwear. "Is it how I touch you here?" He slips a finger over the cloth, rubbing up and down. "Do you want me to stick it in you? Are you going to swallow me in like a good little princess?"

Although his touch and dirty words are maddening, it's the look in his eyes that make me want to free fall to sin.

He looks at me as if I'm the most appetising thing he's ever seen. He's starving and his unapologetic, raw hunger is rubbing off on me.

"You'll come for me, won't you?" he growls. "You'll scream so loud, you'll bring the whole fucking house down, huh? Everyone will know you're being fucked real good, won't they?"

Oh, for the love of Vikings, why does every word he says turn me on even more?

"But first, you want me to see you, don't you? You want me to see that pussy that will soon belong to me. I bet it's all swollen and pink and ready for me, isn't it?"

I swallow, unable to breathe right. Because maybe I do. Maybe I'm crazy and I want him to see me.

All of me.

He angles my legs up and brings my boy shorts down without breaking eye contact.

Those enthralling pale eyes.

Those blue, *blue* eyes.

The intimacy of it undoes me.

Then his gaze strays to what he's uncovered. I lick my dry lips at the feral, intense look on his face.

But I don't get to watch him watch me for long. I don't get to pause the moment and tuck it away for safekeeping.

Because then he's between my legs.

"What are you —"

All thoughts disappear when he runs his tongue from the bottom to the top of my clit.

I open my mouth to say something, but it remains in a wide 'O' as he repeats the onslaught, not giving me time to breathe. I grip the wooden table's edge as my head falls against it.

He sucks and pulls at my folds with his teeth, his stubble scratching at my inner thighs. The sensation is enough to bring me to the edge.

"You taste." *Suck.* "Like." *Suck.* "Fucking sin."

I can feel myself dripping for him. For his words. For his whole damn aura.

Levi owns me in ways I can't begin to explain. I can't even understand them myself.

He nibbles on my clit with his teeth, and I jerk up off the table as if I'm possessed. He pins me down with both his hands on my hips.

My fingers find the golden locks of his hair and I push—or pull—I'm not quite sure. He continues sucking and nibbling and thrusting his tongue in and out of me like he's been starving for me. Like I was made for him to devour.

Something wild and unrestrained builds inside me so fast, I can't register it, let alone contain it.

There's no warning. No damn slowing down Levi and his brutal, unrestrained tongue.

I come so hard, my head bangs against the wood and black dots form behind my lids.

A flash of movement breezes in my peripheral vision. Or maybe that's the orgasm halo.

I return to the world of the living with Levi's lips on mine and his tongue thrusting inside my mouth. The same lips and tongue that had just brought me over the edge.

I almost come right then and there again.

This time, I kiss him back. I clash with his tongue and his teeth, and I give back the wildness he brought out in me.

I become the war he tries to conquer.

TWENTY-FIVE

Astrid

If fate brought us together, then fate be damned.

I tiptoe towards the back entrance of the pool house. It's become an epic sneaking out technique that I've been perfecting. There's no way in hell I'm having breakfast with my evil stepmother and her daughter.

That sounded very Cinderella-ish—and not in a good way.

I spent the entire weekend with Dan at Ally's or playing pool at his place. Oh, and I totally stole Aunt Nora's scones and left Dan with nothing.

Still, I couldn't say a word about what happened at Ronan's party.

Zach, Dan's eldest brother, drove us home that night. By then, I had already run away from Ronan's mum's office and hid by the garden.

Okay, I might have called Zach, too, so he'd come to get us.

I mean, I can't be blamed. Anyone would've freaked out if they were so wanton and vocal about their first orgasm. An orgasm that happened straight on Levi's face.

Jeez. I don't know what the hell took over my body.

He didn't chase after me that night—thankfully—but he sent me a text.

Levi: You can't run away from me, Princess. I'll catch you every time.

He sent another text yesterday morning. Six a.m. on a Sunday. Does he even sleep?

Levi: Let's go for a jog and train those legs to run better.

I ignored both texts.

I wish I could say I figured anything out over the weekend. On the contrary, everything is becoming more complicated than I thought.

Levi is a damn dilemma with no way out. That small part of me that's itching to be pulled into his orbit? Well, that part isn't so small anymore.

It's still too early for Dan to pick me up. They have practice in the evening today, and he's not that much of a morning person. He won't be waking up until it's time for school.

If I want to avoid breakfast from hell, I need to get out now before Victoria and Nicole are up.

Especially Nicole. I've made sure we haven't crossed paths at home since that scene of her between Levi's legs.

Before he ended up between mine.

God. That's so screwed up.

My gaze meets Sarah's from the kitchen's window. I place a finger in front of my lips and beg her with an expression to remain silent.

She rolls her eyes but waves me away. I throw her a kiss and duck around the pool house.

"Not happening. Astrid will not go through that again."

I stop at Dad's voice as I get to the corner of the building. I peek my head around as slow as physically possible.

He stands at the edge of the pool, already dressed in his three-piece black suit. One hand in his pocket, the other is holding the phone glued to his ear.

"I'm her father and legal guardian, Commissioner."

My back snaps in a rigid line. This has to do with my accident.

"She lost her mother in an accident and had a similar one of her own," Dad speaks in his no-nonsense tone that intimidates me even when I'm not the one on the receiving end. "She will not take the fall for your incompetence."

Silence.

Long, thick silence.

Dad looks in the distance for a few seconds that seems like an eternity. "The answer is no and that's final."

He clicks something on the phone and turns around. I duck and run in the opposite direction towards the pool house's side door.

Dad stops in front of the entrance to the kitchen and takes a deep breath, his shoulders drooping as he pinches the bridge of his nose.

I haven't seen him do that since I was a little girl. I thought he'd completely lost that habit.

The moment ends as fast as it came. He straightens like the Lord Clifford everyone knows, opens the door, and strides inside.

"Sarah, is Astrid down for breakfast?"

Shit.

I sprint towards the back entrance, not looking back.

My head is a jumbled mess as I walk down the street and to the park. My fingers tighten around the backpack's straps.

Dad's hiding something that has to do with the police commissioner and my accident.

Astrid will not go through that again.

Go through what?

A finger taps my arm, and I yelp. I was too caught up in my thoughts to notice someone approach me, let alone walking by my side.

My heart rate returns to normal only to spike up again when I meet those sinister pale blue eyes.

Sometimes, it's like they belong to an angel. Other times, it's like the devil is staring down at me.

This morning, it's a mixture of both.

I can't help the spike of my pulse or how heat smothers my body by just looking at him.

Levi has his golden Viking hair that's slicked back today as if he's in a fashion show. His team's royal blue jacket clings to his shoulders like a second skin.

His mouth curves to the side. The same mouth that sucked and nibbled and brought me a pleasure I didn't realise existed. The same mouth that kissed me like a madman with my taste all over him.

"You're blushing, Princess." His grin widens.

"I'm not."

He taps my nose with his index finger. "It's adorable."

I step back until he has to drop his hand.

Dammit. A single touch is all it takes for me to crave crawling into his side.

"Why were you blushing? Are there certain memories pricking your mind?"

"Oh, please. Don't flatter yourself. It wasn't that special." I lower my flushed face as soon as I say the words, not wanting him to see my reaction.

"*It?*" he asks with an amused tone.

"You know."

"No. Enlighten me."

"Stop it."

"Stop what?"

Ugh. He's infuriating. "Can't you just drop it?"

"Are you too shy to say I went down on you? That I ate you up like I've never eaten anything before? That I licked and bit your hot, wet pussy as you came all over my face and —"

"Stop." I place both of my hands on his mouth, shutting him up.

I'm not that worried about the early runners in the park as much as my stupid body's reaction to his crude words.

With every word coming out of his mouth, a rush of heat invades me and pools between my thighs.

When the hell did I become so addicted to his dirty talk?

I look on either side of me. "Why are you here anyway?"

"I came for you."

I came for you.

Just like that. He makes it appear so easy and nonchalant.

"I would've gone to your house, but I'm guessing Lord Clifford isn't a big fan of me."

"No shit, Sherlock." I frown. "How did you know I'd be in this park?"

"I have my ways."

Dan. That traitor. I should be angry with him for spilling my morning routine, but I don't have it in me right now.

Levi might be a bastard, but he's managed to pluck me from the dooming thoughts about Dad and what he's hiding from me.

"Run with me." He nudges my shoulder.

"I'm an artist, not an athlete, remember?"

"You don't have to be an athlete to run."

"I'm good." I flop onto an empty bench. "Thanks but no thanks."

I try to imagine he's not standing right in front of me as I retrieve my sketchbook.

Easier said than done.

His presence always fills the space like a hurricane brewing in the distance.

I pause opening my pad, recalling that my current sketch is from the game. I might have been working on it during the entire weekend.

"Hey." I meet his assessing gaze. "Did you steal my sketch the other day?"

"What sketch?"

"Just some rubbish."

"Just some rubbish, huh?"

"Uh-huh."

There's no way in hell I'm telling him that it was the first thing I've been able to sketch after months.

"Now I see it."

I follow Levi's eager field of vision. He's staring at the end of my sun-moon-star tattoo.

"See what?"

"That's the reason you have all these stars on your phone case, your bag, and even your drawings." He tilts his head. "Do you make wishes upon the stars, Princess?"

"I stopped doing that since Mum died." I narrow my eyes. "You did steal my sketch."

"What's your evidence?"

"Tough luck, Levi. You just admitted to it."

"And how, do tell, did I admit to it?"

I puff out my chest, feeling smug. "You said I have stars on my drawings when you've supposedly never seen one."

"I meant *that*." He points in my sketchpad's direction.

Right. Lie to someone else.

"Let's run," he repeats.

"The answer is still no."

He slides beside me, crowding my space. His eyes gleam with menace and the air shifts.

The park and its runners hush in the background. All I can hear is the thumping of my heart and all I can smell is Levi's clean, intoxicating scent.

"We can sit here and catch up on what happened on Saturday. You know, the whole part about eating you up," he whispers so low, it's sinful. "Do you want to know if I jacked off to your orgasm face?"

I jerk up and start running to hide the heat creeping up my cheeks.

Did he really jack off to me?

Wrong thought, Astrid. Super wrong thought.

Levi catches up to me, chuckling softly. He must be finding all of this too amusing.

Bastard.

While I put every ounce of energy I have into running, Levi seems like he's strolling in the park.

His legs don't flex as much as mine—stupid tall people. While I'm already sweating like a pig, there's not an ounce of sweat on his forehead.

When I glance at him, his hard stare is on me. He's not even putting up an effort to run and is only keeping up with my pace. It'd be suicide to ask him for a race.

His muscles expand and move with ease. Even his breathing comes in and out with ease, unlike how choppy mine is.

After a few laps around the park, sweat coats my temples and my hands. My legs scream to be put out of their misery as if I've just finished a marathon.

I fall against the bench, panting so hard, my heart almost leaps out of my throat.

"I'm done. So done."

Dark laughter fills my ears as a bottle of water is thrust into my face. I don't know where he got it from, but I don't care as I gulp half of it down in one go.

Levi sits beside me, his chest rising and falling steadily while mine nearly breaks down from my erratic breathing.

When I glance at him, he's taking a sip from the same bottle I did, that familiar spark taking over his eyes.

I lick my lips. He's drinking from it on purpose, isn't he?

"How do you aliens do this all the time?" I stare ahead to distract myself from his glistening lips.

Damn his lips.

"It's all about stamina. Besides, you're doing it all wrong."

I wipe the sweat off my eyebrows and my temple. "I'm doing it all wrong because I'm not supposed to be doing it at all."

He smiles. "No, I meant that you shouldn't waste all your energy at the beginning. You have to divide your strength and pick up slowly."

"Like at the games?"

"Sort of."

I peek up at him, not sure if I want to take the bull by his horns. "Then what happened at the last game?"

His face closes until there are only unreadable lines. It's like he had his guard down and now he's closing the fort.

"What do you mean?"

"You didn't play like yourself in the second half."

"You came to one game and now you're an expert on how I usually play?"

"How do you know I didn't come to the previous games?"

"I would've noticed you."

"No, you wouldn't have, Levi. I was invisible to you until that stupid party."

He says nothing. The silence stretches long enough that it becomes uncomfortable. I fidget with my backpack's straps.

"Do you believe in fate?" he asks.

I'm taken aback by his super out-of-character question.

"Not really."

"Me neither, but I'm starting to."

My pulse quickens at the irresistible drop in his tone. "Why is that?"

He fists my hair in his grip so my head is angled up. "I would've found you no matter what, Princess. It was a matter of when, not if."

TWENTY-SIX

Levi

Fight all you want, but you'll never win.

There are two things I learn when I drop Astrid off at school.

A- She doesn't want to be seen with me.

B- I fucking hate it.

As soon as I park the car, she flies out towards the entrance as if her arse is on fire. Although it's a shame to have that tight little arse on fire.

Daniel comes out of his car as soon as Astrid crosses the threshold of the entrance. He must've called her name because she turns around and meets him halfway for a hug.

My grip tightens around the steering wheel.

One more thing I fucking hate.

I watch for a change in Daniel's expression. An excuse to erase him completely out of her existence.

Lucky for him, he only gives her a brief side hug with his arm at her back.

Astrid's smile widens at another man who comes out of the passenger seat of Daniel's car. He's a taller, slightly buffer version of Daniel with a Mohawk hairstyle—who does that anymore?

He opens his arms and Astrid goes right into them. I grind

my teeth at how his hand dips to the small of her back. The sorry fuck grins at her with that unmistakable hunger.

Huh. Looks like someone's going down.

Soon.

No one touches what belongs to me.

Astrid Clifford is already mine. She just doesn't know it yet.

Today's practice goes smoothly now that I don't have to worry about the little princess in the crowd, cheering for someone else.

"Good to have our captain back." Cole winks at me on our way out of the locker room.

"Did I ever leave, fuckers?"

"Uh, yeah?" Xander raises both eyebrows. "You were the living dead on Saturday."

"Shut it, Knight."

"Yeah, shut it, Knight. My party cheered up Captain." Ronan flings his arm around my shoulder, expression cunning. "Were Mum's paintings that inspiring?"

I smirk. "Very."

"Oh, *bordel*." His face falls. "Come on, Captain. In the office? Mum will fucking kill me."

"Rest in peace, little shit," Cole says.

"Don't fuck the corpses when you're dead." Xander laughs and we all laugh with him.

Ronan headlocks both Xander and Cole, making them butt heads. I let them walk ahead as Aiden stalks to my side like the creep he is.

He's focused on his phone, on someone's social media. That's rare. Usually, Aiden doesn't give two shits about such things.

Unlike me, he does have an Instagram account, but he only uses it to paint a fake image.

I angle my head to the side to see who the pitiful fuck is

who has my cousin's attention. I only catch a glimpse of a girl's Instagram before he hits home.

"Are you recruiting someone for a satanic sacrifice?" I ask.

"Maybe." His poker face game is too strong. It's as if he's actually entertaining the idea. Wait. Is he?

"What gives, Lev?"

"About?"

"No fight with Jonathan for the entire weekend. That's a record."

"He's not worth it."

"And you're not speedy." He raises an eyebrow. "Keep doing what you're doing."

My feet falter for a second as Aiden's words sink in.

I'm not speedy—not that I like the term.

Fuck.

I was never able to pull a brake on it before, but now, the wheel is slowing down on its own.

"You coming to the Meet Up?" Aiden asks over his shoulder.

"No, and, Ro!"

"*Quoi?*" Ronan pants, barely escaping Xander's punches.

"Take Daniel with you." I pause. "From now on, always take him with you."

I find Astrid in the car park, frowning at her cell phone.

She needs to stop staying in fucking isolated places like this. If someone has half of my power over here, they'll easily manage to pull some shit like the other time.

"Trouble getting a ride?"

She jerks, wide eyes straying my way before she releases a breath. "You scared me."

"Then maybe you shouldn't stand in isolated places like prey begging to be eaten."

She lifts her chin. "What you did won't dictate my life."

I snatch her wrist and pull her into me. "Stop putting yourself in danger."

"You're the worst danger that can happen to me."

"Worst danger, huh?"

"Duh. Have you seen yourself?"

"Why don't you tell me, Princess?"

She purses her lips for a second too long and I'm tempted to eat her mouth all over again.

Kissing Astrid isn't merely a pleasure; it's slowly becoming a need, like air and food.

"You're like the night," she finally says.

"The night," I repeat.

"Uh-huh. And not just any night. You're like those dark, silent nights where no one knows what will happen."

"Would you like to know what will happen now?"

Her breath hitches. "Now?"

My hand wraps around her throat, and her pulse quickens under my thumb. "When you're being this bloody stubborn, I'm tempted to do —"

"To do what?" Her voice drops, but her gleaming eyes never leave mine.

I run my tongue over the shell of her ear, loving the shiver that takes over her. "Wicked things, Princess."

"You're…" she trails off, clearing her throat. "Whatever. Not that it matters. How did you know I had trouble getting a ride?"

"You're standing on your own at eight in the evening."

"Dan has a meet out with the team." She narrows her eyes. "Is it normal that the captain doesn't attend?"

"They can fend for themselves."

"That's not very captain-y of you."

"That's not a word." I smile. "Besides, I don't feel like being a captain tonight."

"What do you feel like being?"

"Just me."

My lips find hers.

Usually, I'd tear past her defences. This time, I don't. I let her have her little rebellion. I let her fight.

Fight me.

Fight us.

If fighting will give her the illusion that she has a chance at winning, then by all means, let her fight.

She closes her mouth, but her body leans closer into me. Then slowly, too slowly, her lips part. It's only the slightest bit, but it's more than enough.

She's given up that inch on her own.

But she should know by now that an inch isn't enough. I take the whole damn pitch.

My tongue finds hers and I devour her until there's nothing left of her. Until she's entirely sagging against me.

Astrid's fate is sealed.

TWENTY-SEVEN

Astrid

Is this the dance of the predator or the prey?

Weeks pass and my life doesn't feel like mine anymore. Not that it did since the summer.

Levi won't leave me alone, no matter how much I refuse him. If anything, the harder I push him away, the more he's prone to kidnapping me into a dark corner and kissing me until there's no breath in my lungs.

The harder I resist the kiss, the longer he makes it.

It's a game to him.

A push and pull.

Levi is a conqueror. He spends his time plotting his battles and studying his opponent's every move so when he strikes, it's direct and straight to the point.

He's not interested in half-victories. When Levi wins, he eradicates his conquest.

He barely lets me hide this twisted thing we have from the rest of the school.

And by saying he's letting me, I mean I kind of threatened him that I'll paint the windshield of his car again and stuff.

It's not real, okay? This whole thing with Levi will blow over sometime soon, and I don't want to be labelled as his majesty's latest acquisition.

Nope. I'm totally not going to be that girl.

And I might have been paying the price for forcing Levi's hand. In exchange for keeping contact at school to a minimum, he came up with his own conditions.

Double emphasis *conditions*—plural.

He's there in the mornings for the stupid morning runs—that's started to somehow grow on me. And I have to kiss him good morning—a kiss that he always deepens and leaves me breathless in the aftermath.

In the evenings, he drives me home. It's a miracle I manage to convince him to drop me around the corner so Dad doesn't see him.

Dan—the traitor—isn't even putting up a fight to take back his position as my driver.

You'll thank me for it later. His words, not mine.

And you guessed it, I have to kiss the manipulator Levi good night, too. That's the most troublesome one because it usually leaves me hot and bothered all night—that's if he doesn't yank my legs apart and go down on me in his damn car.

But despite all the time I spend with Levi, I'm still clueless as shit about him.

Some days, he's the devil, complete with that black look in his eyes. Other days, he's laughing and teasing and making my life hell.

While the first version scares me, a part of me wants to exploit it and figure out why he acts the way he does.

And more importantly, I need to know how long he plans to keep me on a leash.

Even with the burst of excitement and pleasure he brings to my life, I'm not stupid enough to trust him. Not after he made it blatantly clear that he'll destroy my life if I don't bow to his authority.

Unlike what Levi ordered, my case is still very much alive with the police. True, he hasn't brought it up lately, but that's the reason he approached me in the first place.

Back then, it was so simple. I hated Levi and everything he stood for. But now, I see different sides to him every day.

I see how he holds my hand to pull me along when we run.

I see his nostalgic smile when it rains before he takes me out into it with him.

I see him at practice with his teammates and in class, and it's like he's not the same Levi. While all the other teenagers are high on spontaneity and living in the moment, Levi is the responsible one.

He's usually in a deep internal conversation between him and himself—even when he's surrounded by his closest friends. It's like he has his own world, complete with forts and bridges, where no one else is allowed.

A part of me wants to barge into his secret world, but the other part is scared of what I'll find in there.

What if his world is a one-way ticket and I get trapped?

I take my coffee and thank Sarah on my way out of the kitchen. Phone in hand, I text Dan that I'm going out. It's Friday afternoon and we agreed to meet at Ally's. Usually, we meet on Saturdays, but since Dan became a permanent starter, that plan is now out.

I make a beeline towards the back entrance through the pool house. Dad and Victoria are at some charity dinner, but old habits die hard. It's become natural to sneak my way out of the house.

Near the pool house's door, strange sounds make me halt in my tracks. I inch closer, expecting to find an animal or something.

The sounds raise in volume. There's a moan, then a growl and the unmistakable slap of flesh against flesh.

I should've continued on my way, but hearing such sounds at home is as rare as England's sun. Even Dad never touches Victoria, except for the platonic hand grab here or there. Thank God for that. I totally don't need the image.

Making sure to keep my body out of view, I peek inside and freeze. The first thing that greets me is a man's naked arse. He pounds into my stepsister like a crazed animal.

Nicole's face twists, whether in pleasure or pain, I don't know. Her eyes meet mine, and I jerk back, but not before recognising the guy she's with.

I run out of the house, my head a complete chaos.

Christopher Vans.

Levi's closest friend.

"Earth to bugger!"

I snap my head up from my chocolate smoothie.

"Did you come here for a one-on-one meeting with your straw?" Dan asks with a dramatic tone. "Do you want me to step outside so you can have a moment?"

"I'm just trying to purge a very disturbing image I've just seen on my way here."

"Disturbing?" He slides closer, pushing his iced coffee aside. "Do tell."

"I just saw Nicole having sex with Christopher Vans in our pool house."

His grin disappears. It's only for a split second, but I notice it. I also notice how his face scrunches and his shoulders tense.

He goes back to grinning just as fast. Only, it seems a bit forced now. "Eww. No more Netflix and chill in your pool house."

I roll my eyes. "I just told you I've seen Nicole have sex and that's your first thought?"

"Does Nicole's sex life need commentating?" He's wearing his rare poker face as he speaks. "She's not even a good fuck."

"How would you know that?"

He takes a long slurp of his drink and shrugs. "Looks like it."

"Don't you think this has King's hands all over it?"

"Captain's?"

"I mean, Christopher is his closest friend."

"*Was.* Since Chris was benched, Captain doesn't look in his direction twice. He punched him at the beginning of the year for being useless."

"That's harsh. Isn't a person's worth calculated by how well he plays?"

He lifts a shoulder. "Captain is all about winning and he doesn't sugar-coat anything when it comes to slackers. He even had a few choice words for his cousin the other day."

I fumble with my straw, humming. Something in my gut tells me Christopher sleeping with my stepsister isn't a coincidence. Maybe he's pretending to be on non-speaking terms with Levi in public, but they're plotting something in secret.

"And here I thought you were too dreamy-eyed about your crush." A mischievous look takes over Dan's features.

"He's not my crush."

"I've known you for three years, and I haven't seen you so caught up with someone as you are with Captain."

"He threatened me, remember? I'm doing whatever it takes to protect myself."

"Uh-huh."

"Bug!"

"Admit it. You like him."

"I hate him."

"I bet he hates you, too." He waggles an eyebrow. "Is this some sort of foreplay? Roleplay? Some other kind of kinky stuff?"

I hit his arm. "You're a pig. Does everything have to be about sex with you?"

"It does," he says matter-of-factly. "Tell me you don't think about Captain in a sexual way."

"I don't!" I say too fast, too defensively. But even saying the words bring back how much I look at Levi's lips when he's not kissing me and how much I don't want to break apart when he does.

Damn the bastard for getting me addicted to his lips.

"Yeah, right." Dan takes a long swig of his drink. "I completely believe you."

"Dan!"

"What?" He feigns nonchalance, grinning like an idiot. "I said I believe you."

"If you don't stop right now —"

"Wait," he cuts me off, sliding his iced coffee in my direction.

"What?"

"Cool off a bit. All the talk about Captain has got you blushing."

I hit him again, and I finish his iced coffee, too.

We spend the rest of the evening bowling. Zach, Dan's older brother who's studying at Imperial College, joins us near the end.

He's a taller version of Dan, with a toned body that he devotes a lot of time to perfecting at the gym.

Sometimes, when he's not with his college friends, he joins us. He also helps us sneak out from the parents' grasps since he knows all the 'tricks'.

Dan goes to get us something to drink while Zach and I continue competing. He always gets a perfect score.

"That's so unfair." I huff, watching his hands. "You have some sort of trick to always knock them over, don't you?"

He laughs, revealing pearly-white teeth. "Not a trick, just skill, babe. Let me."

With me holding the ball, Zach comes behind me and snakes his arms on either side of me to help me grip the ball tighter.

"Keep your hands steady. Don't push the shot and take your time." He presses a hand on my back. "Bend slowly and let go."

All the pins fall down in one go.

"Yes!" I jump up, hugging Zach. "I did it!"

"You did it." His arms wrap around my waist.

Suddenly, a strong hand pulls me back by the arm, and I yelp as I trip and almost fall.

Then I come face-to-face with Levi's destabilising pale eyes.

Only now, they're completely black.

TWENTY-EIGHT

Astrid

You don't own me, your majesty. No one does.

That part about being scared of the 'black' Levi?

I take it all back.

I'm not scared of him, I'm terrified. There's this complete disregard for everyone around him when he's in this mood and it seems impossible to carve a path into him.

He's wearing simple jeans and a royal blue pullover, but his entire aura is as black as the look in his eyes.

With a deep breath, I attempt to dissipate the tension in the air. "Levi. This is Zachariah, he's —"

The words die in my throat when Levi slams his lips against mine.

We've had wild kisses before—they're all we've had, actually—but this one is different. Our teeth clash and it's like he's sucking the life out of me.

Claiming me.

Punishing me.

The roughness of his mouth turns my head dizzy. I'm helpless as a marionette in his strong arms, unable to breathe or forge a path out.

I push at his chest, but it's like he doesn't feel my grip.

He doesn't feel anything.

When he finally lets me go, I'm breathing so heavily, I'm afraid my heart will pop out of its cavity.

Levi pulls me to his side with a steel hold on my waist, despite my protests.

I'm tempted to slap him for kissing me in public like that.

Lots of kids from our school come here. If anyone finds out, my already sour reputation will only get worse.

He promised to keep it under wraps. He freaking *promised*.

The clearing of a throat brings my attention back to Zach who had front-row seats to the entire show. Aiden stands not far away, observing us with an indifferent expression.

My cheeks flame at the thought of Zach watching me being kissed savagely by Levi. That's definitely not the image I want to give to him.

I bow my head, unable to look at him. "I…umm… Zach, this is —"

"Levi King and she's mine," he says the words with a coolness that negates his death grip around my waist. "Keep your fucking hands off her."

Before Zach or I can say anything, Levi drags me out of the bowling centre as if I'm a rag doll. I'm too stunned to react or say anything. I can barely keep up with his wide strides, let alone form any words.

Once we're in the car park, I come back to my senses and fight him off, but his hold tightens around my waist until it's painful.

I wince. "You had no right to do that."

He yanks me around until my back hits the side of his Jaguar. It's the first time I get a closer look into his eyes since the show he put on inside.

They're still black with not an ounce of the peaceful blue.

He's like a storm waiting to erupt.

"No right?" he repeats, pushing into me with his entire body until I'm covered with his scent and the hardness of his chest. "So he had a right to put his hands on you?"

"He?" I'm confused.

"That bastard inside."

"Are you freaking kidding me? Zach is like my eldest brother."

"One who wants to fuck you." His words are deadly calm.

My lips part. "Are you insane?"

As if possible, his eyes darken more, rippling with tension. There's barely an ounce of the Levi I've gotten used to. He's evaporating into smoke that's impossible to catch.

The frightening calm on his face puts me on the edge of myself.

I can deal with anger and rage, but how can I pick a fight with deadly calm?

"Are you blind?" He's still in that cool phase of his. "Can't you see the way he looks at you?"

"Like a sister, you mean."

He bursts out laughing, but it's completely humourless. "If he looks at you like a sister, then I look at you like you're a fucking nun."

"God damn it, Levi! Just because you want to fuck me doesn't mean everyone else does. Stop being a caveman."

"A caveman, huh?"

"I don't know what the hell is wrong with you today, but you're hallucinating and overreacting."

He slams his hand on the hood of the car near my head, and I jump at the bang.

I fight the tears of helplessness and anger blurring my vision. I hate him for making me feel like I'm at fault when I didn't do anything wrong.

It's so similar to Dad, and I swore I'd never let anyone belittle me anymore.

"What is wrong with you?" My voice raises.

"You!" he growls. "You're what's wrong with me!"

He grips my chin between his thumb and forefinger and squeezes hard enough that it hurts. "You are mine, so stop acting otherwise."

"I never agreed to be yours, King. You don't own me. No one does."

"Oh, but I do, Princess." He slaps my thighs apart and cups me through my jeans. "I own every part of you, and soon, that won't only be in theory."

His touch awakens my body, getting it all worked up, and I loathe him for it.

"And if I refuse?" I lift my chin.

His jaw clenches as he says in a cool, non-negotiable tone, "You might think you have a choice, but you don't. You will *bow* to me."

"I'm glad you showed your true face, but then again, this has always been you. I was just the idiot who refused to see it." I push him away with all my might and run past him.

Tears blur my vision as I sprint into the street, wiping them with my sleeves.

I should've probably gone back inside for a ride with Dan, but I can't face Zach after what just happened.

I wander down the road with my arms hanging limply by my sides.

The streets are crowded with people heading to local pubs and restaurants. My heart aches and I feel like an emotional mess every time a family comes into sight.

Why the hell do I have to think about my non-existent family whenever I'm down?

My phone rings, and I wipe my nose before answering, "Astrid speaking."

"Miss Clifford," the deputy commissioner says in a friendly tone. "I hope you're doing well."

"I'm good, thanks." My muscles lock as I stand near a tree with my back to it. "Is there something new about the case?"

"Yes and no. We found new evidence in the soil that could be damaged surveillance videos. Our forensics are working to recover it."

My heart picks up its pace as I listen to the deputy explain how this could change everything about the case. He tells me that when they have suspects, I might have to identify them. After I talk to my father, of course.

"What do you mean, after I talk to my father?" I ask.

There's a pregnant pause before the deputy commissioner clears his throat. "Lord Clifford is against you identifying suspects. We were hoping you could convince him."

This must be the reason for the argument between him and the commissioner the other day. It doesn't matter. I'll be eighteen in a few days and by then, Dad won't have any guardian power over me.

But why would Dad be so against me identifying suspects? Isn't that the point of the entire case?

My head hurts from all the drama with Levi and this new thing with Dad.

It's like being caught in a crossfire that's none of my making.

I text Dan to pick me up—without Zach.

Instead of Dan's car, a red Ferrari trails behind me. I stop on the pavement, throwing a curious glance at it.

Aiden King.

He steps out of his car, wearing dark blue jeans and a plain grey T-shirt that complements his eye colour.

I fold my arms over my chest, not knowing how I'm supposed to act near him.

Aiden is as much of an enigma as his cousin—if not more soulless.

"May I help you?" I ask.

"Maybe." He leans against the passenger door of his car, facing me with his hands in his pockets.

"How?"

"I thought you might want to know a few things."

My brows scrunch. "Like what?"

"The words you said earlier."

"You heard that?"

"It's not my fault you were too caught up in your little argument to notice me."

"So what? Are you here to gloat about your eavesdropping skills?" I hate being on the defensive, but this is Aiden King and I don't have a good track record with the King bloodline.

"I just told you. It's about what you said."

"What did I say?" I ask.

"Insane. Hallucinating. Overreacting." His grey eyes turn steely. "It'd be in everyone's best interest if you didn't repeat them in front of Lev again."

My arms drop to my sides. "Why?"

"He doesn't react well to them."

"Why not?"

His head tilts to the side like Levi when he's contemplating something. "You're not stupid. Surely you noticed something."

"I did, but it doesn't make much sense." I pause. "But you do know, don't you?"

"Even if I do, why should I tell you?" he asks in a completely indifferent tone, like I'm wasting his time.

"You're the one who came to inform me that I shouldn't be saying those words. You're supposed to tell me why I shouldn't be saying them."

"Not really. All you have to do is refrain from saying anything about mental stability." He pauses. "Oh, and stop provoking him. The more you push, the harder he pushes back. The more you run, the faster he chases."

He turns to leave and I clutch the sleeve of his T-shirt, halting him in his tracks. "Wait."

His bored look greets me as he waits for me to speak.

Swallowing, I let go of his T-shirt. "Tell me something. Anything."

"What would I gain from that?"

I suppress an inward groan. He's Levi's cousin, all right. After a second of thinking, I say, "You came for a reason. You know I can help or that I'm already helping. You think I'm of value or you wouldn't have come to find me."

He cocks an eyebrow. "One question. I'll answer one question."

"Does he...have a mental disorder?"

"Not him, but if he keeps going down this lane, he'll end up on the same path."

"Whose path?"

"I said one question." He strides to the driver's door. "Bring me something else of value and I might answer a second one."

I stare at his car as it disappears in the distance. Is he even a seventeen-year-old kid? His attitude and certainty don't hint at that.

On the flip side, I found my source of information on Levi.

TWENTY-NINE

Levi

Madness doesn't ask for permission and neither will I.

I hit the bag in the gym over and over until my knuckles bruise and ache. I don't stop.

If I do, I might turn into that dark version of myself again. I might tear through the streets and go find her. I might do things I'll regret.

Thwack. Thwack. Thwack.

I continue hitting the bag until I have nothing left in me. Until my body nearly collapses.

With one last shove at the bag, I let my body flop against the mat as harsh breaths tear out of my lungs.

The world spins around me like a fucking fog.

After what seems like half an hour of staring into the distance, I stagger to my feet and take a quick shower. I throw my jersey and team clothes in a bag and stuff a cigarette in my mouth.

I won't stay at Uncle's house before the game. The first thing I'll do as soon as I get my inheritance is buy a house as far away from him as possible.

Maybe in Scotland.

"Leaving again?" Aiden calls from the corner of the lounge area.

He sits in front of the glass chessboard, playing against himself like a weirdo.

I blow a cloud of smoke. "Tell Uncle I have practice."

"Or I can just tell him the truth. You don't want to see him."

I lift a shoulder. "That works, too."

I'm about to continue my way when he speaks again, "I had a talk with your girl."

The cigarette almost falls from my lips as I whirl around. "What the fuck did you just say?"

"I told her what you wouldn't."

I'm in his face in a second, pulling him by the collar. "You stay the fuck away from her, do you hear me?"

"I would've if you stopped acting like a grouchy dick all the time." He pushes me away and sits back down. He takes the queen between his thumb and forefinger. "Those who don't play chess think the king is the strongest piece, because the game ends when he dies, but they don't stop to think that if the queen dies first, the king doesn't have a chance to survive."

I narrow my eyes at the meaning behind his words. Both of us have been raised on chess, but he has a different perspective. He wouldn't admit it, but Aiden is just like Jonathan. They don't care who they have to crush to get what they want.

Aiden kills the bishop with the queen, leaving his white king vulnerable. I move the black king to the right.

"Even a king can kill a king." I stuff the cigarette back in my mouth. "Checkmate."

On my way out, I retrieve my phone and stare at a text from Daniel saying he went to pick Astrid up.

After the stunt with his brother, I don't trust him as much.

I pause near my car, remembering how her eyes fluttered with fear and disappointment. How those deep greens stared up at me with moisture in them.

Fuck that.

Fuck her trust issues.

I'm done waiting for her to accept this.

If I have to use force, so be it.

THIRTY

Astrid

A pawn isn't supposed to play the king's game.

Monday is my eighteenth birthday.

I'm not celebrating. I stopped celebrating my birthdays after Mum's death.

Her funeral was on my birthday.

And my day starts like a funeral.

Instead of sneaking off as usual, I find Dad waiting right outside my room.

I'm forced to have breakfast with the 'family' and face Victoria's snobbish face and Nicole's glares.

I have a wild guess that she's the one who slipped the 'stay away, bitch' note under my door last night.

Not that I care who she sleeps with.

After an agonising breakfast with Victoria jabbing her fingers in my wound about missing the museum exhibition, I finally head to the door.

I texted Dan to pick me up since Levi disappeared for the entire weekend.

Well, not exactly disappeared. The team went to Kent and returned with a draw. The spirits weren't so good according to Dan.

Unlike his previous away games, Levi didn't send his usual

taunting yet seductive texts. He didn't talk dirty to me, then ask if I was blushing.

Not that I wanted him to text me. I'm still mad as hell about the scene he caused on Friday. However, I couldn't help thinking about what Aiden said. Levi and I need to talk—after he stops being a dick.

Still, I can't help the void I felt. Since the day Levi barged into my life uninvited, we haven't spent two days without seeing each other. He's been slowly creeping into becoming a constant, and his absence feels strange.

Okay, I might have tried to stalk him on social media, but he made that hard, considering he doesn't use it.

Aiden does have an Instagram account. The only thing he posted over the weekend is a black and white picture of a queen chess piece fallen against a blank board. The description: *Long Live the Queen.*

Dan wasn't so helpful either. He posted a selfie with Ronan, Xander, and three girls stuffed between them.

He found his real tribe with Ronan and Xander. They're like his spirit animals when it comes to partying and girls.

Once I get to the park, I get out my sketchpad and try to capture a beautiful scene of an elderly couple walking with a toddler, but I can't get the lines right.

My mind is filled with my routine in the park these past few weeks. I've gotten used to running alongside Levi. It feels funny to be here all alone now.

Dan sends a text that he's right outside.

As soon as I get into the car, the first thing I notice is his stone-cold expression. Dan is the fun type who doesn't let anything bring him down. He's the joker, the player, and the party animal.

I can count the number of times I've seen him so serious.

Even his uniform is dishevelled as if he were just kicked out of bed.

"What's wrong?" I ask carefully. "Did something happen at home?"

He shakes his head. "You didn't check Snapchat?"

"I don't have Snapchat."

"Oh, right." As if possible, his frown deepens. "Astrid, you know I love you, right? I'm here for you no matter what."

Okay, shit is really hitting the fan if he's using my name.

"You're scaring me, Dan. What the hell is going on?"

"Okay, yeah." He retrieves his phone with hesitant fingers. "This means nothing, okay? It'll blow over soon."

"Show me already!"

He continues hiding his phone, but I snatch it from his grip. A gasp falls from my lips when I see the collage of two pictures.

In one picture, my legs are wide open, my head is thrown back, eyes shut, and my mouth is in an 'O'.

Levi's face between my legs is all dark and blurred, it's impossible to recognise him.

That day at Ronan's party.

The second picture is taken from the side. I'm against Levi's car with his hand between my legs.

Once again, Levi and even his car are blurred.

The caption is: *Royal Elite's slut is taking more jobs.*

My cheeks burn and tears blur in my eyes as I face Dan, who's watching me with the same furrowed brow. "Everyone at school saw these, didn't they?"

He winces and I get the answer I need.

"It's nothing, Astrid. Don't let it get to you."

So what if the entire school saw my orgasm face or me being manhandled?

So what if this goes viral and ruins my entire freaking future?

I'm shaking, teeth almost chattering as if I'm coming down with a cold. Tears stream down my cheeks, but I don't feel them. I don't feel the shame.

I'm turning numb like after Mum's accident.

Shock. That's what Dr. Edmonds called it.

"Come here, you." Dan gathers me in a hug and I sob into his chest as the phone falls to my lap.

"W-what if Dad finds out? He hates me already."

"Stop thinking about him or anyone. Fuck whoever did this, okay? Don't let them bring you down."

I try, I really try, but as soon as we get into school, it's a complete shit show.

Everyone seems to have eyes for me. I think I'm strong, but I'm not when half the school hates me and the other half judges me.

"Slut."

"Bitch."

"Whore."

Similar murmurs break out everywhere I go, despite Dan's glares. If he weren't by my side, they would've attacked me full on.

"Hey, Danny!" a senior calls. "Pass over the slut once you're done, would you?"

Dan swings at him with his hand in a fist. I pull him back at the last second, tears blurring my eyes.

I won't cry. I will *not* cry.

"I'll go home," I tell Dan.

Dan's been working so hard to get the grades for engineering in Cambridge. I don't want him to get into trouble because of me. And that's exactly what will happen if someone else provokes him.

He clutches my shoulder. "Are you going to let them submit you into feeling weak?"

"Well, it's not like I can stop this from going viral or go back in time and stop it from happening..." I trail off.

You might think you have a choice, but you don't. You will bow to me.

Levi's words explode into my brain like destructive firecrackers.

It's not a coincidence that he was blurred while my face was clear for the entire school to see.

This can't be happening.

No.

No.

I fly out of the school with tears blurring my vision and my heart breaking into a million pieces.

THIRTY-ONE

Levi

No one messes with what's mine and lives to talk about it.

On late Monday morning, I'm on my way to my car when Aiden, Xander, and Cole block me.

"What is it now?" I massage my temples against the pounding of a hangover.

The weekend was basically all about addictions. First, the high of adrenaline during the game, then alcohol and cigarettes.

I might have gone too far in the shots battle with Ronan. He better be feeling worse than I do.

Coach will kill me if he sees the hangover face.

"You didn't see?" Xander asks.

What a fucking shit show on a Monday.

"He doesn't have social media," Cole jabs Xander.

"Are any of you dickheads going to tell me what's going on or do I need to start punching first thing in the morning?" I pat my back pocket for my cigarettes.

Seems I burned through my last stash yesterday. Another addiction spiralling out of control.

Fucking perfect.

"Promise that you'll remain calm," Aiden says.

I nod absentmindedly. I'm in the mood to say fuck the school and go back to sleep.

"Here goes nothing." Xander holds his phone out for me. "These were posted all over the school's group."

My spine turns rigid as I stare at two photos of Astrid. She's not naked, but the shots don't leave much to the imagination.

I yank Xander's phone and study the pictures.

"It could be Photoshopped," Cole says in an uncertain tone.

"No, that's me." I tilt my head to the side, trying to figure out where the fucker stood while taking the pictures.

The first picture looks like it's been taken outside the left window.

The second picture was taken somewhere near the car park's lift.

Whoever did this is fucking over.

"You promised." Aiden clutches my shoulder and presses down hard. I don't know if he's trying to keep me in line or if he's simply stopping me from going more berserk.

I won't do this with rage. No. That will make things messy. This one will be done with so much fucking calm, they'll wish I was angry instead.

"Have you seen her at school?" I ask.

"You won't like this, Captain." Cole stares between me and the other two. "She showed up with Daniel and she looked like she knew."

I kick a nearby pole, not caring for the pain exploding in my toes. Of course, she showed up. Astrid isn't the type who runs away.

I'm going to fuck up Daniel's face for letting her go through that. "How bad was it?"

"Aside from the slut and whore remarks…" Xander trails off. "Some made suggestive remarks her way."

Those fucking arseholes are dead.

No one messes with what's mine and lives to talk about it.

"We're going to teach the fucking school a lesson." I'm about to head to my car when a black BMW screeches to a halt beside my Jag.

Daniel barges out with a fuming face and his hands clenched into fists.

I look past him, expecting Astrid to come out of the passenger seat.

When she doesn't, the weight that's been perching on my chest since Friday becomes heavier.

"Where is she?"

"That's what I ought to ask you, *King*," he snarls.

"What the fuck is that supposed to mean?"

"After her accident, the shrink said she needed to get out of her shell and I so foolishly believed you'd give her that, but this is over the fucking line. Even for you, Captain."

He lunges at me, but Aiden yanks him back by the shoulders. "Back. Off."

"You think I did this?" I ask with an incredulous tone. "If I wanted to ruin her reputation, I would've done that at the beginning, not now."

"She's been through hell and back. She doesn't need your shit, too," Daniel spits out, struggling against Aiden and Xander. "If you can't be man enough for her, then leave her the fuck alone. I'll find her and you'll no longer be welcome near her. I don't care if you remove me from the team. Actually, I quit. You can take my position and shove it up your arse."

I stalk towards him until I'm a short distance away. "Go back. What do you mean by you'll *find her*?"

"She ran away from school two hours ago and I can't find her anywhere."

I push Aiden and Xan out of the way until I'm toe-to-toe with Daniel. "Where the fuck is she?"

"I checked her home, Ally's, the park, and the school's art studio, but she wasn't at any of them."

"You didn't search hard enough."

"Those are the only places she frequents."

"There must be somewhere you're forgetting." My voice raises and so does my temper.

"If she wants to run away." Aiden's gaze slides from me to Daniel. "She won't choose a place she can be found in."

"Ask Ronan to throw a party," I tell Aiden. "I want the entire school invited."

I'll find Astrid and the whole school will know the consequences of fucking with what's mine.

THIRTY-TWO

Astrid

He thought he broke me, but he shouldn't have let me pick up the pieces, because what doesn't kill me, better run.

My forehead presses against the tombstone as I breathe in the smell of dirt.

I've been crying on Mum's grave for the past hour or so, but the pain inside me feels like a living, breathing being.

It's so alive.

So heavy.

So *real*.

"Make it stop, Mum," I cry in a hoarse voice. "Make it all stop, please."

If she were here, she would've said the right words to make me feel better.

She would've hugged me until I was strong enough to pick up all my broken pieces.

Levi's betrayal dug a deep, black hole in my chest that keeps getting bigger with every breath I take.

It's all my fault.

I should've never let my guard down around him. He's the king and I'm just the pawn he decided to play with.

Why was I stupid to believe there could be something more?

"Astrid?"

My back snaps into a rigid line at the voice coming from behind me.

I wipe at my eyes with the back of my hand, sitting up. "D-Dad?"

His brows draw as he stares down on me. He's carrying red tulips. Mum's favourites.

I'm surprised he remembers that. Hell, I'm taken aback by seeing him in the cemetery in the first place.

In her will, Mum asked to never be visited on the anniversary of her death, but I'm always here on my birthdays.

Technically, I'm not defying her will if I come on the anniversary of her funeral.

In all of the three years since Mum died, I was the only visitor she had.

Or so I thought.

Is Dad the secret visitor who always leaves red tulips at Mum's tombstone?

"What are you doing here, Dad?"

He places the flowers on the tombstone and sits beside me, not caring that his pressed Gucci suit wouldn't be good friends with the dirt. "I should be asking you that. Shouldn't you be at school?"

I wince at the reminder of school.

Dad narrows his eyes slightly. "Are you skipping? Do I need to talk to the principal?"

"N-no." *Think, Astrid, think.* "I just needed to talk to Mum. I miss her."

My voice shakes at the end and I realise how much that's true. Since she left, my life doesn't feel right.

For a brief moment, when I was with Levi, I thought I could be happy again.

But it was all a freaking joke. He only did all that so he could manipulate me.

Dad places a hand on my shoulder. "I know I'll never be

Jasmine, but if you need to talk…" he trails off as if he doesn't know how to finish the sentence.

I sniffle. "W-why are you against me identifying the suspects?"

He lifts an eyebrow. "I see deputy Vans has been telling you things he shouldn't."

"I heard you talking to the commissioner. You said you didn't want me to go through what happened in the past again. Why?"

"Eavesdropping, too," he says with slight amusement.

"Technically, it's not eavesdropping if I hear you on my way out."

"You mean when you sneak out."

Busted. I smile a little. "Semantics, Dad."

He smiles back.

I forgot how young and carefree Dad looks when he smiles genuinely, not like the one he puts on in front of cameras.

I haven't seen him smiling like this since I was seven.

"Don't you want me to find justice?" I ask.

"Justice is unimportant in this case."

"But why, Dad? You closed Mum's case so quickly, too. As if it never happened. You might want to pretend like she never existed, but she did."

"I know that." A muscle clenches in his jaw.

"Then why did you shut off the investigation? Why, Dad? Why?"

"The other person died. There was no need to keep the case open."

My throat closes. "S-someone else died?"

"Yes." He stands up. "So drop it."

"But —"

"Take it as if I'm asking you for a favour and drop it."

After Mum's accident, I looked all over for articles, but Dad's PR team is so strong that they were all wiped out. Then he announced me to the public as his daughter. The articles mentioned that Mum's accident was because of a dog.

This is the first time anyone's mentioned someone else.

My lips thin in a line, despite all the questions I want to ask. I can't deny Dad the first favour he's asked of me.

"Fine."

"Thank you." He offers me his hand. "Have lunch with me."

"Don't you have to work?"

"That can wait."

I take his hand, stunned that he'd want to have lunch with me outside the house.

It's awkward at first with Dad asking about school and all. Then we both order pepperoni pizzas and talk about his future projects. Apparently, Dad plans to make a school for refugees and I feel kind of proud about that.

His assistant calls, but he tells her to postpone all his appointments for the day.

For the first time in ever, I feel closer to Dad, like maybe he doesn't hate having me all that much.

After lunch, he asks me where I want to go next. I choose the amusement park where Mum used to take me on my birthdays.

I thought Dad would only watch as I play, but he removes his jacket and tie and plays with me.

We have lots of fun, trying to win stuffed animals. Who knew Dad had an excellent shooting range? But then again, he still keeps grandpa's shotguns, so maybe it was one of his hobbies. He sure doesn't practice it now.

A few people recognise and approach him. He always introduces me first, as if it's important for him that people know about me.

He only drops me home late afternoon when he receives an emergency call.

"I'm sorry for bailing on our date," Dad says as we both get out of the car in front of the house.

I grin, holding out the stuffed toys we won. "Thanks, Dad. I had fun. I feel lighter now."

"Remember, Astrid. You're a Clifford and no one brings us down."

I try to give him a smile, but at the reminder of how I ran from school today, it comes out as a grimace.

"No one hurts my daughter and gets away with it. Tell me who I have to destroy."

"No one, Dad."

"Are you sure?"

I nod.

He takes my hand in his and clasps something around my wrist. "Happy Birthday, Star."

Before I can say anything, he goes back to his car and disappears down the road.

I look down to find a dainty bracelet around my wrist. There's a sun, a moon, and a star, like tattoo.

My lips curve in a smile, but the weight that somehow vanished in Dad's presence returns.

I go inside the house with a sigh.

Victoria stands at the entrance wearing a scowl and a gown with hideous patterns.

I attempt to ignore her on my way inside, but her venom-filled voice stops me in my tracks. "No matter what you do, you'll always be an outsider."

"Then why are you feeling so threatened?" I tell her coolly and push past her.

Once I'm in my room, I place my stuffed animals carefully on the table and throw my weight on the bed, closing my eyes.

I wake up to someone shaking my shoulders.

"Dan?" I crack one eye open.

"Jesus Christ, Astrid." He exhales deeply and sits by my side. "I searched for you the entire day. Give a man some warning when you run off."

"Sorry. My phone died." I sit up, rubbing my eyes. "What time is it?"

"Around six. I came as soon as Sarah called. Where did you go, anyway?"

I tell him about visiting Mum and my impromptu birthday date with Dad.

"I bet my gift will be better than Uncle Henry's." He reaches under the bed and gives me a box of scones. "Mum's speciality. I helped."

I half-hug him. "You're the best, Bug."

"I know." He grins. "You can thank me by splitting the scones."

"Nice try, but nope."

"Stingy."

"They're mine."

He laughs. "Happy Birthday, Bugger. How do you want to celebrate?"

His phone rings. Dan silences it and turns it off but not before I see 'Captain' flashing on the screen.

My heart aches as if being sliced open. But then I remember Dad's words from earlier.

You're a Clifford and no one brings us down.

I shouldn't be feeling sorry for myself. I should be making him feel sorry.

I should make him feel my pain.

"What does he want?" I ask Dan.

"Forget about him." He throws up a dismissive hand. "Back to birthday plans. I cancelled practice and Ronan's party, and I'm all yours to binge-watch Vikings."

I stand up, my veins thumping with determination. "I have a better idea."

THIRTY-THREE

Levi

You might have won the battle, but the war is far from over.

I pace the length of Ronan's lounge area and run a hand through my already-dishevelled hair.

Searching for Astrid has been the theme of the day. After I went to school and beat the shit out of a few kids who made suggestive remarks her way.

I did it near the back entrance, so there's no evidence—aside from my bloodied knuckles.

Once I was done, I made the entire team help in searching for Astrid.

Aiden sits opposite me playing chess with Cole, but he keeps watching my every move like he's my damn mother.

I flip him off and stuff a cigarette in my mouth.

Daniel sent a text, telling me he found Astrid and he's bringing her to the party.

I thought I'd have to drag her here, not that she'd come of her own accord.

On the outside, this looks in my favour, but it's not.

Nothing good comes from messing up my plans.

I know it so well since Astrid has fucked up every plan I had for her since the day we met.

It's been a whole damn hour since Daniel's text, but they still haven't shown up.

I breathe through my nose and snatch a lighter from Xan, ignoring his protests.

The party is in full-blown mood, despite the Monday part of the deal.

A trendy pop song I don't give a shit about thumps from the speakers. Everyone dances and grinds to it like crazed animals.

Led by Ronan, some of the team players down shots. I'm not even in the mood to stop them. I'll let Coach kick their arses during practice tomorrow.

I pull out my phone and dial Daniel for the hundredth time in the past hour, but his phone's still turned off. I curse and start to light my cigarette.

Some murmurs break out at the entrance.

Ronan taps my shoulder. "Holy shit, Captain."

My attention drifts in the direction where Ronan, Xander, and most of the other kids gawk.

My lips part, almost dropping the cigarette.

At first, I don't recognise her, but one look at those deep green eyes is enough to identify the girl who's been fucking up my life in all the right ways.

A low-cut black dress reaches her thighs, hugging her curves and outlining her full breasts and the pale tone of her skin. Her brown hair falls on either side of her face. Red lipstick brings out the teardrop in her upper lip and contrasts against her unearthly pale complexion.

She's wearing matching red heels like she's out for a party in the club.

I want to kidnap her somewhere so no one gets to look at her the way I do.

I want to blind my teammates so they don't see her glowing as I do.

Maybe she's right. I'm a fucking caveman.

"That's bloody hot," Xander mutters.

"Sure as shit," Ronan says. "Where has she been hiding all those goodies?"

"Hey, fuckers." I glare at both of them. "Hands off. Eyes off. Go stare at someone else."

"Maybe you should, too." Ronan cocks his head. "She's already taken, Captain."

Astrid stops near the entrance and throws a look behind her. Daniel winks and saunters ahead.

She smiles when someone else stops beside her and offers his elbow. She takes it and her grin widens as if she's some fucking film star.

I see red.

Absolute fucking red.

Zachariah.

She brought that fucker to a school party as if she's announcing a relationship for the entire world to see.

"Aha. She's into the mature type." Xander nudges me. "What are you gonna do about it, Captain?"

I start forward, but a strong arm holds me back.

Aiden.

I attempt to push him away, but Cole joins him by yanking back my other arm.

"Let me fucking go."

"Yeah, let him go." Xan jumps like a kid at Christmas. "A hundred says that Captain will win."

"A hundred that Danny's brother will." Ronan shakes Xan's hand.

"You will not start a fight in a crowded place!" Aiden shouts over the music. "My father will find out."

"Fuck your father." I struggle against him as hot, red rage grips me by the gut and shoots through my veins.

Who the fuck does Zachariah think he is to touch her?

How dare he touch what's already mine?

How dare she let him?

Astrid laughs at something he says. My vision blackens until all the colours are suffocated into a deep, dark abyss.

"Hurts like a bitch, doesn't it?" Daniel leans against the marble counter, grinning with malice.

"Mate," Cole warns him. "Stop it."

"What the fuck do you think you're doing?" I grit out. "How can you let her come with that scum?"

"That scum is my brother and as far as I'm concerned, he didn't post pornographic pictures of her for the entire school to see."

"I didn't fucking do that!" I struggle against Cole and Aiden to no avail.

"Doesn't matter." He's in my face in a second. "You didn't stop it either, so you're just as guilty. Oh, and, Captain, you're going to regret losing her."

He walks away after a slight push from Ronan.

"Losing her," I repeat with a bitter laugh. He said I lost her.

Fuck him.

Fuck anyone who thinks that Astrid is no longer mine.

My gaze strays to where the bastard who will soon be dead is offering her a drink.

Even though she made her grand entrance, some of the other kids are still murmuring at her back. She pretends she doesn't notice them as she laughs along whatever the dickhead is saying, but I recognise all her tells.

The way her upper lip twitches. The way she grips the cup tighter.

The princess might think she's over me, but we didn't even fucking get started yet.

"Let me go," I tell Aiden in a calm tone that wraps all the rage inside.

"You won't stir up trouble?" he asks with a suspicious voice.

"No. I'll do this the calm way." I breathe in and out to wean down the raging storm brewing inside me.

By the end of the night, everyone at school will know their fucking places.

Astrid included.

THIRTY-FOUR

Astrid

Your time is over. I'm not your subject anymore.

One would think that changing into a pretty dress and heels would change my perceptive about my image.

It doesn't. Not as much as I wanted it to, anyway.

When I decided to come here, I wanted everyone to see me strong. It's my birthday, and I don't even like this day, but no one will bully me into running away and hiding like I did this morning.

I wasn't born to bow.

Zach stays by my side and Dan joins us every now and then. Even with them around, I feel as if I'm strolling around naked in a room full of people.

The back of my neck itches as I take a sip from the watered down drink Dan gave me. I know *he* is watching me.

I caught a glimpse of Levi on my way inside, although I refused to look in his direction.

If I do, I don't think I'll be able to keep up this façade. I don't think I'll be able to continue my strong act.

I close my eyes for the briefest bit and draw in a long breath. I will not let Levi King ruin this night for me.

I'm not the same Astrid who caved in every time he touched me.

This time, I'll flip him off in front of everyone.

Zach and I are talking about a conference he's attending next week when a bull barges between us.

Jerry Huntington. The judge's son, the one Levi fought.

He's swaying on his feet, already drunk, and the party has barely started.

"What do you want?" I ask.

"The same thing everyone here wants but is afraid to ask." He licks his lips, swinging in my direction. "Your pussy, babe."

Zach lunges forward, but I beat him to it.

I slam my fist into Jerry's face so hard, pain explodes in my knuckles.

He steps back, shaking his head and I punch him again. "Talk to me that way again and I'll ruin your face."

He growls and lunges at me. People gather all around us, gasping. I stand my ground, ready to give him a piece of my mind.

Daniel slams his shoulder into Jerry, pushing him to the ground. Xander and some other player from the football team drag Jerry outside as he spouts profanity.

I lift my chin up and flip him the finger.

"That was badass." Zach raises an eyebrow.

Adrenaline bubbles in my veins like a drug dose. "I want to punch some more people."

He laughs, offering me his hand. "How about a dance instead?"

Jumping up, I take it as *Whatever it Takes* by Imagine Dragons starts playing.

I wrap my arms around his neck and we laugh and chuckle, goofing around on the dance floor.

Zach spins me out and brings me back to his arms again.

"Does everyone always stare at you?" he asks as we adopt a slower pace.

"Only when I'm the school's laughing stock." I try to hide the bitterness in my tone.

"Well, they're missing out." His breath tickles my ear and I can't help the giggle that escapes me.

"You know…" he starts. "I always had a crush on you, Astrid Clifford."

"Y-you did?"

"Uh-huh. I only backed down because Danny would've smashed my face in if I hurt his best friend."

Okay. Wow. I never knew that. Maybe Levi was right.

"Is this your new conquest, slut?" Chloe hisses and barges her shoulder into mine.

I'm about to punch her like I did Jerry, but the music stops abruptly.

Everyone stops dancing and chatter breaks out. Someone shouts to put the music back on.

Then, as if someone flipped a switch, the murmurs cease and the crowd parts to make way for Levi and his four horsemen.

He's wearing the team's uniform and stands in the middle as if he owns the room and everyone in it.

I look away, refusing to be sucked into his orbit.

Daniel leaves Xander and Ronan's side to stand by me. His harsh glare falls on his captain. The same captain he idolised for a long time.

Most loyal best friend ever.

Chloe smiles brightly at Levi like she's seeing a Christmas tree. She pushes her dancing partner away as if he never existed.

"King, I —"

"If you're going to call anyone a slut, start with yourself." Levi looks down at her with dark, calm eyes. "You opened your legs for half the team and swallowed for the other half."

Oohs and *aahs* break out in the audience. Everyone gathers around us like we're the entertainment of the night.

Chloe's face goes red. Her mouth opens and closes like a fish, but she says nothing.

Levi's gaze narrows on Nicole, who comes to stand on Chloe's side. "If you have any slut remarks to say, you might want to start with how you beg for it on your knees."

"That's not true." Nicole glares at him, then at Dan as if he said the words.

"Do you want footage to prove your extracurricular activities?" Levi cocks his head to the side.

Nicole's face twists in pure panic as her gaze bounces between Levi and Dan.

My cheeks flame with rolling anger. Levi doesn't get to do this after he set out to ruin my life.

He looks around him as if searching for someone in specific, but he's not. He's just making eye contact with as many kids as possible.

Everyone—literally everyone—either flinches or cowers away whenever he meets their gazes.

"Does anyone else have another slut remark they'd like to grace us with?" He keeps his cool tone.

But I know that fake coolness.

It's something he uses to pull everyone in just so he can destroy them afterwards.

The best wars are won through calm, not a raging storm.

Aiden, Xander, Cole, and Ronan are like his generals. They're all glaring everyone down like they're soldiers.

It's scary how they can make an entire party submit to them with just a few words.

"I do." Someone raises a beer, pushing through the crowd to make his way to Levi.

Christopher Vans.

He stands in front of me and spits on the ground. All I can smell is alcohol. Black circles surround his bloodshot eyes.

"Is this the new slut you're banging, King? Doesn't look all that something to me."

Dan charges forward, but I pull him back. If anyone will put this scum down, then it's going to be me.

"I'm no one's slut," I grit out.

"Didn't hear you." He laughs.

"Are you done?" Levi's face remains nonchalant, but a muscle tics in his jaw.

"What?" Christopher sways on his feet and hits him with a bottle of beer to his chest. "You're going to call me a slut, too?"

"At least they're useful. You're not." Levi straightens until he's a few inches taller than Christopher. "You're such a fucking failure that even freshman can take your place on the team now."

The kids gasp.

Like me, everyone knows how close Levi and Christopher have been for years.

But it must be true that they've grown apart since the beginning of the year.

Christopher swings a fist at Levi, but he steps back and the drunk boy trips over his own feet and falls on his face.

Everyone laughs and some take pictures, recording the next mess.

"Does anyone else have something to say?" Levi asks loud enough for everyone to stop talking and breathing altogether.

He grabs my wrist, and before I can protest, he pulls me to his side with his hand wrapped tightly around my waist. He places a long, possessive kiss on my forehead, then on my cheek and on my mouth.

Murmurs break all around us, but I'm too caught up in the gleam in his eyes to notice anyone else.

There's that blackness, but there's also a sliver of vulnerability that I've never seen on him before.

With one last squeeze against my hip, he faces everyone. "Astrid is under my protection. Mess with her and you'll have a personal problem with me. I'll bury you so fucking deep, you'll pray for death instead."

They start nodding, but Levi doesn't pay them attention.

The king has issued his decree and the subjects have no choice but to obey.

And just like that, he places a hand under my legs and carries me in his arms, bridal style.

I yelp, then try to struggle. "Where the hell are you taking me?"

"I'm kidnapping you, Princess."

THIRTY-FIVE

Astrid

Surviving you shouldn't mean becoming all entangled in you.

What are you supposed to do when someone kidnaps you?

Kick and claw? Check.

Hit and scream? Also, check.

When I don't stop screaming and hitting him every step of the way, Levi pushes me into the passenger seat of his car and retrieves a piece of rope from his glove box.

"What are you doing?" My frantic vision bounces between him and the rope. Why the hell does he even have rope in his car?

"Are you going to stay calm?"

"Let me go, you arsehole, let me —"

I'm cut off when he yanks both my arms behind my back, pressing his body flush against my front.

I seize breathing when his strong scent fills my nostrils. His hard chest flattens my breasts, making me all warm and fuzzy.

It's only been three days since I've felt this warmth. Three measly days, but it's felt like an eternity.

While I'm distracted by his sheer presence, Levi wraps the rope around my wrists, securing them behind my back. Then he hangs the seatbelt over my chest so I'm unable to move.

He steps back as if inspecting his handy work and taps my nose twice. "Be a good princess."

"Fuck you, King."

His eyes narrow the slightest bit, but he closes the door, hard, and I jump. I wiggle sideways, trying to free myself, but he's already in his seat, securing the locks from his side.

The car's engine revs to life and we're flying down the streets.

I twist my wrists, but that only makes the ropes dig deeper into my flesh. "Kidnapping is a crime, you know."

"I couldn't care less."

I groan from both frustration and anger. "So, what? You think you can act like a villain and kidnap me on your black horse and I'll have no other choice but to forgive you? Are you expecting a kiss in thanks, too?"

He cocks an eyebrow. "I didn't think about it that way, but that can work, too."

"Ugh. I hate you."

"You proved it by bringing that scum." A muscle clenches in his jaw. "You'll pay for that."

"You have no right to tell me what to do. I'm not, and will never be, one of your subjects."

He throws me a dark glance. "You'll learn your place. Eventually."

"How long are you going to keep me? A day? A week? A month?" I taunt. "As soon as I escape, guess who I'll be going back to? Here's a hint. His name starts with a Z."

He steps on the brake so hard, I almost topple over and hit my head on the windshield.

My space is crowded by his body and his face that's breathing menace into mine.

He clutches my chin between his thumb and forefinger, forcing me to look straight into those pale eyes.

There's so much intimacy in this moment—walls falling down and others going up.

I just don't know whether those walls are his or mine.

"You can be upset and angry all you want, but don't bring another man in my presence again."

"Or what?"

"I'll end them. Every last fucking one of them."

My lips part. "You...you wouldn't."

"Try. Me." His breath tickles my skin and he darts his tongue out to lick the shell of my ear before he murmurs in dark, hot words, "I dare you to fucking try me, Princess."

I want to think he wouldn't do such a thing, but he can be damn crazy. He's proven time and again how abnormal he is.

Hell, if I didn't stop him, I don't know how far he would've gone with Jerry all those weeks ago.

"You're a good girl, aren't you?" His lips hover against the corner of my mouth and my breathing turns into choked gasps. "So how about you be a good little princess and stop fucking everything up?"

I want to curse and shout at him. I want to tell him that he's the one who fucked up my life, but I don't trust my anger. I feel like I'll say something that will only backfire on me. Besides, he's too close, it's impossible to concentrate.

He starts the car again and I decide to ignore his existence. If words don't work with him, then the silent treatment will have to do.

I stare out of the car window, pursing my lips. Soon enough, the city's loud life and the bright lights disappear until the road turns deserted.

The way to the Meet Up.

I recognise the area even before we pull over in front of it.

Levi steps out from his side of the car, then opens my door. I look in the opposite direction.

He holds my chin, trying to make me look at him, but I keep my vision directed to the side.

"As you wish, Princess." His words are barely out when he yanks me from the passenger seat and carries me in his arms—with my wrists bound behind my back.

My breasts brush against his chest, creating a maddening friction. His strong arm against my naked thighs shoots tingles straight to my core.

Nope. I'm not going there.

The house is dark, but as soon as we're inside, an automatic white light turns on.

Levi carries me up the stairs and down two halls with his face stone cold. I breathe harshly, both because of the sensations he's eliciting in my body and because I need him to know my displeasure.

Either he doesn't notice or he doesn't care.

My bet is on the second.

He swings open the door leading to a medium-sized bedroom with a large bed and crisp white sheets. There's a small desk and a closet, and that's it.

Levi throws me on the bed and I crawl to the other end, my throat closing.

My courage from earlier is completely gone now. We're all alone here. My shoulder blades snap together at the realisation.

"What the hell do you think you're doing?"

He doesn't answer.

Instead, he removes his jacket, tosses it on the table, and rolls the sleeves of his shirt to his elbows. "You're speaking to me now?"

"Let me go, Levi." I lean against the headboard, my heart thumping so loudly, it fills my space.

"You're calling me by my name, too." His voice is calm. Too calm. It's frightening. "That's progress."

"Is this another one of your games? Are you trying to scare me?" I hate the tremor in my voice. It only proves how much his plan is working. "Go right ahead. Make me hate you for good."

"Don't you already?" The bed dips as he crawls towards me with black, impenetrable eyes.

"I do." I fight the tears blurring my vision.

"You do, huh?"

"Did you think I'd run back to you because you stood up for

me? Newsflash, King. I'm not a damsel in distress. I don't need saving from what you caused in the first place."

He grabs both my legs and pulls me towards him. I yelp when I fall against my bound hands and slide forward.

My legs spread open on each side of his strong thighs and my dress bunches up until my underwear peeks out.

He grips my hips in his merciless, strong hands until I'm half straddling his lap.

"The pictures aren't my doing," he says with fake calmness on his face.

Tears blur my vision as anger and shame roll off me in waves. "Don't lie to me. I deserve at least that."

"I've never lied to you, Princess. If I do something, I own up to it."

"Yeah, sure. Then why was your face and even your damn car blurred?"

"I don't know yet, but I'll find out, and whoever did this will pay."

Every word coming out of his mouth is so sure and confident, I'm starting to doubt myself.

But isn't that what he wants me to feel?

Isn't it his purpose to reduce me to a mindless being?

A hand remains at my hip while his fingers snake up the hollow of my waist. I suck in a stuttering breath at the sensuality in his touch.

I can fight, but then what? He'll just have me back exactly where he wants.

And maybe, just maybe, I'm tired of fighting.

"You'll also pay, Princess." His voice turns deadly and so do his eyes.

"For what?"

"For bringing that fucker when I told you to stay away from him. What were you trying to prove, hmm?"

I swallow as his deft fingers snake a path to the zipper of my dress, slowly pulling it down.

"Were you perhaps trying to prove that you're not mine?" He yanks my dress down my shoulders with one tug.

I gasp as my breasts spill free from the built-in bra. My knee-jerk reaction is to hide them, but it's impossible with my bound hands.

Levi's black gaze turns feral as he takes them in. He looks at me like he wants to devour me and leave nothing behind. A rush of need spirals through me and my nipples tighten and pucker as if begging for his attention.

It's crazy how I'm ready to jump out of my skin whenever he looks at me like this.

Levi and I have always shared this weird, insane connection that I've never felt with anyone else.

A push.

A pull.

A current of power.

His thumb finds a throbbing nipple and he flicks it up and down. His pale eyes meet mine in a challenge. He's teasing me, punishing me, and daring me to do something about it.

Tiny bolts of pleasure shoot between my legs as I bite my lower lip against the onslaught.

His mouth wraps around my other nipple and he bites down. Hard. A zap of electricity starts from his hot mouth on my breasts and ends pooling at my core.

"L-Levi...please..."

"Please what?" he speaks against the sensitive skin of my breast, his breath heating my skin. "Stop or keep going?"

I don't know. I don't know anything at the moment.

My head is dizzy and my legs are turning into puddles around his thighs. Since I can't answer with words, my body takes over and I push my breasts into his fingers and mouth, silently begging for more.

"Do you want me to suck harder on these tight pink nipples, Princess?"

A small, needy voice leaves me as my eyes droop with un-containable lust.

"Do you want me to make them tender and painful with pleasure?"

Oh, God.

His dirty words have always been my undoing.

I nod a little, pushing further into him.

"Not so fast." He smiles with contempt, looking up at me. "What were you trying to prove tonight?"

"That you don't own me!" I shout, my voice hoarse.

"I don't own you, huh?" His smile disappears and he's back to his scary calm façade. "Is that what you really think?"

"You hurt me," I bite out against the agonising mixture of pleasure, pain, and anger shooting through me all at once. "All you ever do is hurt me. You're toxic, Levi, and I won't continue being manipulated like a piece on your chessboard."

He removes his mouth, but his thumb continues swiping back and forth on my other breast.

"All I ever do is hurt you," he repeats as if he's mulling the words over. Only this time, there isn't that usual mocking edge. If anything, he appears genuinely confused.

I recall what Aiden told me the other time and feel horrible for saying what I did.

All the anger from moments ago withers away at the lost look in Levi's gaze. It's like he wants to act out on something, but he doesn't know how.

And I might have said something wrong.

"No. Wait." I wrap my legs around his waist tighter, not wanting to lose him. "I didn't mean that."

He tilts his head to the side. "You didn't mean what?"

"That all you do is hurt me. You…make me happy, too."

He raises an eyebrow. "I do, huh?"

"It drives me crazy, but yeah, you do. You take my mind off things and I feel free with you. And I guess I hate that. I hate how vulnerable you make me feel. I hate that you're able to hurt me so easily like no one else ever could."

There, I said it.

My deepest, darkest fears are out in the open.

I swallow audibly after my confession, peeking at Levi through my eyelashes. I barely get a glimpse before his hand wraps around my nape and he crushes his lips to mine.

A strangled moan escapes me as he pulls me into him. My response is just as violent as his claiming.

I get lost in the kiss and the words hidden underneath the animalistic passion.

He doesn't have to say it out loud for me to hear it.

I make him vulnerable, too.

Unlike me, he gets off on it, making it a strength instead of a weakness.

He tugs my dress all the way down my legs until I'm lying in front of him in only my black underwear.

Tingles erupt on my skin the more he touches me. The more my lungs fills with his scent. The more his pale eyes draw a path down my neck. The more his tongue trails from my ear to my collarbone to the valley of my breasts.

"Oh, God…Levi…"

"You're not going to challenge me this time?" he whispers in my ear.

I buck against his hand as he pulls down the only piece of my clothing left. I lie completely naked in front of him while he's still fully clothed.

"Do you want a challenge?" I breathe.

"I love it when you challenge me, Princess." He licks the shell of my ear and pushes his erection into the soft flesh of my thigh. "It makes my cock so fucking hard."

"Unbind me," I breathe out, fighting the tremor in my voice.

He shakes his head.

"How am I to challenge you then?"

"Your mere existence is enough of a challenge." A sadistic

smirk tilts his lips. "I like you bound, Princess. I like you at my mercy. I like when you're mine."

His fingers hover over my core, threatening but not touching. I may have pushed myself up off the bed, needing any type of friction. Hell, I'm ready to dry-hump his thigh at this point.

"You want me to touch you?"

I nod slowly.

His hand wraps around my throat, squeezing the slightest bit. "And when I do, you'll come for me, screaming my name until you forget all other fucking names. You'll be my good little princess, won't you?"

I bite the corner of my lower lip as he teases my soaking folds.

Levi is the type of predator who plays with his prey. He drives me to the edge, just so he can devour me more relentlessly afterwards.

"Answer me," he growls against my throat.

"Why do you like pushing me, Levi?" I crane my head to the side, silently giving him better access to my neck. "Why do you like playing with me until I don't know whether or not this is real?"

"Because I don't do things halfway. I take everything, Princess."

"Everything?"

"Your tears. Your laughs. Your pain. Your joy." He drags his tongue along my lower lip, then bites it. "Everything you have to offer is mine to own."

He releases me so that he can yank his shirt open, causing a few buttons to fly all around us.

My mouth dries at the sight of the muscles of his chest and the way they flex with every move.

He's so gorgeous, it's unfair.

My body craves his with every breath I take. I'm tuned to him in ways words can't describe.

He undoes his belt and shoves down his trousers and boxer briefs in one go.

My eyes bulge at how his ready cock points in my direction.

Before I can study him fully, his body covers mine, his firm ridges moulding to my soft curves.

Like we were made to fit together.

He reaches into the side table and pulls out a condom, ripping it with his teeth.

My breathing hitches as I watch him in all his naked glory, hovering over me like a god.

A sex god.

I've always had some images about my first time, but never in my wildest dreams did I think it'd be with Levi.

And now, I wouldn't have it any other way.

My breathing hitches as he pulls me by the hips until his cock is at my entrance.

"It's time you were all mine, Princess."

He slams inside me in one long, brutal go. I shriek at the intrusive sensation, my eyes rolling to the back of my head.

Oh, God. That hurts!

I close my eyes, trying to get used to the feeling of being stretched open. He's so big, it's hard to even breathe.

"Fuck. You're a virgin?" He stops, staring down at me with a mixture of confusion and what looks like pain and awe.

"Was," I try to joke, biting my lip against the pain. "Can you move or something?"

His lips find my softer ones, and I'm momentarily lost in the kiss. He starts moving slow and steady as his mouth devours mine.

His hand reaches between us to flick my clit and the pain withers away, leaving something entirely different in its wake.

His fullness.

I can only feel him filling me and it's so intimate.

So...erotic.

Soft moans tear past my lips as he picks up his pace.

"Harder," I murmur.

Levi's brows scrunch as if he's as surprised as me for saying that.

"Do you like a little pain with your pleasure, Princess?" He bites down on the lobe of my ear, drawing a shudder from me.

"I...don't know."

"Let's find out." He grabs my hip with one hand and wraps the other around my neck.

It's not tight enough to cut off my air supply, but it's firm enough to let me know that I'm at his mercy.

A part inside me loosens at the feeling of him being all over me. There's something about relinquishing all of my control to him that makes me feel at peace—or maybe a little powerful, myself.

With my hands bound against my back, Levi rams deeper and harder into me until everything fills with his scent and his presence. A maddening buildup starts at my core and spreads all over my body like wildfire.

"Fuck, Astrid. You're so fucking tight." *Thrust.* "And beautiful." *Thrust.* "And driving me fucking insane."

The sensation swipes over me like a hurricane. This orgasm is so different from all the other ones he's given me with his mouth. This one unravels me from the inside. I can't even think or breathe. I can only scream his name like he told me I would.

I almost black out, but I'm brought back to the moment when Levi's back turns rigid. His Viking hair sticks to his temples with sweat and all his muscles become taut. He comes with a groan, squeezing me into him.

And then, his mouth is back to devouring mine.

Best. Birthday. Ever.

THIRTY-SIX

Levi

You should know by now that I don't play fair.

The bed is empty.

It smells of lilac and sex, but there's no sign of Astrid.

I curse as I jump to my feet, blindingly shoving my legs into the trousers lying on the floor.

It's six in the morning and we're in the middle of nowhere, so she can't reach civilisation unless she has a ride. And judging from the rain beating down outside, she couldn't have gone far.

After last night, I thought she'd be too sore to move, but apparently, I thought fucking wrong.

I shouldn't have unbound her. Better yet, I should've tied her to me when I gathered her in my arms.

I've never slept with a girl after sex.

I've never slept with anyone. Full stop.

Since I lost Dad, I've had insomnia. That's why I started drinking—aside from wanting to piss Uncle off. When I'm hammered, I manage a few hours of sleep. But I had to take it down a notch when I started focusing on football.

Most nights, I'll stare at the ceiling or wear myself out in the gym.

But last night was different. Last night, I had a petite thing sleeping in my arms like a baby.

I might have spent the entire night watching her. Sue me.

Every line of her face and curve of her body is engraved in my memories. As I observed her, lots of dark thoughts barged through my mind, but most of all, it was unstoppable waves of possessiveness.

She only belongs to me now and no one will be able to take her away.

Ever.

I might not know how the fuck Astrid fits in the big picture, but I know that she's mine. I know that I'll feed off everything she offers like the parasite she paints me as.

I don't bother with a shirt as I snag my car keys and fly down the stairs.

It's fucking pouring outside. The rain is falling so hard that the distance is foggy and the vision blurry.

Right in front of the house, Astrid stands in the middle of the rain, eyes closed, head tipped back, allowing it to soak her face. Her arms are wide open on either side of her as if she's an angel about to fly.

I freeze, watching her do exactly what I showed her last time I brought her here.

Her dress sticks to her body, and rivulets form a path from her wet hair to her neck.

I drop the car keys on the porch and stride towards her. The rain beats down on me, soaking me in a second.

She doesn't feel me when I'm right behind her, studying the hickeys I left all over her neck and nape. The angry red marks against her pale skin elicit a primal reaction in me.

I licked her, so she's mine.

My arms wrap around her waist from behind and I bury my head into her wet neck.

She inhales a stuttering breath as her palm covers my connected hands, whether to push me away or keep me there, I don't know.

"What are you doing out here?" I ask near her ear, drawing a shudder from her.

"I was leaving."

My jaw clenches. "Why?"

"Because…" she trails off but doesn't look at me. "It was a mistake, wasn't it?"

"Says who?" I growl in her ear.

"Says me." She rotates her head to stare at me. "I don't know what the hell you want from me and it's driving me crazy."

"Good." I nibble on the lobe of her ear, tasting her and the rain. "You drive me fucking crazy, too."

She turns around in my hold, placing both palms on my chest. "Do you ever intend on stopping?"

"Never, Princess." I pause. "You said you were leaving. Why didn't you?"

"It was raining."

"That's all?"

"You know, it was pouring the day I lost my mum. Since then, I've hated rainy days. Until —" she glances at me with a strange vulnerability "—you showed me how to enjoy it again. Thank you."

No. Thank you, Dad.

I run my fingers through her hair, pushing the wet strands off her face. "So you owe me one, huh?"

She hits my chest. "You just needed to turn the situation in your favour, didn't you?"

"What did you expect?"

"Fine, what do I owe you?"

"Your sketchpad."

"No," she says defensively, her cheeks flushing, even under the rain.

I laugh. Asking for her sketchpad is only a formality. I already went through it a few times when she was struggling to finish her laps in the park.

Hell, when I don't sleep, I spend the entire night looking

at the sketch I stole from her house and imagining her concentrated expression.

"Pick something else," she tells me.

"But I want the sketchpad."

"Pick something else or you're not getting anything."

"Let's start by dancing in the rain."

"Start?" She chuckles. "What happens afterwards?"

"See, that's your problem, Princess. You need to learn how to stop thinking about afterwards." I pull her into me by the waist, my morning wood pressing into the bottom of her stomach. "Live in the moment."

A soft gasp tears past her lips and she stares up at me with wide, lust-filled eyes. "You'll ruin me."

I lick her upper lip over her Cupid's bow. "I promise you'll love every second of it."

Her breath hitches. "What if I don't?"

"At least you'll never forget the experience."

"Can't you be nice?"

"I am fucking nice." I suck her lower lip into my mouth.

She pulls away, smiling. "You could lie and tell me you'll try and take it easy on me."

I laugh and for the first time in years, the sound is genuine. "I'll never take it easy on you. If anything, I'll be more persistent."

"More?" she all but yells. "There's freaking *more?*"

"You haven't seen anything yet." I carry her in my arms and place my forehead against hers as the rain beats down on us. "You can take this as a good thing, Princess, or fight it. It's up to you."

I whirl her around, and she squeals, her arms snaking around my neck in a steel hold like a child with someone they trust. And then she's laughing and giggling so hard, I can't help smiling back.

"Can't you at least tell me what we're doing afterwards?" she shouts between giggles.

"Do you really want to know?"

My lips find her neck and I suck on an unmarked spot on her collarbone until her breathing crackles.

"Once we're done dancing in the rain, I'll —"

"You'll what?" The need in her tone makes me hard.

"I'll fuck you in the shower, Princess."

Her pupils dilate and she swallows audibly as her body leans into mine.

A part of her might still fight me, but soon enough, she'll learn that there'll be no escaping my hold.

Uncle was right. I destroy everything.

But this is the first time I want to keep something instead of shattering it to pieces.

THIRTY-SEVEN

Astrid

It's the queen who sacrifices herself for the king.

I'm panting as Levi and I throw on some clothes after stepping out of the shower.

And by some clothes, I mean, he puts on black boxer briefs and I wear his team jersey.

That was…wow. Mind-blowing is an understatement to describe what just happened in the bathroom.

I feel so used and pleased.

Give it to Levi to make me feel completely different emotions at the same time.

"Number ten never looked so damn good." He drags his darkened eyes from my breasts to where the jersey reaches mid-thigh.

I pull my hair up. "Is that so?"

For the love of Vikings. Am I flirting with him right now?

"You know how it'd look better?"

"How?"

"On the floor."

He reaches for me, but I duck out of his grasp, giggling.

I run down the hall, my bare feet slapping against the wooden flooring.

Thundering footsteps come from behind me. Fear and

excitement erupt in my stomach, and I run faster, harder. Just like the prey Levi wants.

Two arms surround me from behind. I squeal as my feet leave the ground and he turns me around.

His hot, husky words tickle my ear. "You can run, but you can't hide. I'll always catch you, Princess."

"I know," I pant, my heartbeat almost leaping out.

"Then why did you run?"

Because maybe I like the feeling of being chased. Maybe I like walking on the thin line between sanity and insanity with him.

I love the way my heart pounds as if I'm about to have a heart attack.

He brings me to the edge and I love the view.

"It's a secret." I laugh and continue running downstairs.

He catches me by the kitchen, making me squeal.

The only reason he releases me is because we need to eat.

He pulls back a stool. "Sit."

I take my seat, looking around the red and black decorated kitchen. It's open bar style with a closet-like fridge and marble counters.

Then my eyes roam to the most beautiful thing in the room.

His chest is so sculpted, I can easily count each one of his six abs. His muscles flex with every move—like he can crush anything in his path. He can even crush me if he chooses to.

The black boxer briefs outline his strong football thighs, barely leaving anything to the imagination.

Then there's those V-lines.

Now, I understand why all the girls are obsessed with that male perfection. It's not about the V, it's about the place it leads to.

A certain organ that was inside me minutes ago. Hard and thick and —

"Like what you see, Princess?"

My eyes snap to his amused ones. "I wasn't looking."

The arsehole's smirk widens. "Something on your face says otherwise."

I turn around, wiping my mouth. Please tell me I wasn't drooling.

"You're blushing, Princess. Nothing can erase that."

Oh.

I whirl back around, feeling my cheeks hotter than earlier. "Hurry so we can go to school."

He walks behind the counter and throws over his shoulder, "No."

"What?"

Turning to me, he leans over on both hands until his gorgeous face is in mine. "Tell me when you last broke a rule."

He smiles, and when it reaches his eyes, I can't help smiling back. "You're too uptight. What did I say about living in the moment?"

"I did, didn't I?" My cheeks heat, remembering how much I screamed in the shower when he disappeared between my legs.

"Sure did." He taps my nose. "You're fucking adorable when you blush."

I swat his hand away. "I don't need to break rules to live in the moment."

"When was the last time you skipped?"

"Yesterday, remember?"

"That doesn't count. You didn't have a choice. Today, you do."

"And if I do skip, what's the plan?"

He shakes his head with disapproval. "Plans defy the whole point of skipping. We'll just wing it."

"Wing it?"

"Since it's rainy, we'll stay inside and do indoor things."

"Things like what?"

"Like fucking your brains out, Princess."

My cheeks turn into a fire pit and a tingle draws up my spine at the promise.

Jeez. I only discovered this part of myself last night and I already can't get enough. Have I turned into a nympho or something?

"That is, if you aren't too sore?" he asks with a raised eyebrow.

"I'm not." I am. But I won't let that ruin my fun.

Ha. I'm starting to think like Levi.

One night with the devil and I'm already thinking like him.

"How do you like your eggs?" He disappears underneath the counter and the sound of pots and pans clanking fills the space.

"You know how to cook?" I ask.

"I learnt a trick or two from spending time here."

"You don't live with Aiden and your uncle?"

"I do, but I don't call that house my home." He reappears with a frying pan and utensils, and heads to the stove.

"I also don't feel like Dad's house is my home sometimes."

He tilts his head. "Sometimes?"

"I don't know how to explain it. Sometimes it does, but other times it doesn't." When only Dad is there. When I don't see Victoria and Nicole's faces or hear their taunts. When I help Sarah out in the kitchen like I used to do with Mum.

When Dad comes to wish me goodnight.

I hop down from my stool and join Levi behind the counter.

One. The view from here is more gorgeous.

Two. I want to help.

"Just sit down." He pushes me back, but I nudge him.

"This is my way of living in the moment. Let me."

It's an epic failure.

I end up with flour all over my face and arms because Levi's definition of living in the moment is playing around and feeling me up.

At first, I tried to fight it, but there's no fighting Levi. His intensity runs too deep. It's like being sucked whole with no way out.

It's frightening sometimes.

It's thrilling most of the time.

I'm always buzzing out of my skin, waiting for the next thing he'll come up with.

He's a high that I'm not sure I want to come down from.

I know Levi is dangerous. I've seen it in that black gaze and his closed-off features. I've felt it in the way he takes whatever he wishes without looking back. I've heard it in his sinister voice and unapologetic words.

All of that was supposed to push me away. Instead, I keep gravitating towards him like a moth to a flame.

He'll burn me.

He'll destroy me.

But I'll keep coming back for more, anyway.

After breakfast, we play chess. He has this huge glass board in the middle of the lounge area and we sit across from each other.

He narrows one eye before we start. "I'm warning you. I crush my enemies."

"Hmph." I tuck my knees underneath me and puff my chest. "Show me what you got, King."

As if I've lit a fire, his eyes gleam with a challenge. His posture turns uptight, and his entire stance sharpens for the battle.

After fifteen minutes of trying to outsmart him, I lose.

He takes down all my defences and then kills my queen in the most brutal way.

I sulk, staring at his main pieces that remain intact.

He chuckles when I continue sulking. "You're doing it all wrong."

"How?"

"You're protecting your king when you should be protecting something far more important."

"The queen?"

"Could be." He tilts his head to the side. "But if you really want to win, then you need all of your battalion."

"How about sacrificing for the greater good?"

"A true warlord sacrifices soldiers, not generals."

I mimic the tilting of his head. "How did you come to love chess so much?"

He's silent for a moment. "It runs in the family, I guess."

"Your uncle plays?"

"He does, but he didn't teach me, my father did. It was one of the few things he taught me."

I straighten, feeling the tension behind his words. "So you weren't close?"

"We were when he wasn't having his manic episodes, which wasn't very often." He stares at me as if he's surprised he just divulged that.

My lips part.

What Aiden said makes sense now. Levi doesn't have mental problems, but he lived in the shadow of a father who did. Maybe that part of his father rubbed off on him, too.

Before I can say anything, Levi smiles in a challenging way. "Do you want to go again? I promise not to crush you this time."

"Bring it."

We go at it for hours. It's the most time I've spent in one place—aside from the art studio—without going out of my mind. In fact, I have fun.

Even though Levi wins every time.

I try to distract him by pushing the jersey up my thighs or pulling it down or licking my lips. Even though his eyes darken with lust, he wins the game, pushes the board away, and scoops me in his arms.

"Were you seducing me just now, Princess?"

I look away, trying to hide the goosebumps covering my skin. "I don't know what you're talking about."

"You were playing dirty."

"I…wasn't."

"Do you know what happens to bad girls who play dirty?" His lips find the lobe of my ear and he sucks before biting down.

I moan, my head falling against his neck. It's crazy how something so little can turn me into a wanton mess.

Levi isn't someone I should be involved with, but my body doesn't understand that.

All I can feel is the thrill and the desire for more.

I want more.

I want everything.

And that's disturbingly similar to how Levi thinks.

Maybe I've become the devil king, myself.

He lowers me to the sofa and yanks down his boxer briefs. I pull my T-shirt over my head and toss it behind me so we're skin-to-skin. Heartbeat-to-heartbeat.

My nails dig into his chest, drawing long red marks. The same way he left his own marks all over my neck, collarbone, and breasts.

He hisses in pain, but his eyes gleam with undisclosed lust.

"You do like a bit of pain with your pleasure, Princess." He smiles, his sinful lips hovering over mine.

"So do you, Lev." I drag my nails down his back this time, ripping a groan from him.

"Sure do." He smirks and my heart skips a beat.

It's not even funny how gorgeous he is.

His fingers trail down my stomach to my wet folds, leaving scorching tingles in their wake.

He teases my clit until I'm bucking against his hand, begging for more.

The feeling starts at my core and spreads all over my body. Just when I'm about to come, he replaces his fingers with his cock, thrusting inside me in one go.

"Oh, God."

"Not quite." His lips curve as his face turns feral with lust and something else I can't place.

I hold on to his neck as he sucks the tender skin of my breast. Is there even a place he's left unmarked?

He sits up and pulls me into him so that I'm straddling his lap. The depth of this position makes me feel him everywhere.

In my body.

In my air.

In my freaking soul.

His lips find mine and he kisses me hard and wild and totally out of control as he picks up his pace. His thrusts are forceful and unyielding, like he wants to engrave himself deep within my soul.

He hits a pleasurable spot and something inside me shatters.

We're so united that there isn't a piece of me he doesn't own at this moment.

I come with a hoarse scream.

As I fall from the wave, I realise something is so utterly wrong.

He didn't use a condom.

I push at his chest as he picks up his pace, but I can't find the words to tell him to pull out.

Oh, God.

How the hell could I forget about that?

"Pull..." I finally breathe, coming down from my orgasm halo.

His eyes darken as he pounds into me harder and faster with his hands threaded into my hair.

"Levi..." I fight the pleasure building inside me and igniting every nerve ending. "I'm not on the shot or anything."

I didn't think I'd need that considering I was a virgin, but I seriously should've thought about it.

As if I put an idea in his head, Levi's lips quirk up in that contemplative smirk that only means trouble. He doesn't make a move to pull out. If anything, his pace becomes so wild, it's impossible to keep up.

His back turns rigid, and panic grips me like a vice.

"Please...please..." I beg, tears blurring my vision.

His hand shoots up to wrap around my neck, firm enough to keep me in place. "Is having kids with me so fucking sad?"

I shake my head frantically, but due to his hold, I can't move much. "It's not that... I don't want to be another version of my mum... I d-don't... Levi... Please..."

His hold falters from around my neck and just when I think he'll come inside me, he pulls out. "Next time, I'm coming inside you."

Next time, I'll be on the shot.

Harsh breaths leave me with gratitude. Levi doesn't listen to orders or requests, yet he pulled out for me.

His brows are still drawn together as he grabs his hard, throbbing cock in a fist as if he's mad at it.

I scramble to my knees between his legs. My hand covers his hand and I lick my lips. "Let me."

He tilts his head to the side. "Why?"

"Because I want to."

After a beat of watching me, he lets go. I take him in my hand, rubbing his length up and down.

He sucks in a breath. "Fuck, Astrid."

"Tell me what to do." I've never done this before, but I want to do it right for him.

"I need your mouth on it, Princess."

Holy shit. Why are those words such a turn-on?

Tentatively, I lick the precum dripping from his crown. That makes him groan, his eyes darkening and fluttering. I repeat it, licking the side before I take him all the way in. It's a challenge since my mouth is small and he's so big. I lick him tentatively. Levi jerks up, moaning, so I do it again and again.

He threads his fingers in my hair, slightly pulling and pushing. "That's it, Princess. Keep doing that."

I do.

There's a rush about having him at my mercy like this. I should've been doing this since the beginning.

I pick up my pace, sucking him hard and fast. Then he curses, tightening his hold on my hair, as his cock spurts down my throat. I try to swallow it all as he looks down at me with that darkened gaze. He tastes of breakfast and a hint of his natural, sweet scent.

He wipes the corner of my lips and I climb atop of him, crushing my mouth to his. I want him to taste himself on me like he gives me a taste of myself all the time. A groan rips from him as he deepens the kiss.

For what seems like hours, we remain entangled around each

other making out slowly, too slowly. It's like a different type of fuck.

Apparently, Levi has insomnia, but I must've worn him out, because he yawns and laughs, saying it's the first time it's happened in months.

Still keeping an arm around me, he reaches the other towards the table. He snatches a pack of cigarettes and takes one out, then retrieves the lighter.

His eyes are droopy, tired, but there's still that spark of intensity and lust. It makes me hyperaware of everything. Of the smell of sex in the air. Of his tousled Viking hair. Of his hard body against my soft one. Of his muscular leg between mine. Of his semi-hard cock against the tender flesh of my thigh.

But most of all, it makes me aware of him. This beautiful, beautiful guy who's silently battling against his insomnia and the shadow of his father's mental illness.

I want to hug him and tell him it's going to be okay.

But it never is, is it?

It's never okay to lose a parent this young, and the scar will be there forever. It's buried too deep, too far that it's impossible to reach it.

All I can do is stop him from doing stupid shit.

I snatch the cigarette away. "This poison will kill you."

His fingers snake a path along my shoulder. "It will, huh?"

"Uh-huh. So be a good King and stop smoking."

He smirks, and even that is lazy. "What will I get in return?"

"Jeez. Do you always have to get something in return?"

"Always."

I scoff. "What do you want?"

He's silent for a moment, and I can see him running a thousand scenarios in his head. "Open your mouth."

That makes my thighs clench and spasm with need. "W-why?"

"You want me to quit smoking, don't you, Princess?"

I nod.

"Then open that pretty mouth."

I do. Like a hormone-driven idiot, I just do.

Anticipation coils at the bottom of my stomach like a starved animal. He's turned me into a freaking animal.

Watching me with those droopy eyes, he clutches the cigarette between his thumb and forefinger. It's crazy how even his fingers look so sexy right now. They're long and hard like the rest of him.

And then he stuffs the cigarette in his mouth. I find myself craning my head against his arm to get a better view of that firm, kissable mouth. How his teeth tug on the cigarette. How his lips close around it.

Can I be that cigarette, please?

He brings the lighter to his face and sets the cigarette on fire. The smell of nicotine mingles with the scent of sex and sweat in the air.

"You said you'd quit —"

He stuffs a finger against my mouth, shutting me up. Then he removes it. "Open."

With a furrowed brow, I do.

Levi takes a drag of smoke but doesn't release it. Instead, he clutches my jaw, squeezing it between his fingers. His lips hover inches away from mine as he breathes nicotine down my throat.

Holy shit. That's hot.

And burning.

I mean, the nicotine burns at the back of my throat. I cough, but he swallows the sound with a hard kiss. I feel like that helpless cigarette in his mouth. Tugged by his teeth and devoured by his lips.

But he tastes like that cigarette.

He tastes like *me*.

If this is the last smoke he'll have, then I'll let him burn me.

We doze off on that kiss, still wrapped around each other.

When it gets cold, Levi grabs a nearby blanket and covers us with it.

Sometime later, a rustle of noises wakes me up from my peaceful sleep.

"Levi?" I ask.

"Hmm?" he responds sleepily, burying his nose in my hair.

"Is someone there?" I open my eyes to be greeted by a man who looks like an older version of Aiden scowling at us.

My heart falls to the ground when I make out the man standing beside him.

"Astrid Elizabeth Clifford. Get up from there, *now*."

THIRTY-EIGHT

Astrid

When something goes to hell, everything else does.

Dad.

Holy shit. It's my dad.

I curl into Levi's side, bringing the sheet to my chin.

My face heats and I cease to breathe.

"Levi and trouble," Aiden's older version says. "Why am I not surprised at all?"

Levi shields me behind him as he stands to his full naked glory, not caring about the two adults throwing daggers in his face.

He takes his time in pulling his boxer briefs up his legs as I fumble to find the T-shirt and toss it over my head.

I keep my eyes bowed, scared to look Dad in his.

I'll probably never be able to look him in the eyes ever again.

I've been a virgin for life and when I finally do have sex, Dad walks in on me.

Worst luck ever.

"What gives, Jonathan?" Levi's voice is bored, the total opposite of my chaotic insides. "I didn't know you had voyeurism tendencies."

"Levi…" Jonathan warns.

"Even your nephew doesn't respect you," Dad speaks under his breath in Jonathan King's direction.

The Jonathan King. Owner of the King Enterprises and Dad's archenemy of sorts.

"Get away from my daughter. *Now.*" I flinch at the authority in Dad's voice.

"Come here, Levi." Jonathan is deadly calm with one of his hands in his pocket.

The feel of it is frighteningly similar to Aiden's lethal poker face.

Levi tilts his head to the side. "Pass."

"Come here or everything ends." Jonathan pauses and some sort of a battle erupts between him and his nephew. "*Everything*, Levi."

Levi's jaw clenches, but he doesn't move. Not an inch. Even though I don't know what Jonathan's talking about, something tells me it's not in Levi's favour.

"Astrid." Dad's sharp voice causes my shoulders to snap upright.

I push my hair back as I stumble to my feet. The T-shirt reaches the middle of my thighs, but I still tug down on it.

Those pale blue eyes clash with mine for a brief second and I offer him an encouraging smile. His fingers brush against my arm before I drop my head and trudge to Dad's side.

As soon as I'm within touching distance, Dad grips my arm and cages me behind him.

"This is the last time I see a Clifford on my property." Jonathan glares down at Dad, who glares back.

A more ferocious battle than the one from earlier erupts between them and I swallow at the thick tension in the air.

"Keep your spawn away from my daughter." Dad drags me away from the house before I can throw one last glance at Levi.

As soon as we're outside, I stop, trying to pull Dad to a halt. "Are they fighting? Can't you stop them?"

"We have no place in their familial matters."

"But isn't familial matters how you found me?"

"I had a very unpleasant call from Jonathan while I was searching for you. He told me that my daughter could be with his nephew."

I'm so ashamed, but it's not what's pushing me right now. My heartbeat thunders in my ears as I strain to hear what's going on inside. What if Jonathan beats Levi?

"But, Dad, he —"

"It's Father!" he snaps, making me freeze near his car. "How many times do I have to tell you to call me Father? I gave you two rules. Two simple rules. Don't sully the Clifford name and stay away from the King's surname. You broke both of them in one day. *Both*. Every time I think I'm getting to you, it spirals out of control all over again. I don't know what I'm supposed to do with you anymore, Astrid."

Tears fill my eyes and I try to fight them away as I take the onslaught of Dad's words. It's like I'm in the presence of a stranger, not someone who's supposed to be the closest person to me.

"I didn't ask for this either. I didn't want to live with you and your stupid family. I didn't want to be shackled by rules and manners. I didn't want to sneak out every day so I wouldn't be forced into a breakfast with your wife, who insults me and my mother the entire time. But that's not the worst part. The worst part is that you *always* take her side. Mum would've never done that. Mum would've heard me out. Mum stayed when you abandoned us. I wish it was you who died that day, not her."

I regret the words as soon as they come out. My lips tremble as Dad's face turns stone cold.

"I… I —"

He releases me as if I were on fire. "Get in the car."

"D-Dad… I…I didn't me —"

"Get in the car, Astrid."

I flinch at his non-negotiable tone and hurry to the passenger side. I sniffle and wipe my eyes, fighting the onslaught of emotions coursing through me.

When Dad takes his seat and doesn't spare me a glance, I know, I just know that I screwed up any chance I had with him.

If Dad hated me before, then now, he simply doesn't care about me anymore.

THIRTY-NINE

Levi

Our calm is only a delusion to the storm.

I watch Astrid being dragged out. The only thing stopping me from snatching her from her father is her own sake.

If I act on what I want, she might end up in more trouble than she already is with her father. Despite her reservations about him, she looks up at him like he's God.

Or maybe I don't interfere because I'm a coward who doesn't want to see her choose him over me.

I face Jonathan, making sure he sees the tension radiating off my body. This one has his schemes written all over it.

He's wearing a dark brown Italian suit, all complete with Italian leather shoes. Handmade. One of a kind. Just for him.

Jonathan likes to believe the world revolves around him. And why wouldn't he when everything he wants whirls in his orbit?

His hair is slicked back and he wears the usual indifferent expression that Aiden inherited.

"How did you find me?"

"You thought I didn't know about your little hideout?" He throws a glance around the place with disregard before his metal eyes slide back to me. "I told you. You only exist because I allow it."

Although a thousand retorts fight to break free, I rein

them in. I've lived with Jonathan long enough to recognise his provocations.

He feeds off anger. Now, I realise that I've been handling it all wrong. I've been playing in the devil's hands and pretending to be above him.

"See, patterns are my forte, and I knew you'd fuck up at some point. It's written in your DNA. One mistake, Levi. I gave you the right to one mistake and it had to be a *Clifford*." He pronounces the name with disgust, as if he doesn't want to say it.

"She has nothing to do with this."

He raises an eyebrow, and I curse myself for wording it that way. Fuck. I just gave him the reaction he needs.

"I see." Jonathan approaches me with steady steps, his shoes the only sound in the house. "This isn't a meaningless fling you're using to rebel against me. That's…interesting."

"If you have a problem, then you have it with me," I snarl in his face. "Stay the hell away from her."

"I don't have to approach her. Her father will be more than enough to put her back where she belongs." His calm expression morphs into sheer hatred. "Far the fuck away from the King name."

I pause. It's the first time I've seen Jonathan showing such great hatred to anyone. He believes emotions such as hatred, revenge, and holding grudges are a waste of time and energy.

Lord Clifford must've done something unforgivable to elicit such unschooled hatred from Jonathan.

"You recognise that this is your fall, right?" Jonathan stares down at me with that usual 'you're a rock in my shoe' look. "Are you ready for seven years in my company? No more football or your little escapades."

My jaw clenches so hard, I'm surprised it doesn't snap.

The moment I've always dreaded has come.

My football dream is withering away right in front of my fucking eyes.

It's during times like these where people start regretting what they've done.

I don't.

If I could repeat last night and today with Astrid, I'd do it all over again.

"I assume you're not ready." Jonathan shakes his head with what looks like exasperation. "You're persistently defiant like your father."

"Is this the part where you tell me I'll become crazy like him?"

"James was *not* crazy." Jonathan's face and voice turn stone cold. "He had mental issues, but he wasn't deranged. He did everything for you, ungrateful brat."

My mouth parts. Did Jonathan just defend my father?

"I'll give you one more chance and you better seize it because I don't give second chances."

He waits for me to release my clenched fist before he speaks again, "You'll stay away from Clifford's daughter. They're not allowed near our family."

"Why?"

"You don't want to know."

"I'll be the one to decide that."

"You won't like the outcome, punk."

"You're good with patterns, aren't you, Jonathan? Tell me what happens if I know."

Silence stakes claim in the lounge area as he squints.

"Very well." He unbuttons his jacket and sits down on the chair at the middle. He always chooses dominant positions, even when he sits.

"If you find out the reason, it'll break you both. You'll hate yourself, then you'll hate her and you'll hate the day you ever got near her, talked to her, or touched her. You'll spiral into your speedy mode and do something reckless and impulsive, and I'll have to get you out of it. Then you'll have to pay your debt to me, which will give me the chance to dictate your life." He crosses his arms over his stomach. "So by all means, if you want to be stubborn and search for the reason, then go right ahead. Give me the chance I've been pining for."

I want to call him a liar and tell him that nothing will break me from Astrid. That he can't manipulate us into being apart.

But this is Jonathan King.

He didn't lie when he said he's good with patterns. He has a knack of seeing the future before it happens. That's why he scores so many successful deals.

Still, I refuse to believe him.

If he could predict the future, why didn't he use it to save his own brother?

I sit across from him, my shoulders crowding with tension. "Tell me."

"I knew you would insist." His voice drops to a murmur as if he's speaking to himself. "James's stubbornness to a T."

Then he starts talking, and with every word he says, something inside me fucking dies.

Jonathan was right. I should've never known about this.

FORTY

Astrid

I never got a warning before I was crushed by you.

I couldn't sleep.

I called Levi, but his phone was turned off. Gloomy thoughts ran rampant in my head all night, spiralling out of control and hitting me in the chest.

What if his uncle hurt him?

What if he needs help?

I'm probably being a tad more dramatic than usual, but their postures screamed a fight yesterday, not to mention that Jonathan King seemed scary. It makes sense that he's Aiden's father and Levi's uncle. It runs in the family.

Come morning, I rush down the stairs with my backpack over my shoulder. Sarah calls after me to eat something, but I don't stop.

I'm running down our driveway when the sound of an engine behind me penetrates my ears. I turn and freeze as I stare at the blinding lights from the car.

Everything stops.

My heart.

My breathing.

All of it.

I'm plucked from the present and thrown back in time.

Darkness surrounds me and rain beats down on me like a vengeful creature. Small whimpers of pain fill my senses like the gurgling of the dead.

I'm lying sideways, half of me outside the car's window. The other half lies on the passenger seat.

A sob catches in my throat when I glance to my side. I know what I'll find, but it does nothing to prepare me for the shock of what's to come.

Blood covers Mum's chest that's stopped rising and falling. Her eyelids are closed as if she's asleep.

Only, she's not.

"No… No… M-Mum… No…please!" I try to crawl to her, but something hard and cold scrapes my side.

The whimpering continues, but it's not coming from me. Just when I'm about to search around me, something stops me.

A bloodied hand grabs my ankle.

I shriek and fall on my arse, and then I'm back in the present at Dad's house.

A Mercedes that I've never seen before is sitting beside me with the engine running. Nicole is in the driver's seat, glaring down at me after she almost hit me.

I stand on unsteady feet, my breathing rushing out of my lungs in a frenzy.

My chest rises and falls so hard, it's like I'm about to faint or have a heart attack.

"Watch where you're going," she snarls out the window as the car passes me. "This isn't over."

I'm not focusing on what she's saying. I hear her. I see her. But it's like I'm caught in an out-of-body experience.

"Are you okay, honey?" Sarah hurries towards me and checks me out.

"I'm…fine." *I think.* I turn to watch the Mercedes exiting the driveway. It seems super familiar, but where have I seen it?

"Did Nicole change cars?"

"Oh, that." Sarah dusts off my uniform as I watch where the car disappeared to in a stupor. "It's an old one, always huddled in the garage. Miss Nicole wanted some changes made to her car, so she's using that one temporarily. It hasn't been out from the garage in years, I'm surprised it still runs."

Dad must've driven it when he used to visit us. That's why it seems familiar.

"Is something wrong?" Sarah asks.

I shake my head, even though something *does* feel wrong.

I'm on autopilot as I walk towards the street. I keep staring at my ankle as if that bloodied hand will imprison me again.

It's not real. It can't be.

But Dad said there was someone else. Am I remembering them now? Is that the reason behind the bloodied hand?

I need some psychological talk with Dr Edmonds. And since I'm eighteen, I don't need Dad's permission.

A wave of sadness takes over me as I throw one last glance at the house and Dad's car sitting outside.

Yesterday, he didn't drive straight home. He took me to the doctor for the morning-after pill and a contraceptive shot. I tried telling him that I used protection, but it's like my tongue was tied.

I felt more ashamed in that moment than when he walked in on me wrapped all around Levi.

On the way home, he didn't speak a word to me.

For the first night since Mum's death, Dad didn't come to wish me goodnight. I waited and waited and waited, but he never showed up.

I was too cowardly to go and apologise, because if he shut me out this time, I didn't know if I'd be able to pick up my pieces again.

Outside, Dan's car is parked right beside Nicole's and he has his forearm against the hood with his entire body leaning against her window.

There's an unusual tension in his shoulders as he talks in

rapid-fire. It's too far for me to hear what he's saying, but Nicole is staring at him with wild eyes and parted lips.

She looks on the verge of...crying?

Then her blurry gaze meets mine and she turns the wheel and speeds forward. Dan stumbles back, cursing.

For the love of Vikings. Is Nicole trying to kill someone with her car today?

I quicken my pace towards Dan. "What the hell was that all about?"

"Nicole being a bitch, as usual." He runs a frantic hand over his face. When he turns around, he appears less agitated. "How are you feeling? Better?"

I might have spent two hours on FaceTime with Dan last night. I had to vent about everything to my best friend.

"No." My voice catches. "Dad isn't speaking to me."

"Come here." Dan wraps me in a hug and I fight the tears as I put my arms around his back.

"Don't you hate me for bailing on you and leaving with Levi?"

"Bugger, I bail on you for shags all the time. That was nothing."

"Really?"

"Really. You're finally not a virgin, so I no longer have to shoo away all those who planned to sacrifice you to Satan."

I laugh as I pull back. "You're not going to judge me?"

"What's there to judge?" Dan grins, showing his dimple. "Besides, in the best friends' manual, it says in bold capital letters that best friends aren't allowed to be judgy little bitches."

"What manual?"

"I'm sure it exists somewhere."

"I'm surprised you read any manual that isn't a porn magazine."

"I know, right? Aren't you happy I'm your best friend?"

"I am. Life would've been boring without you, Bug."

"That's the spirit." He pauses, the smile and the dimple disappearing. "Full disclaimer, in the manual, it also says that best friends should offer reality checks about any bad shit the other friend is doing. Captain leans towards the bad." He rolls his eyes. "But you already know that."

"Do you think it's weird that I keep gravitating towards Levi despite knowing what he's capable of?"

"Nah." He nudges my shoulder, waggling his eyebrows. "It just means that you have a wild side I wasn't fully aware of."

Maybe he's right.

"Besides, it's not like you can choose who you like. That shit is messed up."

"Since when did you become a philosopher about relationships?" I nudge him back. "Don't tell me you actually like someone."

"I like everyone who opens their legs for me. Or mouths. I'm flexible."

"You're such a pig."

He chuckles. "Come on, let's go to school."

"Wait. Do you think Levi's fine?"

"You don't know?"

Something clenches in my chest. "I don't know what?"

"The team had a party yesterday at the Meet Up."

"They did?"

"Yeah." Dan winces. "I went after you called it a night."

"Was Levi there?"

"He's the one who called it."

"Oh."

I was worried sick about him while he had a party. He didn't even bother to text or check up on me.

"And what did he do?" I ask.

"The usual. Party. Drink."

"That's…brilliant."

"Astrid —"

"No. Dan. It's fine." I force a smile. "Let's go to school."

Hot, red fire courses through my veins as I stomp to the car and throw my weight into the passenger seat.

Levi had a party as if nothing happened yesterday. He didn't stop to ask how it went with Dad. He didn't think we needed to talk or anything.

For Levi, this must be another mind game.

I'm the one who shouldn't have focused on the arsehole in the first place.

Not when I have more important things that I should worry about.

"Actually, Dan. I'm going to see a doctor."

FORTY-ONE

Astrid

You didn't kill me, you destroyed me.

I come out from my session with Dr Edmonds feeling lightheaded.

Everything that I thought I'd figured out is smoke and mirrors now.

Mum's accident. My accident.

Since Mum's death, I've thought that no amount of therapy would bring back my mum or make me move on. So I've been ghosting my shrink.

Dad forced me to see Dr Edmonds at the beginning, but when I started throwing fits and woke up screaming in the middle of the night, he left me alone.

He only made me see Dr Edmonds again after the summer accident.

"Are you all right?" Dan stands up from the seat in the waiting area. "Why did you want to see your shrink?"

"Because —" I look up at him with my heart squeezing in my chest "—I think I've been running away."

He clutches my arm, helping me sit on the bench as the assistant calls in another patient.

"Did the doctor say that?"

"No. He told me that I quit visiting him for a reason and

I also returned for a reason." I grip his arm tighter. "He's right, Dan. I had a flashback."

His brow furrows. "A flashback?"

"From my accident with Mum. Dad said someone else died that day and I think… I think he or she asked me for help." My eyes fill with tears. "What if… What if they died because I couldn't help them?"

"No. No. Look at me, Astrid." He clutches my shoulder. "You had a concussion and couldn't even save yourself, let alone someone else. Okay?"

I nod slowly, more to myself than anyone else. "That's not the problem, Dan. The problem is that I wanted to remember for the wrong reasons. I want to recall what happened at my hit-and-run accident because I'm so mad at Levi right now. It's messed up, isn't it?"

"It's human." He grins. "Let's egg his car and slash his tires. That Jaguar pisses me off."

I snicker. Only Dan would turn an intense situation into a joke.

"So did the doctor say you could remember?" he asks.

"Yeah, but the whole thing is entirely up to me. Apparently, I've been blocking memories."

"Are you scared?"

"No. Maybe. I don't know."

"I'm here. You've got this, you little bugger."

"God. I don't know what would've happened to me if I didn't have you, Bug."

"Probably lots of shit." He twists his mouth. "Buy me lunch?"

"Cheeseburgers," both of us say at the same time.

"How about we skip?" He waggles his eyebrows.

"I know what you're doing, Dan, and no, I'm not running away from school anymore."

I'm done bowing. It's time I stand tall.

***

In school, no one looks in my direction, and when they do, they bow their heads.

Everyone except for Nicole and her wingman, Chloe. They glare at me, but they keep their vapid mouths shut.

Dan walks by my side, winking at his harem of girls.

Me?

I'm counting my steps so I don't trip and fall.

Good or bad, I hate being put under the spotlight.

The only thing I want is to disappear into my art studio and not come out until it's time to go home.

Dan has a meeting before practice with their coach, and as soon as he disappears down the hall, I quicken my pace to the studio.

Someone cuts in front of me and I come to a screeching halt.

Aiden.

He's wearing his football blazer and the uniform's trousers. For a star player, he's in no rush to meet their coach.

"What do you want?" I ask as coolly as I can manage.

I hate how much I want to search around him for the other King, or how much I want to see his cousin in him.

He leans against the wall, crossing his arms over his chest. "Something changed."

"And I'm supposed to know about it?"

He remains as blank as a board. "Have you heard what my father and Lev talked about yesterday?"

I shake my head. "Dad and I left first."

Aiden continues looking me up and down as if he's searching for something. Then he pushes off the wall, about to leave.

"Wait. Do you know why there's animosity between your father and mine?"

He appears lost in thought for a second. "Hmm. It might have to do with that."

"With what?"

"Lev is acting strange."

"Is that why he threw a party out of nowhere yesterday?"

"Perhaps." He pauses. "He ignored you, didn't he?"

I thin my lips, refusing to admit how much that hurts.

Aiden's gaze gets lost in something behind me. It's the first time I've seen his gunmetal eyes project anything but deadly indifference.

As if a demon has possessed him, his eyes darken until they become frighteningly black.

I glance over my shoulder to see who the victim of the young King's wrath is.

My lips part when I make out Kimberly. The same chubby girl who educated me on football during the other game. We ended up sitting together in most home games.

She glances at me and smiles tentatively as she gives me a little wave. I wave back. Then she links arms with a taller blonde beside her, who is trading glares with Aiden.

Being tiny, the first thing I notice about Kimberly's friend is her long legs that go on for miles—okay, that's a bit overdramatic. But they're so toned, like she's an athlete.

She has pale skin and electric blue eyes that shine with malice the more she shoots daggers in Aiden's direction.

She has some balls to glare at Aiden this openly. He's a scary little shit who always gives me a serial killer vibe.

"Do you want to try something?" he asks without breaking eye contact with the blonde.

"Try what?" I ask, confused.

"About Lev."

"What is it?"

He flings an arm around my shoulder and pulls me to his side. "You'll find out."

The blonde breaks eye contact and takes the first turn around the corner with Kimberly.

Aiden continues watching her, even after she completely disappears.

His lips curve in a sadistic smirk before he faces me. "Let me test something about Lev."

I point at his arm. "Does that include you holding my shoulder?"

He nods. "I would tell you to trust me, but I know you won't."

At least he knows that.

A few minutes later, I'm sitting on a bench, watching the practice with Aiden by my side.

I think about shoving his arm away, but his theory about a test stops me.

"Aren't you supposed to be in practice?" I ask.

"I need rest after a minor injury." He tips his head at a passing player.

Me, on the other hand? I keep looking for Levi to come out of the locker room.

Everyone is on the field—including Dan. He furrows his brow at me as if asking, 'What the fuck are you doing?' I don't know myself, but if anyone will force Levi's hand, it can only be Aiden.

Ronan and Cole stare at us with stupefaction, just like the rest of the team. Only Xander laughs and shouts, "A hundred that a King will kill a King today."

I think he even gets a few bets from the other team members, Ronan and Dan included.

My breath hitches when Levi steps out with Coach Larson.

Something inside me ignites at seeing him again after the time we spent all tangled around each other.

I should be mad at him, but I can't help noticing how his athletic body looks in the royal blue jersey and shorts. How his tousled blond hair falls on his forehead and how his pale blue eyes glint under the sun.

Damn how irresistible he is.

He pulls his legs back, stretching while listening to the coach.

He switches to stretching his arm behind his head and turns around. Then his gaze meets mine.

I swallow, the urge to remove Aiden's arm consumes me, but I resist it.

I want to see Levi's reaction. I want to see him lose it like he did with Jerry and at the party.

At least that would prove this isn't a game for him.

Levi pauses mid-stretch, and my heart thumps so loudly, I can't hear anything past it.

As if a robot has taken over his body, Levi turns around and continues walking with the coach towards the other players.

Something breaks in my chest.

If he hadn't meet my gaze, I would assume I was invisible.

Am I invisible?

"Huh." Aiden drops his arm. "That failed."

A sob catches in my throat.

Was everything that happened between us a stupid game? How…could he?

I stand up and stride towards the sidelines. My temper boils, and I know the moment I clutch the metal railing that I'll say something stupid.

"Levi!" I call.

He doesn't turn around or acknowledge me, but the entire team's attention is on me. Dan shakes his head and Xander elbows Levi.

"King!" I shout. "If you don't turn around this second, we're over. Completely over. Do you hear me?"

I wish I'd never said that. I wish he hadn't turned around.

When he does, his eyes are completely washed out. I don't recognise this Levi. Not at all.

It's like an alien has sucked his soul and left this person behind.

He smirks in that cruel, sadistic way. Then his next words undo me.

"We were never something to be over."

FORTY-TWO

Levi

Losing a battle doesn't mean ending the war.

The moment Aiden strolls into the locker room, I throw him against the wall with my forearm crushing his trachea.

"What the fuck were you doing?" I snarl in his emotionless face.

Murmurs from the rest of the team members break out around us. I should've left it alone until we got home, but the fire inside would've consumed me by then.

I was barely able to stop myself from climbing the fence and smashing Aiden's face to the ground during practice.

He dared to touch her.

He put his fucking hands on her.

The corner of his lips curls in a smirk. "It didn't fail, after all."

I grab his arm—the same fucking arm he had around *her* shoulder—and twist it. "Do you want a cast?"

"Captain." Cole approaches slowly. "We can talk it out. No need to break things…or bones."

"Tell. Me," I growl in my cousin's poker face. "What the fuck were you doing?"

He remains silent, meeting my stare with one of his own.

My hold tightens around his already twisted arm. I'm going to fucking break it and to hell with it if Jonathan controls my life.

He already does, anyway.

Xander kicks Aiden's leg. "Whatever it is, tell him, you little shit."

"He'll really break your arm," Cole hisses.

Aiden's expression doesn't change, no matter how much pressure I apply. The fucking psycho has become abnormally resistant to pain since that incident nine years ago.

"Yo, King." Ronan stares at him with bugged eyes. "*Mais tu es fous ou quoi?* Do you want your arm broken?"

He doesn't. But if a broken arm gets him what he actually wants, he wouldn't mind.

"Who told you to keep your conversation with my father a secret?" Aiden finally speaks.

"Go near Astrid again, and I'll fucking kill you."

"Tell me the secret."

"Pass."

He smiles in a taunting way. "If you don't give me what I want. I won't give you what you want either. Guess what, Lev? The game always starts with two kings on the chessboard."

"One-nil to Aiden!" Ronan shouts, then says, "Ouch!" when Cole smacks the back of his head.

I smile and let Aiden go with a shove against the locker.

I could punch him to death and tear him limb from limb, but physical strength doesn't work on this little shit.

He said it himself, *Smarter, not stronger.*

To win, I have to play his way.

"So this is a game, huh?" I ask.

"Sure is." He smirks, dusting his jacket as he starts to leave the room.

"Very well. I'm making my first move today. Meet me in the car park."

"Make it count, Lev." With one last taunting smirk, he disappears behind the door.

I face the rest of the team and speak in my most authoritative tone, "If anyone goes near Astrid, they'll have a personal problem with me. Do I need to repeat myself?"

"No, Captain," they recite in unison.

"Make that apply to the entire school."

"Yes, Captain."

I throw up a hand, dismissing them, and they each go back to their tasks.

All except for one.

Daniel glares at me and pushes my shoulder on his way out. "I don't take orders from a coward captain."

I grind my teeth, but I let it go. It's not my midfielder speaking, it's Astrid's best friend.

After changing my clothes, I get out and stop at the front of the locker room with my back against the wall.

I might put up a façade, but I'm feeling too much chaos, and it's beginning to numb me.

I've tried drowning it in alcohol, but that shit's never good. Not to mention that Coach will have my arse if I come to practice with a hangover.

Smoking is also off the table after the last erotic smoke I had with Astrid.

The look on her face when I told her we're nothing still cuts through me like fucking knives.

Jonathan had to screw up my life in a completely different way.

I need time to figure this whole shitty situation out, but that doesn't mean anyone can have Astrid.

Not Aiden.

Not Zachariah.

No. Fucking. One.

Chris trudges away from me, towards Coach Larson's office. I watch him from behind, tilting my head and narrowing my eyes.

I'll deal with his drunken arse later. He's off the team until he shows up not hungover or as high as a kite.

Once I arrive at the car park, I spot Dan driving out. Alone. Astrid must've gone home first.

She's strong. She fucking has to be.

Because since my eye-opening chat with Jonathan, I'm starting to think I'm broken beyond repair.

"Interesting location for a battle." Aiden's mocking tone reaches me before he slides against his car that's parked opposite mine.

I toss my bag in the back seat and lean against the driver's door, facing him, and cross my arms over my chest.

"What do you want, Aiden?"

"Simple. Tell me what Father told you that's made you become so volatile."

"Why do you want to know?"

"No one keeps me in the dark." He shrugs.

"Seriously? You're bringing out your big guns for something as insignificant as this?"

"Insignificant battles win the war. Now tell me what I need to know."

"No."

"I'm going after Astrid then. Careful, King, your own queen will bring you to your knees."

My knee-jerk reaction is to punch him in the face.

I don't.

I should've known that Aiden would aim for my weakness. But the thing with Jonathan is none of his fucking business and it'll remain that way.

"I look forward to spending more time with Clifford. Maybe I should join her and Sterling in bowling?"

"You do that."

"If you're calling my bluff, it's your loss. You know I'll do it."

"I'm sure you will." I nod towards where a tall blonde walks in the direction of a small green car with her friend. "In exchange, I'll have a go at Ice Princess."

His smirk falls, and although it's not slow, for someone with Aiden's conniving mind, it's noticeable.

"I heard she can be fun and not so icy underneath that exterior."

His right eye twitches.

Checkmate.

I slam my shoulder into his. "Stay the fuck away from Astrid."

I climb into my car as he continues staring at her with darkened, angry eyes.

I don't trust Aiden, but I trust whatever fucked up fixation he's had on that girl since the first time he saw her last year.

She's the same girl he's been stalking on Instagram like a stage five creeper.

Now that Aiden's taken care of, it's time I focus on more pressing matters.

Like Jonathan and his fucking secret from hell.

FORTY-THREE

Astrid

If life punches you, punch right back.

A week passes and life goes on.

I guess.

I've been focusing on my therapy with Dr Edmonds. We're even having two sessions in the same week now.

I still can't remember, but talking to the doctor helps. I get to focus on something that's not the arsehole who shall not be named.

Since the day he pretended he didn't even know me, he's erased me from his existence. When he walks by me, he doesn't spare me a glance.

It's like I've become invisible again.

In exchange, I erased him from my existence, too.

Dr. Edmonds says that I'm evading my problems. He said the same about the fact that I haven't spoken to my father since he flew to Russia last week.

But, well, the shrink doesn't know everything. He just needs to focus on helping me regain my memories.

I know, deep down, that Levi is hiding something from the day of my hit-and-run. That's why he's been so hell-bent that I drop the case.

For months, I've been so blinded by his wickedness and charm that I didn't look harder into it.

Now, I'm not.

Now, I won't stop until I uncover everything that has to do with my accident.

I'll pluck that crown off his head and push him to the edge.

Maybe then he'll realise how it feels to have your heart broken and watch as it bleeds out.

On Saturday, the home team wins and Ronan throws his usual party. Dan invited me to the game. I passed, but I don't pass on the party.

I don't run away anymore.

When any of Levi's groupies calls me a slut, I call her a slut right back.

If anyone attempts to touch me, I punch them in the face.

I'm done being tolerable to their ridiculous bullying.

Dan stopped me from punching Jerry when he started talking shit again last week. He said my artist hands need to be protected. So instead, he punched Jerry in the face, knocking him to the ground on my behalf. He would've gotten suspended if it weren't for my testimony.

"Best friends are made to punch people for you," he said when I found him in detention that day.

"No, they aren't, Bug." I laughed.

"Well, they should be. I'm totally adding it to the manual."

I put my arm in Dan's as we walk into Ronan's mansion. Drunk teenagers fall on either side of us, making out or cannonballing into the kidney-shaped pool.

A loud pop song I don't recognise thumps through the speakers and many of them dance to it, spilling alcohol all around.

One would think that Ronan would try to wind down the chaos, but he's betting with Xander on who can down more shots.

If the howling and the screaming by the pool are any sign, Ronan isn't winding down the party anytime soon.

Where the hell do his parents disappear to?

I grab a drink from a server—because it's totally normal to have servers and butlers at teenagers' parties—and down it in one shot.

"Liquid courage this early?" Dan asks with a slight lift in his lips before he takes one, too.

I run my fingers through my hair. "Okay, how do I look?"

"Badass." He pinches my cheek. "You should've gone wild before."

By going wild, Dan means that I wore the sinfully short denim shorts that he made me buy on a dare last year.

My lips are painted red and my hair is pulled up into a messy ponytail that I spent an hour trying to make look right.

I'm wearing a strapless black top, but against Dan's suggestions, I did put on my matching denim jacket.

I might want to feel powerful, but I still want to crawl back into my comfort zone.

Which won't happen.

Thus, liquid courage.

Dan and I down tequila shots for what seems like half an hour before he starts getting fidgety.

I push him in the direction of a second-year girl who's been watching him the entire time. "Go shag."

He waggles an eyebrow. "Wanna join?"

I make a face. "You suck, Bug."

"I can suck."

"Eww, Dan. Now I need bleach. Thanks a bunch."

He makes two guns with his hands as he walks backwards with a grin. "Call me and we're out of here, okay?"

That's some commitment for Dan.

But tonight is different. I'm not bailing out.

I down one more shot. Whoa. The tequila here is strong enough to make me spin.

Wait. Am I the one spinning, or is the room?

Fun.

I came here to have fun.

Although my feet are unsteady, I keep walking in zigzag lines towards the football team, where Ronan's having his drinking competition.

I steal a shot from a passerby and mumble a sorry here and there when I stumble into someone—or two.

The plan is to watch from afar. Like, *really* afar.

I hide behind a potted plant's huge leaf that adds some shadow to my face.

See, not noticeable at all.

Heat creeps up my neck and my arms. It's freaking hot in here.

I tap someone's shoulder and give him my shot. "Hold this for me."

"Sure thing, love." He's smiling down at me. I smile back, or I think I do as I take off my jacket and toss it somewhere behind me.

Much better.

"Thanks!" I take back my shot. "Oh, Knight! Go Elites!"

"Woohoo!" He pauses. "Wait. Was Danny boy right? Do you have a high alcohol tolerance?"

I tap my chest. "I'm the man."

His eyes glint as he takes me by the arm and drags me to the rest of the team.

"No," I whisper-hiss. "I'm supposed to watch from afar, dummy."

He chuckles, the sound devious as he winks. "Believe me, love, this will be more fun."

Xander uses his shoulder to push through the football players before we stop beside Cole and number thirteen.

I giggle.

I forgot the name of the one who threw the party.

"Look who I found!" Xander shouts over the guys' hoots. "Competition for Ronan."

Yup. Ronan. That's his name.

"Oh, puhleeze, bitch." Ronan wipes alcohol from his mouth, his cheeks red. "I can drink an entire gallon and still fuck two girls into oblivion."

"You're a pig," I tell him in a semi-slurred tone.

Oohs and aahs erupt around us. Cole clutches Ronan's shoulder. "You need to prove your worth, little shit."

"It's on!" Ronan is in my face. "No one can beat the king."

"I can beat any king," I hiss, pushing up my imaginary sleeves.

"Woohoo!" Xander raises my arm. "It's on, team. Let the bets roll."

Aiden walks straight to the middle of the scene and pushes both Xander and Ronan off. "Leave, Clifford."

Determination pumps in my veins as I place a finger on his chest and shove him away. "No King will tell me what to do."

"Hashtag burn." Xander coughs as the others snicker.

I flip my hair back. "Are we doing this or what?"

Ronan offers me his hand. "Yes, my queen."

I smile at the overdramatic tone he uses.

Aiden shakes his head at his friends. "It's your lives."

In no time, Ronan and I are standing on top of a table with the entire team forming a circle around us.

All of them are chanting, "Drink, drink, drink!"

The only rule of the game is that whoever falls is the loser.

My shot supplier is Xander, and Cole is Ronan's reluctant one.

In the beginning, I don't really know what I'm doing until the buzzing of energy gets into my veins.

During the first shots, almost all of the team is on Ronan's side, chanting his number and his name.

Then after a few rounds of my keeping up with his pace,

slamming one glass down after another, many of the team start chanting my name.

There's something contagious about having so many people shouting my name and cheering me on.

"You're going down!" Ronan slurs as both of us sway.

"No, *you're* going down!" The ceiling is spinning, but I blink, bringing the shot to my lips.

I miss it and break into a fit of giggles when alcohol falls down my neck.

"He's out!" the entire team yell, catching a falling Ronan.

"Hell yeah!" Xander shouts at a few guys by his side. "Pay up, bitches."

"I won?"

Cole smiles, shaking his head. "You won."

"I won!" I scream and jump up and down.

Bad idea.

The ceiling spins round and round as I fall backwards. The cheering and hooting stop altogether.

Strong arms clutch me and I crack my eyes open, looking at the face that's been torturing me for two weeks.

Pale blue eyes stare down at me as if I'm the most beautiful thing on earth.

And it does shit to me.

That look. Those eyes.

It hurts knowing I don't have this in my life anymore. Why did he come in if he planned to leave all along?

I slap his cheeks with both my hands. "Oh, you're real."

Tears blur my eyes as I giggle. "Is this a dream or a nightmare?"

"Both, Princess."

FORTY-FOUR

Astrid

Why is it impossible to hurt you?

When I open my eyes, I have two thoughts.

Where the hell am I?

Why is someone digging near my head?

I cradle my skull and wince. Apparently, the digging is *in* my head.

I turn to the side and sit up slowly. On the nightstand, there's a cup of coffee, a bottle of water and paracetamol pills.

I snatch the pills and the water, which soothes my scratchy throat enough to sip the coffee.

Eww. It's bitter.

I sip it anyway because I need to wake up.

Tequila shots—and whatever shots I had afterwards—were a bad idea.

If Dan was going to stop me, he should've done it earlier.

I'm adding that to his friendship manual.

I feel like I'm going to topple over and puke all over myself. Oh, and the hangover will last for a week.

My gaze strays to my surroundings. I'm sitting on a king-sized bed with untidy sheets. The open balcony causes curtains to flap into the room.

I've never seen this room in Dan's house before. And since when do they have gold-rimmed ceilings?

I look down at myself and gasp when I find out I'm only wrapped in a bathroom robe.

With a beating heart, I peek underneath it. Shit. I'm completely naked.

I'm not in Dan's house and I'm naked. Please tell me I didn't do something I'll regret.

The clearing of a throat pulls me from my stupor. My head snaps up. I didn't even realise someone else was in the room.

My breath comes in short gasps. Levi sits in a recliner, one jean-clad leg crossed over the other.

He's wearing a black T-shirt that sticks to his defined abs. His tousled hair is pushed back, giving a full view of the sharp lines in his face and the murderous look in his pale eyes.

My stupid body comes to life and tiny tingles shoot straight to my core.

Nope. I'm not going there.

Tightening the robe over my chest, I jerk off the bed, abandoning the cup of coffee on the nightstand.

A stupid little part of me is wishing for a word from him. A touch.

Anything.

But I'm not that girl anymore.

It's the first time I'm taking the Clifford pride seriously. Levi won't dictate my life anymore.

Tucking in my headache and my shell of a heart, I stride to the door. The moment I open it, a hand slams it shut from behind.

A large—and a very hard—body glues to my back. And the warmth. Damn him and his warmth.

I dig my elbows into his ribs. He doesn't back off.

If anything, he pushes his hips into me, pinning me in place.

Angry tears barge to my eyes.

How dare he do this to me when he already wrote me off?

How dare he play with my body and my heart as if it's some game?

I turn around and punch his chest. "You don't get to do this. We're nothing anymore, King."

His face closes off. "Says. Who?"

"*You!* We were never something to be over, remember?"

"So you decided to drink with my team." His voice hardens. "Is that your way to get back at me?"

That was my way to get back at myself. I planned to drink myself into oblivion. But at some point, I started to have fun with Ronan and the guys. For a moment, I was able to forget about this bastard.

"I'm so over you, King." I laugh with bitterness. "Oh, wait. It wasn't something to be over anyway."

"Fuck, Astrid." He sighs loudly, closing his eyes. When he opens them, there's a chaos of emotions I can't decipher.

What happened to you?

Why did you push me away?

Those questions slip to the tip of my tongue, but I don't ask them, because deep down, I'm afraid of the answer.

I'm afraid he'll cut through the fresh wound and ruin me beyond repair.

"Stop acting like you can belong to someone else." He grips both my hips and pulls me into him. "There hasn't been a moment where you weren't mine."

My fists clench and I hit his chest the hardest I can. "What the hell do you want from me, Levi?" *Hit.* "What?" *Hit.* "I can't do this anymore."

He grabs my wrists in his hand. "You can't do what?"

"I can't pretend like all of this is fine. I can't plot your demise when I'm aching to see you again. Checkmate, you won. You fucking won. Are you happy now?"

"Not even close." He spins me around and I fall backwards on the bed. Then he's on top of me, his body covering mine. My robe falls open at the bottom and his erection presses against my thighs.

I can feel myself crumbling.

My skin flushes, coming alive under the friction of his clothes.

Two weeks. It's been two damn empty weeks without him.

I'm aching to be filled again and only Levi can make that happen.

My fingers fist in his T-shirt. I don't know if it's to bring him closer or to push him away.

"How can I win when I've been losing to you since the beginning, Princess?" There's a strange vulnerability in his eyes that hits me in the chest. "Do you know how I spent the past two weeks without you?"

"I don't want to know."

"Too bad, because you will."

He flips me around and I gasp when I end up on my hands and knees—my trembling hands and knees. I can't process what's happening when his hard body covers mine from behind and his lips find the lobe of my ear. He runs his tongue over the shell and makes a trail down my neck.

I shiver and a zap of pleasure trickles down my thighs. Oh, God. Just one touch and I'm a helpless fool.

"No, Levi… Don't… I can't do this anymore. Stop."

"Do you think I don't want to stop?" he growls in my ear as he yanks the robe down my arms and tosses it away.

"I've been debating against who and what I am for two damn weeks, and guess what?" A zipper sounds from behind me, and I swallow audibly.

"W-what?"

"I can't win when I've already abdicated, Princess."

I throw a glance over my shoulder and suck in a breath. He's hard all over. His abs, his thighs, and his cock.

A full-body shudder goes through me.

I want him inside me.

No. I *need* him inside me.

I'm starting to wonder if I'll ever have this reaction to someone else other than him.

When I'm near him, it's both frightening and exciting. Even though I know there's a dark abyss ahead, I keep walking to it all the same.

It's crazy. It's reckless. But it's ours.

Levi and I haven't started as a fairytale, and I know it won't be a fairytale ending, but I still crave what we have.

My breath still catches in my throat and my heart tries to beat out of my chest.

How can I feel this strongly for a monster?

He grips one of my hips harshly. "I see you, but I don't touch you. I hear you, but I can't speak to you. You've been driving me fucking crazy."

"Good." I lean into his hand, rocking against his thigh. "Because you've made me crazy for a while now."

Levi releases my hip and stuffs his index and middle fingers into my mouth. I suck on them as I ride his thigh. I'm probably making a sticky mess on his muscles, but I don't stop.

I *can't.*

He doesn't seem to mind. If anything, he drags his thigh against my sensitive folds faster, sending me into a frenzy.

"You're soaking me." His voice is raspy. "Fuck. Do you feel yourself on me, Princess?"

I nod.

He flicks his thumb against my nipple and it hardens before he pinches. Hard.

"Do you want me to make you come?"

I moan around his fingers in response. He removes his thigh from between my legs, leaving me empty and aching and so freaking hungry.

"What —"

The words die in my throat when he runs his hard, thick cock up and down my entrance.

Holy shit.

That's even better than his thigh.

My breathing comes out stuttered and short.

"Tell me you're mine."

When he doesn't remove his fingers, I speak around them. "I'm yours."

"I don't care what fucking happens. You're not leaving anymore." He slams into me before I can form any type of response.

I close my eyes at the onslaught of emotions and tears form behind my lids.

This feeling, this belonging.

I thought I'd imagined it the other time, but it's real. Something primal goes through me whenever we're joined like this.

He's mine, too.

His harsh breathing. His relentless strokes. His head-turning scent.

All of him.

He belongs to *me*.

Thrusting into me long and hard, Levi removes his fingers from my mouth to stroke a strand of hair behind my ear.

He wipes a stray tear from under my eye. "I told you no protection next time. I want to feel you bare."

I smile despite myself. "It's not about that. I'm on the shot."

"Thank fuck."

"And here I thought you were trying to impregnate me last time."

"Oh, it will happen someday, but you're not ready for that yet." He sucks on the lobe of my ear and nibbles down my throat.

I'm too lost in his body against mine to form any opinions about what he's just said.

He picks up his pace and I push back into him as his thrusts turn harder and faster and out of control.

With each pound, he hits that sweet spot that drives me nuts.

"Oh, God, Levi... More."

"Are you mine?"

"Oh, please..."

"Tell me you're mine, Princess. Tell me you won't let anyone else touch you the way I do. Tell me you won't change or leave me."

My heart thunders at his strained tone and the way he watches me as if my answer will be either his damnation or his salvation.

I open my mouth to say something, but he stuffs a harsh finger into it.

"Don't lie. If you make a promise, fucking keep it."

"I'm yours, Levi," I whisper, meeting his gaze.

And I mean it.

I've been his for longer than I'd like to admit.

"Promise," he growls.

"I promise."

His thrusts turn animalistic and so do my movements.

His muscles become rigid and he curses, calling my name.

This orgasm hits me harder than any of the others. Maybe it's because it's been so long. Maybe it's because I missed the freaking hell out of him.

Or maybe, just maybe, it's because of all these jumbled feelings in my chest.

I'm completely screwed.

FORTY-FIVE

Levi

If you're a mistake, I'll still make it every fucking time.

I push through the chaos in Ronan's house, carrying a bucket of water.

All the team members left yesterday after I put a stop to the party.

The three I needed to fuck up hid, but there's no running from me.

Xander, Cole, and the little shit, Ronan, are sprawled on the sofas in the lounge area. Their limbs are thrown over each other in awkward positions.

Aiden sent me a video of Astrid hugging Ronan's shoulders while they drank at the same time; Xander, Cole, and the other team members cheering them on.

I've never driven as fast as I did last night.

I had meant to pull her down, beat the guys to a pulp, then go back to punching the bag.

But the moment she fell into my arms, I couldn't leave.

I tried, but the thing about Astrid? She got under my fucking skin and it's becoming impossible to pluck her out.

Then this morning happened.

I told myself it was only one last time. One last taste. One last touch. One last fucking kiss.

But that's impossible, too.

There's no fucking way I'll ever get enough of her.

Fuck the King and Clifford names.

Fuck the animosity.

Fuck everything.

There'll be a change of plans and Jonathan will have to accept it.

I stand in front of the three suckers who dared to defy me and pour the bucket of water over them.

Ronan gasps first, eyes widening. "It's not me. The devil Xan made me do it."

"Screw off." Xan sits up, wiping water from his face. "You're dead, Ro."

"What the fuck?" Cole cracks his eyes open and blinks. "Captain?"

"Outside. Now."

"*Et la merde.*" Ronan stumbles to his feet. "I promise I didn't fuck her… I don't think?"

Xander hits the back of his neck. "You're making it worse, arsehole."

"Not only did you make her drink, but you also took liberties in fucking touching her," I meet their sleepy faces.

Cole raises a forefinger. He's barely standing, and there are red nail marks all over his neck. Someone had a night.

"Correction," he says. "We didn't make her. She wanted to do it."

"Is that so?" I fold my arms.

Xan swats him. "Shut it." He laughs, meeting my gaze. "Won't happen again, Captain. Striker's honour."

"I know it won't, because every time you think about pulling such a stunt, you'll think about the early swim you're about to take."

"But it's fucking freezing outside," Ronan whines.

I raise an eyebrow. "Exactly."

"Captain." Xander shows me his charming smile. "You can't sacrifice me. I'm your ace striker."

"That would be me." Aiden's bored voice drifts through. He leans against the counter, sipping from a black mug.

"Traitor," Cole mutters.

Aiden lifts a shoulder. "I warned you. This is the 'I told you so' moment."

I knew I could count on Aiden's itch for that girl. Now, he won't dare to cross a line with me, because he knows full well that my threats aren't empty ones.

"Outside. Ten laps each." I point in the direction of the pool. It's raining. Perfect.

"I hope you gathered enough money from the bets to admit us into a fucking hospital afterwards." Cole nudges Xander.

"All bad ideas start with X." Ronan slaps him on the shoulder. "*Connard.*"

"Oh, fuck off. You two wanted to see Captain's reaction."

"Glad to fulfill your wish." I smirk. "There will be extra practice later, too."

A collective groan fills the space as they start stripping.

"Can we at least have breakfast first?" Xan asks with a cautious tone.

I shake my head.

He grunts, "Worth the try."

"What's going on?" The voice coming from the entrance stops me in my tracks.

All eyes turn towards her. She's wearing her shorts and one of my T-shirts that I left at Ronan's place.

A wave of possessiveness hits me at seeing her wearing my colours and my number. From now on, I want her to wear only that.

Her hair is still damp from the shower and falls on either side of her face. The bright green of her eyes fixes on each of the guys and they stop stripping.

It's Ronan who runs towards her first with his hands on his belt. "Astrid, my drinking buddy queen. Tell the tyrant captain to stop torturing us."

"You're doing an extra lap, Ronan," I tell him.

"Torture?" Astrid asks, appearing lost.

Ronan and Xander fill her in and soon, the three arseholes surround her, pleading with her to save them.

"I wanted to do it. It was fun," she tells me, chuckling. "Aren't you being a little too hard on them?"

"He is!" Ronan high-fives her.

"Hey, fuckers. Hands off." I step between them and Astrid. "Ten laps in the pool or something else. Your choice."

They know the alternative will be a lot fucking worse.

They all run towards the pool, removing their clothes on the way. Astrid breaks down in laughter when Ronan and Cole push Xander into the water, shouting, "The Devil first!"

When she continues staring at them, smiling as they bitch about the cold. I regret not making them go in with their clothes on.

I don't like that she watches them half-naked. I step into her line of sight, blocking them.

Aiden smirks from my peripheral vision, shaking his head. I flip him off behind Astrid's back and take her by the arm. "Do you want breakfast?" I ask.

"I'll make some if you get them out."

I narrow my eyes. "No."

She clutches my arm and tiptoes, brushing her lips along my cheek. "Please?"

Well, fuck. I can't say no when she puts it that way.

I face Aiden. "Tell them they can come out."

"After one more lap." Aiden continues drinking his coffee leisurely, seeming to enjoy the show a bit too much.

I join Astrid behind the counter while she retrieves eggs and packs of bacon from the fridge.

My hands brush along her hips from behind and she sucks in a breath. There's nothing I want to do more than to kidnap her upstairs and fuck her until she can't walk anymore.

But she said she needs to know everything. I'm not ready for that. I'm not ready to put an end to this peace.

The three wankers come out after they shower and change into dry clothes. Astrid already has breakfast ready for them. Aiden and I helped. Correction. I made the little shit Aiden help.

It's surreal when we all sit down for breakfast. I'm at the head of the table. Astrid is on my right and Aiden is at my left.

"Your parents are never here?" Astrid asks Ronan.

"They work a lot for the European Union and shit." He finishes chewing on his bacon. "C'est merveilleux, my queen."

"Stop calling her that," I warn.

He rolls his eyes at the same time as Astrid.

"Are they okay with all the parties you throw?" She helps Xander to another serving of eggs.

Fortunately, she made extra, because we eat like pigs in the morning.

"They have to be here to care." Ronan scowls at me. "But I'm totally telling them what you did when I get bloody Ebola, Captain."

Xan stops mid-chew. "Isn't that shit deadly?"

"Ebola isn't from the cold," Cole corrects them, but Ronan and Xander aren't hearing him. They continue their overdramatic bitching, painting imaginary scenarios about dying of Ebola.

Astrid laughs and jests with them, and although I hate seeing her laugh with anyone but me, I can't help being mesmerised by her spontaneous energy.

She knows I won't be her prince charming, but she still wants me anyway.

If anything, she wants me because I'm not.

I kick Ronan and Xander whenever they attempt to talk to her and grab her leg under the table.

My hand snakes up her thigh under her shorts. She sucks in a breath, trying so hard to focus on her coffee.

When she meets my gaze with those huge fucking eyes, my breath catches somewhere out of reach.

Will she still look at me that way when she learns the truth?

FORTY-SIX

Astrid

No matter how much you hide it, the darkest truths will always come out.

After breakfast with the guys, Levi tries to shoo them away. When that doesn't work, he kidnaps me to the room upstairs and shows me that I should be only looking at him, not his teammates.

I might get close to them just so he'll *show* me all over again. This part of Levi will always get me in a twist.

I figure I must be heavy, so I try to move from my position splayed out on top of him. But he wraps his strong hands at the small of my back, forbidding me from moving.

He rolls us over so we're lying facing each other. I want to let him sleep since I doubt he got any last night, but his lips find mine and I'm a goner.

We kiss for what seems like hours. We devour each other at a slow, passionate pace, like we're relearning one another again. We don't even come up for air, we just breathe each other in.

I love kissing him. I not only feel his taste in my mouth, but I also feel him all over me and inside me.

Levi and I were made for kissing. We should never stop kissing.

It should be a blasphemy that we haven't been kissing since that party.

After what seems like an eternity, he pulls back, but he threads his fingers in my hair, playing with the falling strands.

I love all the little ways he touches me like he can't get enough of me.

My own fingers get lost in his Viking hair.

"What do you want to do today?" he asks.

"Why?"

"I'm being nice here, Princess." He slides his hand from my hair to wrap it around my throat, squeezing the slightest bit.

I grip his arm, not sure if I want to stop or encourage him. Judging from the shaking of my thighs, it's the latter.

It's crazy how much his intensity wakes something entirely feral in me.

It's like a high that's spreading through my bloodstream.

"Is this your version of playing nice?" I bite my lower lip.

"Oh, I'm playing fucking nice." He brushes his mouth over my cheek. "If it were up to me, you'd be naked all day in my bed."

A familiar need surges through me. Maybe I want that, too. Maybe I don't want to leave his arms until I get enough.

But then again, will I ever get enough of him?

Besides, he's offering me a way to get to know him better, and Levi doesn't offer chances.

"I can ask for anything?" I prod.

He narrows his eyes. "Ask and I'll decide."

"No. You have to agree to anything first."

"Try again, Princess. I don't agree to something without knowing the consequences. That's a terrible negotiating method and a sure way to lose before even starting."

"Make an exception for me."

"Are you going to ask for other people? Because that's a resounding fucking no."

"Aw, man. There goes my chance to have an orgy with Xander, Ronan, and Cole."

His eyes darken as he grips my hip tighter until it's almost painful. "You want to have an orgy with those three fuckers?"

When I remain silent, his demeanour stiffens. The anger radiating off him seeps under my skin, even though it's not directed at me. *I don't think.*

"What did they do to you last night?"

"Nothing."

He continues glaring at me.

"I'm kidding, Levi. Jeez."

"You're kidding, huh?"

"Totally. As if I would ever want anyone other than you."

That draws a mischievous smile from him. "Good save."

I'm really starting to learn the devil's ways.

"So what do you want to do?" he asks. "One last chance. Otherwise, we go with my naked-all-day plan."

I'm tempted to follow his plan and say to hell with it, but something I always wanted to do with him pricks my mind.

"I want a normal date. Maybe a film and the amusement park?"

"That's it?"

I nod, lowering my head. "I haven't really dated before and I want to experience that."

"Wait. Go back. *Haven't really?* As in you've *sort of* dated?"

"I had some awkward dates in middle school when I was with Mum."

"Any sorry fucks I should know about?"

"No, you freak." I laugh. "Are you always this possessive?"

"Only with you, Princess."

I can't help the heat creeping up my neck and into my cheeks. He has this maddening way of making me blush over the smallest words.

"Don't even try to compare me to your previous dates." A shot of possessiveness and jealousy grips me.

"I don't date."

"Oh."

"You'll be my first."

I can't help the stupid grin spreading on my face. "Is that a yes?"

"Not so fast." He lowers his head until his lips hover a hair's breadth from mine. "What do I get in return?"

"What do you want?"

"You in my bed after the date."

"Does that mean I'm paying for the date with sex?"

He lifts a shoulder, amusement glinting in his eyes. "If you want to look at it that way."

"That sounds awfully like you're my sugar daddy."

"I'll be your anything as long as you're mine."

"What if I change my mind?"

He nibbles on the corner of my lip, drawing a shudder from deep within me. "Too bad. The deal with the devil is a one-way ticket."

When I told Levi I wanted to go on a normal date, I certainly didn't mean for him to terrify me in the amusement park.

I'm sweating and breathing harshly by the time we come down from the rollercoaster ride.

Levi laughs, wrapping his bigger hand around mine.

"That's not funny!" I nudge him.

"For someone who won a drinking game against our ace drinker, you're rubbish with thrill rides."

"Whatever."

"You should've seen your face." His voice drips with amusement.

I throw him a glare, scowling.

He clutches my cheeks and pulls them so his face is mere inches away from mine. "You're so fucking adorable when you're angry."

"Is that why you ghosted me for two weeks?" The question comes out of nowhere, but that's probably because it's been at the back of my mind since I woke up this morning.

I won't pretend everything is okay after he spent two weeks pretending I wasn't there.

His expression closes and he lets go of my face. Just when I think he'll retreat and I'll have to chase him all over the park, he entwines his hand with mine.

I run in front of him, but with his hand holding me hostage, it's kind of impossible to get far ahead of him.

"Tell me why." My voice catches. "I have the right to know why you treated me like I didn't exist."

He says nothing, continuing to stride ahead.

"Are you going to do it again? Do I have to sit and wait until you turn against me?"

Levi tugs on my hand, bringing me to a screeching halt. "Believe me, Princess. That won't happen again."

"Why not? If you did it once, what's going to stop you from doing it again?"

He releases a frustrated sound and continues dragging me along. At first, I think we're leaving, but he stops in front of the Ferris wheel and gives the man our tickets before he flings me into the seat.

I fold my arms and sit at the far end from him.

He slides to my side. When I attempt to stand, he yanks down on my thigh with a strong hand.

A groan of frustration rips from me. "I'm angry at you right now."

"You can be angry all you want without leaving my side."

I release an annoyed breath and stare outside as the ride starts moving. The more we go up, the smaller the world becomes. People are so minuscule, they're barely decipherable.

Levi's hand snakes up the leg of my shorts, but I grab it and fling it away. "Unless you're ready to talk, don't touch me."

"That's where you're wrong, Princess." His hand surrounds my throat. "I touch what's mine whenever I damn well please."

"Stop," I hiss, feeling my inner walls crumble. "Just stop playing these mind games with me and tell me, Levi."

His head tilts to the side like it does every time he's plotting something—usually trouble.

"Are you still searching into what happened that night?" he asks.

My brow furrows. "How did the conversation go to that?"

"Answer me."

"I told you, I'm not giving up on my justice." My lips part as I search his face. "Is that what this is about? Did you have something to do with the accident?"

A muscle tics in his jaw and he focuses on the outside world.

I clutch his face with both my palms, forcing him to look at me. "Did you?"

Oh, God. Please tell me this isn't true.

I search his pale eyes for any tell, but they're glassed over. He's sealing himself inside.

"I was there," he says calmly. Too calmly.

A sob tears from my throat.

He was there.

Levi watched me being hit.

"But I wasn't part of the accident."

"Then you were a part of the ones who chased me like I was an animal?" I ask in a stupor.

"No."

"How the hell am I supposed to believe anything you say, Levi?" Everything clicks into place and I stare at him as if he's not real. "This is why you approached me, isn't it? You didn't want me to reveal what you and your little band of friends did—Wait… were Ronan, Xan, and Cole a part of it? Oh my God. Of course they were. Aiden told them to leave me to die, didn't he?"

"Astrid!" He clutches my shoulders and I realise tears are streaming down my cheeks.

I promised myself that I'd never cry for him, but here I am.

Only, these tears are for myself. For the pathetic fool in me who considered trusting him again.

"For the last time, I'm repeating that I had nothing to do with the accident."

"How did you feel when you saw me covered in my own blood, King?" I cry. "Did you get off on it?"

"No!" His grip tightens on my shoulder.

"Then why were you so insistent that I drop the case? Why did you make my life hell for it? And don't lie to me. If you do, I'm erasing you completely. I swear."

"You're erasing me, huh?" He fists a handful of my hair in his fist, eyes menacing. "Do you think you can forget me?"

"Maybe not at first." My voice is filled with emotions. "But I promise that I'll eventually do it. I'm not your plaything, Levi, and I never will be."

He drops his hands from my hair and sighs. "Fuck it."

Fuck it?

What the hell is that supposed to mean?

"Do you remember what happened the night of your accident?"

"The accidental fire?"

"Only, it wasn't accidental."

My eyes widen. "You…"

He nods. "I set my uncle's mansion on fire."

"But…why?"

"Arson leads to prison, Princess. Uncle could've gotten me out of it, but that would've been at the expense of my freedom. That's why I needed you to drop the case."

"No. Why did you burn your uncle's mansion?"

He laughs without humour. "Because I wanted to rebel against him? Because he threatened to take my inheritance and keep me on a leash? Because I wanted to be a dick and take his favourite holiday home right before the summer? Take your pick."

Wow. I didn't realise his relationship with his uncle was that strained.

"Can your uncle take your inheritance?"

"My father listed him as my guardian until I'm twenty-five. If I don't play into his hands, he won't let me touch a dime from the family's money."

"Can he really do that when you're over eighteen?"

"Yeah. Even if he can't, I can't challenge him in court. No lawyer will beat Uncle's harem of hotshot lawyers."

"Why is he doing this to you?"

He releases a long breath. "He doesn't want me to become my father. You see, my father wasn't the perfect King that Jonathan is. James King loved life more and he never engaged in the family business. He played rugby in his early years and had a horrible injury that forced him into early retirement. He became depressed, then manic. While Uncle built the empire, my father either gambled the King's money or spent it on drugs."

Humming energy pulses off Levi the more he talks about his father.

I inch towards him slowly, as if I'm afraid of setting him off. My heart aches for him and I can taste his pain on the tip of my tongue.

No king is born as a king. They're made into one from their childhood. Levi never had a silver spoon. His mother abandoned him without a look back, his father had mental issues, and his uncle is obviously a control freak.

Oh, and his cousin is a psychopath.

"But you told me you had a good relationship with your father."

"I did when he wasn't manic or high, which leaves very little room for father and son bonding." He pauses. "He taught me to be myself. I didn't realise how much he really meant to me until I lost him."

I lean my head against his tense shoulder, squeezing his hand in mine.

This must be why he has prejudices against drugs. It was part of the reason he lost his father.

"Jonathan doesn't want me to be a failure like my father, and Jonathan stops at nothing to get what he wants."

I can see where Levi and Aiden got their ruthless side from.

Levi wouldn't admit to it openly, but he takes after his uncle in more ways than one.

"And what do *you* want?" I ask in a whisper.

His eyes find mine and they soften. "You."

If my heart could escape its confinements, it would be spilling at our feet right about now.

"What else?" The words come out on a breath.

"Just you would do." His lips find mine in the slowest, most toe-curling kiss he's ever given me.

I push him away with a hand on his chest. "There must be something else you want."

He's silent for a beat. "Football."

"You want to play pro?"

He nods once. "I had some calls and interest from Liverpool and Manchester City."

"Wow. Those are big ones."

He narrows his eyes. "How do you know that, Miss I Don't Care About Football?"

"I had Dan educate me." I smile. "But wow, I'm happy for you."

I try to camouflage the breaking of my heart at the thought that he'll be on the other half of the country.

"Doesn't matter. If Uncle forbids it, no good team will accept me." He stares down at our entwined hands. "What about you? Where do you plan to go?"

"Dad is thinking about Imperial College."

"And let me guess, that's not where you want to go."

"I'm an artist. I want to continue being an artist."

"Did you tell him that?"

"Have you seen my dad?" I laugh awkwardly.

"He seemed a lot more reasonable than my uncle."

"Do you really think that?"

"Not really." He shrugs. "But Uncle's enemy is my friend."

I laugh, leaning my head against his shoulder. For a moment, we get lost in the lights in the distance as the Ferris wheel continues its ascendance to the top.

That's when a crazy thought comes to mind. "Levi... Did you see who hit me that night?"

"If I had, I would've told you."

I pull back, staring at him. Then I grab both his arms and feel around them. "Were you there the moment I got hit?"

"I heard the hit."

"Meaning, you were at the road? Did you see anyone?"

"Believe me, Princess, if I knew who hurt you, I'd be the first to fuck them up."

But the thought won't leave my mind.

Could it be...?

I lift his long-sleeved T-shirt to his elbows.

He chuckles, "Am I going to be your sugar daddy sooner than agreed?"

My gaze zeroes on the lines in his veiny forearms. I pull it to the shadows and gasp.

The mole near his elbow looks like a small star in the darkness.

My eyes blur as I look at him. "You saved me."

FORTY-SEVEN

Astrid

Just when I think I have you, everything dissipates into thin air.

Weeks pass and every day is surreal.

Every day, Levi tests my limits and I test his right back.

We're like two pieces of a jigsaw, he and I. It's impossible to have the entire picture without being there.

I walk into the school with Levi's arm wrapped around my waist. Most of the football team surround us as if they're knights.

Dan, Aiden, Xander, Ronan, and Cole are like my own protection and follow me whenever Levi isn't around. I can tell Aiden isn't happy with it, but Levi forced his hand somehow.

Since that pool punishment, the three others keep quiet around Levi. Apparently, their captain has been out for their lives at practice. I've been hoping it's not because of the orgy joke.

But knowing Levi, that probably plays a part in it.

Levi isn't only possessive to a fault, but he's also the petty jealous type when I as much as look at his teammates. I might have done it on purpose a time or two to get a rise out of him.

I smile mischievously as I tell Ronan, "When are we going to have another drinking competition?"

"Tonight if you like…" his grin falters when Levi cuts him

a glare. "Or never. Yeah, never." He leans in to whisper, "Come down when Captain is asleep."

"I heard that." The look on Levi's face is that of pure contempt. I can only imagine all the ideas he has running through his mind on how to punish Ronan.

"You're pathetic." Aiden shakes his head at his cousin.

Levi flips him the finger.

"Twenty-two hundred." Ronan coughs and my gaze immediately flies in his direction.

The blonde girl, Kimberly's friend, is walking by us, hugging her books to her chest and heading towards the library. The guys stare at her, but only Aiden and Levi check her out openly.

"What's the deal with her?" I ask. "An old ex of the both of yours?"

A stab of jealousy hits me. Levi said he doesn't date, but if he has an ex of that level, it would make my self-confidence shaky.

"She's no one's ex or current." Xander laughs. "She's Frozen. An ice princess."

"Unfortunately for this chap." Cole nudges Aiden.

He throws him an undecipherable look and scrolls on his phone as if nothing happened.

"She's sort of like you." Xander snaps his fingers at me. "Captain had his knickers in a twist because of you."

"Piss off, Xan," Levi tells him.

"No." I elbow Levi's side. "I want to know more."

Ronan's playful gaze bounces between me and the girl as she disappears inside the library. "Do you think she's pretty, Astrid?"

"Are you kidding me? She looks like a doll." And I'm glad she has Aiden's interest, not Levi's.

Scratch that.

I shouldn't be glad that anyone has the psycho's attention.

A lustful look covers Ronan's features. "As in, you'd do her?"

Ronan is the type who makes everything about sex—like Dan. However, from the time I've spent with them, I've learned that he's the one with the most heart out of the four horsemen.

Xander is too slippery. Cole's too silent. Aiden is too... Well, nothing. I can't grasp his real character, no matter how much I study him.

"Yes, I would." I keep up with Ronan's game.

"Take my fucking money," Ronan exclaims. "I want to watch. First row!"

"In your fucking dreams." Levi pushes him away with a hand on his face.

"Oh, come on, Captain. You already took away my cake bunny hookers fantasy."

"Cake bunny hookers?" I chuckle.

"Ronan wanted hookers dressed as bunnies coming out of his birthday cake," Cole says. "Captain denied it."

Wow. I don't even have words for that.

"You killed my fantasy once, Captain." Ronan talks in his dramatic voice. "You can't do it *une autre fois*. Two hot girls will be explosive. It's a waste if no one watches."

"Who said no one will watch?" Levi meets my gaze with his darkened, lust-filled one. "I would."

"I would watch, too," Aiden says without lifting his eyes from his phone.

I don't know which one to be more surprised by. Who knew both cousins had this side to them?

When we arrive at my class, Levi pulls me against him by the hips and leans in to whisper in my ear. "Locker room. After practice."

Last week, I snuck into the football team's locker room to surprise Levi. The surprise somehow ended up with me sucking him off in the showers before he fucked me against the lockers.

I still have the bruises and hickeys to prove it.

My body throbs and heats at the mere memory of that day.

"That was a one-time thing."

"I'm making it a multiple-times thing." His tongue slides to the shell of my ear. "Be there, Princess."

"Or what?" I lick my lips, unable to resist the urge to push him.

There's this sick thrill about getting under his skin.

"Or I'll bind you again." He pauses. "Wait. You'd like that, wouldn't you?"

I thin my lips to keep myself from screaming hell yes.

He taps my nose twice. The gesture has become an addiction. "I'll wait."

Like a lovesick idiot, I watch his strong, broad back as he retreats down the hall.

He's just too tall and well built, it's unfair.

My own Viking.

When I turn to get into class, someone slams their shoulder into mine on the way inside. Nicole.

She's been extra aggressive these past couple of weeks. I usually strike back, but I don't want to stir up a big problem with her. If she tells Dad about Levi and me, things will become murkier than ever.

The only reason she's keeping her mouth shut about my relationship with Levi is because I threatened her that her sexcapades with Christopher under Dad's roof would come to light as well.

That kept her in line. Sort of.

She and Chloe still throw remarks my way, whether in the halls or at the games when I go. I decided to tune them out as background noise.

I'm finally living my life as I've always wished, and I won't let them or anyone else ruin it for me.

With every session with Dr Edmonds, I've come to appreciate everything I have. I'm even coming to peace with myself that I might never recall my memories from the night of the accident and that it's completely fine.

My memories or whatever grudge I hold don't define me. My past doesn't define me.

Since that resolution, I've been more comfortable in my skin and I even started getting my muse back. Baby steps, but it's there.

I want to say it's all because of the therapy, but it's not. There's a different type of therapy wrapped in an enigma called Levi.

Ever since I found out he's the one who saved me that night, it's like someone breathed fresh air into my soul. My own type of a second chance.

I've been given that second chance for a reason. I always thought that Levi was my bully and my tormentor, but maybe since the beginning, he's been more.

I'm not naive enough to think that life with Levi is easy. It isn't. While he doesn't have his father's mental illness, he has a suffocating intensity that demands everything out of me.

Whenever he offers a piece of his heart, he confiscates part of mine in return. I'm just hoping it won't be broken beyond repair by the end.

We didn't start as some sort of a meet-cute. It was bloody and gruesome and a part of me knows that Levi will never be the Prince Charming type. I'm completely fine with that. I always preferred the villain, anyway.

I love our morning runs and our non-traditional dates. I love how he models for me just so he'll end up taking my clothes off and I'll be the one modelling for him. In bed.

Every time we have sex, it's like he's engraving himself into my soul, piece by each bloody piece.

It's become an addiction that I can't get enough of.

But more than anything, I know I can't get enough of him.

It's he who's turning my world upside down. The intense sex and the mind games are all a part of what he is.

Who he is.

And I want all of him.

Even with the feud between Dad and his uncle.

When I asked Levi if he wasn't curious about it, he said it was none of our business. We're not our families.

"Earth to Astrid."

My head snaps to Dan, who's been sitting on my desk, chatting about the upcoming game.

"Hey, crazy bugger." Dan jams a finger in my arm. "You weren't listening to me, were you?"

"I was. You're so going to nail it."

"Mrs Jills?" He scrunches his nose. "Thanks for the disgusting image of me nailing our fifty-year-old math teacher."

I break out in laughter. "Sorry, but hey, you do have a sex bucket list, after all."

"It doesn't include fifty-year-old teachers."

"No?"

"Freaking no way." He releases an exasperated sigh, throwing a glance to our right to where Nicole has been shooting daggers at us.

"Do you want a picture?" he asks her with sarcasm.

She flips her hair back. "As if anyone would need a reminder of your trashy face."

"Then stop looking."

"And you stop talking to me."

"Jesus." Dan faces me again, his features tight. "How do you live with her?"

"I sneak out all the time." I grin. "Never mind her."

"If she bothers you, let me know."

"So you'll defend my honour?"

"Hell yeah. It's in the freaking friendship manual that you should've read by now. You're like the laziest best friend ever."

"I'm working on it." I laugh. "Hey, Bug. Do you want to go shopping this weekend?"

He waggles his eyebrows. "Slutty lingerie for Captain?" His smile drops. "Wait. Wrong image."

"No." I chuckle. "I need serious interview clothes for Imperial College."

"Ah. That." He leans in. "You're not going to talk to your father about the Royal College of Art?"

Considering that Dad's been ghosting me in the house and hasn't attempted to force me into those dreadful breakfasts, I don't see the point.

"'This is your future. You're not supposed to make your parents happy at the expense of what will make you happy.'"

"Wow. Since when did you become so wise, Bug?"

His smile is faint. "Since I'm not going into engineering."

"Oh. Why not?" Dan's family owns an engineering company. He and Zach are expected to take over the family business.

Since I've become best friends with Dan, he's always planned to do engineering in Cambridge. He has all the high grades and impressive records to fly him there.

Now, I feel like a horrible friend for not picking up on his change of heart earlier.

"I'm going to be a solicitor."

"That's also cool, but what made you change your mind?"

"Engineers are considered nerdy, especially in college. Besides, solicitors have a more active sex life."

"Please tell me you're not changing your interest because of the sex life."

"It plays a part. Okay, a *huge* part. But no, I feel like I'm more fit for winning verbal arguments."

I hold his hand. "I'm so proud of you. Whatever you choose, Bug."

"Me, too." He removes his hand. "But don't touch me. Captain is fucking crazy about that."

Both of us laugh, knowing exactly how true that is.

My phone vibrates with a text.

Dad: Meet me in the school's car park.

My heart starts beating fast. Why would Dad come to meet me at school?

"Do you want me to go with you?" Dan asks, apparently having seen the text.

"No. I'm cool. It's going to be cool."

I'm lying.

I'm freaking out on the inside.

Dad told me two days ago that he wanted to talk to the

family about something important, but I never thought it'd be so soon.

Maybe he's had enough and will finally adopt Nicole and throw me away.

As I walk out of the school, my chest tightens until it's painful.

All this time, I've convinced myself that I don't care if Dad adopts Nicole. It's not like I want to be Clifford's princess anyway. But now that it's becoming a reality, I feel like crying.

He's my dad, not hers. *Mine.*

Deep inside, there's a part that still longs for the father who used to carry me on his shoulders when I was a little girl.

The sound of rain fills the car park. Since it's close to the afternoon, almost all students' and teachers' cars are gone.

I open my umbrella and step onto the wet pavement.

It's dark and humid and so freaking wet. If I weren't so out-of-my-mind anxious, I'd drop the umbrella and stand in the rain.

I walk into the car park, searching for Dad's Mercedes. It's getting darker and no lights are turned on, so I can't see long distance.

My phone vibrates.

Levi: Practice was cancelled. Come to the locker room.

Just reading his text lifts something heavy and crushing off my chest. The thought of him always puts me in a special mood. It's like I become invincible knowing he'll always be there for me.

Since Mum's death, I've been like the living dead. Until Levi breathed life into me.

I open the text to type back when strong lights blind me. I freeze and a tremor shoots through my limbs.

I continue staring ahead, but I can't see anything due to the light. Just like that day at the party.

My heartbeat speeds up and my hands tremble so hard, the phone clutters to the ground.

Move. Move. Freaking move.

Everything around me disappears except for the sound of the downpour, the smell of the earth after the rain, and blinding white light.

"Honey, give me the phone."

"Is it Dad again?" I can't help the disregard in my tone.

Mum smiles. "We have big news for you, honey."

"Is it about Grandpa's death?"

Her brow furrows. "Well, yes, but this means something more for us. For our family."

"Family? What family, Mum? He's married and happy with his blondie aristocrat and daughter. He's not a part of our family."

"Star." Her voice softens. "Everything isn't what it seems."

"Yeah, sure thing, Mum. Dad didn't leave us for another freaking family."

"Didn't you say you wanted to live with him?"

I rummage in her bag for the phone. "That was eons ago. I'm never living with him without you."

She draws in a deep breath. "I'm done running, hon. I'm ready now."

"For what?"

"Shit. Fuck!" Mum curses as she swerves the car.

I look up through the rain-covered windshield as she claxons for a long second.

"Move!" she shrieks and I watch in horror as she tries to swivel past a dog in the middle of the street.

When she turns the car around the dirt side, the first thing I see is a man.

It's funny how such moments happen in slow motion, even though it's a mere fraction of a second.

The man has his hands apart, his eyes closed, and his head tipped back as the rain beats down on him.

He looks so...at peace.

Mum hits the brakes, but we don't stop. Then I don't get a chance to scream as something thuds against the car and we flip over.

I'm thrust back to the present, gasping for air. I'm on my knees on the concrete floor, clutching my head between shaky hands.

"Astrid?" A hand clutches my arm.

I look up slowly. Dad is staring down at me with a furrowed expression.

"Are you okay? What happened?" He pulls me to my feet and I hold on to his arm with all my might as if he's my safety net.

"D-Dad," I cry, tears streaming down my cheeks. "Please tell me the other person who died during the accident wasn't James King. *Please.*"

His mouth clamps shut and it's all the answer I need before the world goes black.

My mother killed Levi's father.

FORTY-EIGHT

Levi

There's no warning when everything comes crashing down.

Astrid doesn't show up in the locker room. Either she's playing hard to get or something's wrong.

I sure as fuck hope for the first option.

I call and she doesn't pick up. I ask Daniel about her whereabouts and he says she met her father and must've gone home with him.

She answers none of my texts or calls.

My mood blackens when she doesn't show up for school the next day or the next.

She's been ghosting me for three whole fucking days.

If this is payback about those two weeks from hell, then I'll take it. But Astrid isn't as black-hearted as I am. Sure, she's a complete nut job when she wants to be, but she's not vindictive.

Unless…something really wrong is going on.

After practice, I'm in the car when my phone beeps with a text from Uncle's security company.

This could and will get back to him, but I'll take that risk. I kept that smashed footage of the summer party, but after that day on the Ferris wheel, I want to know the truth more than Astrid does.

I knew Jonathan's company would get it done even before the police, that's why I asked for a favour from Uncle's people.

My brows crease as I watch what happened that day.

Astrid banged on my door after I kicked her out. If I hadn't kicked her out, that accident wouldn't have happened.

She danced under the moon all alone like a fucking angel.

My jaw clenches as she starts running. I go through all the other cameras, trying to get a view of the two who are running after her.

Him.

I knew it.

I continue watching the footage, but the cameras stop right at the road. There's no footage of Astrid being hit. There's only a side view of the car that's speeding down the road.

I'm about to close it when I notice something.

Wait a fucking second.

I replay it back and then forth. Back and forth.

Well, fuck.

This changes everything.

Aiden, Xan, Ronan, and Cole stand by my side as Chris shivers on the ground alongside his minions.

My knuckles are bleeding from beating him to a pulp. He just admitted to being behind the photos that Xander showed me. He wanted to get back at me, so he ruined my '*plaything*'. That got him a punch that broke his nose.

The two juniors, David and Michael, remain huddled in the corner, stammering that they didn't do anything.

I pull Chris by the collar until I'm breathing in his face. "Now, tell me everything."

"You told us no fucking mistakes," he snarls, showing bloodied teeth. "She heard us talking and I had to shut her the fuck up."

"So you planned an accident?"

"What the fuck?" He coughs blood. "We had nothing to do with the accident. We only chased her to shut her up."

My hold falters on his collar. I planned the fire. I had Chris and the two juniors execute it with me because I didn't want Aiden and his gang to get a whiff of my rebellion against Jonathan.

The trembling juniors in the corner who keep repeating that they only did what they were told aren't to blame. I am.

I knew that Chris was volatile and had a knack for danger, but I still used that to my advantage. Michael and David are just pawns who would do anything for their captain. Including arson—and possibly murder.

I might not have driven the car that hit Astrid that night, but I played a role in it.

"We only did what Christopher said." Michael looks about ready to pee himself. "I wanted to tell the police everything, but my stepfather will kick me out of the house if I have a criminal record."

"We're sorry, Captain," David stammers. "P-please forgive us."

"That depends." I push Chris up when he almost falls to the ground.

"On what?" Michael asks.

"Tell me everything you saw that night." I glare down at Chris. "And you. Tell me why the fuck you've been sleeping with Astrid's stepsister."

When the three of them are finished, the image starts forming in my head.

I'm only missing one link.

Just a little something.

And I have to risk my future to see the end of it.

For Astrid, it's fucking worth it.

"K-King?" Nicole stares up at me with wide eyes as I stand in front of their door.

I spent all night watching footage after footage of that party and keeping screenshots and short clips for evidence

There are a few interesting things that came to light.

Nicole casts a cautious glance over her shoulder, then closes the door and steps outside. "You're not supposed to be here, my stepfather will kill you."

I glance behind her, even though the door is shut. "Is Astrid here?"

She twists her lips. "You should leave."

"Not going to happen." I start to push past her, stop, and look down at her. "There's something I'm curious about, Nicole."

She licks her lips, flipping her blonde hair back. "What is it?"

"Did you fuck Daniel after you put something in his drink?"

Her face turns white. "I-I don't know what you're talking about."

I pull out my phone and show her two clips that prove her implication. She put pills in two shot glasses and offers one to Daniel. Then he takes the other and shoves it in Astrid's hand.

Nicole begins shaking and swallows hard.

"Now," I continue, "there are no cameras inside the rooms, so tell me, were you fucking Daniel while Astrid had her accident?"

"K-King, I... I...didn't mean for it go that far, I promise."

I barge into her space. "I have enough evidence for Daniel to charge you with rape."

"That... That's not..."

"What was your plan exactly? Have him and Astrid fuck? Are you a voyeur or is this some other fucked up kink?"

"That drink was supposed to be mine, not Astrid's! Daniel is supposed to be mine, not hers. But he had to snatch my damn drink and give it to his stupid Astrid. I studied with him all my life, but she waltzes in here one day and he becomes best friends with her overnight. What does she have that I don't?"

"So you decided to rape him?"

Her lips tremble. "I...I didn't. You don't know what happened, so shut up."

"Then you mind telling me why you whored yourself to Chris after?"

"I only did that to make Daniel jealous."

"Let me guess. It didn't work. So you used Chris to find out if anyone knew what you did that night or if there was any footage to implicate you."

"No. I didn't even know there were cameras. Do you think I'm stupid enough to have done it if I did?"

Huh. That changes things.

The door opens and Nicole wipes her cheeks, murmuring, "Please."

"Is something the matter?" a woman asks in a posh voice.

Victoria Clifford, Nicole's mother, stares between us with a cool yet welcoming expression.

"Nothing's wrong, Mother." Nicole pleads with her eyes again.

She'll end up falling, but I don't have time for her now.

"May I help you?" Victoria asks me.

"Yes. I'm here to see Lord Clifford."

FORTY-NINE

Levi

The king always falls down without his queen.

Astrid's father stares down at me, even though we're both sitting in his office.

Uncle says that aristocrats are like that. They like to look down their noses at people. They like thinking they have royal blood and whatnot.

At the end of the day, moguls like those at King Enterprises are the real royalties.

However, it's not my name that I take pride in as I meet Lord Clifford's icy stares.

It's not my past or my present.

It's the future. Mine and Astrid's.

Lord Clifford listens with a blank expression as I tell him everything I've uncovered.

Once he finishes watching the clips of footage I've sent, he closes the laptop. Aside from the slight tightening in his jaw, he doesn't show any reaction.

Man of steel. Just like Jonathan.

His desk is large and made of mahogany wood, but aside from the laptop and his glass of scotch, there aren't many belongings.

"You do realise that there's enough evidence to implicate you

CRUEL KING | 297

for arson and withholding evidence. You're already eighteen, so it'll be full charges," he speaks in a calm and composed tone as if he's in a meeting at the House of Lords.

"Actually, there's no proof of me doing any arson. I know all the cameras, so I made sure to move in their blind spots. As for withholding evidence, the police lost the footage. Their incompetence isn't my fault. Last I checked, recovering a spoilt flash drive I found lying about on our property isn't a crime. Putting all that aside. In case of any charges, Jonathan will make sure I come out unscathed."

Lord Clifford's lips pull in a sardonic smile. "You're that scoundrel's blood indeed. Did he teach you to be a dick?"

"It's natural. Comes with the family name."

He raises an eyebrow. "But he's holding you on a leash. What you just did will ruin your future and force you to spend seven more years under that tyrant's hand."

"How…" I clear my throat. "How did you know that?"

"You think I wouldn't search the background of someone I found in bed with my only daughter?"

"Touché."

He takes a sip of his drink without breaking eye contact. "You chose to process this evidence despite threats from Jonathan?"

"Yes," I say without a sliver of doubt.

"Why?"

"Because I want justice for Astrid."

"How about justice for your father?" His calm question catches me by surprise.

I look down, trying to school my expression. Since Uncle told me about the accident three years ago, I've been having a constant battle with myself.

What I want and what I need.

What I lost and what I can have.

The past and the future.

But I already made the choice.

"You already know." Lord Clifford puts his glass on the table with a clank.

I nod. "But I still want to see where this goes with Astrid and —"

"Absolutely not," he cuts me off, standing.

"With all due respect, Astrid and I have nothing to do with what happened in the past or the feud between you and Uncle. We're our own people and deserve to be treated as such."

"You're not naive enough to think that, are you?" He strides from around the desk to stand in front of me. "The feud between me and that scoundrel, King, is because he blamed Astrid's mother for the accident, saying she killed your father. I've been trying to prove that something suspicious happened. Jasmine was a careful driver and never got a ticket in her entire life."

"It was an accident in which both of them died." I grind my teeth. "It's over. It's in the past."

He releases a sigh. "Tell that to my daughter, who's locked herself in her room for days since she remembered the accident."

I stand up slowly. "She remembers?"

"Yes."

"Let me talk to her." I swallow and say the word I never thought I would say, "Please."

He shakes his head.

"Astrid and I are the same. We both lost our parents that night. I understand her the best."

"You understand nothing, son. Astrid is locking herself up because she thinks that her mother killed James. She feels guilty towards you. Seeing you is the last thing she needs."

"Fuck," I curse under my breath, using the desk's edge as support.

Does this mean I've lost her once and for all?

No. I won't accept that.

"One time," I ask Lord Clifford again. "Let me see her just one more time."

"Seeing your face will only remind her of her guilt. It'll hurt her and I promised that wouldn't happen anymore." He pauses. "Besides, it was indirect, but you participated in her accident. It's best if you both go your separate ways."

"I don't want that," I grit out.

"You can't always get what you want. Welcome to life."

At home, I stand in front of the glass chessboard and stare down at the black king piece.

Dad always liked playing in black and I picked up the habit after he taught me how to play.

On my way out of Lord Clifford's house, I stood outside, looking at all the windows, hoping Astrid would peek out from one of them.

She didn't.

"I'm so sorry, Father," I tell the king piece.

I chose the future over the past, but I lost both of them.

"Look who's graced us with his presence."

My shoulders droop as Uncle sits on the white king's side. He must've just returned from an all-nighter in the office. Or two nights, judging from his unshaven face and his missing tie and jacket.

"Care for a game?" he asks.

I sit down and rearrange Aiden's last game that he played against himself.

Uncle reaches behind him and pours us two glasses of cognac.

I raise an eyebrow when he offers me one. "What did I do to earn a drink from Jonathan King himself?"

He clinks my glass. "You were born a King."

"I'm more of a vodka person myself, but oh well…"

He narrows his eyes. "Now I know where all those bottles disappeared to."

I shrug and take my first swig. The bitter taste leaves a burn at the back of my throat. Placing my drink on the side of the board, I push my first pawn forward, mimicking Uncle's first move. It'll be good to receive the news of my fall to hell while playing chess.

"I had a call from the deputy commissioner."

Here we go.

"I'm guessing it's not because I beat his son to a pulp?"

"You did that?" He fixes in on me with his impenetrable gaze, twirling his drink. "What did I say about violence?"

"It doesn't solve anything." I grin. "But it sure answers questions."

He shakes his head. "You're so much like James, it's uncanny."

"My father wasn't a violent man." After a few moves of my pawns, I push my knight forward.

"Sure was when he was a punk your age."

Huh. Maybe Father and I are more alike than I thought.

"Did you hate him for that?" I ask.

"James was my oldest brother and only sibling. I never hated him."

"But you were always breathing down his neck."

"Because he was slowly committing suicide with all those drugs and parties and whatnot."

"Let me guess, you've been keeping me on a leash so I don't grow up to be like him."

"Of course." He swallows my knight in a full dick move. "What did you think it was?"

"Anyone ever tell you that you have a shitty way of showing you care?"

He shrugs and takes a drink of his cognac. "I do what it takes to protect my family."

"By being a dictator?"

"The methods don't matter. The results do."

I scoff. Some things never change.

While he's drinking, I notice an opening and use my queen to kill his bishop.

He raises an eyebrow, probably since I left my king unprotected. It doesn't matter. My rook is in place and if he makes a move, his queen will be unprotected.

"You made a mess," he says, and something tells me it's not about the game.

"I'm ready for the consequences."

"You know." He chuckles with nostalgia. "I could never beat James in chess. It drove me insane."

"No way. You actually lose."

"I actually lose." He brings his drink to his mouth, then stops. "I was the nerd in the family while James was the popular one. He got all the attention, all the stardom, and all the girls. And yet, he kept beating me at chess, which was supposed to be my speciality. One day, I asked him how he did it, and he said, *You're too uptight, little brother. Don't play the game —*"

"Play the player," I finish for him.

He nods. "I understand the full meaning behind his words now. I shouldn't have controlled you. It was an epic failure and I lost my holiday home because of it."

I go to attack his queen but stop. "I'm...sorry?"

He scoffs. "We both know you don't mean that."

"I would if you drop the entire case against Lord Clifford's ex-wife."

"There's no case to drop. Both Clifford and I buried the accident for a reason. He didn't want his ex-wife's name in the press, and I didn't want the press to broadcast that my brother was drunk and high at the time of his death." He points his glass at me. "Clifford and I agreed to make each other's lives hell since then, though. I'm winning, by the way."

"Of course you are. You always win, Uncle."

"Not always, punk. No matter what I did, I lost my brother." He pushes me back using his rook. "I won't lose you as well."

I hesitate before clutching my bishop. If this is a tactic to make me doubt my next move, it's fucking working.

"You want to play professionally? You have what it takes."

"I…do?"

"On one condition."

I eat his queen and grin. "Ha. I'm listening."

"Checkmate, punk." He grins back. "Sacrificing the queen for the king is a pleasure."

No. It's not.

I stare at my king surrounded by Uncle's rook and knight.

The bastard couldn't protect himself or his queen and now their entire kingdom is all fucking over before it properly started.

I shake my head, focusing back on Uncle. "You'll really let me play professionally or was that a ploy?"

"Both." He smiles. "Here's what you have to do in return."

FIFTY

Astrid

Everything ends. Even a war.

A harsh breath leaves my lips as I watch Levi's retreating back from the window of my room.

An itch urges me to run after him and hug him.

I want to hug him so badly and not just because I need a hug myself.

When Sarah told me someone by the last name King had come over, I nearly had a heart attack. It took everything in me not to go and protect him from Dad.

But I couldn't face him.

I doubt I ever will.

Levi had a deep connection with his father and once he knows the truth about what happened three years ago, he won't look at me again.

I hang my head against the window's frame and hit my forehead against it over and over again.

A hug. I totally need a hug right now.

Fetching my phone, I open it. I'm bombarded by the notifications. I attempt to ignore them, but then I read a notification from the school's students' group.

'There's a murderer's daughter in RES.'

My heart almost leaps out of my throat as I open the original post.

Someone from the journalist group says that he received a tip that there's a murderer's daughter studying in RES and he'll soon reveal the name.

My breath becomes shortened and the room starts spinning.

How... How could they have found out so soon?

Only Dad and I knew.

And...Jonathan King. Could this be his way to destroy my father through me?

But wouldn't that also sully the school's name?

He owns most of the shares, so why would he destroy it?

I'm about to call Dan when someone bangs on my door so hard, I flinch.

Before I can react, Nicole barges inside and closes the door behind her.

She's dishevelled. Her eyes are bloodshot and tears stream down her cheeks. Her hair is in all directions.

"What's going —"

"I had nothing to do with whatever happened that night," she blurts, eyes shifty. "I really know nothing about your accident, I just wanted Daniel. That's all."

"You wanted Daniel?" I repeat, incredulous. "As in, my best friend, Dan?"

"Yes, yes, that Dan!"

"But...you always insult him and look down on him."

"Defence mechanism, idiot." She sniffles. "I didn't mean to drug you. I gave him one shot and the other was supposed to be mine, but he had to snatch it from between my fingers and give it to you."

Oh.

"Wait. Dan was also drugged?"

"Yes, and he spent the night with me." She lifts her chin.

"Oh. My. God." I stomp towards her. "What the fuck did you do to him, Nicole?"

"It's all because of you," she snarls back. "Since you came into my life, my house, my school, everything became fucking hell. He was mine first. I saw him *first*! Why can't you just leave so everything can go back to the way it was?"

She storms out before I can say anything.

I don't have time for her anyway.

Oh, God. I've been so blind this whole time.

I wasn't the only one traumatised that night. Dan was assaulted, too. Why didn't he say a word about it?

I call him, but he doesn't pick up.

"Dammit, Dan," my voice chokes out. "Pick up."

I continue calling him as I throw on a hoodie. I need to find him, then strangle him for hiding this—after I hug him.

On my way out of my room, I run into Dad. I step back, my head lowering.

"Uh, Dad—Sorry, I mean, Father. I have to see Dan."

"Can that wait for a bit?" He walks inside. "Besides, Daniel is with the council."

"F-for what?"

"His school orientation," Dad says. "He mentioned it to Sarah when he came by this morning and you didn't want to see anyone. He said he'll drop by later."

"Oh, right. Okay." I release a breath. I don't know why I thought he was in danger.

Dad continues walking into my room as if he's seeing it for the first time.

I swallow. "Is there something you want to talk about, Dad?" I wince. "Sorry, I mean, Father."

"Dad is fine." His eyes soften. "I'm sorry I made you call me something you didn't relate to, Astrid."

"O-okay." I don't know why I feel more nervous now that Dad is allowing me to call him Dad.

It strangely feels like the last meal they offer to inmates before their death sentence.

Will he announce that he's adopting Nicole now?

He settles on the edge of the bed. "Do you want to sit down?"

I realise I'm hugging the doorframe as if I'm looking for an escape. With a reluctant heart, I release it and step towards my father.

I sit as far away from him as I can while still on the same bed.

My heart beats so loudly, I can only hear the buzzing in my ears. It's like that time when both my parents sat me down to tell me that Dad wouldn't be visiting us as often anymore.

I'm bracing myself for the bad news. No matter how much of it I receive lately, it doesn't get any easier.

Before he can speak, I blurt out what I've been too much of a coward to say all these weeks, "I'm sorry, Dad."

"For what?"

"For saying what I said that day. I was angry. I didn't mean that I, you know, wanted you dead. I don't. You're my...dad. I just miss my mum and I wish I had both of you beside me."

He releases a long sigh. "Me, too."

"Really?"

"Yes. Jasmine and I decided to reunite officially right before her accident." A sheen of sadness covers his gaze. "It remained as a dream, after all."

"Wait. You planned to divorce Victoria? But wasn't she your wife since I was seven?"

"On paper, yes. She's the perfect wife chosen by my parents, but she was never my wife. Your mother is the only woman I wanted to marry."

"Then why didn't you?"

"I did." He scratches his forehead and clears his throat. "In Vegas."

"Vegas? As in Las Vegas?"

"Yes. That's the one."

Whoa. I somehow can't imagine my dad, Lord Henry Clifford, heir to the Clifford household and a member of the House of Lords, visiting Vegas, let alone having a Vegas wedding.

"Mum never mentioned that."

"But she told you that you weren't illegitimate, didn't she?"

"Yeah, she did." Her version was that they registered their marriage secretly and that's it.

"What is it?" he asks, when I remain quiet for long beats.

I smile awkwardly. "Sorry, I'm still wrapping my head around the Vegas part."

"I wasn't always so put together, you know. I was quite wild in my youth. How do you think I met your mother?"

"She left that part vague. She mentioned something about a party?"

"I guess she could've called it a party." He shakes his head with a nostalgic smile. "That was probably her PG-13 version. My friends and I partied and gambled all night. In our drunken minds, we decided it was an epic idea to get skull tattoos. We went to this parlour down the road and Jasmine was there. She was…stunning. And I may have pushed my mates aside so she'd tattoo me. Only, she made fun of my skull idea and how 'unoriginal' it was. So I gave her free rein to do anything as long as it could be hidden by clothes." He pauses as if tasting his own words. "She looked out of her skin with joy. I've never seen someone look so happy before. Apparently, it was the first time someone had given her artistic freedom. She promised that I wouldn't be disappointed."

I inch closer to him. "And what did she do?"

I didn't realise Dad had a tattoo. Or maybe I did from when he lived with us and forgot about it.

He stands up and unbuttons his shirt. "I'll show you instead."

My jaw would've dropped to the floor if it weren't attached to my mouth.

A black and red phoenix tattoo covers the middle half of Dad's back in a 3D style sketch. Its tendrils resemble flames.

"Wow."

I've seen so much of Mum's work, but this is her most passionate one. I strive to sketch like her one day.

"That's not all." He rolls up his sleeves to show me small

tattoos in a vertical line along his forearm. A sun. A moon. A star. The sun on Dad's arm is black.

"Like mine." I show him my tattoo at the same place as his. However, in mine, the star is coloured black.

And in Mum's tattoo, the moon is in black. I chuckle. "She got us matching tattoos."

"I was against it since you were only fifteen, but I'm glad she did it anyway." Dad smiles as he buttons his shirt and sits beside me again.

"How long did she take to do the phoenix?"

"About a week. We talked so much during that time. It was the first time someone had genuine interest in me and not in my family name. So afterwards, I hid my real identity from her. We stayed together for months before I took her to Vegas."

"How did Mum find out about who you are?"

"The horrible way. My parents got involved and it wasn't pretty. People like me aren't supposed to be with people like Jasmine. Even though I knew that, I couldn't lose her. Especially when she was pregnant with you."

I continue itching closer until there's no space left between us. "What did you do?"

"I struck a deal with my father. The marriage would remain under the radar, and so would you and Jasmine. If I'd refused, they would've done it the harsh way and it would've hurt Jasmine." He stops meeting my eyes with his identical ones. "Those seven years I spent with you two were the happiest times of my life, Star."

A sob catches at the back of my throat. "Then why did you leave? Why did you end up marrying Victoria and tossing me and Mum aside?"

"Your mum did the tossing, actually. Now, I realise it must've been a ploy from either my father or Victoria or her parents. Or all of them. I had to leave. I'm the only heir to my family and I knew if I didn't obey, my parents would've buried you and Jasmine until I could never find you."

"Bad things for the greater good."

"No, Astrid. No." He holds my shoulders. "There was no greater good about leaving you and your mother. There hasn't been a day that I didn't regret it. But every time I went back, Jasmine pushed me out. She allowed me to see you sometimes, but she cut me off from your lives, saying you two didn't fit into my world. Her constant rejections were my punishment."

"You really planned to reunite with Mum?"

"Yes. After my father's death, I was done with the masquerade. I finally convinced Jasmine to give me another chance and she agreed." His face turns rigid. "But it never happened."

"She was really happy that night, Dad." I smile, fighting the pressure at the back of my throat. "I'm the one who threw a tantrum."

"It wasn't your fault. You didn't know." He pauses. "Astrid, this period will be hard for the family. I need you to be strong. Can you do that for me?"

I nod slowly, my voice catching. "What will happen?"

"Some people will pay." His demeanour hardens.

We remain silent for long seconds until it almost becomes awkward.

"Can I tell you something, Dad?"

"Anything."

I gather all my courage and blurt, "I don't want to go to Imperial College. I want to study art like my mum."

"All right."

"All…right?" My mouth hangs open.

"Of course. I won't make you study something you dislike. Besides, you have too much talent to waste."

I don't know which part should surprise me the most. The fact that Dad saw my sketches or that he's letting me study art.

"Thank you," I murmur, my voice catching in my throat. "All this time, I thought… I thought you hated me."

"Oh, come here, Astrid." He opens his arms and I dive into them, wrapping my hands around his waist. A sob tears from my throat and I can't help the tears.

"I'm sorry, I'm so sorry I made you feel that way." He strokes my hair back. "I was scared I'd lose you, too, so I was stern. Now, I realise that's not what you needed."

"I just… I just miss Mum so much and you're the only one who reminds me of her."

"I miss her, too." He kisses the top of my head. "I'm sorry I couldn't grieve with you. I wanted you to move on with your life, but that was wrong, too. You needed to grieve properly first. I promise to learn from my mistakes and be a better father for you."

I look up at him through blurry eyes. "You won't throw me away and adopt Nicole?"

He laughs. "That nonsense was never on the table. You're the only daughter I have. Nicole will leave after her mother is sent away."

"What do you mean by sent away?"

Dad opens his mouth to speak when the door barges open. Victoria walks inside with Grandpa's antique shotgun pointed towards us.

"No one will send me away."

FIFTY-ONE

Levi

Was it all just a fantasy?

I stare up at Lord Clifford's mansion.

Logically, I should've given Astrid time to cope, but patience has never been one of my qualities.

If I have to climb through a window and search every room to find her, so be it.

We're going to talk, then I'll kiss the living hell out of her. Or it can be the other way around. The order doesn't matter.

Astrid and I aren't something decided by an accident three years ago. We're more. We're a lot fucking more.

Astrid didn't only engrave herself in my soul, she's also become an inseparable part of my core. And no fucking one can take that away from me.

Not even her.

"Captain?" Daniel calls from my side. "What are you doing here?"

"The same as you. To see Astrid." I narrow my eyes. "But I came first, so wait for your turn."

He releases a sigh. "She's going through a lot. Maybe you should give her some time to cope. Ever heard of that term?"

"Whatever coping there is to be done, Astrid and I are doing it together." I push past him towards the entrance.

He grips my shoulder and pulls me back with a force I didn't realise he had.

"Fucking stop. She's not like you. Astrid isn't the type who goes forward, not caring about those left behind."

"Is that what you think I am?"

"That's what the whole team thinks you are! They're just too scared to say it to your face."

"Yeah? What have I been doing?"

He throws his hands in the air. "You've been torturing us more than Coach for the championship."

"So now we don't want the championship?"

"We do, but we started this to have fun. Not all of us are going pro. Hell, not even half of us." He releases a deep breath. "This is the last season we'll ever be able to compete in football before it all becomes corporations and politics."

Huh. I never looked at it that way.

"Nice talk." I pat Daniel's shoulder. "Let's finish after I see Astrid."

"Captain!" He runs alongside me. "You're not hearing a word I'm saying. She needs time. Once she's calmed down, she'll come out on her own accord and talk to you."

"What if she never does?" I meet Daniel's eyes. "What if she spends distance away and realises that she doesn't fucking want me anymore?"

He remains silent for a second too long. "Then it's her choice. Another word you need to learn."

I jab a finger at his chest. "That's not going to fucking happen."

Daniel tries to stop me again when a loud sound slices through the silence.

We both pause and stare at each other with wild eyes.

A gunshot just came from inside Astrid's house.

FIFTY-TWO

Astrid

Everyone falls. Including the king and his queen.

I shriek when the gunshot reverberates all around us.

My fingers dig into Dad's forearm as my frantic gaze slides over him, looking for any injury.

"I'm fine, Astrid." He motions behind him to a hole in the wall.

My heartbeat skyrockets until it's impossible to focus on anything but the buzzing in my ears.

"Put the shotgun down, Victoria," Dad speaks in a calm yet firm tone as he cages me behind him.

Still, I peek around him.

Victoria stands at my door, her finger trembling on the trigger. For the first time in my life, I see tears streaming down her cheeks.

I've always joked with Dan that she was an unfeeling robot, considering she didn't show emotions. But I should've known that those are the most dangerous types.

"I stood by you." Her voice is shaky and she seems on the verge of a nervous breakdown. "I was the perfect wife for you. I did everything from those dinners to those stupid wives' gatherings. How dare you throw me away?"

"We had a deal, Victoria," he tells her slowly. "I told you the marriage was a contract. I provided a home for you and your daughter and paid your dead husband's debts. In return, you played the wife's façade. You agreed to those terms."

"I thought you'd come around." Her finger remains unsteady on the trigger, and I shrink further behind Dad's back. "I waited for you. We could've been a real family..." She smiles in nostalgia, but then it drops. "If it weren't for that slut."

"My mother wasn't a slut," I grit out.

"And you!" She points both her gun and manic expression at me. "The Clifford name is my daughter's right. You don't deserve anything except for rotting with your whore of a mother. But you just refuse to fucking die."

My lips part as I choke on air. My gaze slides from her to Dad. His jaw clenches, but he keeps his calm. "So you did it. You hit Astrid at the party."

"Yes, I *did* it. I went to pick up Nicole, and this little bitch was running in the street, begging to be hit." She laughs. "I slowed down, about to stop, but then I thought that if you joined your mother, we'd finally be a real family."

My eyes blur as I stare at the monster in her eyes. She planned to kill me. It wasn't an accident. She did it on purpose.

Anger bubbles in my veins like a hurricane, and then it hits me. The old Mercedes Nicole drove the other day was the same Mercedes I saw parked near our house the day before Mum's accident.

"You manipulated my mother's brakes, didn't you?"

"I did that, too." She smiles like a psycho. "Henry was planning to divorce me and remarry her, so I decided to erase her. Pity you didn't go down with her like a good little bitch."

I scream and push past Dad towards her. I'm going to murder her. I'm going to choke her with my bare hands.

Dad yanks me back as Victoria's stance widens in menace.

"Let me go!" I cry, tears streaming down my cheeks. "Dad, let me go!"

"Yes, let her go, Henry." Her voice is soft, motherly almost. "If you do, we'll finally be a family."

"We were never going to be a family!" Dad's voice rises. "The only family I wanted was Jasmine and Astrid."

"No." A tear slides down her cheek. "You only felt duty towards her because she trapped you with a baby."

"There was no duty about Jasmine. She's the only woman I ever loved."

"No. Henry. We're a *family*."

"Not anymore." His voice turns to steel.

"You!" she screams, aiming her shotgun at me. "It's all because of you. I'm going to kill you this time."

I swallow, my limbs trembling until it's impossible to control them.

Dad stands fully in front of me until I can barely see anything.

"Drop the gun, Victoria," he speaks low. "Don't make this worse than it already is."

She shakes her head frantically.

"The police are on their way," he enunciates. "It's over."

"No! No! That little bitch doesn't get to live her life while I rot behind bars."

"Mother."

All our attention snaps to the voice coming from behind Victoria.

Nicole stands on wobbly legs with Levi and Dan behind her. They came.

Tears fill my eyes. Levi returned for me. He didn't give up on me.

Our eyes meet for the briefest second and in his light blue ones, I see concern and longing. Desperate, intense longing that matches my own.

"N-Nicole?" Victoria stammers. "Go back to your room, darling. I'll take care of this and come fetch you, okay?"

"Mother, stop." Nicole's voice shakes with every word like she's finding it hard to speak. "Please."

"But, honey. I'm doing this for us. For your future. You'll be a Clifford soon."

"I don't want to be a Clifford. I love Dad's name just fine."

"What are you talking about? That's what we worked for."

"That's what *you* worked for. I only wanted to be free of all these shackles and protocols and wearing masks." She hiccoughs. "I only put up with this life for you, Mother."

"But…what about your future and the doors the family name will open for you?" She pauses. "We'll talk about this later after I finish this."

Dan nudges Nicole, and she winces before stepping forward.

"Mother, *please*." She reaches a trembling hand towards her mother. "Uncle Henry has always given us everything we wanted. You can't hurt him."

"I won't hurt him. It's his daughter that I'll kill."

"Stop!" she shrieks. "Just stop it, Mother. I already lost my father. I can't lose you, too."

Victoria lowers her gun, tears shining in her eyes. "I… I did all of it for you, darling. I did everything so you could have a better life."

"I know," Nicole cries, pulling her mother into a hug. "I know."

I gasp as Levi steps forward and grabs the shotgun out of Victoria's fingers.

For a second, I think it'll go off and kill him, or Victoria will put up a fight and shoot him.

I only breathe in relief when it remains inert in his hand.

Dad tugs me to his side, his arms clasped tightly around my back in a protective hold.

I hug him back, even though a part of me wants to run to Levi and kiss him.

Officers barge inside with the deputy commissioner in tow. An officer yanks Victoria's arms behind her back and handcuffs her.

"Victoria Clifford, you're under arrest for the attempted

murders of Jasmine Green and Astrid Clifford. You have the right to remain silent…"

As the officer reads Victoria her rights, Nicole sobs, begging them to let her go.

Even though I don't feel the slightest sympathy for Victoria and I'm happy she's finally getting what she deserves, I can't help feeling bad for Nicole.

Life as she knows it is over. She's lost both of her parents and there's nothing she can do to stop it or turn back time.

Daniel clutches Nicole's shoulder, pulling her back, when she keeps holding on to her mother. She tries to fight him, but Victoria shakes her head.

In true Victoria style, she stops crying and lifts her chin like the aristocrat she is.

Dad pats my hand and walks towards her. He nods at Dan to take Nicole away. Once my stepsister's sobs disappear down the hall, Dad stares down at Victoria with the most furious expression I've ever seen on his face.

"You took a life from me and I promise that I'll take yours in return," he speaks with pure contempt that causes my skin to crawl. "I'll make sure you rot in prison until the day you die."

Her breathing hitches as she shakes her head again.

Dad exchanges a look with the deputy commissioner before they all walk down the hall.

I go to follow them when Levi blocks my path, staring down at me with a crease between his brows.

He must've given the shotgun to one of the officers, because his hands are empty. When he opens his arms, I want to dive into them so hard.

I want to cry into his embrace and tell him how much I love him.

But that would only be torture for the both of us.

Our fate was decided on a rainy night three years ago by a stray dog. Nothing short of a time travel machine would change the past.

Maybe then, Mum would be alive and married to Dad. Maybe then, Levi's father would be alive, too.

Maybe there wouldn't be a feud between Jonathan King and Lord Henry Clifford.

Maybe we would have met under different circumstances.

But there are no maybes in my life. There are no time travel machines either.

Truth is, we were over before we even started.

And that hurts.

"Astrid..." he trails off as if he can't find the words. "I love you. I'm fucking crazy about you, Princess."

Tears surge into my eyes, but I push them back.

Be strong.

You have to be strong.

"And I love you, Levi," I murmur the words as if I'm afraid of them.

I'm afraid that now that they're out there, I've doomed myself to a harder fall.

He smiles as his lips capture mine.

It's impossible to resist him. I can't.

I'm crashing and burning, but I still enjoy every hit. Every lash. Every spark.

The kiss is filled with so much passion and so many unspoken words. It's like he's begging me to stay with him. To never leave him. And I'm tempted to do just that.

But I can't.

I place both hands on his chest and push him away, shaking my head.

"No."

"Why the fuck not?" He ruffles his hair, almost ripping it out. "We love each other."

"That's never enough. It wasn't for my parents, and it's certainly not enough now."

"You said that you wouldn't leave me no matter what. I told

you not to say something you don't fucking mean, but you still promised. You fucking promised, Astrid."

I fist a handful of my hoodie over where my heart lies. "It hurts, Levi. Seeing you hurts so much."

His body freezes as if someone has thrown ice water on him. That someone is me.

His shoulders droop and he nods before he turns around and leaves.

My knees crumble and I fall down, realising that I've succeeded.

I've broken us apart for good.

FIFTY-THREE

Astrid

We might be over, but is it the end?

The two weeks after Victoria's arrest go so fast.

Nicole went to a relative's house in South West London. Dad offered her to stay, but she refused.

Victoria pleaded guilty, but even with that, I know Dad pulled all his weight in the political ring to have her behind bars as long as possible.

After my time off school, I decided to go back. According to Dan, the entire story about a murderer's daughter was slipped by Victoria to the journalism club, and since it's all over the press, it blew up in Nicole's face and now she's the secret murderer's daughter.

I don't think she'll ever return to RES or finish her senior year. And for some reason, I feel bad for her.

Like me, Nicole didn't want this life. She only accepted it for her parent. It's wrong for her to pay for her mother's sins, even if Nicole can be a total bitch herself.

I've never seen her so broken as the day she packed her suitcases and said goodbye to Dad and me while Daniel stood by my side.

She didn't look him in the eyes as she bowed her head and walked out the door.

"Are you ever going to tell me what happened between you two that night?" I asked Dan once she was gone.

His jaw tightened. "Doesn't matter."

"Dan... I'm your best friend. You're supposed to tell me these things. I'm supposed to be there for you when you're hurt."

"That's a tad bit dramatic, crazy bugger. Tone it down a notch."

"Nope. It's written in the friendship manual. I finally read it."

He laughed. "About time."

"So? Why didn't you tell me?"

"One. It's fucking embarrassing to tell you I was drugged and might have drugged you. And, oh, wait. You had an accident that night."

"Well, we had time after. Why have you never brought it up?"

"You make it sound like a disaster or that I'm traumatised."

"You aren't?"

He continued staring at where Nicole disappeared from. "I'm not."

"But didn't she...assault you?"

"Not exactly."

"Not exactly? What is that supposed to mean?"

"Nothing you need to worry about. Nicole is over."

But something told me that wasn't the case.

I sit at my desk in my room and stare at the sketchbook. I'm supposed to find a few sketches that speak of me and my style so I can send them to colleges, but I got lost somewhere.

For the past hour, I've been studying multiple sketches of Levi. There are a few of him scoring, running, or just standing over the team with crossed arms.

I can't get him out of my head.

Since that day he walked out on me, I keep replaying the final look in his eyes. The hurt. The defeat.

I broke his wings, but I'm the one who's bleeding.

I've been dreaming that he'll come back to knock on my door or sneak in from my window.

But that's all they are. Dreams.

Even if he comes, it'll only make it harder to push him away again.

Because I said the truth. He'll only see me as the daughter of the woman who killed his father. And while Mum had nothing to do with it, his father died that day.

I can't live with having him look at me that way.

That doesn't mean I can stop thinking about him, though.

That doesn't mean I can stop my muse from sketching him.

A few months.

It'll be less than a few months before we go our separate paths.

Dan mentioned that Jonathan King is allowing Levi to play professionally.

He'll pick either Manchester or Liverpool and live at the other side of the country while I continue studying in London.

My heart aches and bleeds at the thought of never seeing him again.

"Those are really pretty."

I startle and meet Dad's gaze. I fumble with the notepad, slamming it shut and fight the embarrassment creeping up my cheeks.

Thank God Dad didn't see the half-naked sketches.

"I knocked," he says. "Three times."

"Oh, I'm sorry."

"It's fine." He pulls out a chair and sits beside me. "I mean it. You have a special talent that's different from your mother's."

I smile. "Thanks, Dad."

"Are you returning to school?"

I wince. "It's time, I guess. I can't run away forever."

No matter how much I want to.

"I know it's been crazy around here recently, but you're strong and I trust that you'll get through this."

"I know, Dad, it's just…"

"That King boy?"

I swallow. "It's over between us. Don't worry."

"I'm not worried. My feud with Jonathan isn't something you two should worry about."

"Dad…are you approving of Levi right now?"

"He had the balls to meet me head-on and even risked his future to process evidence about your accident. That grants him some points." He scrunches his nose. "He still has that loathsome King pride, but it can be wrenched out of him."

"But…but what about Mum and his father?"

"They both died, Astrid. It was an accident. Neither you or Levi had anything to do with it." He holds my hand in his. "All this guilt is coming from inside you and you're the only one who can fight it."

"I don't know how." My voice breaks.

"Ask yourself. Are you living for the past or for the future?"

I'm speechless, not knowing how to respond to that.

Dad stands up and pats my hand. "For what it's worth, that boy seemed infuriatingly set on the future."

FIFTY-FOUR

Levi

It isn't over until it's over.

The sound of the spectators is deafening.

We're on our way to the championship.

Coach Larson looks at me like a hawk and points at his watch. Five. We only have five minutes left.

I motion at Ronan and Cole to push back to defence. I know they want to go out with a bang, but it's been a bitch to defend our two to one against Manchester, even though we're playing on our ground.

I scored the first goal and Aiden scored the second.

The prick Daniel's words from the other time have stayed with me. For the last few games, I've been giving the team more leeway to have fun as long as the results are there.

Being the captain doesn't only mean leading my team to victory. It also means being there for the fall and listening to them when they talk. Like every responsible general would do.

We lose the ball, and Aiden slams his shoulder in mine on his way back.

"You're sloppy, Captain." His eyes shine with contempt as he runs backwards. "I'd be surprised if you impress any scouts with your safe ways."

Fucker.

He laughs, exchanging glances with Xander.

Sometimes, I think Aiden only allows himself to let go during the game. For ninety minutes, he transforms into an unstoppable beast, playing the opponent's defence until he wears them out.

Cole snatches the ball from a midfielder and passes it to me. I keep possession, studying the pitch.

I can defend our score and win the game for sure. I can play as Coach wants. As everyone expects.

But I'm not a coward.

I'm a King and we don't play fucking safe.

I sprint forward, and I can almost imagine Coach yelling profanities in my peripheral vision.

I focus on the crowd going wild, the adrenaline pumping in my veins, and my team, who follow me.

Aiden and Xander run on either side of me to form a triangle. I dribble past one from defence and pass the ball to Xan who changes the direction with one masterful touch to Aiden.

I push in the last defender's back and make sure we're at the same line.

Aiden surges forward like a bull in between two defenders and passes me the ball. I don't bother to keep it in place. I shoot it while it's still in the air.

The crowd goes wild. I don't even get a chance to see the ball inside the net. Aiden tackles me to the ground and the entire team plus the bench form a pile on top of me.

It's impossible to breath, but I laugh anyway. It paid off. The gamble paid off.

This isn't only about the game anymore. This is about the fucking zombie I've become the last two weeks.

After I walked out on Astrid and never looked back, because I was playing it safe.

That's not me.

And it'll never be.

Xan and Ro carry me on their shoulders and I shout alongside them.

This victory is for us, not only me.

That's probably the difference between me and Aiden. He's too individualist to play the game right.

And the reason I'll make sure he's not the captain once I'm out of here.

The guys lower me when we reach Coach Larson. He stares at me with a disapproving glance, and all the guys grow silent.

"That was a dangerous stunt, Captain." Coach grins. "But a damn good one at that."

He headlocks me and I accept the taunting punches from everyone.

"Coach."

He and the rest of the team straighten at Uncle's voice.

"Mr King." Coach Larson shakes Uncle's hand. "You should be proud of your son and your nephew."

"Right. Of Course." Jonathan's voice is completely neutral.

Aiden and I exchange a look and roll our eyes.

"Someone is here for you, Lev." Uncle points to a man dressed in a three-piece suit, who looks so much like the type Uncle hangs out with.

Wait. This is…

"Mr Jeremy?" Coach Larson, who's always composed, almost stumbles on his words. "It's an honour to meet you."

"The honour is all mine, Coach." Jeremy shakes Coach's hand. "You've built an impressive team."

He turns towards me. "Levi King?"

"The one and only!" Xan shouts.

Jeremy laughs. "I've seen exceptional captaining skills today. Your leadership and ability to make decisions in a split time are exactly what we're looking for. That finish only proved how much we need to have our hands on you." He meets Jonathan's gaze. "You didn't tell me you were hiding a gem, King."

"It comes with the family name," Uncle says.

Jeremy smiles, eyeing Aiden. "We'll be talking to the second King soon, too."

"Yeah, that won't happen, Jeremy." Uncle takes him away before the assistant coaches start bugging him.

I gulp a mouthful of water and spill some over my head.

One problem out of the way.

"Victory party at my place!" Ronan yells, gripping me by the shoulder. "Captain, man of the hour!"

"You'll have to do it on your own." I shrug him off.

"Why?" Cole snatches the bottle from between my fingers.

"I have an important place to be." *A place that's two weeks overdue.*

"Uh, you don't have to." Xander waggles his eyebrows, motioning behind me.

My breath hitches when I turn around.

The guys' cheers, the spectators, and the entire fucking world disappears.

The only thing that remains is the girl walking across the pitch.

She's wearing my T-shirt with the number ten on it. Her hair falls like a fucking halo around her face.

Air rushes back to my lungs, and it hurts.

Feeling so much life after suffocating for two weeks fucking hurts.

I'll make sure it never hurts again. For the both of us.

Astrid once told me I was a dark night. It's on dark nights that stars like her shine the brightest.

FIFTY-FIVE

Astrid

Mine.

My heart tries to punch its way out of my chest as I stare at Levi.

Sweat and water make his gorgeous Viking hair all tousled and shiny. He runs towards me in that agile, stunning way that made me put up with his morning runs.

His chest muscles strain against his jersey and his strong thighs nearly burst out of the shorts.

He stops in front of me, his handsome face slightly flushed from the heroic game he just finished.

I only came in the second half, after trying to convince myself for the thousandth time that this was the right thing to do and praying that I didn't shatter us for good.

"Congrats," I murmur, almost stammering like an idiot. "That was a great game."

"Fuck that." He breathes hard, approaching me slowly. "Why are you here, Astrid?"

"I…" *I was an idiot? I want a second chance?*

Where the hell do I even begin with my jumbled thoughts?

He barges into my space. His chest brushes against my breasts and I'm so full of him. Of his height. Of his natural scent now mixed with adrenaline. Of his sheer presence.

God, I missed him. I missed him so fucking much.

He clutches my shoulders with strong hands, and I briefly close my eyes against the sensation. His touch has always been my undoing, and I've been starving for so long.

"Tell me you couldn't sleep either. Tell me I've been driving you as fucking crazy as you've been driving me."

I nod, fighting the pressure building in my throat. "I know there's a dark past between us, but I'm choosing to be selfish. I'm choosing the future, Levi."

"Thank fuck, because I'm never giving up on you, Princess."

I release a long breath. "I thought you already had."

"Nah. I have to live up to my devil reputation."

I throw myself against him, my hands securing tightly at his back. Levi wraps his arms around my waist and pulls me into him. We're so close that he's crushing me until I can't breathe.

Scratch that. I can breathe. I breathe him. His embrace. His warmth. The future I want with him.

Levi and I have been something special since the day I stumbled into that private room, drugged, and he kicked me out just so he'd save me later.

We've been something special since he made me his target and I fought back.

The past won't define our lives. The future will.

"Now say it," he whispers against my ear.

"Say what?"

"That you're mine."

"I'm yours." I chuckle, looking up at him. "Even if we have a long-distance relationship."

"Fuck long-distance relationships."

My heart breaks as if he jammed a knife into my chest. Does Levi only plan to spend the rest of the year with me and then we go our separate ways?

He taps my nose. "Kiss for your thoughts?"

"So, what? It's over once you go to Manchester or Liverpool?"

"Nothing will be fucking over."

"But you're going —"

"I'm going nowhere, Princess. Uncle brought his friend who happens to be Arsenal's CEO to make sure I stay in London."

"Arsenal. Wow."

"I know. Jonathan is being manipulative until the very end."

"No. I mean, I'm happy for you… If you decide to stay in London, of course."

"Fuck right, I'm staying. I go wherever you go, Princess."

He seals his lips to mine in a passionate, all-consuming kiss that steals my breath away. I moan, threading my fingers into his hair as the guys cheer all around us.

I kiss him back, rising on my tippy toes to reciprocate what he's thinking.

Mine.

EPILOGUE

Astrid

One year later

"This isn't funny."

My heart almost beats out of my chest even as I try to keep my voice light-hearted.

The sound of the rain beats down all over the King's mansion, soaking the fountain in the middle of the back garden and the trees in the distance.

I should've known he was up to no good.

Levi is always up to no good.

"Levi?" I call in a hesitant voice as my steps falter near the covered hallway of the King's mansion.

I search around, expecting one of his distasteful pranks where he jumps me from behind.

I'll probably never admit this to him, but I love that part of him the most. There's never a dull moment with him.

He makes my days unforgettable and my nights as thrilling as a rollercoaster ride.

Yesterday, he saw me having lunch with a few of my college friends who somehow all ended up being males. Levi decided to be a dick and kiss me in front of all of them until I had to apologise and leave.

I'm still feeling sore from the way he took me hard and fast against the door as soon as we entered his flat.

It's his type of punishment. A game he plays with my body that I don't ever want to end.

As soon as we graduated, Levi chose to live on his own. He still didn't touch his trust fund and is living off his overflowing career with Arsenal. It amazes me how he can play and study at the same time. I feel so overwhelmed with the art classes alone.

On paper, I still live with Dad, but in reality, I crash in Levi's flat more often than not.

We practically live together now.

"Are you going to be petty for long?" I ask, rubbing my arms.

A chill covers my bare limbs and it's not because of the cold. A part of me is bubbling, itching and almost jumping out of my skin for what he plans to do.

Levi might have grown up, but he's still the same unpredictable arsehole who's out to flip my world upside down.

The only difference is that I love it. No, I crave it. Sometimes, I feel like his madness mirrors mine.

And when I wake up in the morning with this face next to mine, I say a silent prayer to always wake up next to him.

He might rock my world, but he's also the only one who's able to balance it. He's my anchor and my peace. He has some possessive and controlling issues, but that's part of who Levi King is.

In fact, after getting to know his uncle and his cousin, I can say Levi is the safest amongst them—shocker, I know.

They have something all screwed up in the family's blood.

They're all twisted in their own ways and they're unapologetic about it.

A sound catches behind me. I stop and glance sideways, my breathing hitching.

"Levi?"

Nothing.

I wait for a few long seconds and then release a breath. I'm going back inside. To hell with Levi's games.

Something crashes into me from behind. I shriek until I recognise his warmth and his unmistakable scent.

"What did I say about letting your guard down, Princess?" he speaks against my ear before he nibbles on the lobe. "That's when I'll always strike."

"You're awful." I try to control my heartbeat.

"You still love me for it."

"Maybe I don't anymore," I taunt. "Maybe I'm falling for someone else from my class."

"Do you really want the blood of all your classmates' on your hand?"

I gasp in mock reaction. "You wouldn't."

"Oh, I very much would."

Yup. He's crazy enough to do it.

Before I can say anything, he picks me up in his arms. I gasp as he runs straight out to the rain, and I squeal with pure excitement as the water soaks us.

His lips slam into mine as he kisses me until I can only breathe him. It's desperate and robs my sanity and my entire surroundings.

He still consumes every inch of me with a single touch.

The feeling of being in the rain with him never gets boring. It's one of my favourite things to do with him.

Instead of spinning me around in his arms, he puts me down on my feet and steps back.

Before I can make out what's going on, he gets on his knees and fetches a ring with a huge diamond on top from his pocket.

"You gave my life meaning and I want to spend every single moment of it with you." He looks up at me with his wet blond hair sticking to his temples and his pale blue eyes shining with intensity. "Would you marry me, Princess?"

"Yes! A million times yes, Levi!"

I pull him to his feet and crush my lips to his as he slides the ring on my finger.

"I volunteer to be best man!" Ronan's voice shouts from behind us.

Levi and I stop kissing, but he's still holding me in the rain.

The four horsemen—Elites' current forward line—cheer with a lot of snark thrown in between.

In fact, only Dan, Xander, Ronan, and Cole cheer. Aiden leans against the wall with his ankles crossed and a bored expression written all over his face as he scrolls through his phone.

Last year, I thought Aiden could be mildly psychopathic, but now, I'm almost sure he has clinical antisocial disorder.

Nothing holds any value to him.

The only time I see him lose the bored expression is when he's around a certain Ice Princess.

"Oh, shit!" Dan exclaims with astonishment. "Does this make me the maid of honour?"

I laugh, the sound carefree and happy. "Sure does, Bug."

Dad walks out the front door, wearing a proud smile. Jonathan stands by his side, staring between his son and his nephew.

Sometimes, I think he wants Aiden to be more like Levi. At other times, it seems the exact opposite.

I wouldn't call Dad and Jonathan friends, but they tolerate each other enough to visit one another's homes when we invite them.

"I'm happy," I whisper to Levi. "Thank you for existing, my king."

He smiles. "Thank you for being mine, Princess."

And then he's kissing me again.

BONUS SCENE

Astrid

Right before the wedding

My body nearly shuts down from exhaustion as I push the flat's door open.

I've spent the entire day with the wedding planner, the flowers planner, and all the other planners.

Honestly, if I'd known a wedding would be this hard, I would've opted to have a small ceremony. Levi insisted that he wanted our wedding blasted all over the world so everyone knows I'm his—typical Levi.

Dad also wants a suitable wedding for his only daughter. I couldn't say no to that.

It's too late to turn back now. There's only a week until the big day. Let's hope I don't collapse before then.

Don't get me wrong, Levi does help. He's even more enthusiastic about this planning charade than me. However, I'm the one who has to go through endless dress fittings and whatnots. As our planner, Mrs. Hudson, keeps saying, 'the wedding is all about the bride'.

What if this particular bride doesn't like the spotlight? Well, there's nothing to do about it.

I'm stuck.

My phone pings. I sling my backpack over one shoulder

and shuffle my groceries and Mrs. Hudson's brochures to retrieve my phone.

A smile breaks across my lips. It's a text from my best friend.

Daniel: I rock the maid of honour role. Guess who's going to steal your spotlight, Bugger?

He's attached the picture we took at the fitting room yesterday. I'm in my wedding dress and he's in a dashing black tuxedo. He has a smug look all over his face as he fingers his bowtie and wraps his other arm around me.

God. He's such a dork.

But seriously, if Dan hadn't been there for me this entire time, I would've gone bonkers.

I type with one hand, still juggling too much stuff.

Astrid: You're welcome to steal the spotlight anytime, Bug.

Daniel: You can't take that back. I'm holding you to it, screenshot and everything.

I'm about to reply when a deep voice cuts through the silence of the house.

"Princess?"

I quickly turn off the phone and slide it into my bag. I don't want Levi to see the wedding dress yet, no matter how much he pesters me.

It's not because of that stupid superstition. It's about something I've seen in Mrs. Hudson's collection.

She has a photo album where she captures shots of the grooms when the brides walk towards them. Their expressions are often filled with awe, love, and utter happiness.

I want to see that look on Levi's face on the wedding day. Hell, this might be the only reason I'm willingly continuing this entire planning nightmare.

That's why he needs to see the dress for the first time next week.

I drop my backpack on the leather sofa and abandon the brochures on the counter.

"Where are you?" I ask, tiptoeing down the hallway.

Although we've been practically living together for the past year or so, I've been spending more time with Dad lately. It's like I'm telling him goodbye before I move out for good.

Of course, Levi hasn't been thrilled about that idea. He keeps sending me texts about his empty bed, empty heart, and empty soul.

I smile like an idiot at those.

Today, I've decided to stay the night for the last time until the wedding.

"In here," he calls, the sound coming from the last room down the hall.

The room Levi turned into my art studio as soon as he got the flat. Actually, the first thing he chose in this house was the location of my art studio.

But what is he doing in there now?

Oh, gosh. Please don't tell me he saw the painting. He's not supposed to lay eyes on it until the wedding night.

It's supposed to be a gift.

I jog down the hall and push the door open. My feet come to a screeching halt as soon as I'm inside.

Levi lies on the sofa, cradling his head, his massive body dwarfing the space.

Oh, and he's naked.

Completely fucking naked.

For a moment, I'm speechless. My greedy eyes take in his sculpted abs, his muscular thighs, and that delicious V that leads to his semi-erect cock.

I shake myself out of my stupor and focus on his face—his tousled blond hair, his arrogant smirk, and his pale blue eyes.

Damn those blue, blue eyes.

"What are you doing?" I mean to interrogate him, but it comes out in a whisper that's barely audible.

"What does it look like I'm doing?" He grins, eyes shining. "I'm modelling for you."

"Modelling for me?"

"I know you've been painting me and taking peeks at my body while you think I'm asleep."

I gasp. "You saw the painting?"

"No. I'll wait until you show it to me."

A breath of relief heaves out of my lungs. Okay, we're safe. But how the hell did he know I was painting him? More importantly...

"What makes you think it's a nude?" I narrow my eyes.

He chuckles, and it's deep and rough and fucking hot. I love it when he laughs like that.

Unless it's in front of other women. That, I don't like.

"You only watch me when I'm sleeping naked. Besides, you're blushing, Princess."

"I am not. It's just the heat of the room."

"The heat of the room, huh?"

"Oh, shut up."

His laugh echoes after me as I storm to my canvas and flop down on the seat.

Despite his dick attitude, I won't miss the chance of having him model for me. Besides, he's right, I've been working on a nude for him.

When I mentioned nudes to Levi a few months ago, he was surprisingly for the idea as long as he's the first and last and only nude I'll ever draw.

Truth is, I'm not interested in other nudes. It takes a lot of intimacy to sketch someone in their initial form, uncovered and raw.

Since our days in Royal Elite School, I've been sketching Levi half-naked behind his back. The idea to make a nude portrait of his magnificent body has been running rampant in my head since that time. So I thought, what's better than to give him a nude sketch as a wedding gift?

I've been working on this for months, carefully adding one detail at a time. Having him entirely naked in front of me will save me a lot of energy and sneaking around.

I took so many photos of him, it's stalker-level, but I still couldn't get a few things right.

This is my golden opportunity.

I remove the cover and retrieve my charcoal. In no time, I'm in the zone, sketching along the ridges of his abs, the curve of his neck, the line of his collarbone.

Then I retouch some parts in his muscular arms and the veins in his hands. Those hands that carry me so effortlessly every time. The hands that grab my thighs under the table whenever we're out, slowly going up and —

I shake my head inwardly.

Focus, Astrid.

I move down to the ridges of his stomach and to the V line leading down to his cock.

A spark of longing hits me out of nowhere. Hell, isn't he more erect than when I walked in?

Jeez. It's hard to be professional when all I want to do is put my mouth on him and let him fuck all the stress out of me.

"You're blushing again, Princess." His gleaming eyes capture mine in a spell, potent and strong.

"Stop looking at me like that," I grumble, my hand quivering.

"Like what?" he drawls.

"Like you want to…you know."

"Fuck you? Make you scream with the force of your orgasm?"

A spark of pleasure races down my spine and pools at the bottom of my stomach.

Why do I want that so much?

He jerks up, and I do, too, quickly covering the canvas. "What are you doing? Models don't move."

"This one does." His wide strides cut the distance between us in a few seconds.

He wraps his arms around my waist. Our lower halves grind against each other, and I hiss a breath as the hardness of his cock nestles against my shorts.

Why the hell am I even dressed?

"I've been wanting to do this since the moment you walked in," he rasps, breathing me in.

Before I can make out what's happening, he captures my lips in a fervent, hard kiss that steals my breath away.

My arms wind around his neck, uncaring that I've got charcoal all over my hands.

Without breaking the kiss, Levi places a hand under my arse and pulls me in his arms. The act is so effortless and natural as he marches out of the studio.

"Aren't you supposed to model for me?" I ask breathlessly against his mouth.

"Later," he grunts, his voice husky with arousal. "We can do that later."

Not that I'm complaining about the turn of events.

He barges into the bedroom—our bedroom—and slams the door shut with his foot.

He puts me on the bed and nearly tears my shorts and T-shirt off. I fumble with the buttons and help him undress me.

In pure Levi fashion, he rips my underwear, and the friction of his fingers against my most sensitive part leaves me breathless, aching for more.

I pant, showing him my charcoal-covered hands. "I'm all dirty."

"Oh, I'm going to make you dirtier, Princess," he whispers against the hollow of my neck before he places an open-mouthed kiss on the curve of my throat.

He doesn't stop there, though.

As he throws off my bra, my last piece of clothing, he sucks on my collarbone and the delicate skin of my breast.

My back arches off the bed, letting the overwhelming sensation sweep over me, capture me in its depths, and unravel me.

"Levi…" I sink my fingers into the short hairs at the back of his neck.

"Fuck, I love the way you say my name." His mouth covers an aching nipple and sucks it inside as his finger twirls the other one. "And I love these tits. They were made for me, weren't they, Princess?"

I groan a "Yes." He's touching my breasts, but I feel his ministrations straight to my core.

"Wrap your legs around my waist," he orders in a hoarse voice.

Something about his authoritative tone turns me on even more. I do as I'm told.

"Tighter," he commands.

I comply, even though my thighs tremble.

Levi lifts his head from my breasts and whispers, "I love you."

Then he's sheathed inside me, all the way in. I'm so full of him that I don't think I'll be empty ever again.

My air fills with his scent, his musk and his fresh breaths. My body, heart, and soul jolt with every deep thrust.

He's not rough and fast, but he's not slow either.

It's the perfect rhythm to send sparks down my belly and all over my body. All my emotions escalate and somehow settle in the space between us.

He's worshipping me, I realise. And that brings happy tears to my eyes.

"Why are you crying?" He wipes a stray tear with the tip of his thumb, a frown settling between his brows.

"I'm just happy." I place a kiss on his mouth. "So happy."

"You are?" He grins, his thrusts picking up pace.

I nod as he hits the right spot. Then when he slides out and slams back in again, I lose it.

All of it.

"I love you," I pant as the orgasm hits me with a force I've never felt before.

As if my words are an aphrodisiac, Levi curses. His abs tighten with the power of his thrusts as he comes inside me with a rough, masculine groan.

Our breathing is rugged and rough, pulsing between us as we both fully come down from the high.

He pulls me into him and nestles my head at the crook of his shoulder.

The room is full of sex, dopamine, and peace.

So much peace.

If I'd known he'd purge all the stress out of me like that, I would've spent all the previous days with him.

"Are you feeling better?" He wraps his large palm around my cheek, combing through the sweaty strands and stroking my jaw.

I stare up at him. "Better about what?"

"You were on the verge of a breakdown these past few days." He watches me intently, putting all his weight into his gaze.

My throat works with a swallow.

"You...knew that?" I murmur in the silence.

"I know everything about you, Princess."

"I thought you were too busy with practice and school."

"I'm never too busy for you." He kisses my forehead, soft and tender. "You'll be my wife, remember? I'll always know everything about you."

Wife.

That word fills me with a giddiness I haven't felt since the day of the proposal.

I want to be his wife. I want to wake up to his face every day and steal shots of him so I can sketch them later.

There's no doubt in my mind that Levi is the man I want to spend the rest of my life with.

"And you'll be my husband." I plant a kiss on his shoulder where I smudged him with charcoal.

"Fuck." His pale eyes shine with potent possessiveness and affection. "Repeat that."

"Husband?"

He nods sharply.

"My husband." I flutter kisses over his neck, jaw, and the curve of his mouth. "My love, my life, and my everything."

A low growl rips from his throat as he grips my hips and climbs atop of me. "My wife. My everything."

A week later, he seals that promise with a deep kiss.

THE END

WHAT'S NEXT?

Thank you so much for reading *Cruel King*! If you liked it,
please leave a review.
Your support means the world to me.

If you're thirsty for more discussions with other
readers of the series, you can join the Facebook group,
Rina Kent's Spoilers Room.

Next up, you can read Aiden's angsty, new adult story in
Deviant King or Jonathan King's age gap, enemies to lovers
story in *Reign of a King.*

Deviant King's Blurb

The villain isn't supposed to be king.

I have a simple plan.
Finish Royal Elite School and get into my dream university.
One glance from the school's king blows my plan up in smoke.
One glance and he suffocates my air.
One glance and he issues his death sentence.
His first words spiral my life into irreparable chaos.
"I will destroy you."
Everything about Aiden King is black.
Black mind.
Black heart.
Black soul.
I should've remained quiet and endured the time I had left.
I didn't.

I made the irrevocable mistake of provoking the king on his throne.

The devil in his hell.

And now, I'll pay the price.

Being hated by Aiden King is dangerous.

But being wanted by him is lethal.

Reign of a King's Blurb

Nothing is fair in war.

Jonathan King is every bit his last name.

Powerful.

Untouchable.

Corrupted.

He's also my dead sister's husband and way older than me.

When I first met him as a clueless child, I thought he was a god.

Now, I have to confront that god to protect my business from his ruthless grip.

Little did I know that declaring a war on the king will cost me everything.

When Jonathan covets something, he doesn't only win, he conquers.

Now, he has his sights on me.

He wants to consume not only my body, but also my heart and my soul.

I fight, but there's no escaping the king in his kingdom...

ALSO BY RINA KENT

For more books by the author and a reading order, please visit:
www.rinakent.com/books

ABOUT THE AUTHOR

Rina Kent is a *USA Today*, international, and #1 Amazon bestselling author of everything enemies to lovers romance.

She's known to write unapologetic anti-heroes and villains because she often fell in love with men no one roots for. Her books are sprinkled with a touch of darkness, a pinch of angst, and an unhealthy dose of intensity.

She spends her private days in London laughing like an evil mastermind about adding mayhem to her expanding universe. When she's not writing, Rina travels, hikes, and spoils cats in a pure Cat Lady fashion.

Find Rina Below:

Website: www.rinakent.com

Newsletter: www.subscribepage.com/rinakent

BookBub: www.bookbub.com/profile/rina-kent

Amazon: www.amazon.com/Rina-Kent/e/B07MM54G22

Goodreads: www.goodreads.com/author/show/18697906.

Rina_Kent

Instagram: www.instagram.com/author_rina

Facebook: www.facebook.com/rinaakent

Reader Group: www.facebook.com/groups/rinakent.club

Pinterest: www.pinterest.co.uk/AuthorRina/boards

Tiktok: www.tiktok.com/@rina.kent

Twitter: twitter.com/AuthorRina